# Praise for Jill McGown's Inspector Lloyd and Judy Hill mysteries

### PICTURE OF INNOCENCE

"[A] fantastically intricate murder plot . . . It's a pleasure watching McGown's wheels of justice grind."

—*Kirkus Reviews*

### VERDICT UNSAFE

"A cleverly constructed, realistic courtroom drama that keeps you totally involved."

—ANNE PERRY

### ━━━━━━━━━NCE

"Con━━━━━━━━━━━━━e devious, cunn━━━━━━━━━━━y wicked. . . . Lloyd━━━━━━━━━━━eir form."

━━━━*ly*

### T━━━━━━━━━━━━USTIN AND

"Sopl━━━━

━━━━━*uirer*

By Jill McGown

# PICTURE OF INNOCENCE

## Jill McGown

FAWCETT CREST • NEW YORK

A Fawcett Crest Book
Published by The Ballantine Publishing Group
Copyright © 1997 by Jill McGown

www.randomhouse.com/BB/

Library of Congress Catalog Card Number: 98-94834

ISBN 0-449-00251-9

Printed in Canada

First Ballantine Hardcover Edition: July 1998
First Mass Market Edition: May 1999

10   9   8   7   6   5   4

# CHAPTER ONE

"DEATH THREATS? AWAY, MAN." MIKE McQUEEN'S Tyneside accent had been modified by years of working and living wherever he saw the potential for building development and by the wealthy lifestyle he had thus acquired, but he liked to remind people of his working-class roots from time to time. His wife wished he wouldn't. He raised his eyebrows at the good-looking young man who was helping his cameraman attach the microphone.

"Window'd be favourite," muttered the cameraman. "Trees in the background, blossom on the grass, raindrops on the window."

"Death threats," repeated Curtis Law. He was one of the reporters from Aquarius TV, their regional network, his light brown hair cut and styled in a way that only media people could be bothered to keep their hair, his suit sober but stylish. And he was whippet-thin, of course. Mike had been like that once, thirty years ago.

"He's been getting them since January. You must have heard about them, Mr. McQueen, even in this desirable ivory tower of yours."

Mike smiled. He had once been *very* like young Mr. Law. Eager, sharp, a bit on the cheeky side. A barrow boy, really, with the polish that even a state education gave you, if you put it to good use, but a barrow boy all the same. Sixty years of staying alive had knocked a lot of it out of him, and it would knock it out of Curtis Law, too, in time. "Yes," he said. "I've

1

heard about them. But I doubt if there's anyone in this village who hasn't wanted to kill Bernard Bailey at one time or another. I also doubt that they're serious, unfortunately."

Law grinned. "Wait till we've got the videotape running," he said.

Mike smiled again. "I won't *say* anything like that when you've got it running. You should know that by now." He took a cigar from a box on the desk, then belatedly, and with no expectation of acceptance, offered the box to the other two.

He didn't overeat; he didn't drink to excess; he was kind to animals and small children. Smoking was, when he came to think of it, his only vice, though he would succumb to another if he was given the chance. Not that he would be—she didn't think of him like that. He was an old man as far as she was concerned. She called him Mr. McQueen.

The cameraman shook his head, but Law, to Mike's surprise, took out a packet of cigarettes. "I'll stick to these, if that's all right," he said.

Mike waved away the gold lighter which Law held out; you needed a match to light a decent cigar. "Surely the death threats are old news," he said.

"These ones are different," said Law. "They're obscene. And explicit as to how he'll die."

Mike knew that, too, but he feigned slight, and uninterested, surprise. "Is that right?" he said. "Fancy."

"But who would actually issue death threats over this business?" Law asked, the cigarette burning between his lips as he concentrated on what he was doing. "That's the sort of thing I'll be asking you. I mean—you want his land, he doesn't want to sell . . . you seem a prime suspect. Scare him out."

Mike sat at the desk as instructed by the cameraman, side on to the view of the trees silhouetted against the pale grey sky, and drew thoughtfully on his cigar. "I don't mind telling you that I'm pissed off with the whole business," he said. "You wouldn't believe the sort of money Bailey's turning down just so he can hang on to a piece of land he doesn't farm anymore.

2

But I'm not creeping round his farm in the middle of the night leaving death threats."

"Oh, bugger," said the cameraman. "Is that guy going to clear away the blossom?"

Mike saw his gardener walking purposefully across the lawn with a rake, and nodded. " 'Fraid so," he said, with no intention of disrupting the man's work to suit a couple of TV types. He'd have thought a gardener clearing the fallen blossom would have been fine, like a scene from a thirties musical. But it was, it seemed, merely distracting. After some discussion, he found himself sitting at the desk like a schoolboy, with the cameraman to his right. The background was his bookcase.

"Do you read a lot?" asked the cameraman.

"Yes," said Mike. "I read several books at once. At the moment, I'm reading—"

"Right," he said. "Level's fine. We're ready."

Mike laid his cigar down in the ashtray, and placed it beyond the camera's range. These days it was more than your life was worth to be seen smoking on the box, even something as civilized as a Havana cigar.

Law reached over, stubbed out his cigarette, and began the interview. "Mr. McQueen, who do *you* think is responsible for these death threats?" he asked, and tilted the microphone in Mike's direction.

"Well, I understand that I'm the prime suspect," said Mike, smiling broadly. "But all I'm doing is offering to buy Mr. Bailey's land—whether or not he sells it to me is entirely up to him."

"But you are very keen to buy?"

"I have to build a road to the Rookery. The alternative is to go through a large tract of woodland whose owners are quite willing to sell. It's costing me time and money trying to persuade Mr. Bailey to sell me his land instead."

"Why spend the time and money?" asked Law. "Why not

just go ahead with the alternative route? Wouldn't that make more business sense?"

"I have no wish to make any more impact on the environment than is necessary," Mike answered, smoothly and expertly, right down to the concerned look. "Even the environmentalists agree that unused fields are better candidates for development than much-loved and ancient woodland—perhaps they're sending death threats. All I can tell you is that I'm not."

"And you are prepared to take a loss in order to conserve the countryside?" The tone was faintly mocking, the eyes cynical. "It wouldn't be because you actually live in Harmston, and you don't want this road in your *own* back yard?"

"Partly," said Mike, with what he hoped would be seen as disarming honesty. "My wife and I have lived in this community for almost eighteen months, and we very much enjoy it here. I've no wish to be responsible for the loss of a natural amenity."

In previous interviews on the subject of Bailey's Farm he had been on the side of the angels for possibly the first time in his life. But the death threats had put a new spin on the story; now it was Bailey himself who was under threat, and the tone of the interview had altered. Bailey was being seen as a man persecuted, driven to breaking point by the pressure to sell land which he had every right not to sell. And Mike was the property developer who had brought about this unhappy state of affairs, who was plundering the countryside for his own gain, and who was attempting to shift the blame for that on to Bailey, whose only crime was to own land that he wasn't farming. Once again, Mike was wearing a black hat. But he was used to that, and he parried the questions with ease. He had appeared on more regional television news programmes than young Mr. Law had, he was sure.

"Mike McQueen, thank you very much," said Law, wrapping up the interview. He stood up. "Would it be all right to do a few reaction shots?"

"Of course," said Mike, retrieving his cigar. "I'll leave you to it."

He left his study by the French window, going out into the warm, wet May morning, relighting the cigar under the shelter of the roofed terrace and watching the smoke as it drifted through the soft, fine rain that fell on to the lush grass of his lawn, now cleared of the blossom his gardener found untidy. The grass had had its first few mowings of the season, and was still cut high. Soon, the blades would be set lower, then lower still, until it was at its summer height. He smiled a little at himself, at his surroundings.

He had grown up in a back-to-back in Newcastle with a concrete yard and an outside toilet. He had left school at fifteen, and had got a job as a tea boy on a building site. He had seen even then the potential in property, and had learned everything he could about building and builders. By the time he was twenty, he had bought his first derelict row of cottages, and by the time he was twenty-two, he had had money in the bank, something his father had never achieved. That was when he had met and married Shirley, a service widow with a three-year-old daughter. They had tried for another baby, but it wasn't to be, and thus it was that when Shirley's daughter left home, they had found themselves with just one another for the first time. If, since then, the marriage had evolved into one merely of companionship, it didn't really bother Mike. He had become a rich man, which had always been his true objective, and when his final project was complete he and Shirley would retire in luxury, and remain companions until death did them part.

The media were leaving; they came out past him, thanked him, got into the cars that sat in his gravelled driveway and roared off down towards the big cast-iron gates.

It was fate, he supposed, that had led him to Harmston, and the greenfield site that the county council was keen to develop, because here, by pure chance, he had found something for which he had long ago stopped looking, and he had used every ounce of guile he possessed, every trick of persuasion he had ever learned, to have his plans accepted, to sweep aside the objections, to get the Rookery built.

And now, it needed a road. He had established that Excelsior Holdings, a company based in London for whom the woodland was a distant and costly irrelevance that they could turn into hard cash, would be prepared to sell. And then, when that news was greeted with horror by the villagers, he had made it known that he had already made an offer to Bailey, and had been turned down. Now everyone knew that all Bailey had to do was sell to him, and the road wouldn't go anywhere near the woodland. If it had to, it would, but he sincerely, honestly, devoutly hoped that it wouldn't ever come to that.

Not because he gave a toss how many people would be deprived of a natural amenity, how much flora and fauna would lose its home. And not because he had any deep sense of community, for he and Shirley had deliberately kept out of village life. Apart from Bailey, they knew about half a dozen of the inhabitants by name, if that. Some of them he employed; he had had dealings with just two others, and that only because they had approached him.

So it was for neither of the reasons he had advanced to Curtis Law that he was holding fire on felling the oaks and the elms. He simply wanted Bernard Bailey's land, and he would do just about anything to get it.

"Death threats?" Detective Chief Inspector Lloyd's tone of voice, and the exaggerated Welshness which ran the words together with just a single *th*, indicated that he was less than impressed. "Can't the uniforms deal with it? Sir," he added, smoothing down the dark hair at the back of his head, the only place he really still had any, and it needed a trim. His boss had become slightly more insistent on deference since the Chief Superintendent rank had been abolished, and the gap between him and Lloyd had been reduced to just one rung.

Detective Superintendent Case, with a full head of hair, although he, too, was looking at fifty from the wrong side, shook his head. "They were dealing with it," he said. "If you can call it that. But it's a bugger, Lloyd. He had the whole place ringed with alarms because his machinery was being vandalized. And someone's got through not once, but over and over again, and left death threats all over the place. The man was getting them on a weekly basis at one point. Now it seems they've turned even nastier. I think CID needs to take a look, at least. The reporter who's been covering the story just rang the press officer to ask what we intend doing about it. I think his words were, if whoever it was could deliver death threats, he could deliver death. And you can't really argue with that."

They sounded like reporters' words, thought Lloyd, but he supposed Case was right. "I'll send someone," he said.

"Do. And not a DC, either," added Case. "Send someone with a bit of experience, and a bit of rank. Bailey's an awkward customer at the best of times."

Lloyd shook his head. "Is this all because he won't sell his farm to a property developer?" he asked, puzzled. "Since when were they the good guys?"

"Since the alternative meant the rape of the countryside," said Case. "According to the conservationists."

"Aren't people's jobs more important?"

Case shook his head. "Not now," he said. "They would have been up until a couple of years ago. But just after his first wife died, Bernard Bailey—what's the word they use nowadays?—downsized what he actually farms. He's got seventy-five per cent of his land doing nothing, uses casual labour when he needs it for the rest. It would mean the loss of three or four full-time jobs at most."

"Is he a friend of yours?" asked Lloyd.

"Not a friend, exactly. We've met. You know how it is. The thing is . . ." he said, and paused.

At last. Case always took forever to get to the point. You always had to have what Lloyd thought of as the Case history first.

"We haven't exactly acted like greased lightning over the vandalism," Case went on. "And as far as I can see, we've done sod-all about the death threats. Bailey's getting meaner by the minute, as you can imagine. And—well, we'll both be attending a function tonight, and I'd like to be able to look the man in the eye rather than spend all night avoiding him."

Case and Bailey belonged to the same Lodge, no doubt. Lloyd had never been introduced to the arcane rituals of Freemasonry, and never wanted to be. But Case had, and you didn't really need to be a detective to work out why Mr. Bailey's problems had a special significance.

"It goes on until the small hours, and I can think of better ways of spending the time than being told I can't do my job. Take pity on me, Lloyd. Send someone who'll keep him off my back for tonight, at least."

A public relations exercise. Lloyd disapproved, basically, of the Brotherhood, but the man was nonetheless receiving death threats, and someone ought to be doing something about it. He rather thought he might go to see Mr. Bailey himself. Bailey could hardly complain about his rank, and Lloyd fancied he came over quite well on the box. He could certainly handle a reporter who spoke journalese.

"Not you," said Case, in an accurate assessment of Lloyd's unspoken thoughts. "You and I are going to headquarters." He picked up a fax. "To discuss the—and I quote—'eighteen-month-long spate of drug thefts from chemists, hospital dispensaries, hospices, research establishments, doctors' surgeries, et cetera, the clear-up rate of which is far from satisfactory, and the seriousness of which means that they must be given top priority.' The ACC is still suffering from verbal diarrhoea, poor chap." He looked up. "But we have to go. So send someone else, Lloyd. Even if you do like being on the telly."

"It's not like it was in Sherlock Holmes's day," Lloyd said, ignoring the jibe. "Hasn't anyone told the ACC that? They don't smoke Turkish cigarettes with distinctive ash—they don't leave behind them the tell-tale aroma of Arabian body-oils.

They're just junkies looking for pills to pop or something to sell."

"Mm. He thinks it might be more organized than that. It seems that this reporter—the same one that's covering the Bailey business—has been critical of our—and I quote again—'piecemeal approach.' "

"Which reporter? Curtis Law?"

"That's him. Do you know him?"

"He's been going on about this for months! *He*'s the one who thinks it's organized, not the ACC. If that's what this conference is about, it's a complete waste of time."

"Fifteen minutes, my car, waste of time or not."

"Yes, sir," said Lloyd, knowing when he was beaten.

He went downstairs to the CID room, and considered Tom Finch, who was a sergeant, and therefore of a rank regarded as suitable. Of course, he looked about fifteen, with his curly fair hair and his cheeky grin, so he wouldn't do, despite the fact that he was thirty, married with two children, and a very able officer. Besides, Judy had never been bloodied in the sport of TV interviews. "Is DI Hill back from court?" he asked, jerking his head at Judy's door.

"Yes, guv," said Finch, who liked to think that he was in a TV cop show. "Her new wheels can shift a bit, can't they?"

Lloyd knocked on Judy's door, and smiled at her. What more could Case and his fellow Masons want? A detective inspector, no less. One with twenty years' service. One with clear-eyed common sense, and brown-eyed, brown-haired, exceedingly pleasing looks. One with instinctive dress sense, and a knack of getting to the bottom of little puzzles, which this surely was. One who would not only talk intelligibly to Bailey and the media, but intelligently, and in a middle-class, educated accent at that. The education had veered a little too much towards maths and logic for his taste—he preferred language and literature—but all in all, as packages went, Judy was a very elegant one.

"Oh, God," she groaned.

9

He looked utterly innocent. "What? I haven't said anything yet."

"You don't have to. You want me to do something I won't want to do."

"It's a doddle. You just have to go to a farm—"

"I hate farms."

He sighed, shaking his head. "You city girls are all the same. One hint of mud, and you get the vapours."

"Just have to go to a farm and do what?"

"Talk to a nice man called Mr. Bailey about death threats."

"Death threats?" repeated Judy.

Death threats, thought Jack Melville, land-owner, country gentleman, old Harrovian, dabbler in stocks and shares, financial consultant to the already very rich. Death threats. Whatever next?

His long face, youthful for its thirty-eight years, was serious. Surely Terri's friends on the Save Our Woodland Sites committee hadn't started sending death threats? There were one or two he wouldn't care to vouch for, and who he fancied were responsible for the curiously middle-class graffiti to be found scrawled on Bailey's ludicrous, ten-foot-high security fences. But death threats? Jack was the *spokesman* for the Save Our Woodland Sites committee, for God's sake. They couldn't start doing that sort of thing. You could end up in prison for that.

He had just given an interview in his capacity as spokesman to someone who had introduced himself as Curtis Law, *Aquarius 1830,* as though Jack should have heard of him. He hadn't. And it had taken him a moment or two to work out *why* he was being interviewed about Bailey's death threats. He usually found some frightfully important work to do when the all-female group had its interminable discussions, and frequently forgot that he *was* its spokesman. He had been press-ganged, a man being deemed to have more gravitas. They were a little impolite about Bailey at times, but surely Terri wouldn't condone the sending of death threats?

10

He loved his wife dearly, and by and large he sympathized with her aims for preserving the village way of life, but she did rather take the whole thing too seriously. She had got up the committee to object to the development in the first place, and they had fought against planning permission being given for an access route at all, which would have effectively stopped the whole thing in its tracks. They had lost that battle, and now that land of some sort *was* to be sacrificed to the earth-movers, the fight had become personal. Bailey's land was the lesser of two evils, and he must be made to sell. The veiled suggestion by the reporter that the SOWS might be behind the death threats—Jack was never sure whether the acronym had been intentional or not—had bothered him a little, though he had laughed it off.

He had acquitted himself pretty well in the interview, he thought. He had explained that while roads were of course the greatest evil since the plague, and every day the countryside was threatened with more and more of them, they were a *necessary* evil. The development had to have an access route, and therefore, if there was a choice, surely fallow fields were better victims than woodland which had been enjoyed for generations? Yes, he wished that Bernard Bailey would just sell the land to the developers, but neither he nor any member of the SOWS would stoop to scare tactics.

The door opened and Terri came in, her curly salt-and-pepper hair tousled and damp from the drizzly day. "June says the television people are here again."

"I know," said Jack. "I've just given them an interview. Bailey's getting death threats now, apparently."

"Oh, that," she said.

Oh. He had hoped she might at least be surprised. "You know about them?" he asked, flipping the computer back on, establishing a link with the stock-markets again.

"Everyone knows about them. He's been getting them for months."

The reporter had said that. "He's had more this morning. Rude ones. Why is it that everyone knows about them but me?"

"Because you've always got your head buried in that thing," she said, waving a dismissive hand at their livelihood. "You never watch television. It was on the local news for weeks until they got bored with it."

"It's . . ." Jack paused, not wanting to hear the answer. "It's not anyone on your committee that's sending them, is it?"

"Not as far as I know. But if it is, who cares?"

Oh, dear, oh dear. "I care! It's against the law."

"Against the *law*?" said Terri, all wide-eyed mock shock. "I didn't know that. Thank you, Uncle Jack."

"Well," he said, on the defensive. "You're not condoning that sort of stuff, are you?"

"Why not?" she said. "Laws were made to be broken. And Bailey isn't going to force McQueen to take that road through Bluebell Wood, not if I can help it."

Bluebell Wood. The damn place didn't have a name, not one that anyone knew. The committee had called it Bluebell Wood when they had decided to save it, and they had a lot more in common with McQueen than they would like to think. His development was called the Rookery, and was marked on the plans in pseudo-medieval lettering. McQueen had christened it that himself, just as they had christened Bluebell Wood. Real country people didn't give places names, twee or otherwise, unless they had to.

Jack had lived here all his life; he liked the woodland. But there was plenty of it. "Bluebell" wood was just one part of a real wood, with a real, unromantic name. Sharpe's Wood. It had once, long ago, belonged to a Mr. Sharpe, so Sharpe's Wood it was. When he had mentioned this to Terri, she had pointed out that it was the thin end of the wedge. Bluebell Wood today, Sharpe's Wood tomorrow. Sharpe's Wood, she had reminded him, had once been part of a forest. A forest that had belonged to no one, and which, bit by bit, had been consumed by commerce.

"You give someone like McQueen an inch," said Terri, "and he'll grab everything, develop it all into housing estates and

12

golf courses. Real villagers won't survive. Just people like that lunatic Bailey."

Real villagers. Jack *was* a real villager, unlike Terri. His great-grandfather had owned most of Harmston in his day; he and Terri lived in what had been the manor house, and he still owned some of the land round about. Come to that, Bailey had more claim to being a real villager than many of the people who wanted him out; his family had farmed that land for generations. But Bailey had been born and brought up in Yorkshire, and had come to claim his grandfather's inheritance a mere twenty-five years ago; he was regarded as an incomer. And he had never been popular. Villages could tolerate a fair amount of nonconformity, but Bailey had long since passed the eccentricity high-water mark, and Terri's description of him as a lunatic wasn't so wide of the mark. The villagers would heave a collective sigh of relief if he were to disappear from their midst.

So Jack hadn't been reassured by her denial of any knowledge of these death threats; Terri wasn't above underhand methods to get her way. But then, that was probably why they had such a successful marriage despite everything, he thought. Because neither was he.

Judy had had to negotiate an electronically locked and controlled gate, and was driving slowly and distastefully over the mud about which Lloyd had been so scathing; it was a roadway, but one which had been driven on by tractors, walked on by cows and sheep, that sort of rural thing, and Judy did not like rural.

Stansfield was a town of sixty thousand people—it had never occurred to her when she moved there that the division would police villages and farms miles away from the place. She was used to city streets. Before Stansfield it had been Nottingham, and before that London, where she had been born and brought up. She liked tarmac and paving stones.

At last she could see buildings, and made her way towards

them. In one, she could see a youth spreading what she assumed to be straw in what she took to be a cowshed, largely because an older man was leading a cow into it. Parking beside a Land Rover and a startling bright red BMW two-seater, she got out of the car to see a dark, weather-beaten man approach her, sleeves rolled up to reveal muscled arms. He could have been any age at all; she understood that he was in his mid-forties.

"Mr. Bailey?" she asked, smiling. "Judy Hill." She withdrew her hand when it became clear that it was not going to be shaken. "My DCI tells me you've received some rather upsetting communications."

"Aye." He jerked his head towards the house, turned, and walked up the steps to the open door.

Judy glanced again at the sports car parked incongruously beside the Land Rover, and at the six-foot-plus Mr. Bailey's retreating back with its broad shoulders. Not his, surely. He'd hardly be able to get into it, for one thing. She presumed that she was supposed to follow, like the old sheepdog that walked at his heel, looking up at him anxiously. He patted the dog's head absently as he went into the house.

The dog stopped on the wide, railed veranda, but Judy imagined that she was allowed in. The film of thin watery mud which covered the courtyard had splashed over her shoes, and she could see nothing on which to wipe them before entering. She shrugged at the dog, and followed Bailey into a wide hallway at which, beside the door, there was the entry phone for the gate, and some sort of switchbox, its cover hanging open.

Ahead were dark green carpeted stairs with a black cast-iron railed banister curving off to the right, then going straight up; against the stair wall stood a long, low, black-lacquered telephone table with a dark green velvet seat over which a quilted jacket had been thrown despite the row of pegs, black cast-iron like the railings above them, between it and the door at the other end of the wall. Big, bold, colourful oil-paintings hung on the rest of the rough, whitewashed walls.

Immediately on her right was the door to the sitting room,

14

sparingly and airily furnished, the fine, cream-coloured vertical blinds closed, producing a soft light from the watery sunshine which fell on to more of the dark green carpeting and soothing colour-washed walls, enlivened by more paintings by the same artist. The centrepiece was a dramatic black stove, pale peach armchairs facing it from three angles. Along the wall, under the window, was a long, matching sofa, and in front of it, a black coffee-table. At the far end, through a stepped archway, a dining table and chairs stood on a raised polished wood platform, lit by the same diffused light from another window. What had once been a rather poky dining room and front room had been opened out into one airy, inviting living space, and it wasn't at all Judy's idea of a farmhouse, especially not one presided over by Mr. Bailey.

To her left, she could see into an office with scuffed striped wallpaper, a metal desk, an open safe containing documents, and a chipped and dented filing cabinet. The only reference to the rest of the house was the cream vertical blind which covered the window. That, she presumed, was Bailey's domain, and she expected to be taken in there to be shown the X-rated communications, but he walked past the office, opened a cupboard, reached in and pulled out two pairs of black rubber boots, handing a pair to her, and began unlacing his shoes.

Judy's heart sank. It had been the wettest spring since God knew when, and she was to be shown the death threats *in situ*. She slipped off her shoes, noticing the mess she and Bailey had made of the hall floor just by coming in from the courtyard, and grimly stepped into the boots. They were two sizes too big and cut down so that they came to mid-calf, catching the hem of her skirt, which sat on them like badly fitting curtains.

They came back out, got into the Land Rover, and, for the next hour, she was driven round the entire farm, stopping to be dragged into hedges and ditches, squelching through God knew what, hostile bushes snagging her jacket and catching her hair, malevolent trees reaching out their branches to rub their wet bark against her, until she had seen and taken down each and every one of the death threats which had been nailed up on trees, stuck up in barns, pinned to bushes . . . all over the damned place.

Back in the relative comfort of the Land Rover, as it jolted and whined its way through mud that would have given a hippopotamus second thoughts, she looked at them properly. They all carried much the same message, to the effect that Bailey was going to die a particularly grisly death if he didn't sell up. The text, liberally sprinkled with four-letter words, was accompanied in each case by an amateurish drawing. They had been done on a computer.

"A lass shouldn't be readin' that," he said. "Wouldn't let th'wife see 'em."

Judy was startled by the number of words he'd managed to produce, but chose to ignore the sentiment. "They appeared overnight?" she asked.

"Aye."

"And your alarms are activated at night?"

"Aye."

The gate was controlled by the panel on the entry phone, unless it was opened with a remote-control "key"; in either event it would close automatically when the visitor passed a certain point, whether on foot or in a vehicle. Vehicles and pedestrians leaving the farm could press a button to open it, and it closed automatically once they cleared a certain point.

"The gate," Judy said. "Who has a key for it besides you and Mrs. Bailey?"

"Th'wife's not got one."

Judy frowned. "Isn't that a bit inconvenient for her?"

"Happen."

Oh, well, none of her business. "Does anyone else have one?"

"Paxton and t'lass."

Paxton, she had already discovered, was his foreman. "Lass?" she queried.

"Daughter. She's t'vet. Sees to th'animals."

16

She knew what a vet was. "What about your employees?" she asked. "How do they get in?"

"Paxton sees to 'em."

"And visitors?" she asked. "Deliveries? Do you sometimes leave the gate open for them?"

"Nay. They use t'phone. Th'wife's allus in th'ouse."

She would be. But the woman must sometimes go to the loo. "There must be times when Mrs. Bailey isn't available to answer the entry phone," Judy said. "What happens then?"

"They don't get in."

Was this any way to run a farm? Judy might not dabble in things rural very often, but she doubted it. "Is your daughter's practice in Harmston?" she asked.

"Aye."

"Does she have employees . . . a partner?"

"Husband. Nowt to do wi' practice. Unemployed."

They pulled back on to the roadway behind the red sports car, which was also returning to the farmhouse, having been somewhere a lot less muddy than they had. Things were looking up, thought Judy; her ordeal was almost over, *and* she was going to find out who in this Godforsaken place drove a two-seater. Both vehicles parked in the courtyard, and Judy clambered out, a process made even more difficult by the ill-fitting wellies, looking up only when she made landfall.

Getting out of the car was a girl in her late twenties, dressed for her surroundings, but elegantly and expensively; she wore little or no make-up, and her blond shoulder-length hair was natural, straight, and well cut. And, for a reason Judy could not pin down, she was quite the most wickedly attractive woman she had ever seen. She reached back into the car and took out a carrier bag, then walked towards the house.

"Your daughter?" said Judy.

"Th'wife," said Bailey. "C'mon."

And Judy, waddling behind him towards the delectable Mrs. Bailey, her clothes muddy and wet, her outsize Wellington boots banging against the backs of her legs, would *garrotte* Lloyd for this.

"Hello," said Mrs. Bailey, turning as she reached the porch, smiling as slowly as she spoke, a long dimple appearing. "You Inspector Hill? You goin' to get to the bottom of all this, then?"

And she had a voice like Devonshire cream. "I hope so," said Judy. "But the flaw with entry phones is that someone—"

"Who let thee in?"

"One of the men watched out for me," his wife said, her voice as soothing as balm. "He was workin' down that way anyway."

Bailey took the carrier bag from her, and looked inside.

"Went into Stansfield. Got a nice bit of salmon. We got no fishmonger in the village," she said to Judy, by way of explanation.

Bailey handed back the bag, and Judy presumed the conversation was over, and reminded herself that she wasn't here to probe the depths of this strange marriage.

"As I was saying," she went on, "the problem with entry phones is that anyone leaving can admit someone, and—"

"Get t'shoes," Bailey said to his wife, with a jerk of his thumb towards the open door, and sat down on one of the wicker seats.

Mrs. Bailey went inside and reappeared minus her shopping and with their shoes. Bailey extended one leg, an indication, it transpired, that his wife should remove his boots. Judy didn't suppose the service would be offered to her, but her boots were so huge that she had no need of assistance anyway. She stepped out of them, and thankfully slipped on her own shoes, as Mrs. Bailey picked up both pairs of boots and went to a standpipe, where she washed the mud off them and her hands.

"Fetch Paxton," he said, with a jerk of his head towards the buildings in the distance, and Mrs. Bailey dried her hands on her designer sweater, and obediently trotted off.

Judy dragged her thoughts away from the Baileys' domestic set-up and opened her mouth to continue.

"C'mon," he said, getting up, going into the house.

Once again she followed him into the hallway, where she was shown the switchbox, which proved to be the alarm system, and Bailey explained how it worked.

Fort Knox should be so lucky. There were fourteen alarms altogether, consisting of the perimeter fence alarm, an alarm which was triggered if the gate remained open for more than thirty seconds, and twelve separate infra-red alarms for the un-fenced boundaries. If one alarm went off, they all did. But if they weren't cancelled, they would cut off after fifteen minutes and reset themselves; the suggestion had apparently been made by the officer called out this morning that Mr. and Mrs. Bailey might have slept through them, so Bailey intended giving her a demonstration. He closed up the box, locking it, thus setting the alarms. He, Judy established, had the only key.

A pick-up truck rumbled into the yard, and Bailey's wife re-turned with the man Judy had seen taking the cow into the cowshed. "This is Steve Paxton, our foreman," she said.

"Hello," said Judy. "I'm—"

"Test th'alarms," said Bailey, and Paxton nodded, walking purposefully off somewhere. "Get in t'kitchen," he said to his wife. "Make thissen useful."

Mrs. Bailey smiled at Judy, and went down the hallway, and through the door at the end.

Judy was still trying to work out the Bailey relationship when suddenly the air was filled with deafening noise, which Bailey allowed to continue well past tolerance levels before he finally opened the box, cancelling the alarms, and let the lid hang open once more.

Paxton came back as Judy's hearing was returning to normal, grinning at her. "I was leaning on the fence," he said. "That's what happens if you put any real weight on it. Happens if anything higher off the ground than a cat crosses the infra-reds, too."

"Thank you," she said, her ears still ringing.

"They can hear them for miles," Paxton went on. "We get

complaints from the neighbours when we test them like we've just done."

Judy could believe it, though their only neighbours were a mile away. At night, they would seem louder.

Paxton left them then to go about his more usual duties, and Judy turned to Bailey. "Whoever it is might be—"

The entry phone buzzed as she spoke, and Bailey reached past her to answer it. "Aye, all right," he said. "If tha must." He hung up, and went back outside, sitting down at the table on the veranda.

Judy followed him out. "Whoever it is might be slipping in on foot through the gate as someone leaves," she said doggedly. "Then waiting until after dark, putting the threats up, and then just leaving by the gate again." She explained as tactfully as she could that it needn't be someone with no right to be there. Someone on the premises legitimately could do the same thing. "I don't know if you—"

Bailey left her in mid-sentence as a small hatchback drew up, going down to the car, and taking something from its woman driver after a brief conversation. The car drove off, and he came back up the steps and sat down again.

"I don't know if you want us to speak to—"

The entry phone interrupted her again, and he got up to answer it. "Right, lad," he said, pressing the button, and came back out.

"Would you like me to have a word with your employees?" asked Judy.

"I can do that missen," he said. "Don't need a lass to do it for me. I want t'bugger caught. That's what I need thee for."

"It won't be easy," Judy told him honestly. But he was fond of security, she thought, and he clearly wasn't short of a bob or two, so she would advise some more. "You might want to consider closed-circuit television," she said, feeling as though she were advising Heathcliff to bug Cathy's bedroom, so little did Mr. Bailey appear to belong to this century, but he seemed to know what she was talking about. Mrs. Bailey reappeared with a tray, and poured two mugs of coffee, handing one to Bailey. "A camera over the—"

An elderly coupé arrived, followed by an estate car, and Judy had once again lost her audience, as a vaguely familiar young man emerged from the former, greeting the Baileys by their first names.

"Police," Bailey said to the young man, with another nod of his head in Judy's direction.

"I'm Curtis Law, *Aquarius 1830*," the young man said to Judy. "You must be DI Hill. Bernard said you'd be coming. You will give us an interview, won't you?"

That was where Judy had seen him. He was on the telly. He reported for the local news at half past six, and he had his own series on policing in the region, called *Law on the Law*. He wasn't overcomplimentary about the constabulary, and if she refused to be interviewed, he would say that the police had declined to make any comment.

"Of course," she said, and turned back to Bailey, determined to finish what she was saying before she was drawing her pension. "A camera positioned over your gate would let you know exactly who was coming in and going out," she said. "Its presence might stop the threats altogether. But if it doesn't, you should be able to catch whoever it is on video, since they have to leave by the gate. I can give you the address of a place in Barton, if you like."

He didn't reply. She wrote the address on a sheet of paper from the unofficial notebook which she took with her everywhere to compensate for the unreliable memory that had almost halted her CID career at the outset. She tore out the sheet and handed it to Bailey, who pocketed it in silence.

"Closed-circuit TV, is that?" said Law. "I could give you a hand setting it up, if you want."

Bailey nodded. "Aye," he said, setting down his mug.

"I would like to interview you and Rachel after the inspector, if I may," Law went on.

"Nay. I've dog to tek to t'lass. Afore lunch."

21

"Well . . . perhaps I could interview you all together?"

"Suits me."

Law turned to Judy, his eyebrows raised.

"I don't mind," she lied. She was under orders to offend no one, and she had probably already offended Bailey. She had better not offend Law as well. She was nervous, and trying not to show it. She was totally unprepared. She knew that she looked as though she had been pulled through a hedge backwards, because she had been, several times. And now she was to be interviewed standing right next to Rachel Bailey.

It seemed interminable, with stops and starts all the time, before Law and his sidekick had decided that they had got enough. Law asked if they could do some general shots of the farm, then come back to do a few reaction shots; Bailey agreed that they could, to Judy's surprise, and they walked off.

"If tha's done, tha can see thissen out," Bailey said to her, taking his wife's arm by the elbow.

Judy watched, intrigued, as Mr. and Mrs. Bailey went into the house, and the old, heavy door closed behind them.

Some puzzles weren't really puzzles at all, she thought, as she thankfully drove off. There were gaps in even Bailey's overkill security. But how Bailey had ended up with a wife like that—that *was* a puzzle. One look at the car and clothes, and she could see what his attraction was for her, but Bailey didn't seem to have married someone twenty years his junior for the usual reasons. She doubted if he even knew what a gorgeous creature he was harbouring.

Bernard kept an iron grip on Rachel's elbow as he locked the front door, and pulled the office door shut, leaving the hallway lit only by the high skylight in the roof. No one could see in, no one could hear anything through the thick stone walls. Rachel knew what that meant, had known ever since she had seen the Land Rover pull on to the road behind her, that she would be getting what Bernard called a hammering. She had thought she could get back before he'd finished with the policewoman; she had been wrong.

"I just had to get your lunch, that's all," she said, her tone conciliatory and quiet and slow. "You were busy. I wasn't gone long. Didn't think a half an hour'd hurt."

A short, hard, back-fisted blow to her ear made her cry out with pain, and for the next few moments, punches landed on her head and back as Bernard administered swift, practised, painful punishment for her disobedience.

"But it does hurt," he said quietly, releasing her. "Doesn't it?"

She furiously blinked back tears, her hand covering her ear, waiting to be told she could go. But without warning he caught her wrist, pulling her hand from her ear, twisting her arm up her back, so that he was behind her, and her heart gave a dip of fear. This wasn't routine.

"Tha went sneakin' out to t'chemist, didn't thee?" he said quietly, his mouth at her still-throbbing ear.

"No," she said. He couldn't know. How could he? She supposed even paranoid guesses must sometimes be right.

"Liar. Tha's not come off pill. I told thee what would happen."

"I'm not *on* the pill." She spoke with the same, slow delivery she always used, though her voice shook with apprehension. "I'm not usin' nothin', Bernard. I told you last time. I swear to God, I'm not."

He dangled something right in front of her eyes. "Tha lost this while tha was out," he said, his voice soft. "June Archer saw it fall. Couldn't catch thee up, so she followed thee back here with it. Tha lost it in t'chemist."

It took her a moment to focus on it in the dim light, and then she could see, swinging gently from his fingers, her gold pendant. Her hand went to her neck, where it should have been, and wasn't.

"So what did tha want wi' chemist that tha had to lie?"

She swallowed the sob that rose to her throat as her arm was

23

twisted further. It still wasn't right from last time. "Tampax," she said. "I left them down in the barn 'fore I drove up here."

Bernard let the pendant fall to the floor. "Pick it up," he said, letting her go.

She might have got away with it, she thought, rubbing her shoulder as she knelt to retrieve her pendant, when his foot between her shoulder blades sent her sprawling face-down, and a second kick just missed her as she desperately rolled away from him, into the stair wall. She got to her knees, rolling herself into a ball for protection.

Bernard reached down and dragged her arms away from her knees, holding them high above her head as he prodded her stomach painfully with the toe of his shoe. "Tampax— pill. It's all t'same," he said. "Tha's no use to me while there's nowt happening in *theer*." And he drew his foot back to deliver a kick.

"There might *be* somethin' happenin'!" she shouted desperately.

He froze, his foot still poised.

"I'm late," she said, her eyes never leaving his. "It might be your son you're goin' to lay into this time."

"Then what would tha want wi' tampons?"

"Just in case."

For a moment, he didn't move, didn't speak, as he thought about what she had said. Then his eyes narrowed with suspicion. "Does tha *still* tek me for a fool? It's nobbut ten days sin' tha said it were tha time o' t'month."

"It was. Didn't say I'd come on."

"Then tha's a lying bitch," he said softly. "One way or t'other."

Her heart was pounding, her voice unsteady, as she desperately fought the tears. "Maybe I am," she said, her eyes still on his, her tones still measured, despite the fear. "But I'm late, all the same, and you better stop this right now if you want your baby born in one piece."

He held her there for a long, long time, as his eyes searched hers. Then he let her go, and his forefinger extended from his clenched fist, his head shaking a warning. "Tha'd best be pregnant," he said. "Or God help thee."

"I just said I was late." Sobs of relief were overtaking her. "I can't promise nothin'."

"I said."

He reached over to the telephone table, and picked up his jacket, shrugging it on. "Don't cook owt for me. I'm going into Barton, see about this closed-circuit TV. I'll get summit out." He went to the door, unlocking it. "I'll likely not want supper neither," he said, and nodded. "Happen I'll go to this do tonight, after all." He turned and looked down at her. "Get up, woman. There's nowt wrong wi' thee."

She got slowly to her feet, holding on to the banister railings, her legs shaking too much to support her.

Bernard looked at the dusty, dried mud on her clothes, and down at the floor. "And get this cleaned up afore I get back," he said. Then he opened the door, whistled for the dog, and walked away.

Rachel clung to the railings, and watched through the tears as Nell jumped into the back of the Land Rover, and Bernard swung himself into the front, driving off. When she felt she could let go, she picked up her pendant, went into the kitchen for the mop and bucket, and washed the floor. Upstairs, she made herself stop crying, showered, changed, and went back downstairs, out on to the veranda. Their cars were still there, and she went down the steps, crossing the courtyard to the cowshed.

The surroundings were really quite comfortable, considering they'd been designed for cows to sleep in, she thought. Today, there was a tenant, but she was at the far end, and there was clean straw in the other stalls, ready for the rest of the small dairy herd. The walls and ceiling were insulated against the weather. She'd lain down in a lot worse places in her time, not least of which was Bernard Bailey's bed.

Bernard was desperate to have a son, and for good reason.

25

He had inherited the farm from his grandfather, but the bulk of the inheritance would be paid over if and when Bernard's first son was born, providing that he was Bernard's natural son, legitimate, and Bernard still owned the farm in its entirety. The old man had made a fortune on the stock-market, and that fortune had been earning interest for almost twenty-six years while Bernard Bailey had been desperately trying to have a son.

His first wife had died, and he had asked Rachel to become his second. Once she had given him a boy, he had said, he would give her a divorce, and he had promised to pay her more money in settlement than Rachel had ever dreamed of having in her most extravagant fantasies. But she hadn't been so dazzled by this prospect that she had lost her common sense. She might have half a dozen kids before she had a boy, she had said, and he had said that in the meantime she could have anything she wanted for the house, for herself. What if something happened to him before she had given him a son, she had asked, and he had said that he would make a will, leaving everything to her. On these mutually acceptable terms, she had married Bernard Bailey.

To start with, things had been all right. She had found Bernard hard going, but she had thought that if all she had to do to be financially secure for the rest of her life was to keep house and endure his silent thrustings until a son was produced, she could live with it. And he had kept to his part of the bargain; she had had a free hand with the interior decor, getting ideas from magazines and watching the modest little house blossom under her direction. It had been full of workmen and tradesmen who couldn't do enough for her, and it had been fun.

But the first punches had landed six weeks into the marriage, and her crime had been her failure to become pregnant. She had always been almost as regular as the moon itself, and when she had found herself overdue, she had thought that with her mother's fecundity she had conceived straight away. She had told Bernard, but it had turned out to be a false alarm. He had said she had lied to him, and the punishment for that imagined lie had lasted seconds, and had left her black and blue for a week.

She had been going to leave him there and then, until she had sat down and considered her position. She had no money of her own, no home to run back to. All she had was a pendant that she could pawn when the going got rough, and she hadn't been convinced that the going had got rough enough. She was bound to get pregnant soon, she had told herself.

But the very regularity that had caused her to believe she had become pregnant had been, in Bernard's obsessed mind, grounds for suspicion that she was on the pill, that she was milking the arrangement, taking all she could from him before she had to start giving him babies. So almost anything she had done or said had constituted an excuse for yet another short, sharp reminder that she was supposed to be giving him a son. She had learned from experience not to fight back, not to utter aloud the names she called him under her breath, not to leave before she was dismissed, because that prolonged the proceedings. He'd hammered obedience into his lass, and he'd hammer it into her, he would tell her as the vicious little punches landed, and to some extent, he had. Because she hadn't left him, unwilling to give up on her fortune. She might be married to a raving lunatic, but he was going to be an incredibly rich raving lunatic, and she was on a percentage.

And as summer had approached, she had finally missed a period, but she hadn't told Bernard, by that time unsure of what she intended doing. Bernard had been expecting a visitor, and she had been sent up to the bedroom as she always was when business was to be discussed; she had been giving long, hard consideration to her future, had decided that she would have to leave, when she had heard the voices.

At first they had baffled her, scared her, apparently coming out of thin air. Then she had realized, from the monosyllabic responses, that one of them was Bernard's, and she knew where they were coming from, and why she had never heard them before. It had been the first day since she had moved in that there had been no fires lit in the non–centrally heated farm-house. And it had been eavesdropping on that one-sided conversation, floating up through the chimney breast from the empty hearth in the office into the empty hearth in the bedroom, that had determined Rachel's course of action.

It was someone called McQueen who had come to see him; Bernard had told him to get out, but he had stood his ground. Men could; Bernard wasn't so brave with men. And McQueen had said that he knew why Bernard had let most of the crops go and had concentrated on animals; which had, as things had turned out, been a wrong move, with the beef ban.

She had already known that Bernard was having a difficult time of it with the export ban produced by the beef health-scare; half his profits had gone at a stroke, and the cows weren't being auctioned at anything like their proper price at home. He had had to slaughter some of the cattle, and was still waiting for compensation; he had been told he might have to slaughter a whole lot more. Nothing had been settled about that, and he was having to feed and water them until it was. Couldn't sell them, couldn't do anything with them.

What she hadn't known, what she had found out, was that Bernard had risked almost all his capital in some financial venture; not long after his first wife died, it had failed, and he had lost it all. That when the beef ban had come along, he had had nothing to fall back on, and had borrowed money, then more money, then more, until now one missed payment on the loan meant repossession of the farm. That he was paying it back with money he didn't have, living on credit that he couldn't repay. That despite the impression he gave of solid wealth, the truth was that he was broke, and the farm couldn't carry on for more than a few months longer.

But McQueen wanted Bernard's land, and the amount he was prepared to pay for it had made Rachel's eyes widen. Bernard had turned him down, of course, because he had very much greater expectations. But Rachel had already decided

28

that she wasn't going to tell him about the baby she was carrying; once she had heard McQueen's offer, she knew she had to get rid of it altogether. If there was no baby, he would have no incentive to keep on juggling his money around; he would *have* to sell, and she would still be able to salvage something from her dreadful mistake of a marriage. Because, while her share wouldn't be the spectacular amount that giving him a son would net her, it would be a great deal better than nothing.

So she hadn't left him. She had made arrangements to terminate her pregnancy, quietly and discreetly, under the guise of a visit to her fortunately uncontactable family, had really gone on the pill, and had returned to Bernard to await developments. But what she hadn't reckoned on was Bernard holding out as long as he had.

For almost twelve months she had hung in there, her eyes on the prize, the hammerings growing more frequent as Bernard's frustration with her lack of productivity grew. In January, he had installed the security fencing, and she had discovered that she was not to be given a key for the gate. She couldn't take her car out and be certain of getting back in, not without Bernard's permission; effectively that meant that she was stuck in Harmston, which not only didn't have a fishmonger; it had no chemist, no outlet for family-planning requisites. Bernard accompanied her on shopping trips to Stansfield, watching her every purchase. Rachel, convinced that he must sell any day, had simply made alternative arrangements, and her nonproductivity had continued until Bernard's suspicions that she was on the pill had hardened to certainty. Then one night, six weeks ago, she had been dragged from bed and subjected to a brutal and prolonged assault designed to discourage its use.

Her feeble, barefooted attempts to defend herself had proved useless, and the careful, deliberate violence had gone on until she had finally collapsed, wrenching her shoulder as Bernard's grip had refused to yield to her body weight. She had best get pregnant soon, he had said, as she half knelt, half hung there in agony, because if there was no sign of a baby in the very near future, she'd get the same again. Then he had let her fall barely conscious to the floor, had got undressed, got into bed and gone to sleep.

When he had got up next morning, she had managed to pull the duvet from the bed, and wrap herself in it; eventually, she had stopped shivering. And when he had left in the afternoon to go on his rounds with Steve Paxton, she had telephoned Nicola for help. Nicola had been horrified, but useful, with her medical knowledge. She had given her first aid, but had insisted on taking her to casualty in case of cracked ribs or worse. There, Rachel had told a pack of lies to account for the state she was in, and had been examined. Very extensive deep bruising, they had said, but no internal injuries, no broken bones. She could have told them that, because that had not been Bernard's intention.

Before leaving Barton, Rachel had asked Nicola to take her to the station, where she had shut herself in the photo booth and taken photographs of her injuries before time took care of them. Bernard might try to prolong the divorce proceedings, and she had wanted ammunition.

Now she had been caught out in a lie, and her plan of action had changed once more. He had been going to do that to her again; she couldn't have taken another beating like that, and telling him that she might be pregnant had been a desperate measure that at least called a halt to the violence while she worked out where to go from here.

And there was only one way that she could see.

"She's fine," said Nicola, scratching Nell's head as she threw the syringe in the bin, having given the old dog her annual check-up. Animals were the only living things her father cared about; she had inherited her love for them from him. She hoped she had inherited nothing else.

"Tha can tek 'er back to t'farm," said her father. "There's a cow Paxton doesn't like t'look of. Tek a look at her while tha's theer."

It was perhaps her father's stage Yorkshireness that upset Nicola most of all; he hadn't set foot in the place for a quarter of a century, and she doubted very much that he'd ever heard anyone under eighty speak like that even when he'd lived there. He'd picked most of it up from the telly, she was sure.

"Well, I . . ." she began.

"I've business in Barton," said her father. "Can't tek dog in wi' me, can't leave 'er in t'car. Tha's doing nowt else."

Nicola pushed her short dark hair behind her ears, a habit she knew she had when she wanted to say no and couldn't, because her husband had pointed it out to her. "The thing is, Gus is making—"

"Tha's been told," he said. "And don't forget t'other beast. She's in t'cowshed." He pushed open the swing door.

"What's wrong with her?"

"Tha's t'vet. Thee tell me." The door swung back behind him.

The outside door banged shut, and Nicola heard the Land Rover start up and drive off. He had deliberately come at lunchtime, so that she couldn't plead a patient. She looked at Nell, who was looking back at her with the anxious expression she always wore, and sighed. "Come on," she said to the dog. "Let's go and find Gus."

"Oh, Nicola!" Gus said, irritated, when she told him.

"What else could I do? He just left her and went."

He shook his head, and stooped to tickle Nell's chin. "Shall we hold you hostage until he pays her something?" he asked the dog, who wagged her tail.

Nicola could never resist the top of Gus's head, its short fair hair growing almost in a circle from the crown. She kissed it. "We'd just end up with another mouth to feed," she said, then wished she hadn't, when she saw Gus's reaction.

"And I can't even feed the two of us, is that what you mean?"

"You know I don't," she said. "You'll get a job eventually. And we'll be all right even if you don't get one for a while."

"All right? I do your accounts, remember."

"There are people worse off."

"Not many vets," he said, straightening up. "You could tell your father you don't run a taxi service for retired sheepdogs. You could send him a bill now and then. It isn't all my fault we're broke."

"It isn't your fault at all." Nicola knelt on the floor and absently patted the dog. "He wouldn't pay them if I did send him bills," she added. He wouldn't just not pay them, she thought. He would take it as a personal insult. "And I do have *some* paying customers," she said with a smile, trying to lighten the prevailing mood a little. "I'm quite a good vet, you know."

"He spends money like water, Nicky—I'm sure he just doesn't think about it because you don't send him bills. Of course he'd pay them. He doesn't expect your gratitude for the rest of your life, but he's not going to pay you if you don't ask him. He buys her BMWs, for God's sake, and he doesn't pay you!"

They had had this conversation several times since Gus had been made redundant. And they had felt the loss of his income very keenly, but they would survive. Nicola smiled. "He's got to keep Rachel happy," she said. "She's going to give him a son and heir, isn't she?" She ruffled the dog's hair. "Maybe we should kidnap *her*. What do you think, Nell?"

Gus crouched down and covered Nicola's hand where it rested on the dog's head, and gave it a little squeeze. "Go on, then. Go and mend his cow. I'll keep your lunch warm."

"You'll make someone a wonderful wife," she said.

"I know," he said. "I didn't know I had it in me." He stood up. "What did you eat before?" he asked. "When I was still in the ranks of the employed?"

She shrugged. "Pot Noodles. Or, as we in the veterinary trade like to make clear, Not Poodles."

"I think I'd *prefer* poodles," said Gus. "What do I do if I get an emergency?"

"In the kitchen? Don't ask me."

He pulled a face. "An emergency call for you," he said.

32

"If you can't get me at the farm, ring Willsden and Pearce."

"How come," he asked, as he went into the kitchen, "both Willsden and Pearce run round in brand-new Range Rovers and you can't even afford a mobile phone?"

She was going to be told the answer. She put Nell's lead on.

"Could it be because they get your business while you're doing people favours you don't even want to do them? Because you fall for any sob story you hear? Because you treat that stingy old bugger's animals for nothing? Because you don't know how to say no to any—"

She ushered Nell out and closed the door. She had heard the lecture, and Gus knew that she wouldn't be waiting to hear it again. Their old car shuddered into life, and she headed out for the farm, windscreen wipers protesting because the fine rain that misted her windscreen wasn't wet enough for them.

The odd thing was that, despite what he had just said, Gus might just be the only person in Harmston who got on quite well with her father. If you didn't count that reporter, whose support her father had deliberately courted. Her father had spent his entire life alienating people very efficiently indeed.

At the age of twenty-one, just after he had inherited the farm his grandfather had left him in his will, he had got her mother, then just fifteen years old, and a Saturday employee in the farm office, pregnant. They had announced their intention of marrying as soon as she was sixteen, still a month away. There had, of course, been a huge row with both sets of parents, and her mother's parents had said that they would refuse consent. Her father had, in typically melodramatic fashion, eloped with her mother to Scotland, established residency, and had married her there. Nicola had been born in Scotland. Then he had come to Bartonshire and taken possession of the land his grandfather had left him.

And it wasn't *just* melodrama; the fact was that she had never known any of her grandparents, whom he had cut off completely from that day on. The tentative attempts she had made after her mother's death to trace the family had ended in failure, and she hadn't tried again.

Her mother had produced her prematurely within two months of their marriage. It had been a difficult pregnancy, and she had been advised not to have any more children. Which she hadn't. Just miscarriage after miscarriage, and the occasional stillborn baby, until she had been worn out. And her father had blamed her for failing him. He'd married her so she'd give him a son, he'd said. And what had she given him? Her. A lass. What use was a lass to him?

He had taken over a successful farm, and had made it more successful. And, like his grandfather before him, he had played the stock-market, and played it well. So well that he had gone into a sort of semi-retirement already. He was well off by any standards in his own right, but he had been and still was obsessed with the millions that remained just out of his reach.

Nicola had escaped his brutal discipline when she went to veterinary college, and had married Gus almost as soon as she had come back to Harmston. She had never told Gus what he was really like; Gus was so gentle, so unlike her father, that she thought it would hurt him to know. Her mother had died at thirty-nine, miscarrying her umpteenth child, less than two years ago.

And her father had been married to Rachel for almost eighteen months.

Curtis Law stood in front of one of the outbuildings, and nodded solemnly, then smiled and nodded. "Will it look all right?" he asked. "It's raining now—it wasn't when I was interviewing them."

"No one'll notice. Trust me, I'm a cameraman."

Curtis carried on with his nods and smiles. Reaction shots. How he might have looked while they were answering his questions. He repeated one or two so that they could edit him in, and he wouldn't just be a voice coming out of the ether.

He had been right in the middle of a big story for *Law on the*

*Law* when *Aquarius 1830* had taken it into their heads to base him at the Stansfield regional office. He had been less than pleased to get sent to some outpost of empire, and the first thing he'd had to cover had been some rich crank with a load of land he didn't want to part with, and the equally well-heeled villagers who opposed his stand.

That was all it had been to start with, the human-interest bit at the end of the proper news, the always entertaining sight of the middle classes getting their dander up. But the dead donkey had got up and walked a few times since that first story, for which Curtis was truly grateful. Vandals had started raiding Bailey's Farm, putting sugar in petrol tanks, slashing huge, expensive tractor tyres, daubing the vehicles with paint, which had provided *Aquarius 1830* with several nights' bulletins, and then Bailey had proved to be a genuine nutcase, which was always good news for local media. He had ringed his farm with more alarms than a high-security prison, and the villagers had objected both to the eyesore of a fence and to the ear-splitting alarms, which could be heard for miles. But practically as soon as he'd installed them, Bailey had got up one morning to find death threats pinned up all over the place, and he had been finding them ever since.

For several weeks, Curtis had become a fixture at Bailey's Farm, and he couldn't have been happier about that. But his last visit had been three months ago, the death threats having become so commonplace as to be no longer news. Now, thank God, Bailey had had more explicit death threats, so he was back.

But the really big story was for *Law on the Law*. He didn't know whether his interest in things criminal had been as a result of his surname, or if some ancestral voice had been calling to him, but it had done no harm to have a name they could play with in the title. Now he was on the brink of the big time. His producer had gone out on a limb for him, spending about forty per cent of the programme's budget on that story alone, and it really could be his passport to national television, to rescuing

*Law on the Law* from its Monday late-evening regional slot and getting it networked in prime time.

He had a false identity, a mobile phone, a hired Jag—the lot. He even had a disguise. The criminal fraternity had a tendency to watch programmes about the police, and though his face was rarely on screen during *Law on the Law*, the make-up department had devised a disguise for him that had worked, albeit briefly, on his mother.

The scam had been his idea—he had thought that the increase in break-ins at premises where drugs were held wasn't just random, and it looked as though he was right. The rendezvous was tonight, and if it worked, he would hand the cops Mr. Big on a plate. The cliché wasn't his; it was a direct quote from a senior policeman, who had been shrugging off the suggestion that organized crime was behind the raids. So, "Operation Mr. Big" it had become.

The interview with DI Hill and the Baileys had taken forever; his attempts to interview Bernard Bailey always did. It was odd how someone who said nothing took much longer than someone you couldn't shut up. He was late already; he should be in Barton now, because he had a busy afternoon's work ahead of him, getting himself ready for this evening. It could lead to glory, or it could lead to his being found up some alleyway if he was rumbled. They had to be sure that everything was right if they were to avoid the second possibility.

He said he had to go, and Gary packed up, got into his car, wishing him good luck for tonight, and drove off.

"You look a right prat doin' all that noddin' and stuff, you know that?"

The lazy voice was right behind him. Curtis turned and looked at Rachel. She stood smiling at him, her hands in the pockets of the full skirt of a dress which would have been demure, with its long sleeves and its buttons right up to the neck, if she had been wearing a bra, which she wasn't. He could see her nipples through the rain-dampened silk, and his mouth went dry.

"I got the keys to the flat today," he said, taking a key from his pocket, holding it out to her. He tried to sound casual, but it was hopeless, and he found himself gabbling. "It's on lease until October—when Mr. Big's all over, it'll be sitting there empty for weeks, I know it will. I might have to hand them back, so I got copies made. I don't know if you'll be able to get away, but I thought if I could ring you when I've got an hour or so, maybe if you could give Ber—"

Her mouth was on his. "I'll get there," she said, kissing him and talking at the same time. "Just try stoppin' me."

She took the key from him, slipping it into her pocket, and now her tongue was pushing gently, irresistibly, into his mouth, sending a shudder of desire through his body.

"But we got the cowshed right now," she said, catching his tie, pulling him gently as she walked backwards towards the shed. "Bernard's gone into Barton. We got most of the afternoon, I reckon."

He was supposed to be in Barton, getting ready for tonight, but Curtis allowed himself to be led through the doorway of the building, out of the drizzle, stopping dead as soon as he was inside. "There's a cow in here."

Rachel smiled. "You get that now and again in cowsheds," she said, leading him into an unoccupied stall. "She won't peek."

He should be in Barton, he shouldn't be here, he thought, as he kissed her gently on the mouth, then kissed her face, her neck, his hand caressing her breast through the silk. "Oh, to hell with Mr. Big," he said, drawing her down with him to the soft straw, pushing up her dress. "To hell with everything."

# CHAPTER TWO

RACHEL DREW IN HER BREATH, MORE FROM THE pain an involuntary movement had caused her bruised body than from pleasure at Curtis's touch. This was the last thing she wanted to do, but she had been given the chance, and Bernard didn't give her many chances, not these days. If she could do it with Bernard within days of that dreadful beating, she could do it with a few routine bruises and Curtis.

He unbuttoned her top button, and kissed the triangle of skin at her neck. She smiled, loosened his tie, and undid his top button, kissing his throat. The next buttons; another exchange of kisses. But that was when she realized the implication of what he had just said.

"What do you mean, 'To hell with Mr. Big'?" she asked, her voice slow and suspicious. "You supposed to be workin' on that?"

"Sort of. But the meeting isn't until tonight."

His evasive answer didn't fool her. "You said to hell with it," she said. "You're supposed to be doin' somethin' now." Her eyes widened, as she pieced it together. The meeting. That was what the whole thing had been working up to. "Is it tonight you get the drugs, and all that?"

"Yes," he said, tackling her third button.

She smacked his hand away before he got her blouse open any further. If he saw the old bruises from that beating now she would never get rid of him, and he was supposed to be in Barton, getting ready for tonight.

He smacked her hand back, in the spirit of the game. "Why have you stopped me?" he asked.

"You don't have time for all that. You said that this was the most important part, settin' it all up. You said if you didn't do it right, you could get hurt."

"I don't *care* about that." His voice was agonized, his eyes pleading with her.

"You said it was the best thing that ever happened to you." Rachel didn't want him losing this chance. "What do you mean, you don't care about it?"

"*You're* the best thing that ever happened to me."

"Don't be daft." It was said as sharply as she ever said anything.

"You *are* the best thing that ever happened to me. And I never get the chance to be with you."

He never got the chance to screw her, in other words. But Curtis really did think he was in love. And he thought that she was, too, come to that, but that was his problem. She had never said she was. She needed him, that was all. And she hadn't known that his meeting was tonight; that was the last thing she wanted to jeopardize. But she couldn't just send him away. It had been three months since she'd seen him; she was lucky he hadn't given up on her already.

"A quickie," she said. "Then you got to go."

Curtis accepted the compromise with alacrity, abandoning the foreplay much to Rachel's relief. The sooner it was over the better, as far as she was concerned.

Nicola had deposited Nell with the other two dogs, and now she parked in the courtyard, and walked into the cowshed. She heard them before she saw them, in the gloom. And before they saw her.

"Oh, shit," said Rachel, letting her arms fall away from her companion.

He turned to look behind him then, and Nicola could see that it was the TV reporter who was with her, who was jumping to his feet, frantically pulling up his trousers, brick-red with embarrassment.

"Don't mind me," she said. "Carry on."

He fled from the cowshed, but Nicola had seen nature in the raw far too often to let the sight of copulation bother her. Rachel was apparently just as unconcerned; she stood up, her skirt falling back down to cover her bare legs, her blue eyes on Nicola's.

"He wanted me to look at a cow," Nicola said.

Rachel smiled her slow smile. "You're lookin' at the wrong one," she said. "The one you want's down the bottom there."

Nicola smiled, too, and walked along to her patient, who was supremely unimpressed by the goings-on. But she felt anxious, as Rachel went to restore her boyfriend's dented dignity. It was none of her business what Rachel did, so she hadn't said anything, but she was taking a terrible risk.

Nicola thought again of the appalling beating her father had given Rachel, much, much worse than anything he had ever done to her, and didn't know how Rachel dared. She had begged her to leave him, but she wouldn't; Nicola had no idea why not. She wasn't frightened to, not like her mother had been; Rachel was frightened of nothing.

Rachel had come to work as a part-timer in the farm shop, just three months after Nicola's mother had died. He had at first asked her to look after the house and cook his meals, then he had asked her to marry him. Nicola had told him what she thought of the haste, and of the difference in their ages, a gap much wider than mere years. Her father belonged to another age, another era, possibly to a world known only to writers of gothic romances. She should have known better than to question her father's actions, but in the end she was given an explanation, of sorts. "She's got time on her side," he said. "She'll bear me a son." Nicola was surprised he settled for the word "son," but even he drew the line at "boy-child."

Time on her side. He could say that again. She was only two

years older than Nicola herself. But Rachel seemed to be working to her own agenda, hanging on as long as she could before she started having babies, and now she was playing around with the TV reporter. Nicola addressed herself to the much less complex problems of the other cow, smiling again at Rachel's little joke, just hoping that she took more care in the future.

Judy had gone home and changed before going back to work. She had got on with what she regarded as more important things until it was time to clear her desk and let it all wait for tomorrow. Then she walked along the corridor, knocked on Lloyd's door, and went in.

He grinned when he saw her change of clothes. "A bit muddy, was it?" he asked.

"A bit."

"I did warn you that it might be."

She nodded, and sat down. "There were a few things that you didn't warn me about," she said.

Lloyd looked all injured innocence. "Such as?"

"Such as, there was a television reporter there."

"Was there really?" he said. "Are you going to be on the telly?"

He looked as though he really hadn't known about that. And if he had, he would have gone himself, Judy reasoned, since he was fond of appearing on television. She forgave him very slightly. "Yes," she said.

"Oh, we'll have to watch."

"And such as, Bernard Bailey is a complete lunatic who only says one word at a time."

"I don't know Bailey, so I didn't know he was a complete lunatic who only says one word at a time," Lloyd said. "Anyway—what's your plan of action?"

"I've got Alan seeing if we can get any sort of lead on the computer program from the print or the graphics, but he says they all do that sort of print, and they all have a drawing capacity, so he's not exactly optimistic about our chances of success."

"Have you ever known Alan Marshall to be optimistic about anything?" Lloyd said, mimicking Marshall's polite Glasgow drawl.

"I thought they seemed a bit adolescent, but he says he thinks it's someone trying to make it look like that, so that's not much of a lead. And even if we do narrow it down to a particular program, ownership of such a program won't exactly prove anything, will it? I've suggested that Alan ask a few obvious hostile factions politely about their computers, and I've asked if the area car can put in an appearance up there over the next few evenings—more so Bailey can see that we're doing something than for any other reason. I doubt very much if they'll catch anyone in the act. I've advised him to think about closed-circuit television."

Lloyd tipped his chair back. Judy had watched him do that for years, and he had never fallen yet. But she was always waiting for the crash. It was how he thought: gently rocking on two legs of a chair. Sometimes quite useful ideas came out of it.

"No one else lives in at the farm? Just Bailey and his wife?"

"No one else. But his daughter has a key to the gate, unlike his wife."

"Did you speak to his wife?"

"Not really, other than to say hello," said Judy, with what she felt was positively heroic understatement. "I tried to see the daughter, but she was out. I spoke to her husband. Nicola Hutchins does all the veterinary work for her father—that's where she was when I called at the surgery. He'd hardly give her all that work if there was any bad blood."

"Probably not," said Lloyd. "But families are funny things. What about the foreman? Your notes said he had a key."

"Unlike Mrs. Bailey," Judy said again. She must surely resent that, but it had been very obvious that Mrs. Bailey was not to be approached, so she hadn't spoken to her. "I didn't speak to him directly about the death threats, because Bailey didn't want me to," she said.

"Could someone's key have been copied?"

"No. They're electronic, and they're issued under some sort of licence system. Only three were ever issued. But it doesn't have to be a keyholder. Anyone could be doing it, providing they stay out of sight, which is why I suggested CCTV. You can *leave* without a key, though that's about the only thing you can do. In effect, anyone could be doing it. *Mrs.* Bailey, for instance, which wouldn't surprise me. Come to that, it could quite possibly be Bailey himself, trying to drum up sympathy."

"Do you think that's likely?"

"Not really. I think he's scared. The security has to be seen to be believed. But it was all in place before the first lot of death threats, even, so that's not what he was scared of to start with."

"Does Bailey have any theories?"

Judy sighed. "You don't *get* theories from Mr. Bailey," she said. "You get 'aye' and 'nay' and 'happen.'"

"Do I gather that you aren't exactly keen to head this investigation?"

Judy ignored him. "The real question is, do we think they are serious threats?"

"And *do* we?" Lloyd let the chair fall back.

"No," Judy said decidedly. "If you're going to murder someone, you murder him. You don't leave him notes about it. Someone is trying to scare him, upset him . . . hoping to make him sell the land. I don't believe that they're serious death threats."

"But you said he was scared of something before all this. Does *he* think someone's going to kill him?"

Judy tried once again to explain that she hadn't the faintest idea what Bernard Bailey thought. "I just know he's got the place wired up as though he has the Crown Jewels there," she said. "If you think you can devise a method of communication that will reveal what he's frightened of, feel free. I won't be a bit offended."

Lloyd smiled. "Never have got on with the strong, silent type, have you?"

No. She preferred the talkative type, like Lloyd, like her father. You could judge their moods, catch nuances. Someone like Bernard Bailey was a closed book to her. "Feelings are running high about this road, and this sort of thing happens," she said. "The death threats are on a par with the graffiti, I think. Just less refined."

"Right. Let's call it a day," said Lloyd. "Let's face it—we were being used as a sop to soothe one of Case's Freemason buddies, and we've done that now."

"*We've* done that now?" said Judy. "*We?* I didn't see you up to your knees in mud."

"And I didn't see you." Lloyd shook his head sadly. "That's something I will regret for a long time."

"Closed-circuit television?" The end of Mike McQueen's cigar glowed red, and he blew out the match.

Rachel Bailey nodded. She sat at the other side of his desk, as Curtis Law had done that morning; Mike always kept the desk between them, in case she might actually see the effect his libidinous thoughts were having on him.

He remembered the first time he had seen her, when she had turned up at his door just over a year ago, and had introduced herself, first to Shirley, then to him. Curtis Law was right about his ivory tower; he had known Bailey had married again almost immediately, but it hadn't occurred to him for one moment that his new wife would be nineteen years younger than him and look like Rachel. He still couldn't believe it; Rachel married to Bernard Bailey was an impossible notion, like an Escher drawing.

"Brought the man back with him," she said, in her honey-drenched voice. "He's there now—sortin' out where all the cameras'll go and that. Shows he's rattled."

There were no *tees* at all the way she spoke the word, not even the Geordie glottal stop that he had employed as a child. In her mouth, it entirely lost its onomatopoeic quality, and Mike wondered what her tongue had to do to produce the delightful sound it did make, then dragged his thoughts back to business, feeling foolish. Rachel Bailey had awakened dreams and desires in him that he had thought were long gone, and she didn't even know she was doing it, which made it all the more potent.

"Yes," he said. "But he'd hardly go to all that expense if he was thinking of giving up and selling as a result, would he?"

"Maybe not. But he's not ignorin' them. Won't even let me see them, this time," she added, with a wicked smile.

Mike had said that he *would* ignore them, when she had first suggested it. But she had been right; Bailey had called the police in the moment he had seen them. They had overplayed their hand, however, and Bailey had begun to accept them as a fact of life, until she had suggested that a few obscenities would shake him up. She had been right about that, too, but it seemed to Mike that it had backfired, if he was getting security cameras put in. It seemed incredible that Bailey could actually be afraid for his life as a result of this nonsense, but it seemed he was; Rachel Bailey knew her man.

She leant forward. "How's he going to feel if he gets another lot *after* the cameras are in?"

Mike drew reflectively on his cigar, his thoughts far away from Bailey's closed-circuit television. And ludicrous, he told himself sternly. She was over thirty years his junior, for God's sake. He'd thought he was immune to all this; he hadn't given it a thought after Shirley had switched to twin beds, or for a long time before, come to that, which was why she had felt justified in doing it. But when Rachel Bailey was here, he was able to think of practically nothing else, like an adolescent. His long abstinence had made him vulnerable to sexual stimuli, he supposed, and all she had to do was smile at him.

"Will you do some more for me?" she asked. "Sayin' cameras won't keep him safe?"

Mike shook his head. "If the cameras don't pick up any strangers going through the gate, it will become blindingly obvious that whoever's putting them up must be someone who doesn't have to leave the premises," he said.

"Supposin' the cameras *do* see a stranger?"

"And when was the last time Bailey let a stranger through the gate?"

"He has to let some through. Ramblers. They got right of way—he can't refuse them. 'Tisn't worth the hassle, 'cos they won't go away. Easier just to let them in. They walk right through the farm. Come back through, when they're done ramblin'. No way he's goin' to see nothin' till next mornin', and I could've put them up by then."

"Give him half a dozen strangers to worry about at once?" Mike shook his head. "No," he said. "It's too risky."

Her face fell. "But it would make him believe that someone can get right past his cameras and kill him any time they want," she said. "Please, Mr. McQueen."

"No," he repeated, firmly. "These cameras pan and scan. You'd get caught." He shook his head at her through the heavy cigar smoke that hung in the air between them. "No," he said again.

"I wouldn't get caught," she said scornfully. "You think I can't dodge a few cameras? And he'd be scared, Mr. McQueen. He would."

"Not scared enough. It wouldn't make him sell up."

"But he thinks someone's out to get him," she said. "And closed-circuit TV don't come cheap. So what when *it* don't work? What next? Guard dogs? Security men? They all cost money. He must be gettin' close to his limit. Just needs nudgin', maybe."

"And what makes you think this road is important enough to me to help you do the nudging?"

She sat back. "You don't want a *road,*" she said. "You want

46

Bernard's land. Trouble is, you're buildin' an estate, and you *need* a road. So if he don't give in soon, you'll have to give up."

Mike nodded acknowledgement of that, a little surprised at her neat summing up of his situation. "You're right," he said. "Work has to start on a road by the beginning of August. And if he's still hanging on by the end of July, I *am* going to have to take the other route."

"And I'd lose my gamble," she said. "Reckon we both would. You goin' to let him win without a fight?"

He had fought. So had she. But sometimes you had to accept defeat. "I don't know how he's made it this far," he said. "But he has, and I don't think two more months will break him."

"*Might* break him," said Rachel. "If he's payin' for all sorts of security, he must be gettin' in deeper and deeper. Maybe the next lot'd do for him."

He still shook his head, but he knew that he would do it for her. She could persuade him to do anything, and had, with that voice, that golden, shining hair, and those dark eyebrows and dark-lashed blue eyes, and that long dimple when she smiled her slow smile, as she was doing now. Besides, her visits to him had brought him back to life, to an extent that he would not have believed; even getting Bailey's land seemed less important than it had. But it was still very important to her that Bailey sell, and he might as well give her a last throw of the dice.

He smiled back, a little reluctantly. "All right, pet," he said. "You've talked me into it." He sighed his disapproval of his own actions, put down his cigar, and switched on the computer. "Again," he added.

Judy's image appeared on the television, uncharacteristically windswept, slightly muddy, and very wet.

Lloyd smiled. He called her his gun dog sometimes, because she positively pointed when she got on to anything in an investigation. And surely gun dogs were *supposed* to be wet and muddy on occasion? He listened as she gave coolly professional answers to Curtis Law's questions, as he had known she

47

would, and sneaked a look at her as she watched herself on television, saw the slight flush in her cheeks.

They were in her flat, which was highly unusual, but it had been the only way he was going to get to see her watch herself on television for the first time. He resisted coming to her flat very often; it seemed to him to be sanctioning their separate lives. But she had refused point-blank to come home with him this evening, so he had turned up here just before her debut, relieving her of the remote control as she had threatened to turn off the TV.

He and Judy had been involved, one way or another, for twenty years, and for the last seven or so he had been trying to get her to move in with him without success. She had agreed, after a long campaign, to marry him when he retired from the job, but he still wasn't convinced she would move out of her flat even then.

He got his first look at Bailey, a saturnine man with a face like granite, who did indeed communicate one word at a time. And then he got his first look at Mrs. Bailey, and discovered that it wasn't just the chance of TV stardom that he had missed. "You didn't tell me about her, did you?" he said, his voice accusing.

Judy glanced at him sideways. "I wanted you to see her for yourself," she said. "So you'd understand."

"Understand what?"

"Why the next death threat's going to come from me," she said, turning to face him. "You ever do that to me again and I'll kill you."

Lloyd really didn't know what he'd done this time. "What? What did I do to you?"

"When I met her I felt—and looked—a complete idiot."

Lloyd frowned, then his brow cleared, as he realized. "You *weren't* wearing the wellies!" he said, delightedly.

"Yes," she said. "I'm standing there looking like a refugee from a Marx Brothers film, and *she*—" She pointed to the television. "*She* gets out of a BMW sports car!"

48

"You can't blame me for that," Lloyd protested, and looked again at Mrs. Bailey, trying to analyse what it was about her. Item by item, Olivia-style, her face was like anyone else's. *"Item, two lips, indifferent red; item, two grey eyes, with lids to them; item, one neck, one chin . . ."* Rachel Bailey's eyes were blue, if Judy's television was to be believed, and she was beautiful, certainly. She had a wonderful smile. But there was something much more than that there.

They'd given it names over the years. It. Sex appeal. *Je ne sais quoi.* It was something that both men and women saw, and recognized, and found very attractive. Something the camera loved. It couldn't be acquired. And whatever it was, Mrs. Bailey had it. He stared at the screen, mesmerized by this goddess who chose to live in the back of beyond with someone like Bailey.

"What on earth does she see in him?" he asked.

"I'll give you three guesses."

Lloyd smiled. "What a cynical person you are. She's probably deeply in love with him."

"It's a weird set-up," Judy said. "She hasn't got a key to her own front gate. He talks to her the same way he talks to his dog. She looks like that, and she behaves like a nineteenth-century serving-girl. She fetches his shoes. Takes off his muddy boots for him. Washes them."

"See? That's a labour of love," said Lloyd, with a grin. "If I'd been there, I'd have cleaned the mud off yours with a gladsome heart."

Judy left the room. When she came back, a pair of shoes caked with a thin layer of dried mud dropped in his lap.

"Then you can clean them," she said.

Not bad, thought Jack Melville, when he appeared on the screen. Not bad.

Terri smiled at him. "You look good on TV," she said.

Yes, he'd thought that himself, immodestly. Maybe he could interest *Aquarius 1830* in giving him a regular spot on stocks and shares, to explain them to the masses—give them tips on buying and selling. After all, lots of them owned shares in this and that now that everything had been privatized. He'd give that some thought. It would do no harm to think about the odd income supplement.

"And I liked the bit about roads being a necessary evil," she said. "Shows we're not all fanatics."

The acceptable face of anti-road campaigning. But how long for? If the road did go through the woodland they would get the mob here, chaining themselves to trees, lying down in front of the earth-movers, looking for a fight with the security men.

It occurred to him later, as they sat down to dinner, and he was entertained to the iniquities of civilization, that Terri would undoubtedly support them, might even join them. But they wouldn't win. They never did; he'd explained that to her when she and her conservationist friends had made a fuss about McQueen's development in the first place. He told her again, now. All fanatics did was alienate people, he said.

And she said that if it wasn't for fanatics, women still wouldn't have the vote. Come to that, most men wouldn't. Just people like him. If it wasn't for fanatics, wrongs would never be righted. Fanatics brought publicity to a cause, and non-fanatics gradually realized that something had to be done.

He hoped he wasn't going to discover at this late stage that he was married to a fanatic, however worthy they were. She had remained on the fringes of fanaticism thus far, and during her history of campaign and opposition and demonstration had had the odd brush with the law, a concept for which she had no little contempt. She admired even less its administrators and enforcers, but basically it had been nice, middle-class, hobbyist rebellion, and he wanted it to stay that way. He didn't want her to go off and live up a tree in Bluebell Wood.

But she might.

At half past eight, Curtis, currently short-bearded, long-haired, brown-eyed, bulkier, and rigid with fear, met his contacts, and told them that he was not going with them to the rendezvous, that he expected the supplier to come to him.

He was wired for sound underneath the padding; if the heavies smelt a rat, the idea was that his colleagues would prevent any damage being done to him. Curtis didn't have a great deal of faith in that, conversing, as he was, in an alley behind a pub, a long way from the van.

The two men were not happy. Their time, they said, had better not be being wasted.

Curtis—Roger Wheeler—said that he wasn't getting into a car with a couple of minders and that sort of cash. He hadn't brought the money with him; the supplier would come to his flat, alone, and hand over the stuff there. Then he would be paid. And that was where and how he would deliver it every month.

He was thankful that they couldn't see the perspiration; that was the plus side of finding himself in an inadequately lit alley in the swiftly gathering dusk with a pair of people-punchers. One of them took a drag of his cigarette and dropped it on the damp cobbles, stepping on it as he moved towards Curtis, standing right in front of him. "You trying to be funny?" he asked, smoke streaming into Curtis's face with the words.

"You'll know when I'm trying to be funny," Curtis said steadily, looking into the other man's eyes. "I laugh." Knowing that his colleagues were parked in a van listening to his gangster impersonation didn't help, and for a dreadful, heart-stopping moment, Curtis thought he *was* going to laugh. But he didn't.

And it didn't matter that it was obviously an act; theirs was, too, in the menacing way they stood close to him, their studied use of props, like the cigarette. It was all body language and striking attitudes, and he was better at it than they were. He had started out as an actor, before TV presenting had beckoned and had seemed a safer way to earn a living. It didn't seem very safe now.

"The deal was, we took you to him."

"Then it's off," said Curtis, and turned away, walking back down the alley to where the Jag was parked, forcing himself to walk slowly, deliberately, not to look behind him to see where they were.

"Hang on."

The voice was right behind him; he stopped, his eyes closed, then turned, half expecting to see a baseball bat coming down on his head.

"We'll ask him. Where is this flat?"

"Not far." He told them where it was, and walked to the Jag, getting in. They were still watching; he drove away, unable to see his colleagues' van, just hoping that it was still in contact with him. A five-minute journey later, he let himself into the flat, lit a desperately needed cigarette, and waited, not looking out of the window, as he longed to do, not daring to expect anything, not knowing what *to* expect. He sat at the table, taking quick, nervous puffs, turning the lighter over and over between his fingers.

Fifteen minutes after he had arrived back, the doorbell rang. Curtis stood up, went to the cupboard, opened it, pressed the record button on the equipment, closed it, and went to the door.

Mr. Big's representative had arrived. He came in without speaking, and the package, encased in plain brown paper, was laid on the table. His hand hovered over it. "Let's see the cash," he said, and pulled just enough of a pistol out of his jacket pocket for Curtis to see what it was.

Curtis, the man who policed the police, was already putting together a programme on the accessibility of guns on the streets. Curtis, the man being thus warned, swallowed hard, and pulled a roll of notes from his pocket. It joined the package on the table. "OK?" he said. "Can we talk now?"

The man sat down, and they discussed Roger Wheeler's future requirements, the conversation relaxed now that the money was there and Mr. Big's representative knew he wasn't having his time wasted. The talk was easy, but Curtis wasn't. He was uneasy, and, though the lighting was purposely dim, horribly aware of his wig and fake beard, and of the pistol his visitor was packing. He hadn't thought of that, and no one could get him out of this if it went wrong.

The other man never lost his watchfulness, his wariness; any minute, Curtis kept thinking, any minute, he's going to twig, and he's got a gun, for God's sake. He surreptitiously moistened his dry lips as his supplier picked the money up and counted it. He wondered if he ought to have opened the package to make sure that it contained what he'd paid for. But there was no reason why he should be a seasoned drug-dealer; he had been posing as someone with a bit of spare cash wanting to get in on a lucrative market. He had a feeling that he should have done, though, to be convincing. Too late now.

The other man nodded, and stood up. "It's a deal, Mr. Wheeler," he said, pleasantly enough. "See you next month."

Curtis shook the hand that was held out to him, glad that his palm wasn't sweaty. It ought to be. He closed the door as his visitor left, locked it, and put the chain on, leaning against it as his whole body suddenly went limp. He'd done it. He hadn't been found out, he hadn't been beaten up, he hadn't been shot. He had done it.

Then the limpness was replaced with a surge of triumph, and he threw his head back, fists clenched. "Yes!" he shouted, and he didn't want to stay here, however luxuriously it had been kitted out for the moneyed Roger Wheeler. He wanted to celebrate; he wanted to get things moving. But he couldn't. He had to stay. He had to stay the night, just in case they were watching, in case they *had* smelled a rat, and wanted to see what he did next. And nothing, but nothing, would have taken him back out into Barton's dark streets, so he was stuck here.

He went back into the living room. It wasn't half past nine yet; he could hardly believe that. It had been the longest hour of his life. Oh, well, he hoped it was a good night on the telly. He grinned at one of the cameras, and picked up the package, kissing it like a sporting trophy. "Gotcha," he said, putting it back on the table, and went to the cupboard, stopping the tape.

Then he removed his jacket to enable him to unhook himself from the recording gear, which he also put in the cupboard, locking it. His shirt was soaked with sweat in the odd places where it actually touched his skin; he peeled it off, and undid the padded waistcoat that had altered his build, going into the bathroom, where he removed the wig and beard and the contact lenses, and had a shower. He towelled himself dry, and stood for a moment, puzzled. He had thought that the make-up department had supplied him with a robe. He shrugged, pulling on his jeans, and came out of the bathroom, stopping dead when he saw the open bedroom door.

"You got them, then," said a slow, lazy voice from the darkness.

He almost passed out. When he had recovered his wits, he went to the bedroom, and switched on the light. She was sitting on the bed, wearing his bathrobe crossed over high at her neck, feet curled under her. He stared at her. "Have you been here all the time?" he asked.

"Came in after you went out. Just as well you told me what you looked like in your disguise, or I'd still be out there waitin' for you." She smiled. "I like you better the way you come."

"What if he'd heard you, or something? Realized there was someone in here?"

"Don't drug dealers have girlfriends, then?"

He supposed they did. But he still didn't understand how she had got away from Cold Comfort Farm. "What have you told Bernard?" he asked.

"He thinks I'm at Nicola's. He's gone out. Some sort of do his Lodge is havin'. They laid on a minibus—it isn't bringin' him back till two in the morning. Told him I didn't want to be there on my own."

"Nicola knows you're here?"

"She knows I'm not there," said Rachel. "Don't worry 'bout it. She won't say nothin'."

"She will if he asks her!"

"But he's not goin' to ask her, is he?" She lifted herself up

54

from her cat-like position, and knelt on the bed. "We got all night," she said, drawing out the vowels slowly, deliciously.

All night. He'd never had more than an hour with her, and now he had all night. He was going to celebrate his success, and he would bet that no drug dealer had ever had a girlfriend like Rachel. He went to her, and lifted her hand to his lips. The wide sleeve of the bathrobe slipped up her arm, and he caught a glimpse of the beginnings of a bruise just below her elbow, and sighed. She always had bruises.

"Forget it," she said, pulling the sleeve down again, and they kissed.

"Can I see them?" she asked, when they drew apart.

Curtis frowned. "See what?"

"Them drugs you got."

He smiled. "Sure," he said, going back out into the hallway, into the sitting room, and picking up the package. He brought it to her, and sat beside her on the bed as she unwrapped it, feeling a little like he had on Christmas morning as a child, when he and his sister had opened their presents, a highly inappropriate thought as polythene bags containing pills and powders, crystals and capsules, spilled on to the duvet. "If the police raid this place tonight, Roger Wheeler could get life," he said.

She smiled. "They dangerous?"

"Not unless you take them."

"Never tried takin' drugs."

Curtis felt a stab of alarm. "Well," he said, getting off the bed and gathering them up, heaping them back on to the table, "you're not going to start now."

"Don't want to," she said. "I'm just interested." She slid off the bed and stood beside him, riffling through the packets. "What all you got?"

"Everything. He's got people breaking into laboratories, hospitals—everywhere. They steal to order, just like I said."

"So what did *you* order?"

"Methadone, phenobarbitone, Nembutal, Tuinal. Amphetamines, all the usual stuff. But I also ordered chloral hydrate—that's the stuff they used to put in people's drinks to knock them out. It's a sedative—acts like a barbiturate. And it's going to prove they steal to order, because it's not the usual sort of merchandise."

"Which one of them is it?"

"That's it." He pointed. "And there's cocaine, morphine, codeine—"

She turned and kissed him, her parted lips just brushing his. "Does anyone else know what drugs you got?"

"Only Mr. Big and his representatives, and I doubt if any single one of them knows exactly. That's how they've been getting away with it. There's no big haul. Just dribs and drabs, here and there."

"So you don't have to give *all* of them to the police, do you?" she said, her tongue fleetingly touching his eyelids, his nose, his mouth, as she spoke. "No one'd know if you kept some back."

"You said you didn't want to try drugs," he said. He wasn't sure how good he'd be at refusing her some speed or whatever it was she wanted, as the tiny licking kisses moved to his neck, his shoulders. He wasn't sure that he could refuse her anything.

"I could use some of them knock-out drops," she said, her voice as lazy as her tongue was busy. "Put some in his whisky. Then he'd fall asleep and not come upstairs to me."

Curtis closed his eyes, his arms round her. He hated to think of Bailey with Rachel.

"Will you give me some?" she asked.

He opened his eyes wide. "I *can't*, Rachel," he said. "You can't go putting stuff in—" He broke off. She knew that; she hadn't been serious, he realized, as she smiled her slow smile and her eyes twinkled with mischief. But even as a joke, her request bothered him. "Is it that bad?" he asked.

"No—don't look so worried," she said, leaning back, letting

56

his arms support her. "It's not *bad*. He don't do nothing weird to me. He just does it all the time, that's all."

"How do you mean?"

She shrugged a little. "He sits there all evenin', watchin' TV. He don't talk to me or nothin'. Just sits and watches TV till the news is done. Then I got to get him a whisky, and go up and wait for him." She was drawing circles on his chest with her fingers as she spoke. "After he's done all the lockin' up, he comes upstairs, gets into bed. He still don't say nothin'. Then after a bit he gets on top of me, gets off when he's done. Don't want me sayin' nothin', don't want me doin' nothin'. I just got to lie there."

"Why?" asked Curtis, mystified.

"He don't want *me*. All he wants is to get me pregnant."

"Why?" asked Curtis again.

"He wants someone to pass the farm on to."

"What's wrong with Nicola?"

"She's a girl. She's not even in his will. He wants a son, and he's sowin' seed every chance he gets. If he don't do it when he comes to bed, he'll most likely wake me up three, four in the mornin' for it."

"But it's not every night, is it?"

"Near enough. Don't take a lot out of him. Don't reckon he even enjoys it." She smiled. "He'd be happier just freezin' it and injectin' me with it like the cows."

Curtis smiled, too, at the little joke, but it sounded awful. "I thought farmers needed their sleep," he muttered.

"He don't do no farming. Not real farming. Most mornings he don't leave the office. Won't come out to answer the phone or the entry phone or nothin', not if I'm there to do it. Just sits and does all his paperwork till I get him his lunch, and then he drives round with Steve, checkin' up on everything. So he's got lots of energy left over for me."

"Can't you tell him no? Does he hit you if you won't?"

She shook her head. "It don't bother me. It's what I agreed.

57

I didn't know it'd be like it is, but . . ." A little shrug. "It don't matter."

"Then why do you want to slip him a Mickey Finn?"

"Because he's started askin' me how come I'm not pregnant when he's doin' it to me all the time. If I could put something in his whisky, he'd fall asleep downstairs, and it wouldn't all be my fault I wasn't gettin' pregnant."

"Is that why he hits you? Because you're not pregnant?"

She looked over her shoulder at the drugs again, then turned back to him. "Reckon there's enough there to put him to sleep every night for weeks," she said, kissing him, pushing him gently down until he was sitting on the bed, and she was kneeling at his feet.

"Mm," said Curtis.

"Maybe even enough to put him to sleep for good." She reached up to kiss him, her tongue teasing his tongue as she spoke.

"Yes," said Curtis, slipping his hands under the towelling as she reached for the bedside lamp, and they were in darkness.

"You could have me to yourself, then," she said, covering his chest once more with little licking kisses. "I could sell the land to McQueen, and you could have me. And we'd have all that money."

"Who needs money?" Curtis was happy just having a job he loved and this wonderful creature making love to him. The desire for money that kept her married to that violent, stone-faced statue baffled him.

"How much would it take?" she asked.

"How much would it take to do what?"

"How much of that stuff would it take to kill him?"

"*I* don't know." He had thought she was talking about money. "It's just a sedative."

"You said it could kill him." Her voice was accusing, between the tiny kisses.

"I said *it* could. I didn't say *you* could." It wasn't easy to be

58

masterful when someone was licking your ribcage. "You'd be the first person the police suspected."

"They'd have to prove it, though, wouldn't they?" she said. Slowly. Sexily. From somewhere near his navel.

"They'd prove it," he said. Briskly. Sternly. From the intellectual high ground.

"How?"

"I'm making a *television* programme—that's not exactly a secret, is it? Chloral hydrate is the star of the show—they would notice that I had had access to it. Like I said—it's not a very common drug. And Nicola caught us at it this afternoon in the cowshed." He felt embarrassed again at the memory, glad of the darkness for the second time that evening as he felt himself flush again. "You're best placed to poison his whisky. The police can put two and two together, you know."

The lecture might have carried more weight had she not unzipped his fly while he was speaking, her subsequent activities causing the pitch of his voice to be less than secure on the last sentence.

He heard her chuckle, and laughed at himself for taking her seriously, if only for a moment. He shifted a little, the better to allow her to remove his jeans, then swung his legs up as she joined him. She knelt beside him, and he pulled away the tie of the bathrobe, opening it, slipping it off her shoulders, and drew her down to him. He didn't know how many times he could make love to her when he had all night, but he intended finding out.

"The police didn't put two and two together about Mr. Big," she said. "Did they?"

"No."

"So they're not so clever."

"They wouldn't *have* to be clever."

Bailey had called her the wife, and Curtis's mental image of her had in no way prepared him for what he had seen when he had finally met her. She had told him frankly that she thought her husband was mad not to sell; on camera, she had said that she was behind him, whatever he wanted to do. Curtis had found her entirely convincing both times.

"Maybe someone else'll kill him," she said. Her delivery was still tantalizingly slow, even when her breathing was quickening. "He is gettin' death threats, after all."

"Maybe."

"Bet you could do it without gettin' caught," she said, her voice husky now.

"Maybe."

"You ran rings round Mr. Big," she said. "*And* the cops."

"Yes."

He let her ego-boosting words wash over him, muttering hopefully appropriate responses as she produced almost unbearable sensations in him. She was quite able to carry out the two proverbial activities at once and always did; he wasn't so good at the talking part. But Rachel talked; she talked all the time, her voice growing whispery and breathless as her excitement mounted, sexier than ever. The idea of those loveless, wordless couplings with Bailey appalled him.

"Bet you could do anythin', if you put your mind to it," she said, the words coming in little gasps. "Bet you could kill him so no one'd ever know it was you."

"Yes," he said. "No." He was no longer able to give the conversation his undivided attention.

"*Would* you kill for me?" she asked.

"Yes," he said, the word just a groan. "Oh, yes."

On the day they had met, he had told her about Mr. Big in an attempt to impress her, but there had been no need; they had both known what was going to happen. She had taken him into the cowshed, and it had been good. It was always good. But this was better than it had ever been, and he kept it going for longer than he had ever done, before the agonizing tension in his body found glorious, ecstatic release in hers.

But when his pulse rate and breathing had returned to normal, when the subsequent inertia had worn off, when the twin triumphs of the night had begun to assume some proportion, Curtis considered the situation in which he found himself in a rather more rational light. Had he at some point in the proceedings agreed to kill Bailey?

He sat up, switching on the light, and turned his head to look at Rachel, to see if she had just been teasing him, if she was laughing at him for taking her seriously yet again. She lay facing him, eyes closed, perhaps asleep, the bathrobe pulled loosely round her once more. Curtis frowned, and leaned over to pull it aside. There were the inevitable bruises, some very recent, some not so recent, but that wasn't what she was hiding from him; he expected them, had grown, like her, almost used to them.

It was the old bruises that made his eyes widen in horror and disbelief. The faded, yellow bruises that covered her torso from her shoulders to her hips. Masses of them. On her breasts, her ribs, her midriff, her back, her thighs, her buttocks. At some time during his enforced absence from her, she had been given a sadistic, systematic, merciless beating by that bastard, and *still* she hadn't left him.

She opened her eyes. "Didn't want you to see them straight off," she murmured. "Said he'd keep on doin' it if I didn't get pregnant. Was goin' to do it again today, so I told him I was."

Curtis stared at her. "But what, when he finds out you're not?"

She moved her shoulders in a shrug.

"You have to leave him, Rachel," he said. "You have to."

"I'm not givin' up. Not now."

But she had to leave him, he thought, as he stared helplessly at her battered body. She *had* to. But he knew she would never leave him, not without the money, not if it was important enough to her to put up with that sort of abuse. And it was. He knew it was.

*"Come away with me,"* he had said as they had got their breath back after that first time.

*"Where to?"*

61

*"Anywhere you want. My place. Leave him and come and live with me."*

*She had smiled. "Can't do that," she had said.*

*Because Bailey had money?*

*She had agreed, readily, candidly. What had he got? she had asked.*

*A future, he had told her.*

*"Can't buy shoes with a future," she had said.*

He gathered her up, and held her in his arms, tears in his eyes. She would risk that again, he knew she would, and he couldn't let her do that. She had asked if he would kill for her, and his answer would have been the same, whatever the circumstances of the question.

Yes. Oh, yes.

# SUMMER

# CHAPTER THREE

IT HAD BEEN A STUPID, WICKED THING TO DO AND he hadn't meant to do it. It had just happened.

Mike McQueen hadn't been able to sleep, because the conscience that so many well-meaning conservationists did not believe he possessed had troubled him too much. He had risen with the sun at four-thirty and had worked on his plans for the second phase of the development, but his heart hadn't been in it, and his thoughts kept returning to what he had done, to what the consequences of his actions might be. He didn't know where she was; there was no way he could warn her.

Two hours later he was looking out of his study window at his trees, now in their summer livery, the sun glinting on the leaves, and wishing with all his being that he could call back one moment of time.

Yesterday's promised anti-road demonstration hadn't materialized; he had had high hopes of dozens of professional agitators swarming all over Bailey's farm, setting off his alarms, making rude gestures at his cameras, threatening him with violence and vandalism. And it might, had it happened, have frightened Bailey enough to reconsider the stand that was exciting all this hostility. But it hadn't happened. The day had passed sunnily and peacefully, with no sign of any marchers, any protesters.

It was the last week in July. There was no more time left, and the road would have to go through the woodland. Shirley had gone away for a long weekend to her sister's before he made the announcement, not wishing to be around when the villagers heard that their wood was doomed, when the protesters came to try to stop it. But nothing had happened. Nothing at all.

And last night, he had gone to see Bailey, and he had done something dreadful. He had just felt so . . . frustrated. So let down. His allies had all failed him. It had been a stupid, stupid thing to do, and it had been truly wicked. Bailey's threat still echoed in his head, and he had looked as though he had meant it. Shirley was very fond of Rachel; if anything happened to her, she would never forgive him.

It had been a stupid, wicked thing to do.

Rachel had croissants and coffee, flirting madly with the head waiter, who was trying to persuade her to have the full English breakfast. "Ees good," he enthused. "Eggs, bacon, sausage, fried bread, mushroom, tomato . . ."

Rachel smiled, shook her head. "I couldn't eat nothin' like that," she said. "I could manage another cup of coffee, though."

"Hey, José! Some more coffee for Mrs. Bailey!" he shouted to a passing waiter, his hand gestures wildly exaggerated.

He probably comes from Clapham, thought Rachel.

"Your 'usband . . . he ees not breakfasting this morning?"

"He had to go back last night," she said.

"He left a beautiful woman like you alone in London?"

She smiled. José arrived with the coffee, and the head waiter went to greet some other old friend that he'd known for two days.

This weekend was the first time she and Curtis had been together since the night in the flat. Even if she could have got away, it would have been no good, because once Curtis had handed over his haul of drugs and the tapes of the meetings, the flat had been crawling with police, and they had made it out of bounds until they finally made their arrest and decided they had finished with it. It was still on lease to Aquarius, sitting there doing nothing as Curtis had predicted.

He had been at the farm at the beginning of June; but he had been helping set up the closed-circuit TV, so he had been with Bernard all the time, not her. She had planted her death threats after the first ramblers of summer had made their appearance, but it had been some woman they had sent from *Aquarius 1830*, not Curtis, because he had been tied up with filming on *Mr. Big*. There had been no point in trying again.

With the rumours of an anti-road demonstration, the television had come back, as had Curtis, and they had snatched a moment to talk. She had told Bernard that she didn't think she ought to stay if there might be trouble, and he hadn't been able to pack her off fast enough, in case any harm should come to the baby.

She finished her breakfast, such as it was, and left, nodding to the American couple she and Curtis had chatted to in the bar on Friday afternoon when they had arrived, both wishing they could just go through to the suite, but having to exchange pleasantries about the weather, about London, about anything and everything before they could leave. When they had finally made it to the suite, they hadn't emerged until Saturday morning.

Curtis had stayed here before, but Rachel had never seen anything like it. She couldn't get over having a suite. And Curtis had tried to look as though he was unimpressed, but even he hadn't been in this part of the hotel before. It was small, but the idea of having what amounted to a whole little luxury flat right inside a hotel tickled Rachel, and she didn't care who knew it. Sitting room, bedroom, bathroom, and Curtis had made love to her in them all. It was, as she had pointed out to him, a bit of a step up from the cowshed.

It was on the ground floor, in a part of the hotel called the Executive Wing, which had three little suites like these. It even had a private entrance from outside, for which guests were issued a plastic card, like the ones for the rooms. You got a new one every day for the outside door, though. She pushed through the swing doors to the corridor which led to the Executive Wing, and let herself into the sitting room.

Bernard had paid for it all, of course, getting the money from somewhere. Paid for the huge double bed they had gone to as soon as they had got away from the other couple, paid for the shopping they had done on the hot, busy Saturday. She had had her purchases delivered to the hotel, and had taken a long walk along the river before going back for a late à la carte lunch, after which they had collapsed on to the sofa and fallen asleep. They had woken up in the late evening; Curtis had made love to her on the sofa in the dark, and then they had gone to the bar and got mildly drunk before going back to bed.

Sunday had been a little more subdued. Curtis *had* had the full English breakfast, which was how Rachel had known that she could never face it, then they had talked, had a quickie in the shower to complete the set, and had dinner sent in. Curtis had had to go back to Bartonshire, but she hadn't gone with him. The rumours had said that the demonstration was going to be held on Sunday and that they would be going to the farm.

She hadn't wanted Curtis to go; he had had physically to detach himself from her in order to leave. She hadn't slept until daylight; at half past three in the morning she had called room service for tea, grateful for the contact, however fleeting, with another person. She had been afraid to go to bed; she wasn't sure if she had ever before slept on her own. She had slept crowded in to a van with too many other people; she had slept outside in a makeshift shelter, other bodies close to hers for warmth; she had shared sleeping accommodation when she was living-in on farms; slept with men during brief liaisons and during longer, but just as doomed, relationships; always, always, with someone else in the room, if not in the bed, and the idea of sleeping entirely alone had frightened her.

But when she had finally gone to it, that big bed had seemed even more luxurious, with no Bernard lying immovably beside her, no apparently tireless Curtis making love to her every time he opened his eyes; she had discovered that she liked it much better that way.

All her life, men had used her. To cook their meals, to wash their clothes, to muck out their barns, to warm their beds. And it wasn't until she had been conned by one who had failed to mention that he had a wife that it had been pointed out to her that she had the wherewithal to use *them*. His wife had said that someone like her could have any man she liked, so why had she taken someone else's? And Rachel had realized then that she just about *could* have any man she liked. Most men couldn't wait to get her between the sheets, and that was power, of a sort, if you learned, as she had, to give them what they wanted once they got you there. The problem was that she had never met one that she did actually like, so now she had settled for using them instead.

Curtis thought he loved her, but he didn't. He wanted to possess her, physically, emotionally. She was some sort of prize that he had won, and when the day came that he discovered he couldn't take her home and put her on his mantelpiece, what he thought was love would just evaporate.

And her brief holiday was over; now, she had to pack her suitcase, and get all the stuff she had bought into the car, and go back to the farm. And Bernard. She sighed, until she remembered that she didn't actually have to do either of the first two things. She rang for someone, and it was all done for her. Half an hour later, she checked out of the hotel, and the car was brought to her, the stuff much more neatly stowed away than she would ever have managed.

She drove out of the hotel courtyard, through the early morning streets in which the rush hour was building up, but not to any real extent, not yet, and out, on to the motorway, looking clean and bright in the already hot summer sunshine. She made good time once she was free of the city; the motorway was quiet, going north, the lines of slow-moving cars all heading into London. She took the turn-off that led to the new M1 link road, and just over two hours after leaving the hotel, she was driving up to the farm gate. She had told Bernard that she would be back at ten; one of the farmhands was waiting to let her in, and she gave him a wave of thanks as she drove past.

She parked in the courtyard and got out of the car, walking slowly up the steps towards the unusually closed door, outside which Nell sunned herself. She stepped over the dog, letting herself into the hallway, closing the door again. The office door was also closed, as it always was when Bernard was working in there, a strip of light showing from under it. She took a breath, and opened the living room door.

The smell hit her first, then the heat, and then her whole body went rigid with fright, her hand flying to her mouth, when she saw Bernard. He was lying on the sofa, quite dead, and there was blood, blood on his shirt, blood on the sofa. For a moment, she stood motionless, not even able to think, then gasped painfully as she breathed again, and her heart began to pound, hurting her. But she could move now. She backed out of the room, into the hallway, and stared at the phone, trying to remember how to use it. Her hand trembled as she punched three nines.

"Emergency. Which service do you require?"

"Police," she said. "Police."

They seemed to want to know a dozen things before they would *do* anything, but at last they said they would be there, and she should stay where she was. She pressed the rest, and stared once more at the phone. Nicola. She had to tell Nicola. Gus answered, listened in shocked silence, then told her that Nicola was on her way to an emergency, and was uncontactable until she got back, because he didn't know where she was. He offered to come over.

"No—no, you stay there, in case she rings you."

Steve. She had to get Steve. She forced herself to calm down, to think what she was doing. He would be at the café now, having breakfast; he didn't eat with the other farmhands, never having quite got over losing his own farm. She knew the café number; she had rung the café daily when she worked in Bernard's shop, which supplied June with eggs and poultry, and she still rang her now and then, just for a gossip. But her brain wasn't functioning. She would have to look it up.

Jack Melville was in the café-cum-newsagent, buying illicit cigarettes. He was supposed to have given them up.

"Can you give me change of a tenner?" he asked.

"Yes, of course," said June, the plump, pretty proprietrix, taking his money and going to the till. The phone rang just as she got there; naturally, answering it took precedence over his transaction. He looked over at the tables, and saw Curtis Law and his cameraman. The cameraman was eating breakfast; Law was engrossed in the crossword.

"Is Steve Paxton still here?" asked June, trying to peer round the partition.

"Here!" shouted Steve, like a child at school.

"You're wanted on the phone."

Steve performed the waltz steps necessary to get through the tables in the little shop, and lifted the counter flap, letting June out as he went in, there being room only for one person of reasonable bulk behind the counter.

Jack resigned himself to wait for his change. "No demonstration after all," he said to the cameraman. He had been deeply relieved when Sunday had passed without a whiff of civil unrest. He tore the cellophane off the packet. Better smoke it here.

"No. I pointed the camera at everyone that went near the farm. There were a couple of long-haired weirdos, but if there were hordes of rabid road protesters, I didn't see them." He shot a look at Law. "If some reporters got their facts right, it would help," he said. "He swans off for the weekend, and leaves us with the demo that never was."

"Don't blame me," said Law. "I just report what I hear. And I was entitled to a weekend off after all that work on *Mr. Big*." He took out cigarettes and matches.

"Do you mind?" said the cameraman. "Some of us are eating."

"Sorry, sorry," said Law, putting them away again.

Jack looked sadly at his packet, and wished Paxton would hurry up and let June get him his change.

"So here we are again," the cameraman went on. "Golden Boy here reckons they'll still be coming, and no one's going to argue with him, not now he's a hero who took on the mob single-handed."

"Pack it in," said Law, good-naturedly.

"It's all right for some." June looked round her little shop. "Don't any of you lot have work to do?"

Law grinned. "We are working."

"I can see that. Getting to grips with one across must be hell for you."

He laughed. "But we're ready to spring into action at a moment's notice."

"Your demonstrators won't be demonstrating in my shop," June pointed out, and turned to Jack. "What's your excuse?"

"I'm a professional gambler," said Jack. "I can work with a phone and the starting prices. And if it's a hot, sunny day and I fancy a walk, I can take one." It was just as well, he thought, that he didn't have to punch a clock, the time Paxton was taking on that phone call. "Would you rather we *weren't* here?" he asked her, with a grin.

Steve Paxton was pale when he put down the phone and came out from behind the counter.

"Is there something wrong?" asked Law.

Paxton blinked a little, looking round at the assembled company. "Bernard Bailey's dead," he said. "Mrs. Bailey's just found him."

Jack saw Curtis Law fold his paper, slide it into his jacket pocket, then he and his cameraman moved like greyhounds, out of the little shop, into their estate car, and off, with a squealing of tyres and puff of exhaust.

They *were* ready to spring into action at a moment's notice, Jack thought, as he watched them drive off.

"I'm going back to the farm," Paxton said to June, then looked at Jack, his eyes widening, and jerked his thumb at the door. "That's where these bloody vultures have gone, isn't it?" he said, in sudden angry realization.

Jack nodded.

"If they're bothering Mrs. Bailey, I'll knock their bloody heads off!" Steve banged out of the shop, into the pick-up truck parked outside.

"I'll be off, too," Jack said absently, opening the door.

"Hang on," said June, waving his tenner at him. She opened the till. "I *thought* it was Rachel," she said. "But I wasn't sure—she sounded so odd. Must have got a terrible shock, poor lamb." She handed him his change. "Well, God forgive me," she added, in a loud, defiant tone, "but *I* won't be sorry to see him six feet under."

No, thought Jack. Not many people would.

Lloyd and Case were in the Assistant Chief Constable's office at HQ once again. The last time, Lloyd had made his feelings clear on the matter of the various break-ins, and Case had agreed with him. They were, he had declared, separate, unconnected incidents. Last week, Bartonshire police had arrested someone whom the police of three counties knew to be deeply involved in organized crime, but on whom they had never had so much as the proverbial parking ticket. Now, the drug-trafficking and extortion charges alone would probably net him life.

As a result of Aquarius Television's activities, they had been able to trace and target Curtis Law's contacts, mounting a huge observation exercise which led them right to the very top, with more than enough evidence to arrest and charge the man at the centre of it all. They were still arresting the smaller fish swimming round in the ripples made by that arrest.

That, their youthful ACC felt, was a coup that should not have been left to a television reporter to bring off, and Lloyd and Case could not but agree with him. But what could they do about it now? These whizz-kids worked too hard and worried too much, in Lloyd's opinion. Didn't get out enough, if the young man's pallor was anything to go by. Fewer of them sitting behind desks and more officers on the ground, that's what they needed if they didn't want TV reporters upstaging them.

The ACC held up a videotape. "This is a preview of a programme which will be going out tonight on Aquarius Television," he said. "It's an account of the events leading up to the arrests made, with their not inconsiderable assistance, over the last few days. I'm far from happy with it."

"Well," said Lloyd. "We knew they'd be doing that—that was the point of the exercise, after all."

"What we didn't know," said the ACC, pouring himself some water from the carafe on his desk, "was that they would be offering it to the network. But they did, and as a result, it will be shown nationwide in due course." He put the video in the machine. "You are quite widely quoted during this programme, Chief Inspector. The impression given is . . . unfortunate, to say the least. I want to know if remarks have been taken out of context, if interviews have been unfairly edited, that sort of thing. If they have, we could possibly get an injunction to stop it being shown as it stands."

He pressed the play button, and after a few moments of blank screen, the station call sign came up. Then Lloyd saw himself in close-up.

*"These are random break-ins, not the work of some Mr. Big,"* he said, his voice sounding very Welsh, and very scornful. The picture froze. Over the still, the words MR. BIG? WHAT MR. BIG? were apparently typed out letter by letter. Then *A Law on the Law Special.*

The three men watched in silence as the fifty-minute programme unfolded. Curtis Law detailed the various break-ins in the Stansfield division in which drugs had been stolen, with quotes from Lloyd, as the then head of Stansfield CID, as to how the various investigations were being handled, showing clearly that no overall strategy had been adopted, that each one had been regarded as a one-off.

True, they were giving the impression that these break-ins

were occurring daily, one after the other, in an area the size of a postage stamp, and that Lloyd had been too dim to notice what was happening, whereas the investigations had sometimes been weeks, months apart, in towns miles apart, and carried out by a dozen different officers from three different stations, but Lloyd didn't think the slight misrepresentation actionable. They were giving the dates and locations on the soundtrack. Certainly, most viewers would not be aware of that, but he doubted that they could object.

The programme pointed out that at this point *all* serious crime in East Bartonshire had been given to Stansfield CID, and that this had resulted in Detective Superintendent Case being brought in to head the department. Had this reorganization of resources helped? The question ended part one.

The commercial break was heralded by Lloyd's freeze-frame close-up, with his words, now given a slight echo, played over it, and MR. BIG? WHAT MR. BIG? typed out once again. The second half opened in similar fashion.

No, was the answer given to the question asked before the break. Case's role was to direct the efforts of the personnel under him, and to take command of major investigations; he had left the day-to-day investigation of serious crimes to his second-in-command.

So Curtis Law had decided to put his theory to a practical test. In disguise, using the name Roger Wheeler, driving a Jaguar, he had set himself up as a man looking for a good, reliable supply of prescription drugs. The soundtapes of his various meetings with sundry shady characters were played, and his request for specific drugs, some widely available, some less easily located, was subtitled, in case the sound quality made it difficult to catch. The subsequent break-ins in which such drugs were stolen were detailed. Then the covertly filmed meeting at his flat was shown, when his order was filled. His contact's just visible handgun was highlighted, the still shot enlarged until the pistol butt filled the screen, and part two ended as part one had, and as part three began, with Lloyd's dismissive response.

The programme then covered the resultant major investigation mounted by Case which in the end had involved not just Bartonshire, but two neighbouring counties; the dawn raids carried out last week, and the arrest of the man behind the organization, all of which Curtis Law had been invited to witness, and to film.

In silence, over a black background, the most serious charges being brought against the man arrested were rolled up the screen, with a note of the maximum sentence allowed on each, followed by the number of other arrests made as a direct consequence. Over this rolling list of iniquities, Curtis Law's voiceover said that perhaps the problem society had to face in the twenty-first century was less one of organized crime than one of disorganized policing.

The black faded up to the freeze-frame of Lloyd's face, and the silence in which the credits went up was broken by his voice: *"These are random break-ins, not the work of some Mr. Big,"* now with multiple echo effect, so that the last seven words repeated several times as the soundtrack faded to silence again. *An Aquarius Television Production* rounded the whole miserable thing off.

"Well, gentlemen?"

Lloyd had been mocked once before, in his childhood, because he had a first name that other children found hysterically funny. The mockery had made him want to cry then, and now he had discovered that it still made him want to cry. But he was a fifty-year-old man, and his colleagues would find it more than a little odd if he did. Besides, he had embarrassed them enough already by making the bloody remark in the first place. He was aware that his face was flushed, and wished he smoked, like Judy did in times of emotional stress. He knew why now.

"It's a bit slanted," said Case. "And sensationalized. But I imagine they've made damn sure they're watertight." He did

76

light a cigarette, having waved the packet at his senior officer by way of asking permission, the gesture answered by a brief nod. "But," he added, "I think that the programme's presentation amounts to a totally unwarranted personal attack on Chief Inspector Lloyd and I would urge the Chief Constable to seek an injunction on those grounds."

The ACC nodded, and turned to Lloyd, his eyebrows raised, waiting for his comments.

Lloyd swallowed a little. "I . . ." he began, and cleared his throat. Mr. Law's programme had exposed a nerve that hadn't seen the light of day since he was thirteen years old. He took a breath. "I said what I said, and I said it in reply to a direct question about organized crime—there is no misrepresentation there. As to the other point—Mr. Law wanted to make a fool of me, and he has. But if it's up to me, I would rather we didn't try to stop them showing it for that reason."

The ACC ejected the video, and put it carefully back in its slipcover. He looked from Lloyd to Case and back again.

"Mr. Law's approach may be objectionable," he said. "But he has indicated a huge hole in our defences. No overall pattern was seen because the cases were buried amongst many others being investigated, and the large network of thieves and suppliers muddied the waters as far as MO and so on. No individual is to blame for that, but as a service, we must address the problem."

As far as MO and so on *was concerned*, Lloyd corrected him, silently. The man used so many bloody words in the first place, you wouldn't think he'd balk at two more. He watched as the ACC poured another glass of water. Oh, God. The man was going to give a speech.

"Other industries are using new technology to produce better results with reduced manpower," the ACC went on, "and we must do the same. The system must be made to work for us, not against us." He picked up two sets of papers, and handed one each to Lloyd and Case. "To this end, as you will see when

77

you read this document, it is proposed to set up a service-wide system to be known as LINKS, which stands for Local Information Networked Knowledge System."

Acronyms. Everything was fine as long as you could think up a good acronym. Lloyd glanced at the document and mentally filed it under wastepaper basket as the ACC described how it was intended to work. There was, of course, to be a working party.

"The composition of the working party will have been decided by the end of the month," said the ACC. "It will be given twelve months to complete its task, and it is proposed to second a CID officer full time to head it. I feel it's important that it be headed by a working detective who knows what is and is not feasible with regard to investigation practices, whose experience will enhance and inform the entire project."

Yes, yes. Get on with it.

"I think that one officer in particular has that experience, the necessary authority, and the analytical skills that we need for the job. Before offering the post to her, however, I would welcome your comments. I'm referring, as you may already have worked out, to WDI Hill."

Lloyd stared at him. He hadn't already worked it out; he had hardly been listening, still smarting from the treatment he'd received at Curtis Law's hands. This had to be the worst Monday morning he had ever endured. They couldn't take Judy. He would fight it. He needed her at Stansfield. Besides, she wouldn't want to do it, and she would blame him if he didn't try to get her off the hook.

But someone had to do it, and her logical mind would ensure that whatever system they came up with was as simple and as effective as possible. If the scheme had flaws, which it surely would, she would find them. She was, in short, perfect for the job.

"I think she would be an excellent choice," he heard his own voice saying. It sounded traitorous. She would kill him. But it was true, and it would do her career no harm to get a bit of administrative experience.

"Couldn't do better," said Case. "She's got a good head on her."

The words "for a woman" hovered in the air, but weren't actually spoken. Possibly because Case assumed that that qualification would be taken for granted.

"Good. Sergeant Sandwell will be acting DI in the interim," said the ACC. "It is anticipated that Mrs. Hill will return to Stansfield at the end of the secondment, and slot into the restructuring which will, with luck, be in place by then, in view of Stansfield's increased responsibilities. Any questions?"

Lloyd had a question. How was Stansfield CID supposed to operate one more under-strength for a year? They had the increased responsibilities *now*. But he'd caused enough trouble for one day. "She might not be too keen on a desk job. She may take some persuading."

"Unless it means promotion," said Case.

"It does," said the ACC. "As you will see in the document I've given you, the post will carry the rank of Detective Chief Inspector."

She wouldn't kill him after all. She'd caught him up. She had always been going to; she had passed her promotion board first time. But Lloyd had secretly and guiltily hoped that she wouldn't get a post until he had retired, or got promotion himself. Now he was going to have to deal with his regrettable tendency to male chauvinism on top of everything else.

And Judy would be coming back to Stansfield a DCI; it didn't take too much brain power to see that this secondment was in order to achieve just that, and that early retirement was on the cards for him. And it was not impossible that Curtis Law's programme had played a part in that decision.

"When will DI Hill be told officially?" he asked.

"Oh . . . next week some time, I think. You can tell her yourself now, if you like. There's no reason why not." He closed his copy of the report. "Thank you for your time, gentlemen."

* * *

Judy was back at Bailey's Farm, looking at a body and trying not to breathe, her second least favourite part of the job. Everyone's least favourite was telling someone that their nearest and dearest was dead, and at least she was being spared that with this one. For one thing, it had been his wife who had found him, and had told everyone who needed to know, and for another, Bernard Bailey seemed to have been near and dear to a very limited number of people, as she had discovered when investigating the death threats. Death threats that she had, to all intents and purposes, dismissed.

But now he was undoubtedly, though not yet officially, dead. That conclusion had to await unnecessary confirmation by the forensic Medical Examiner. There were blood stains on his shirt and part of the sofa, a number of tears in his shirt indicating a stabbing. He had evidently been unwell at some point, a fact probably not unconnected to the bottle of whisky, about two-thirds full, which sat on the coffee table, a full glass beside it, and the empty bottle which lay on the floor. The smell of the whisky mingled with the other odours in the hot, airless room, its windows shuttered and locked, its radiators full on, for some reason. A browning apple sat amid the coffee-table clutter, roughly cut in two, the sweet smell making matters worse, but there was no knife. The duty inspector was organizing a search of the immediate grounds; they would have to draft people in if they had to search the whole place.

Judy wanted to talk to Mrs. Bailey, who had apparently discovered her husband's body, but she was being seen by her GP, who had been summoned by the officers first on the scene. They had arrived to find Steve Paxton trying to hit the Aquarius TV cameraman, the cameraman fighting back, Curtis Law trying to separate them, and Mrs. Bailey in near-hysterics, screaming at them all to stop.

A blood-smeared copy of *The Times* lay on the floor beside the empty bottle, the crossword half done, as though Bailey had been surprised in the middle of doing it. Judy turned her head to one side to read the date, to discover that it was that morning's paper.

She thought of her father then; she couldn't imagine why, except that it had been a long time since she'd seen either of her parents. It was ridiculous; it was only a couple of hours away down the motorway. You'd think they lived in Australia. She didn't even ring them all that often. She should go and see them. But then again, she thought, now might not be the best time, and she didn't want to think about that. She had work to do.

The officers first on the scene had cordoned off Bailey's office; they had found the safe open, and had thought it might have been a burglary gone wrong. It didn't do to rule anything out, but his safe had been open the last time she had been here, and it was hard to see how a burglar could have got into the grounds, never mind the house, without Bailey knowing. The alarms were set, and the windows were all shuttered on the inside. The lights had been on in the sitting room and the office, and off everywhere else. She'd get the SOCOs to check the office out. If they ever arrived.

She left the body and went up the steps, through the archway, to the dining area. A hatch to the kitchen was on her left; she looked through it to see by the sitting-room light a big, working, farmhouse kitchen, equipped and decorated with the same eye to design. Gleaming, state-of-the-art kitchen units lined the walls under the two windows. The dark red quarry tiles of the floor contrasted with the pristine whiteness of the walls and the woodwork. Beyond that was the area that housed the big freezer, the washing machine and dryer, and the deep Belfast sink in which nameless dead rural things got unpleasant things done to them, she supposed. Not, she imagined, by the farmer's wife. She could see from there that the back door was locked, the key still in it.

She turned back, the smell hitting her again as she went back down the steps, and forgot not to breathe through her nose. The room which had struck her as light and airy the first time she had seen it had been rendered claustrophobic and oppressive by the inordinate heat, the shutters, and the foul pot-pourri of sudden, violent death; Judy knew she had to get out of there. Now. She picked her way over the vomit, past the body, ducked under the blue and white ribbon barring the doorway, and went out into the hot morning, taking deep breaths.

She had thought, in her probationer days, that she would get over the revulsion, but she never had. She had simply learned how to control it, and she was never entirely convinced that she would always manage that. And outside was, she realized, not that much of an improvement. Nameless farmyard smells hung in the motionless air, only marginally better, to her nostrils, than the room she had just left.

Paxton was sitting at the table on the veranda; Judy took out her cigarettes and sat down beside him, lighting one as he glowered over to where Curtis Law and his cameraman stood with Tom Finch.

"Bloody vultures," he said. "That girl was in a right state, and they're filming, trying to ask her questions? They'd no business being here!"

"A complaint will be made to Aquarius Television," said Judy. "But, to be honest, a video of the murder scene might be useful to us."

"If you give a bugger who did it," said Paxton.

"You don't, I take it?" Judy said, expelling smoke with the words. It crossed her mind that maybe she shouldn't be smoking, but she dismissed the thought for a dozen different reasons. She hardly ever did, anyway. Only when she really felt the need. And when had she ever felt the need more?

"He was a nasty piece of work. There won't be many who'll mourn Bernard Bailey."

Much what she had already surmised. "Why did you work for him?"

"There aren't too many jobs in a place like this."

"How long have you worked here?"

He sighed. "Six years. I had my own farm, but it didn't survive the recession."

82

"So you were here when the first Mrs. Bailey was alive?"

"If you can call it that," he said. "She was always pregnant—lost I don't know how many babies. That's how she died. She looked fifteen years older than she was, I can tell you that. And scared stiff of him, she was. At least this one stands up to him."

That hadn't been Judy's impression. "Does she?" she asked.

"As best she can," said Paxton. "I mean, she's got more about her than the first one. And she's a nice girl—friendly, you know. There's no side to her. She'll muck in with everyone else if there's a job to be done."

Perhaps she did do nameless things to dead creatures in that big sink, thought Judy. She had obviously got a slightly misleading impression of Mrs. Bailey.

Paxton shook his head. "The way she looks, she could have done anything. Why she wanted to marry that nutcase, I'll never know. I mean, all right, he's got a lot of brass, but even so. He was a nutter. I mean," he said. "Look at this place. Like bloody Alcatraz. And she didn't even have a key to the bloody gate."

"Do you know why he had all the security put in?" she asked. "*Was* it because of the vandalism?"

Paxton shrugged. "That's what he said. But he wanted her where he could see her. He told me if he caught anyone letting her in without his permission, he'd get his cards. And I know he didn't like folk just being able to walk in," he said. "Let his shotgun off at McQueen first time he came here."

Judy's eyebrows rose.

"I'm going back a bit now," Paxton said. "To when the first Mrs. Bailey was alive. I was with some of the lads, heard the gun go off. We ran up here, thinking there's been an accident, or that Mrs. Bailey has finally let him have it between the eyes, and find McQueen having a real go at him, shotgun or no shotgun. Bailey's scared stiff. Yells to us to get McQueen off him and throw him out." He grinned. "We let McQueen get in a few before we grabbed him. Mind, he saw him again after that, and there was no trouble that time. And that was a while before the alarms went in, so it might not have had anything to do with that. Or with her. It could have been the vandalism, I suppose. But that's what he was like," he said, tapping his forehead. "He was a nutter, I'm telling you."

"Tell me about yesterday. We were told there was going to be some sort of demonstration here."

Paxton nodded. "Your lot were here, for a while. Till they decided it wasn't going to happen. TV was here all day. No demonstrators, though. Bailey had the alarms set all the time, and all the windows locked and shuttered all day. God knows who he thought was coming. Genghis Khan at the very least."

"What about the front door? Had he locked it?"

"No. It was closed, but it was unlocked. Has to be, really, so that he can get in and out to the office. And the entry phone's in there, of course. He had to answer it himself, with Mrs. Bailey being away."

So, Mrs. Bailey had been away. Judy was instantly suspicious of spouses who happened to be away at the material time.

"Did he let anyone in?"

"Not while I was here. I let the others go at five, and I knocked off at six." He smiled sourly. "He didn't want me to go," he said. "He was scared shitless." He put a hand to his mouth in mock disapproval of his language. "Sorry. But he was."

He quite possibly had been, thought Judy, remembering the smell with unwelcome clarity. "Did he have the radiators on in the sitting room?" she asked.

"Radiators?" he repeated. "I didn't even have the sheet over me in bed last night, so I wouldn't have thought so."

"Did you notice anything unusual when you got here this morning?" she asked.

He shook his head.

"When does the morning paper get here?"

Paxton looked slightly puzzled. "Half six or so. They arrive in the village about six, and the lad does the farm first, I think.

He leaves the paper in the mailbox by the gate. But you'll be able to find out from the video exactly when it came."

Judy had yet to see what the video had picked up from the camera that watched Bailey's gate. Tom Finch had stopped the tape when he arrived, intending to check it, but for the moment he had his hands full. DC Marshall was on his way; she'd get him to look at the tapes, which had to be their best witnesses.

Fourteen alarms, six cameras, shutters on the windows, and Bernard Bailey had somehow contrived to be stabbed to death on his own sofa. The monitor was in the hallway, so he could check who was at his gate before he opened it for anyone. The front door had been unlocked, but the alarms had been set, and she knew from personal eardrum-rattling experience that they could not have gone off without alerting everyone for a mile in every direction.

Bernard Bailey had let someone in, and that someone had killed him, or he was killed by someone with a key to the gate. Or he was killed by someone already in the house, whatever Steve Paxton believed about Mrs. Bailey being away. Had Mrs. Bailey stabbed her husband to death when he was in the middle of having an apple for breakfast, and doing the crossword? A number of things argued against that. Did he have whisky for breakfast, too? He had not, as far as Judy had been able to see, attempted to defend himself, which suggested that he had been asleep, probably drunk. And she couldn't really imagine Bailey doing a crossword.

Her father did crosswords; so did Lloyd. And they had something else in common; they both loved talking. They could talk for England. Well, Lloyd could talk for Wales. Her money would be on him, if he and her father staged an international, but it would be a close-run thing.

She felt homesick again, as she looked round this green, alien, rural world with its organic smells and distant animal noises, and longed for London's traffic-ridden, fume-filled, people-thronged streets. But that wasn't what she was supposed to be thinking about. How had she got on to that? The crossword. Yes. The crossword. And the fact that the word-sparing Mr. Bailey didn't strike her as a crossword-doer.

"Was he a crossword man?" she asked Paxton.

"Wouldn't know. I doubt it." He looked at her, squinting in the sun. "Why'd you want to know that?"

She smiled, not answering him. "Why did no one find him before his wife came home?" she asked. "Didn't anyone think it odd that he wasn't up and about at that time in the morning?"

Paxton shook his head. "We never saw him till afternoon," he said. "And she keeps the blinds closed anyway, because of the paintings, so no one coming up this way would notice the shutters."

"Thank you," said Judy. "I can let you get back to work. I might want to speak to you again, though." The entry phone buzzed, and she went back in, answering it to the FME, thank God. She hit the gate-open button. "On second thoughts," she said, calling Paxton back. "You couldn't man this thing for me, could you? Just keep out anyone who isn't police. Tell them it's a crime scene."

"Yes, sure, if you want."

She looked round for somewhere to extinguish her cigarette, and Paxton took it from her, grinding it out on the veranda, and took up his post as the Baileys' GP came downstairs.

"How is Mrs. Bailey?" asked Judy, taking the doctor out into the courtyard where they could not be overheard.

"She's not too bad now," she said. "But she's still very agitated. If you can leave it for an hour or so before you speak to her, it would be better. And if it's any help, I believe she really did get a terrible shock."

Judy smiled at the implied assumption that Rachel might have wanted to stab her husband to death. "She's not the only candidate," she said.

"Oh, no—of course. He was getting all those threats earlier in the year, wasn't he? Do you think someone killed him over this business about the road? Surely not."

Judy sincerely hoped not. There hadn't been any threats in

recent weeks, but perhaps that was because the sender had got serious. She gave a little shrug, and watched the doctor leave, thinking about that day when Bailey had dragged her through every muddy inch of his precious land. *Now,* now when a few muddy footprints might help, where was all that mud? Now, everything lay rock-hard and dry in the heat wave that was now nearly a fortnight old and showed no sign of passing.

The FME was arriving, the two doctors' cars passing on the roadway, and Judy prepared herself to go back into the house, into the room. At least Mr. Bailey was about to be pronounced officially dead, which was a step in the right direction. But finding enough people to interview employees, watch videos, check on keyholders, search for the murder weapon—all that was proving very difficult, at the start of the summer-holiday season.

"Just doing our jobs, officer," said Curtis, sounding a lot jauntier and cheekier than he felt, when Sergeant Finch had finished reading them the riot act about contaminating scenes of crime, looking a little like an offended cherub.

"Yeah, well, when your job starts interfering with my job, mate, my job wins."

Curtis smiled. "I suggest you watch Aquarius TV at ten-forty this evening and see if you still think that at eleven-thirty."

Finch frowned, but ignored the remark. "Were you filming when you went into the house?" he asked.

"Yes." Curtis felt a bit guilty about that. "Sorry. But you know cameramen."

"What did you expect?" said Gary. "It was a story. And stories on TV need pictures, don't they? What did you *think* I'd do? Memorize it all, and draw pictures when I got back to the studio?"

"We'll want the film," said Finch. "And there's no way you're going to be allowed to show it."

"Not now. But after, maybe. And it's not a film," Gary added, removing the tape from the camera. "It's a video. You can have it. But you'll have to watch it in the studio in Stansfield—it won't play on an ordinary VCR."

Finch took it, and Gary reloaded. Curtis was worried about Rachel—she had looked so awful when they went in. Her face had been white, and she had been trembling from head to foot. He had wanted to hold her, comfort her, but he couldn't. And then that oaf had come in and started a barney, the police had arrived, and she had started screaming.

"Is Mrs. Bailey all right?" he asked.

"Wouldn't know," said Finch. "Shouldn't think so, not if her husband's just been stabbed to death. Someone will be in touch about having a look at this," he said, "but I don't think we need detain you any longer."

Curtis wanted to be detained; he wanted to see Rachel. He tried desperately to think of some good reason why he should stay.

"You don't mind if we hang about, do you, mate?" said Gary. "I mean, we'd be here anyway by now, right?"

"Yeah, all right. But don't get in the way," said Finch, and walked off.

Curtis hadn't realized it was that simple. He had to remember that he was here as a journalist.

Nicola drove towards the farm, urging the old car to go faster. Gus sat beside her, trying to calm her down.

"What else did she say?" Nicola asked.

"Nothing else. Just what I've told you. She walked in this morning, and found him dead on the sofa." He put his hand on hers where it rested on the steering wheel. "You don't have to go so fast, Nicky," he said gently. "Slow down. Look—stop. Let me drive. You shouldn't be driving."

She braked and brought the car to a halt, suddenly in tears. Gus was holding her, rocking her like a baby, saying all the things you would say to someone who had just lost her father.

But that wasn't why she was crying, and she couldn't tell Gus. She couldn't tell anyone.

# CHAPTER FOUR

LLOYD HAD ARRIVED BACK AT STANSFIELD TO DIS-
cover that this Monday morning had yet more in store for him.

"Bailey's been what?" he said, when Case told him.

"You heard. Stabbed several times, according to Inspector
Hill."

Poor Judy. She always seemed to get the bloody ones.

"And," said Case.

Here we go again, thought Lloyd. If he hadn't asked for no
calls while he considered how he intended approaching his colleagues tomorrow, Judy's message would have come through
to him. Now he was going to be given lengthy Case notes. But
these turned out to be very short indeed.

"He was found by his wife, who called us. But Curtis Law
and his cameraman beat us to it and went in there all cameras
blazing."

Lloyd stared at him. "How did that happen?" he demanded.

"Combination of circumstances. They were a lot closer than
we were, and they heard about it at more or less the same time.
And they're still there, covering the story, obviously. Finch tore
them off a strip, but we can't actually stop them reporting the
murder. Look, Lloyd, if you don't—"

"Don't say what you are going to say."

Case sat back. "All right," he said. "All right. If you think
you can handle it. But don't lose your temper, Lloyd. We don't
need any more adverse publicity. And the man was receiving
death threats, remember. Law told us that if someone could get

in to leave threats, they could get in to kill him. He'll be gunning for us over this as well as the other business."

And Lloyd had thought that today couldn't get any blacker. "I'll be on my very best behaviour," he said. His quick temper and injudicious tongue had got him into trouble with everyone from very senior officers to innocent bystanders, but he could keep his cool when it was important that he do so. He hoped.

He arrived at Bailey's Farm at the same time as Freddie, who was standing by his elderly, beloved, open-topped sports car, negotiating with whoever was manning the phone entry.

"No—I'm the pathologist." He sounded it out, syllable by syllable. "Look—is Chief Inspector Lloyd there? Or Inspector Hill? Just tell one of them that Freddie's here—all right?"

Lloyd watched, unobserved.

"Freddie," Freddie repeated. "Never mind the last name—she'll know who you mean. It's a Polish name, you wouldn't—"

The gate said something which to Lloyd was unintelligible, but Freddie understood it, having been conversing with it for some time, evidently.

"I'm the *pathologist*, for God's sake! I'm *supposed* to be at the crime scene!" He turned and saw Lloyd laughing. "Who the hell have you got manning this thing?" he demanded.

"Don't ask me," said Lloyd. "I've just got here. But you've cheered me up, Freddie—not something you often do, and something I would have thought impossible today."

"Sorry, Freddie," said the gate, now with Judy's voice. "Hello, Lloyd."

Lloyd realized that there was a camera high on a post, and smiled weakly at it. He had so many things to tell Judy that he had no idea where to start, and now it was all going to have to wait. The gate swung open, and he and Freddie got into the cars and drove through, arriving together in the courtyard, where Freddie parked beside the BMW, and leapt out over his pride and joy's low door. Lloyd got out of his car to see an estate car with AQUARIUS TELEVISION painted on the side, and a camera pointing at him, but Curtis Law wasn't evident. He joined Freddie, who was admiring the BMW.

"Not a traditionalist, then, our Mr. Bailey?" he said. "This is not your average farm vehicle."

"It's his wife's," said Lloyd, with the knowing look that irritated Judy.

"Ah. *Cherchez la femme?* What's your theory this time, Lloyd?"

"No theories," said Lloyd, truthfully, for once. "All I know is that he's dead, he's wealthy, and he has, in Judy's words, a drop-dead gorgeous wife. And she is drop-dead gorgeous—you wait till you see her."

"She's certainly got a drop-dead gorgeous car," said Freddie, patting it the way other people patted Labradors. "Ah, well. Let's go to work."

Lloyd followed Freddie up the steps, into the house. The scene-of-crime people were working in an office, where there was a safe with its door standing open. Perhaps Bailey had been robbed. Lloyd didn't know if that would be good or bad. He ducked under the tape, going into the room, where the smell was awful, the stifling heat was unbearable, and the body was a far from pretty sight. Lloyd found a photographer, another scene-of-crime woman examining the sofa, and Judy, looking green. Freddie was greeting her effusively, as ever, as he took out his tape recorder.

"No lovely assistant with you today?" she asked, manfully joining in Freddie's banter.

"No. She's off sick. I'm not going to be able to fit Mr. Bailey in until Wednesday morning, I'd better warn you. I'm going to be away almost all day tomorrow, and there's no one else to do it."

"Life was pronounced extinct at eleven-fifteen," said Judy. "The FME left some notes."

"Good, good," said Freddie, smiling at the SOCO as she went off to join her colleagues in the office and informed him that Mr. Bailey was all his. He told the photographer what angles he wanted, and stayed out of the other man's way until he'd got his shots before beginning, as ever, with an eyes-only examination, noting the position of the body and the circumstances in which he had been found, speaking into a tape recorder. "Deceased smells strongly of alcohol, and there is evidence of vomiting round the mouth, on the deceased's clothing, and on the carpet," he said happily. "One, two, three ... four visible wounds to chest ... some bleeding has occurred, but haemorrhage very unlikely to be cause of death. Respiratory failure a possibility."

He began taking temperatures then, and Lloyd waited until he had noted the second lot, fifteen minutes after the first. "Well?" he said.

"Rigor is quite advanced," Freddie said. "A very rough estimate would be six to twelve hours."

Lloyd looked at his watch. Seven minutes past twelve. It was now Monday afternoon, he told himself comfortingly. The worst Monday morning of his life was over. And he supposed Mr. Bailey had had a worse Monday morning even than his, because some time between midnight and six A.M., he had lost his life. Lloyd had only lost his DI, a measure of his not inconsiderable self-esteem, and in all probability, come the reshuffle, his job.

"Could it have happened at, say, seven o'clock this morning?" asked Judy.

"Well, the body temperature doesn't entirely preclude its being as late as that, but the heat in this room will have affected the cooling rate considerably. I have to take his temperature a few more times before I can work anything out from that."

"Do you think the radiators were put on to confuse the time of death?" Lloyd asked.

"Could be, could be. Then again ... perhaps Mr. Bailey felt cold."

"In this weather? It was a very warm night."

"I don't think he was quite himself, even before he was

stabbed, do you?" said Freddie. "Was he on any sort of medication, do you know?"

"I don't know," said Judy. "But I'll ask his wife. *Could* it have been as late as seven?" she asked again.

"Rigor's a very unreliable guide," Freddie said, "but as a general rule, its onset is six hours after death. With a heavy build like Mr. Bailey's, I would actually have expected it to take even longer than usual, so if it had happened as late as that, I wouldn't have expected to find rigor at all, whereas, as I said, it is quite well advanced. But I might be able to give you a better estimate once I've opened him up. I certainly won't know how he died or what he died of until I do. It's an odd one."

Alarm bells rang in Lloyd's head with Freddie's final, almost throwaway, remark. Odd ones he could do without.

"Why seven o'clock?" Freddie asked Judy.

"That's today's paper," said Judy, indicating *The Times*. "It's delivered at half past six, and the crossword's half-done."

"You see, Lloyd?" said Freddie. "That's a real detective for you. No theorizing. Just facts." He opened Bailey's shirt, slowly, carefully, and examined the wounds.

"What sort of weapon?" asked Lloyd, ignoring Freddie's teasing. How he could be cheerful in these dismal circumstances was beyond him.

"You want me to tell you that from some cuts in his chest? How should I know? Wait until I've had a proper look."

"If you're not doing the post mortem until Wednesday, it would help if we could have some indication of what we're looking for out there," said Lloyd, looking out at the small team of people going over the ground. "It looks as though someone might just have picked up a kitchen knife and stabbed him—is that possible?"

Freddie relented. "Yes," he said. "At least, it was something with a blade, not a screwdriver or anything like that. Broader than that. Say half an inch wide at the point to which it penetrated. But not very sharp. Whatever it was didn't go in cleanly."

He grinned. "But the apple could be a red herring, if you see what I mean. It needn't have been cut open in here."

Lloyd knew that. He glanced at Judy to find that she had retreated as far as she could from the foul-smelling body, and he could see that she had already spent more than enough time with it. "You carry on with the interviews," he said to her. "I'll catch up with what's been going on when we've finished here."

She smiled her thanks. "Right," she said. "I think it's time I had a word with the widow. She's supposed to have been away, and came home to find him like that."

The drop-dead gorgeous Mrs. Bailey. "Could a woman have stabbed him?" Lloyd asked Freddie.

"Before I've had a chance to see the depth and force of the wounds, as far as I'm concerned, anyone could have stabbed him. He was a big, powerful man, but he might not have been awake, or even conscious. My guess is that he was lying in this position when he was stabbed. There are no defence wounds, so I expect he knew nothing about it."

A domestic? That had to be the simple explanation. And simple explanations made life simpler all round. Because although Judy had been, unlike him, extremely diplomatic when interviewed, she had indicated that the death threats were not something that she believed would result in Mr. Bailey's death. The man had even received another lot after he had put in the cameras. He would die if he didn't sell, cameras or no cameras, they had said. Cameras might be watching his property, they had said, but the writer was watching him. He hadn't sold; McQueen had indicated on Friday that he would be taking the other route; Bailey had died on Monday morning. Was that just coincidence? The press wouldn't see it like that.

His money, for the moment, was on Rachel Bailey having come home to someone who had drunk so much that he had made himself ill before passing out on the sofa. She had picked up a knife and stabbed him, for reasons which would probably become clear. Simple.

But he had a feeling that it wasn't going to be *that* simple.

94

Rachel had hung everything up in the wardrobe, or consigned it to the washing basket, and now she was going through them all again. She had emptied what was left in her weekend bag on to the bed; she had been through everything. She had known that the clasp wasn't reliable—why hadn't she had it seen to?

"Come in," she said distractedly to the knock on her door.

The woman who had seen Bernard about the death threats came in, looking considerably more elegant than she had then.

"Hello—I don't know if you remember me. Detective Inspector Judy Hill—I'm with Stansfield CID."

Rachel straightened up. "Bernard'd been draggin' you all over the farm last time I saw you," she said.

"Yes," she said, smiling a little. "How are you feeling?"

"I'm all right. Don't know why I carried on like that. Got a shock, that's all. The blood and everything. Then they came in filmin' everythin',' and Steve started fightin' with them. It just got to me."

"How did they get in?"

"I let them in. Didn't care who it was. Just wanted someone with me. And . . . and I know Curtis and Gary from when they came here before." Rachel shook the empty bag, felt in the pockets. Why hadn't she packed herself? She felt tears coming again, tears of bewilderment.

"Mrs. Bailey? Are you all right?"

She unzipped compartments, feeling in them, pulling the lining out. Maybe it had fallen into one of the shopping bags. She picked one up, tipping it out, tears streaming down her face, then picked up the next and did the same. Where was it?

"Mrs. Bailey?" The inspector sounded alarmed, and came to her, taking the empty bag from her. "Rachel? What's wrong? Are you looking for something?"

Rachel looked at her. "A pendant," she said. "I've lost a pendant."

"Well—just take it easy," she said, sitting her down on the bed.

"I know what you're thinkin'." She wasn't going to pretend.

95

Not to anyone. "You're thinkin' all she's worried about's losin' a pendant. You'd think losin' her husband'd be more import—" She was unable to control the huge, shuddering sob that had welled up.

"I'm not, Rachel, believe me."

The inspector put her arm around her as Rachel shook with the sobs she had been holding in since she had found Bernard. At last, they subsided, and there was a few moments' silence before the inspector spoke again.

"I'm very sorry about your husband," she said.

"Are you?" replied Rachel, dully. "I'm not."

Inspector Hill didn't look surprised. She looked concerned. "Aren't you?" she asked, her voice slightly disbelieving.

"Why should I be?" said Rachel. "You knew him 'bout as well as I did, 'cept he didn't fuck you all the time." She coloured up as soon as she'd spoken. "I'm sorry," she said. "I'm sorry. I shouldn't have—" She began to cry again. "I'm sorry."

It was this room, this bed. That was all it meant. Bernard silently and sullenly mounting her, thrusting into her, grunting when he came. She had told Curtis she hadn't minded it, and that had perhaps been the only real lie she had ever told him. She had hated it, dreaded it. On the only occasion she had refused he had just held her down and done it anyway.

"It's all right," Inspector Hill said. "I've seen grief affect people too many ways to take any notice of what they say."

Grief? No. She felt bewildered. Lost. Frightened. The inspector thought she was still in shock. And perhaps she was right, Rachel conceded, because she still couldn't get the scene downstairs out of her mind. Her system hadn't recovered, which was why everything seemed so hopeless.

She blew her nose, shook her head. "He married me because he wanted a son," she said. "I married him because I wanted a big house like this and money to spend on clothes and . . ." She waved a hand round the room that she had transformed. "All this." She wiped her eyes. "I'm not goin' to pretend I loved him," she said. "Nobody'd believe me if I did. That pendant means more to me than he ever did."

The inspector nodded, reminding Rachel of Curtis doing all his serious nodding to the camera after he'd finished an interview. She wanted him here, not some policewoman who thought she understood and didn't, could never, understand.

"It was my mother's," she went on. "Only thing she ever owned that was worth anything."

"Are you from Devon?" asked Inspector Hill. "Is that where your family is?"

Rachel shrugged. "Not from anywhere in particular," she said. "I'm Cornish, really, but we travelled all round Devon and Cornwall." She looked at the other woman, wanting to see her reaction. "My family are travellers," she said. "Tinkers. Gypsies. Whatever you want to call them."

There was no reaction. Just polite interest.

"Didn't ever like it. People callin' you names, movin' you on, not lettin' you into shops nor pubs."

"How did you end up in Bartonshire? It's a long way from the West Country."

"Usual way."

"A man?"

Rachel nodded. "He was in Torquay on holiday with some other folk, and we got together. Saw my chance to get out, took it, came here, moved in with him. Forgot to tell me he had a wife. She moved back in, threw me out. Always checked after that. Never took nothin' to do with the married ones. More trouble than they're worth."

"What did you do after you got thrown out?"

"Well, I wasn't goin' back to travellin'. And there're plenty of farms round here. I can do anythin' on a farm," she said. "I can bale hay, I can drive a tractor, I can pluck chickens, dip sheep—I can even milk a cow without a machine to help me, which is more'n Steve Paxton can do."

She looked down at the clothes-strewn duvet, and her finger drew little circles on an empty bit. "I was workin' on a farm, saw they needed people for the shop here. Had to be better'n muckin' out, I thought, so I went after it, got it. Then . . ." She shrugged a little, looked up. "He asked me to marry him. But he didn't love me or nothin'. Never said he did. Just—just wanted to breed from me." She explained the terms of Bernard's grandfather's will. "I said I'd do it. But it was a mistake." She looked up. "He never spoke to me, never said nothin' to me that wasn't an order. Never even called me by name. Just tried to get me pregnant near every night in life, and never said a word then, neither."

The inspector listened gravely to the speech, jotting things down in her notebook. "Can I ask you about this morning?" she said.

Rachel nodded. She felt better now. Even the pendant didn't seem to matter so much. And maybe it was at the hotel. "I came home just after ten o'clock," she said. "I went into the living room, and—" She broke off, took a deep breath. "And it was like a furnace, and there was this awful smell, and he was lyin' there in all that blood." She felt the panic again, but she controlled it. "I rang the police." She shrugged. "That's it."

"I understand the front door was unlocked—was that usual?"

"Yes. More often than not, stands open in the summer. Well—you saw yourself, when you were here. But it was closed."

"Does it get locked at night?"

Rachel nodded. It was the last thing Bernard did before he came upstairs. She could hear the heavy old-fashioned lock being turned, feel the tension in her body that that sound had created. "He changed the tape and shuttered all the downstairs windows and locked the door 'fore he come to bed," she said, with an involuntary shudder. "Half ten. When the news had finished."

"I'm sorry if this is difficult for you."

Rachel shook her head.

"You found him when you came home, you said. Can I ask where you had been?"

Rachel gave her a severely edited account of her weekend in London, leaving out any mention of Curtis. Then she had to go through what she had found when she got into the house. She hadn't touched anything but the phone, and the phone book, she said, in answer to the inspector's question. The alarms had been on, the shutters down and locked. She had used the light from the living room to do her phoning.

"Was your husband on any sort of medication?"

"No," said Rachel. "He was as healthy as an ox."

Inspector Hill looked up from her notebook. "Do you know what your husband kept in the safe?" she asked.

Rachel shook her head. "Just papers and stuff. He never closed it, so I don't think he had nothin' worth much in there. You can check it, if you like—look at anythin' you want, anywhere."

"Thank you. And . . . this may sound unimportant, but what newspapers do you have delivered?"

"The *Mail*," said Rachel.

"Neither of you took *The Times*?"

Rachel closed her eyes as a wave of panic caught her. "No."

"Thank you," said the inspector. "Rachel—we're going to be in and out of here for a while yet. Is there somewhere you can go rather than stay here? Your stepdaughter's perhaps?"

Rachel smiled at that description of Nicola, and shook her head, then the smile went. "You'll be takin' him away, won't you?" she asked anxiously. "And the sofa?" She couldn't have that blood-stained sofa in the house. She couldn't. "I heard someone say they needed a van for it. Does that mean they're takin' it away too?" She had listened to the conversations through the chimney breast.

"Yes. It'll go to forensic."

"And can I clean up the carpet where he was sick?"

"Yes, when they've finished. Once they take the crime-scene tape down, you can do what you like."

She gave a little sigh of relief. "Then I'll be all right here," she said.

"If you're sure. Would you like us to try to contact your family?"

She shook her head, and the inspector left the bedroom, but not the house, as Rachel discovered when she watched from the window. She saw Aquarius TV's estate car; Curtis must still be around somewhere. But he'd be busy. He'd come back tonight, when everyone had gone.

Judy had come downstairs to find Lloyd and DC Marshall in the hallway, with the TV monitor and recorder, watching the tape. Steve Paxton had been relieved of entry-phone duty; Lloyd had had the alarms switched off once the SOCOs had finished, and now the gate stood open. A crowd of local reporters had gathered in the courtyard behind a cordon.

She told Lloyd what she had so far learned; he told her that Bailey's morning paper had not been collected from his mail box, and was indeed the *Mail*.

The tapes ran for twelve hours, and it appeared to have been Bailey's habit to change the tape sharp at ten-thirty in the morning and ten-thirty in the evening, which tallied, as Judy told Lloyd, with what Mrs. Bailey had said. He had two tapes for each day of the week, so that Monday's tapes would be reused the following Monday, if there was no reason to hold on to them. The tape found in the machine was marked SUNDAY 1; SUNDAY 2 was still on the shelf. Bailey had obviously not changed the tape at ten-thirty yesterday evening, nor bolted the door, and yet Freddie had indicated that he had died later than that.

"So that's a little puzzle, isn't it?" said Lloyd. "Why didn't he change the tape, bolt the door, and go to bed like he always did?"

Judy nodded, noted it down. Lloyd's little puzzles were always worth investigating. But Bailey had been drinking; he had been expecting marauders all day, and may have thought he was still at risk; and Rachel hadn't been there. His ten-thirty ritual may have had more to do with trying to get her pregnant than with a desire to sleep. His routine had already been broken, so perhaps it wasn't so puzzling.

"If the tape doesn't get changed," Lloyd went on, "it rewinds itself. Which it did. So practically the whole of yesterday from ten-thirty in the morning has been wiped with the new recording, and there's nothing on the few minutes at the end of the tape."

"What have we got on it?" asked Judy. "Anything?"

"The tape ran itself back at ten thirty-nine P.M., and started recording again at ten forty-three. The first thing we've got is at ten-fifty P.M., when an estate car came through the gate without using the phone. We had the number plate checked, and the car is registered to Mrs. Nicola Hutchins."

"That's his daughter," said Judy.

Lloyd nodded. "It leaves again just after midnight. So far, its driver is our best bet. And nothing whatever was happening anywhere else there's a camera."

"Hello," said Marshall. "Look at this."

He rewound the tape, and played it in normal time. As far as Judy could see there was still nothing whatever happening on any of the six boxes into which the screen was split.

Marshall rewound the tape again, and replayed it. "Don't watch the pictures," he said. "Look at the time."

And this time Judy saw the figures at the bottom right of the screen jump from 02:23:43 to 02:37:04. Marshall paused the tape.

"Well, well, well," said Lloyd, sitting back. It was a swivel chair; it wouldn't tip back. He contented himself with swaying gently to and fro. "So someone arrived here at about—call it two twenty-four in the morning, and then, to wipe out the recording of his or her arrival, thirteen minutes later he or she ran the tape back, and started it recording again." He smiled. "But," he said, "he or she would still have to get out again, unless, of course, he or she lived here."

Marshall ran the tape in normal time, this time with all three of them watching. At 02:40:23, the gate opened, and a figure on foot, slim, wearing jeans and a hooded jacket, face turned away from the camera, walked quickly through it, away from the farm.

The camera was high, so that no one could use the gate without being picked up by it, and they only had a back view to work with, on a black and white picture lit by a security lamp.

The tape was put back on fast forward in vision, and they watched the sun rise on Harmston, but that was all that happened until a few minutes to six, when Paxton arrived, and waited for the farmhands. He let them in, and they went about their business, none of them ever out of camera range for more than a few seconds. At six thirty-five, the paper was delivered. At nine-thirty, Paxton left in the pick-up to go for breakfast, dropping off one of the farmhands, who waited at the gate, eating his sandwiches. Rachel Bailey's BMW arrived at two minutes past ten, and the farmhand opened the gate for her. Seven minutes after that the Aquarius TV estate car pulled up and Curtis Law got out, used the entry phone, and was admitted. That was followed shortly by Paxton in the pick-up, using his key. Then the two police officers who had responded to the 999, then Tom Finch and Judy herself. A few minutes after that, the tape reverted to the night shots for the last nine minutes of its length.

Marshall switched it off, and got up stiffly from the crouching position he had necessarily adopted, since Lloyd was occupying the only chair, swaying to and fro as he thought.

"We could look at the other cameras' output more closely, I suppose," Marshall said. "But I couldn't see anything going on."

"I'll put someone on to it, but I think we can safely concentrate on the camera over the gate for now," said Lloyd. "And we'll want a copy of the tape." He got up, and beckoned them to follow him into the office, where their conversation would be less public. The SOCOs had finished in there, and the DC looking through the safe had found papers which showed that

Bernard Bailey had, contrary to popular belief, been on the verge of bankruptcy. Whether that had a bearing on his death remained to be seen.

"Comments," Lloyd said.

"This farm is a long way from anywhere," said Judy. "Even the village is two miles away. Whoever that was, was on foot."

"Someone could have driven here and parked on the road beyond the gate," said Marshall. "No one would see a car parked way out here at that time in the morning."

No, thought Judy, they wouldn't. They probably *all* went to bed at ten-thirty. She had quite often been known to go to bed at ten-thirty herself, but she liked to feel that life was going on outside her window, that the odd late-night reveller was creeping home at half past two in the morning. And even if such a thing ever occurred in Harmston, she thought, no late reveller would be creeping home via Bailey's isolated farm. She could no more live here than she could live on the moon, never mind with the uncommunicative Bailey trying to get her pregnant all the time. But she didn't want to think about that, she reminded herself, so she put it out of her mind. Again.

"Now, who might want to erase the record of her homecoming, if that was several hours earlier than she's prepared to admit?" asked Lloyd. "And who could have used that thirteen minutes to murder her husband, drive her car out, come back, wipe the tape, and leave on foot, making sure the camera didn't catch a glimpse of her face? She could have spent the rest of the night in the car, then driven back in to be recorded on video at the time she does admit to coming home."

"Oh," said Marshall, a little surprised. "I thought it was a man on the video."

Lloyd looked at Judy, eyebrows raised.

"I wasn't sure," she said. "Someone slim, certainly. And young. But I wouldn't put money on either sex."

"Alan," said Lloyd. "See if you can get an idea of his or her height. Check the other videos for someone whose height you can check."

Marshall went off to comply, and Lloyd looked back at Judy. "It could have been Mrs. Bailey," he said. "Couldn't it?"

Lloyd's instant theories were legendary. So was Judy's equally instant disproving of them. She couldn't actually see anything wrong with this one so far, but the newspaper still puzzled her. "Who brought *The Times* in?" she asked. "And who did the crossword? And when? There's blood on it."

"Ah, yes—the SOCO thinks the paper fell on to the sofa, and got blood on it that way, if that's any help," said Lloyd. "How it got here in the first place is another little puzzle for you to ponder."

"Thanks."

They went back out into the hallway, and she saw Curtis Law hanging round outside waiting for an interview. That was when she remembered that he had offered Bailey help in setting the system up; he'd know how to tamper with it, she thought. He was slim. Young. But she didn't suppose he had taken to murder just so he had a story to cover.

She felt Lloyd tense up as he saw him, and frowned a little. She knew that Curtis Law had stolen a march on them with this drugs business; she knew that it had not gone down very well with Lloyd, who had never been very enamoured of him in the first place. She would have understood if he'd been irritated—angry, even, about Law succeeding where he had failed. But he hadn't been, not really. He was always quick to admit his mistakes; he had accepted that he had been wrong, and Law had been right. So that wasn't it.

Lloyd was nervous of only one thing that Judy knew of, and that was heights. He pretended to other people that he wasn't, and his would-be air of indifference upon finding himself on the top floor of a high-rise fooled them, but she knew him too well not to be aware of the waves of discomfort. She was aware of them now, as he talked to Marshall, looked at videos, did anything he could to delay going outside.

Lloyd was *nervous* of Curtis Law, and that didn't just puzzle her; it worried her.

* * *

Terri Melville was, as she unoriginally put it on the phone to her Save Our Woodland Sites committee members, over the moon. Oh, of course, she had said, it was dreadful, but she didn't suppose that it would be too long before McQueen was offered the land, and that was a great relief. But yes, a terrible thing to have happened, in Harmston, of all places.

Well, yes, she supposed Rachel might have done it herself, which was what most people thought must have happened. It had always been a very strange setup. A girl like that, and a man like Bailey.

Oh, yes, really beautiful. And always very pleasant, and easy to talk to, which was more than you could say for her husband. But what reason could she possibly have had for marrying Bailey if it wasn't for his money? And she'd made the most of it. There was that car, for a start. And the clothes. Designer dungarees for mucking out, she supposed. But seriously, she had some wonderful clothes. But then, she was that kind of woman, wasn't she? She could wear anything and make it look fantastic. Then if you rushed out and got the same thing, you just looked like a sack of potatoes in it.

No—Terri had wondered why he'd married her, too. He had certainly never seemed like someone who would want a girl nearly twenty years younger than him for *that* sort of thing. Of course that poor wife of his—no, his first wife—well, she was hardly ever not pregnant, so maybe he was more interested in that sort of thing than he seemed.

Jack Melville gloomily listened to variations on this theme eight times. He had given up trying to work; for some reason, the many telephone calls had to be made in his presence, despite the fact that these days they had a phone in every room, in each car, a cordless one in the hall, and a mobile.

And of course, Terri was saying for the umpteenth time, who knew what went on behind closed doors?

Jack did. He knew what had been going on behind Bailey's

105

closed doors. He knew a great deal more than he should know, or wanted to know.

Or in the Baileys' case, Terri was saying, what went on behind umpteen alarms and God knew how many television cameras?

Jack stiffened. He'd forgotten about that. Oh, dear God. The police would know he'd been there. He shot a look at Terri, but she was engrossed in gossip, thank God. He had to think. He had to think very, very carefully. He mustn't panic. He must think of a good reason. One he could offer Terri. Any reason. Anything but the truth.

Curtis walked towards Chief Inspector Lloyd and Inspector Hill, who were coming out of the house at last, ducking under the cordon. "Any particular lines of enquiry yet?" he asked. The question was directed at Inspector Hill, who shook her head in reply. "Have you revised your opinion on the death threats?"

"Not yet," she said. "But nothing has been ruled out."

"We would like the public's help on this one," said Lloyd. "If we can use your airwaves, it would be a big help."

Curtis wondered if he'd seen *Mr. Big* yet, and decided that he couldn't have, or he wouldn't be being that friendly. They had never been bosom buddies in the first place, and Lloyd wasn't going to like *Mr. Big* one little bit. Presumably his bosses had seen it, though. He had thought the police might try to stop it being shown, but they hadn't. Which was a pity. An injunction got you on the news, doubled your viewing figures when you did show it, even if you did have to take out the naughty bits.

"Just along the lines of anyone who was in this area yesterday to come forward, that sort of thing," Lloyd went on.

"I was in the area," said Gary.

"This is my cameraman, Gary," said Curtis. "Say hello to the police officers, Gary."

Gary shook hands with Lloyd, and nodded to Inspector Hill.

"I was here," he said. "Taking shots of anyone who came to the farm, right up until the light went, really, so I can let you see who came here up to about eight."

"That's good news," said Lloyd. "I'd like to see the tape when it's convenient."

"Anytime, really. Your sergeant's got the one I shot this morning—just come in anytime. There's always someone there in office hours."

"Anything you can tell us now about his visitors? Did he let anyone in?"

"Only one. McQueen, the developer who wants this place for his road. Struck me as odd, him calling on Bailey. I thought he'd get short shrift like everyone else, but he was let in."

"Did you see him leave?"

"No. He came just as the light was going. I packed up then."

"What about Bailey's CCTV?" asked Curtis.

"Not as helpful as it might have been," said Lloyd. "Thank you very much." He turned to Curtis. "And you, Mr. Law. I take it you would like an interview?"

"Please," said Curtis. "Do you want to go over the ground before we start?"

"Well, I'm prepared to say that he was found with knife wounds, and that we're treating it as murder. The usual stuff. And that any information will be treated in the utmost confidence, in view of the use to which these secluded lanes are put now and then," he added. "Nothing too specific, but you wouldn't expect me to be, not at this stage. At the moment we need all the help we can get." He smiled. "I don't know how the police managed before television," he said.

Curtis smiled inwardly at the irony of that remark.

"And we might want volunteers to help us search for the weapon." Lloyd waved a hand in the general direction of the fields. "There's a lot of land to cover."

"You might never find it," said Curtis.

"If it's here, we'll find it. You can be sure of that, Mr. Law. We'll find it, whatever it is, wherever it is."

"Excuse me," said Inspector Hill, and walked off in the direction of the old brown estate car that was pulling into the courtyard.

Curtis was barely aware of the visitor, his mind still on what Lloyd had just said. Was it his imagination, or had that conversation turned a little sinister? Probably his imagination. He realized then whose car the inspector had gone to meet, as he saw Nicola Hutchins disappear into a crowd of police and reporters. "We'll want a shot of her," he told Gary, running forward. "The dark-haired one. That's the daughter."

They got their shots, but she hadn't said anything. Curtis prepared to begin his interview with Lloyd, glancing up at Rachel's bedroom window.

He hoped she was all right.

Nicola had been startled to see the number of police vehicles there, as they had got out of the car. What seemed like a dozen cameras were pointing at them. Why all the media? She supposed it was because her father had become something of a local celebrity.

"That's the inspector that called about the death threats," said Gus, as a woman approached them, and saw them safely through to the other side of the cordon.

Inspector Hill said hello to Gus, and introduced herself to Nicola. "I'm very sorry about your father," she said, leading them up the steps to the house.

"Thank you," said Nicola, a little uncomfortably. "How's Rachel?"

"She's been seen by her doctor," said the inspector. "I think she just needs to rest a little."

Nicola was sure Rachel wouldn't be in mourning for too long, and neither would she, come to that. But she would miss him, in an odd sort of way. She felt a little as though an ugly factory chimney that she passed every day had been demolished; she was glad to see it gone, but it would take her a while to get her bearings now that it wasn't going to be there.

Inspector Hill took them into Bernard's office, and Nicola didn't want to be in here. Why were there so many police? The inspector sat behind the desk, and indicated that Nicola should sit on the other chair. Gus perched on the safe, closed for the first time Nicola could remember. She swallowed hard. Could she weather this?

"You called on your father at about ten to eleven last night, is that right, Mrs. Hutchins?" asked the inspector.

The closed-circuit television, of course. Nicola nodded.

"Was it usual for you to call on him that late?"

"No. He'd rung me earlier. About a sheep." She supposed they had to ask questions. It didn't mean they suspected her of anything.

"Oh, yes," said Inspector Hill. "You're the vet, of course."

"He rang at about half past ten. He said a sheep had got on to the road and been badly injured." She noticed that Inspector Hill was writing down what she was saying, and became a little self-conscious. "He wanted me to deal with it."

"Wouldn't a sheep getting out set off the alarms?"

Oh, God. There was no sheep. There had never been a sheep. "Yes, but the alarms weren't on, for some reason," she said. "He told me where to find it, but when I got there, there wasn't any sign of a sheep. I thought he must have given me wrong directions."

The inspector looked a little puzzled. "Wrong directions?" she queried. "I would have thought your father knew every inch of the land round here."

"He does. Did. But he'd had a lot to drink."

She looked interested. "Was that unusual?"

"Yes," she said. "He always had a whisky at night before he went to bed, but that was it. Just one. He never drank the rest of the time. Well—not unless something had really upset him."

"Would you have any idea *what* might have upset him?"

Nicola hesitated, then said, "Not really."

"Which means you have," the inspector said.

Her voice was gentle, but it held a slight warning, and

109

Nicola reacted to that automatically. "Well, I don't know for a fact," she said. "I mean, I don't really know at all. I just think that he must have been upset to have been drinking so much."

"And you think you know what *might* have upset him," Inspector Hill persisted, her voice quiet, sympathetic, but somehow remorseless. "Don't you?"

"Yes," said Nicola reluctantly, horribly aware that she was not going to get off the hook until she told her. "I . . . I think he may have had a row with Rachel."

"Did he often have rows with her?"

"I wouldn't know," she said, uncomfortably. "Yes," she said, when the inspector still hadn't spoken. "I think he probably did."

"What makes you think that?"

It was a reasonable question. Nicola sighed. "I just think it's a possibility," she said. "It didn't strike me as a match made in heaven."

"Where did he say you'd find the sheep?" asked Inspector Hill, changing the subject completely, much to Nicola's relief, even if it was to the non-existent sheep.

Nicola hadn't thought about any of this. She had thought she would find Rachel, and maybe a couple of policemen. Not swarms of them. They were searching the grounds. Why? And why were they asking so many questions?

"On the road just behind the farm," she said. "When I couldn't find it, I came on up to the farm. And when I got here I saw that the alarms weren't on."

"Was the front door locked?"

"No."

"Did that surprise you?"

"Not really. He locks up when he goes to bed, I think. And he hadn't gone to bed. He was out." The inspector wrote that down, too. Word for word. "I don't know where he was," she said. "I thought . . ." She changed her mind about what she had been going to say. "I thought perhaps he'd gone to meet me, but I'd gone to the wrong place, so I thought I'd better wait."

"Was the Land Rover here?"

"I don't know. He locks it up at night ever since the vandalism, so it might have been. Or he might have taken it out—I don't know. I didn't look. When he didn't come back, I left."

"You waited for over an hour," said Inspector Hill.

"Yes."

"Were you worried about him?"

Nicola shook her head.

"But he'd had a lot to drink, and you thought he might be driving. He'd left the house open, the alarms off—didn't that bother you?"

"I . . . I thought it was odd, that's all."

"Did you switch the alarms back on when you left?"

"No. I wasn't going to interfere with them. I just left them the way I found them. Look—why are you asking all these questions?"

Inspector Hill's eyebrows flickered in the tiniest of frowns. "Mrs. Hutchins," she said carefully, firmly. "Your father has been found dead, with several stab wounds to his chest. I think we do have—"

Nicola stared at her. "He was stabbed?" she said, uncomprehendingly.

"What did you think had happened, Mrs. Hutchins?" she asked, her voice quiet, sympathetic.

Nicola swallowed. "I just . . . well, I thought . . . No. It was silly. I just thought he—" She was gabbling. She had to say something, for God's sake. Something sensible. But nothing sensible came out. "It was just, with the drinking and everything, I just—"

"Take your time."

Nicola took the inspector's advice, and waited for some moments before trying to speak again. "Gus said that Rachel had rung, said that something awful had happened, that my father was dead. But I—I thought he'd, well . . . killed himself. I had no idea—"

111

"Killed himself?" Inspector Hill looked up from the note-book in which she was writing. "Was he suicidal?"

Oh, God. She appeared to be writing down every single word Nicola was saying. Weren't they supposed to caution you or something? Maybe she should refuse to say any more until her solicitor was present. No, no. *You* didn't stab him, for God's sake, she told herself, trying to gather her wits while the intelligent brown eyes watched her, and her patient, polite, per-sistent interrogator waited for an answer to her question.

"No, I just—" Nicola pushed her hair behind her ears. "It was just that the last time he got drunk was just after my mother died." It had the merit of being entirely truthful, unlike some of her other answers. "And, that time, he *did* make a sort of suicide attempt."

"A *sort* of suicide attempt?"

"I think it was just a melodramatic gesture, like everything else he ever did. He shut himself up in the barn with the Land Rover engine running. It would have taken him about three weeks to die, and he'd have had to keep going out for petrol."

Inspector Hill smiled. "So what happened?"

"Someone heard the engine, opened the barn door, and found him sitting there. Nothing wrong with him at all. But he was very drunk. I thought he might have got the same idea this time, and succeeded. I had no idea that he'd—" She stopped talking.

Inspector Hill nodded. "I'm very sorry," she said. "I as-sumed you knew what had happened."

Nicola waved away the apology.

"What made you think he had committed suicide?"

"I just thought . . . I thought he'd had a row with Rachel," she said.

"Why?"

"No reason. I just don't think they got on very well." She wished with all her heart that the interview would stop, and perhaps she had sold her soul to the devil last night, because her wish was immediately granted.

112

"One more thing," said Inspector Hill. "You might find this question a little odd, but I need to know. Did your father do *The Times* crossword at all?"

Nicola almost laughed, not only at the unthreatening nature of the question, but at the very idea. "No, he never did a crossword in his life." She frowned. "Why?"

"Just checking something," said Inspector Hill. There was a tiny pause. "Why did you believe that your father had had a row with Rachel?"

It was for all the world as though she hadn't asked the question before; Nicola pushed her hair behind her ears as the silence that followed it went on and on, and the inspector waited for an answer.

"I didn't mean a row, not really."

"What did you mean?"

With considerable reluctance, Nicola answered. "I thought he might have been hitting her again."

"What?" said Gus. *"Bernard?* I've never seen him lose his temper with anyone."

"He didn't lose his temper."

"Well, then. What makes you think he hit her? Did she tell you that?"

Nicola shook her head. "I know he hit her."

"And you think that this would be a fairly regular occurrence?" asked the inspector.

"Yes," sighed Nicola, turning back to her, away from Gus's bemused look. "He did it all the time."

"If he did it all the time, that wouldn't be what you thought had made him get drunk," said Inspector Hill. "Or that he might have committed suicide. Why did you think that?"

Nicola shook her head.

"Mrs. Hutchins," said the inspector.

"Once," Nicola said slowly, reluctantly, "he gave her a terrible beating. I mean—really, really terrible. I had to take her to casualty. I thought he might have done that again, or tried to, and she'd got away from him."

113

"What made you think he might have done it again?"

It was still none of her business what Rachel had got up to in the cowshed. Nicola didn't want to answer her, but she knew she would, sooner or later, and it might as well be now. "I . . . I think Rachel may have been—"

"Think I may have been what?" asked a lazy, almost unconcerned voice behind her.

Nicola turned quickly to see Rachel in the doorway. "Oh, Rachel," she said. "I'm sorry. I didn't mean to—"

"It's all right." Rachel smiled slowly, a little sadly. "Can't tell no one where to get off, can you, Nicola? Reckon he hammered all the guts out of you."

Nicola felt tears pricking her eyes.

"Nicky?" said Gus. "What does she mean?"

"And you just come gutless, didn't you?" Rachel said to him. "Or you'd've been helping her out, 'stead of lettin' folk walk all over her."

Nicola burned a painful red.

Inspector Hill looked up at Rachel. "Is Mrs. Hutchins right?" she asked. "*Did* your husband hit you?"

"No," said Rachel. "He didn't hit me. Any more'n he hit Nicola. He took his fists to me. Gave me what he called a hammerin', every time he felt like it, just like he gave Nicola ever since she could walk. Did it to me 'cos I hadn't given him a boy. Did it to her 'cos she *wasn't* a boy."

Tears streamed down Nicola's face as she looked at Rachel, praying that she would stop. But Rachel's voice went on remorselessly.

"Lasted seconds, hurt for days. Wasn't even anger," she said. "He knew what he was doin'. Knew where it'd hurt the most, never left no marks where you couldn't cover them up with clothes. But we all got to take our clothes off sometime, right, Nicola?"

Nicola saw Gus's horrified face; he got up, pushed past Rachel in the doorway, and left the house, the front door banging shut behind him.

"You didn't mention any of this when I spoke to you earlier."

"No," said Rachel. "I didn't. Because you would've thought what Nicola thought. That I'd had enough of it. That I'd stabbed him."

"I *didn't* think that!" Nicola sobbed. "Truly, I didn't." She hadn't had time to think of any explanation for it at all.

"I told *her* this morning," Rachel said, nodding over to the inspector, her voice made all the more attractive by being slightly hoarse, "and I'm tellin' you, and anyone else who's interested—I'm not sorry he's dead. But I didn't kill him. I left here on Friday morning, and I didn't get back until ten *this* morning." She looked across at Inspector Hill. "And I don't know nothin' about dead bodies," she said, her voice as slow as syrup. "But he looked like he'd been one for a long time 'fore I got back."

Nicola wiped the tears. Oh, God. This was getting messier by the minute. She really hadn't thought that Rachel had stabbed him, but now ... now, she didn't know what to think. Her knuckles were white with tension, and she had to talk to Gus. "Can ... can I go, please?" she asked.

Rachel looked over at her. "You got to start doing what you *want* to do, Nicola," she said. "You don't have to ask nobody's permission. She can't stop you leavin' here." She looked at Inspector Hill. "Can you?"

"No. You can leave any time you like, Mrs. Hutchins."

"See?" said Rachel. "Bernard's gone, Nicola. He can't do nothing to you anymore."

Nicola got up. Rachel held her eyes for a moment, then moved aside, and Nicola went out to find Gus leaning against the railing of the veranda, staring ahead of him. He didn't turn round. He didn't speak. She went down the steps to the car, getting into the passenger seat. It was a long time before he left his contemplations at the rail, and joined her, driving her home in silence. They pulled up in the little surgery car park.

"Is it true?" he said.

"Yes."

Gus got out of the car and slammed the door.

"Sergeant Finch, Stansfield CID," he said, holding out his warrant card, which Mike had already seen, when the waves created by Stansfield CID's recent, much publicized arrest of an acquaintance of his had lapped disagreeably round his feet.

"I remember you," he said. Fortunately, he had been astute enough to bury his less than ethical dealings under so much legitimate stuff that they could prove nothing, except that he had some dodgy friends. "Come in," he said.

He showed Finch into the study, invited him to sit, but he said he would stand. Mike sat. His legs were shaking. This might be more questions about backhanders to town councillors, or unsecured, unrepaid loans to back-bench MPs, but he doubted it.

"I believe you called on Mr. Bernard Bailey yesterday evening," the sergeant said.

Mike's eyes closed, as his fears were confirmed. "What's happened?" he said, his voice almost failing him, and opened his eyes.

The young man frowned. "Were you expecting something to happen?" he asked.

"I . . . I just—" Mike broke off, and made himself calm down. "Policemen don't usually inquire into people's business *unless* something's happened," he said. "The last time you had arrested a friend of mine. What's happened this time?"

"Would you mind telling me what your business was with Mr. Bailey?"

"I'm trying to buy his land."

"But Mr. Bailey already knew that, sir," said Finch. "Could you tell me what your particular reason was for calling on him yesterday?"

No, he couldn't. It had been the stupidest, most reprehensible thing he had ever done in his life, and there was no way that he could discuss it with Sergeant Finch. The repercussions had already come about, and he didn't know if he could bear this.

"A last-ditch attempt to make him change his mind," he said. "No particular reason. Just . . . hoping I could talk some sense into him, I suppose."

"So what was he like, when you spoke to him?"

"Like he always is," said Mike, his mind in a fog of panic, startled to hear himself give a comprehensible answer. "Surly. Uncooperative. Rude." Oh, God, what had he done to her?

"Had he been drinking?"

Mike shook his head. "I don't think so."

"Were you in the sitting room at all?"

"No. I saw him in his office." He shook his head, bewildered. "Why do you want to know that?"

"Did you notice the alarms?" said Finch, totally ignoring him. "Would you know if they were on or off?"

"Haven't the foggiest. On, I should imagine. He had the shutters down, so I suppose all the security systems were on. Look—what's happened?"

"When did you leave?"

"I don't know! I was there for ten, fifteen minutes. I left at quarter past eight or something!" He couldn't stand it any longer. "For Christ's sake, man, tell me what's *happened*."

"Mr. Bailey was found murdered earlier this morning."

Mike's eyes grew wide, as he stared at the young man with the killer punch. Mr. Bailey? *Mr.* Bailey?

Oh, Jesus *Christ*, he thought, when it all began to fall into place, to make sense. He felt the colour drain from his face, and he looked down at his desk, at the papers on which he had done no work at all, despite being up since dawn. All that soul-searching. All that guilt. All that panic. For what? Someone who had rolled him over. Jesus Christ.

"I'm sorry if it's come as a shock," said Finch, not sounding one jot sorry about it. "I didn't think you were particularly close to Mr. Bailey."

"Close?" said Mike, looking up again, feeling dazed. "No."

"But this news *has* come as a shock to you?"

Mike nodded slowly, then realized that it had been a question which required a rather more vehement answer than that. "Of course it does, man!" he shouted. "You don't think *I* murdered him, do you?"

Finch shrugged a little. "I don't know who murdered him," he said. "But I do know that you knew that something was going to happen at Bailey's Farm last night. And I believe, Mr. McQueen, that there's a bit more to all of this than you're prepared to admit."

Mike nodded. "Maybe there is," he said. "But that's my business, Sergeant Finch."

"It's mine now," said Finch. "We may want to see you again, Mr. McQueen, but thank you for your time."

Mike rose automatically.

"No, no, don't get up. I'll see myself out."

Mike sat at his desk for a long time after the sergeant had left. Then he took a cigar from the box, and rolled it between his fingers. He was only allowed to smoke them in here or in the garden, and even when Shirley was away, he did as she wanted, as he had been told. He had always done women's bidding. He had only vague memories of his father, who had been killed in the war; he had been brought up by his mother and sisters, various aunts and sundry female neighbours, all telling him what to do.

Then he had married Shirley, and he had had a whole new set of regulations, like not smoking in the sitting room, and how to hold his knife, and that he mustn't spoil Margaret. But he had spoiled Margaret, of course. She had had him wrapped round her little finger, and he had done her bidding too. She had left home the only time he had refused her anything. They had come to live here because Shirley wanted it; the Rookery project had been for her, in a way. But she had had no stomach for the fight in which he had subsequently engaged, and had gone off to her sister's until it was all over. It was all over now, but he doubted that she would be hurrying back.

And then there was Rachel Bailey . . . he closed his eyes, and dropped the cigar back into the box. My God, Rachel Bailey. There really was no fool like an old fool.

# CHAPTER FIVE

RACHEL HAD EXPANDED A LITTLE ON LIFE WITH Bernard after Nicola had left, and had gone upstairs to get the photographs she had taken of what Bernard had done to her that night.

Through the chimney breast she could hear the inspector talking to the man who'd been in the office earlier, the one who had said he thought she had killed Bernard. The Welsh one. They were talking about her again, and they didn't sound like colleagues having a discussion, Rachel thought for the second time, as she listened; they sounded like a couple having an argument.

Why, Inspector Hill was asking, would anyone stay with a man who treated her like that? The money she stood to gain, the man said. But he was going to lose the farm, she argued, and no farm meant no inheritance. Perhaps Mrs. Bailey didn't know that he had gone bust, he said. She told you Bailey didn't talk to her. But she was only going to get the money in any event if she gave him a son, the inspector pointed out, and she hadn't had a baby of either sex. Well, he said, they would just have to ask her why not. Rachel smiled, and opened the bottom drawer of the dressing table, taking out the agreement.

When she went back down, the man introduced himself as Chief Inspector Lloyd. He was about the same age as Bernard, maybe a little older; not as tall, but dark, like him, though the Chief Inspector had lost most of his hair. Unlike Bernard, he smiled readily and often, and he looked like there would be a quick temper ready to surface if things weren't going his way. Bernard had never got angry, had never said or done anything he hadn't meant to say or do. Rachel would bet Chief Inspector Lloyd did that all the time, then wished he hadn't.

He was wearing clothes that suited the weather, but didn't exactly suit him or one another. Was he the cool, collected, colour-coordinated inspector's type? Perhaps not, thought Rachel, but there was a lot more between them than just their shared occupation, her type or not. Fate wasn't too fussy about mixing and matching.

Rachel handed Inspector Hill the envelope with the photographs in it, then pulled the chair away from the desk, sitting down. The inspector looked up when she saw the first one, her eyes troubled, and glanced at Rachel before she looked through the rest, pushing them one by one over to the Chief Inspector, like you did with holiday snaps. He kept one out when he closed the envelope, and raised his eyebrows. The inspector nodded. A lot of communication went on without words, Rachel noticed. You had to be close to someone before you could do that.

Chief Inspector Lloyd looked over at her then, the photograph in his hand, and took a breath before he spoke, like people did when they were going to tell you something you didn't want to hear.

"Mrs. Bailey," he said. "Did you know that your husband was in a very bad financial position?"

Rachel nodded. "Oh, he didn't tell me or nothin'," she said, in answer to his surprised look. "He didn't want no one knowin'. Even Nicola thinks he still had money. But I heard someone talkin' to him."

"There are county-court judgements against him. His creditors were threatening to distrain upon his goods," he said. "And he was almost certainly going to lose the farm."

"I know. That's why he got all them alarms, case he couldn't make a payment. Said he'd shoot them if they tried to get in."

"I take it you overheard that as well?"

121

She nodded again. "Only way I found anythin' out was by overhearin'," she said. "Bernard never told me nothin'."

"Do you know *how* he was meeting the payments?"

No. She had no idea how he'd managed it. "Just shuffled his credit round, I suppose," she said. "Reckon that's why he owed so much to everyone else."

"But he couldn't have gone on like that forever," said Lloyd. "And if he lost possession of the farm, he wasn't going to fulfil the conditions of his grandfather's will."

He came round the desk, sitting on the edge of it, looking over at her, and Rachel saw the look in his eyes. Oh, not as naked as it was in Mike McQueen's. Not as eager as it was in Curtis's. But it was there. She glanced at Inspector Hill, and she was looking back at her, her face a little speculative. Rachel was right about them, she knew she was.

"Do I gather that he did this to you?" he asked, holding up the photograph.

She nodded again.

This time he nodded, too, and there was just the ghost of a smile. "My question is simple, Mrs. Bailey," he said. "Why did you continue to stay with him?"

"McQueen's offer," she said. "He was offerin' him four times what this place is worth, and I thought he'd have to sell in the end. I had to stay with him until he did." She reached into her back pocket, and pulled out the agreement, handing it to Lloyd.

He took out glasses, read it, then looked up at her over the frames. "This says that he will pay you ten per cent of his net worth as at the date you quit the marital home," he said. "If you had this, why didn't you sue him for divorce as soon as he started abusing you?" He handed it back to her.

"He wasn't worth nothin' like he was goin' to be if I gave him a son," said Rachel. "Even before he went broke. I didn't want to divorce him, not then."

"But you *didn't* give him a son," said Lloyd.

122

"I was tryin' to get pregnant," Rachel said. "To start with. Just didn't happen, that's all, 'cept he wouldn't believe that."

"What made you stop trying?"

"If he was goin' to lose the farm, reckoned I might as well be on the pill. Was gettin' knocked about regular for it anyway."

"Knocked *about*?" said Lloyd. "Is that what you call this?" He held up the photograph.

Rachel shook her head. "Reason for that was he hung on like he did. Knew I *had* to be on the pill. One night he drags me out of bed, beats me so bad I can't stand up. Says he'll do it to me again if I don't get pregnant soon."

Lloyd put the photograph down, pushed himself off the desk, and began to walk round the little room, picking things up, examining them, as though they were far more interesting than anything she had to say. Rachel watched him until Inspector Hill spoke again.

"The money was that important to you?" she said, incredulously. "You were being beaten, practically held prisoner—"

"Wasn't no prisoner," said Rachel, with a smile. "I could've walked out of here any time I liked. Just couldn't get back in again."

"Why would you *want* to get back in again?" she asked, picking up the photograph.

"This." Rachel held up the agreement in a counter to her photograph. "Had to be there if I wanted my ten per cent when he sold."

"What if he hadn't sold?" Lloyd asked. "What if McQueen had used the other route? What then?"

"I'd've left him," Rachel said, with the tiniest of shrugs, looking back at him. "Divorced him. Wouldn't've got nothin' out of it, though, 'cos he wouldn't have had nothin' to pay me ten per cent of. It was a gamble, that's all." Lloyd understood, a little, she thought. But Inspector Hill didn't.

"That sort of beating could have done you lasting damage," she said,

Rachel shook her head. "He didn't *want* to do no lastin'

123

damage," she said. "He needed me fit. Didn't put his weight behind none of them kicks—just kept on doin' it till I couldn't take no more. Thought he could scare me off the pill."

Inspector Hill shook her head in disbelief. "You're saying you were virtually *tortured*, Rachel! How could you stay after he'd done that to you? How could money *ever* be worth ending up like this?"

Rachel looked at the inspector's clothes, less expensive than her own, but no less elegant. At her hair, probably just as expensively cut. She smiled at her, and sat forward, her hands clasped on her knees. "You wore cut-down rubber boots for one hour, one day of your life," she said. "A wet day. A muddy day. On a farm. A day anyone with any sense would wear rubber boots, whatever they looked like. And you know how that made you feel."

The inspector flushed a little, and Chief Inspector Lloyd smiled.

"I wore 'em every day, all day, on my bare feet. Days like this. In hot, dusty, city streets. Beggin' for money." She paused, and sat back. "You never begged," she said.

"I thought gypsies—"

"Looked after their own? Maybe they do. But look at me," she said, with another little shrug. "I'm not a gypsy." She smiled. "Happened at one of them rock festivals. This guy come over to the field where the travellers were, stoned out of his mind. Couldn't even speak English. Gave my mother some stuff to try, got her stoned too, got himself laid. Never even asked his name. No way she could pass me off, not once her old man realized I was a blue-eyed blonde and I was stayin' that way. So he threw us out, and we didn't belong nowhere. I learned to look after myself."

"Did you?" asked Inspector Hill, with a glance at the photograph. She put it on the table, face down.

Rachel nodded. "In the end, I got six half brothers and sisters to look after, too. We'd trail around in an old VW camper, sometimes joinin' up with other travellers, sometimes on our

124

own. We'd pick up some man, she'd get pregnant again, he'd leave, we'd have another mouth to feed, and I'd have another year of rubber boots and sleepin' outside and beggin' in the streets to look forward to. Didn't own a pair of shoes till I was thirteen years old. But I worked for the money, and I bought them myself."

Inspector Hill smiled. "What were they like?" she asked.

"They were gold," said Rachel. "High-heeled sandals. Put them on, wouldn't take them off, not for no one." She smiled broadly. "Cut my feet to ribbons." She sighed. "But you don't get rich muckin' out cowsheds. And I couldn't do no real job. Can read 'n' write, but that's 'bout it. Never had no real education. Bernard Bailey offered me a fortune for somethin' I *could* do."

"But it wasn't going to happen, was it? And I'm told that farm work isn't all that easy to come by. What would you have done once you finally did leave him?"

"That pendant?" Rachel said. "The one I can't find? My father gave it to my mother. Took it from round his neck and gave it to her 'fore he left. Had it valued a few years back. Solid, twenty-four-carat gold, they said. My mother couldn't get over that when I told her. She'd thought it was junk jewellery—only kept it 'cos she liked him. I got it when she died, and it's my insurance. It's been in and out of more pawn shops than a burglar, and I always get it back."

But she might not get it back this time. She must ring the hotel, see if they'd found it. Why hadn't she had the clasp fixed?

"But it might as well've been junk jewellery, far as he was concerned," she went on. "Just somethin' he gave a gypsy girl to remember him by. 'Cept he gave her more than that. He gave her me. And maybe I got more'n just his blond hair and blue eyes. Because *I* wanted that kind of money to throw away."

The inspector looked totally baffled. "How many more beatings like that did you intend to put up with in order to get that sort of money?"

"Few as possible," said Rachel. "He *was* going to do it again, the day you were here. Asked me if I'd been to the chemist, and I said no, but someone'd seen me. So he knew I was lyin,' was goin' to give me another kickin' for it. But I told him I was pregnant. Didn't dare touch me then."

Lloyd continued to look at Bernard's books and files as he spoke. "You *pretended* to be pregnant, knowing that he would have to find out you weren't?" he said. "Knowing what he would do to you when he found out?"

"Was goin' to do it to me anyway," Rachel pointed out. "And he didn't lay a hand on me after I told him I was havin' his precious baby, never mind his boot. Not once." She gave a short sigh. "All the while I was married to him, Bernard Bailey was either trying to get me pregnant, or knockin' me about 'cos I wasn't," she said. "Don't know which I liked least. I got eight weeks free of that. This is the first time in eighteen months that I got no bruises on me."

Lloyd turned to look at her then. "Why did you come back here this morning?" he asked.

"I was *due* back this mornin'. Bernard couldn't afford no more nights in a place like that. No way I could've stayed there any longer."

"But you didn't have to come back here," said Lloyd. He came over, sat on the edge of the desk again. "McQueen had said publicly that he would take the woodland route if he hadn't acquired this land by the end of July. You had already lost your gamble. And yet you came back here, when you could have gone anywhere."

"Why not?" said Rachel.

Lloyd sighed. "Being dragged out of bed without warning and beaten until you can't stand up is one thing. Calmly walking back into this house in the full expectation that your husband would do it again when he found out you'd lied to him is quite another."

Rachel smiled. "And someone came here and stabbed him

126

to death 'fore that could happen," she said. "So you reckon that makes me suspect number one, right?"

"You are an intelligent, articulate woman, Mrs. Bailey," he said, sounding Welsher than ever. "And nothing you have told me suggests that you do anything without careful consideration of the consequences. The risk far outweighed any possibility of gain. It makes you *a* suspect, certainly." He got off the desk. "I think that's all for now," he said. "Thank you for being so frank with us."

"Wouldn't've been. If Nicola knew how to stand up for herself. But she don't." She looked at Inspector Hill, as she got up to leave. "Bernard Bailey did that to her," she went on. "And Gutless Gus was lettin' you walk all over her."

The inspector didn't argue with that. She got to the door, and turned back. "Rachel," she said, a little tentatively. "You said her father couldn't do anything to her now he was gone. Was he *still* abusing her?"

"Only saw him knockin' her about the once. Don't reckon he had to do it too often, the way he'd got her trained. They were in the barn. They didn't see me."

She could still see it. See Nicola cowering in the corner as the blows had landed on her head, her shoulders. That had shocked Rachel more than anything else Bernard Bailey had ever done. This time she picked up the photograph, held it up. "You want to see lastin' damage?" she said. "Don't look at this. Look at Nicola."

The inspector frowned a little.

"He never did nothin' like this to her," Rachel said. "She never ended up in casualty. But he hurt her. He hurt her every time she tried to speak up for herself from when she was two years old, and he did her lastin' damage, all right. That's why she can't make a decent livin' out of bein' a vet, 'cos she's frightened to make people pay her what they owe. That's why she married someone who's so soft he can't get a job no more'n I can, and he's a qualified accountant. But she thinks he won't hurt her."

"And you think he will?"

"Not by punchin' the back of her neck, he won't. But he won't be no use when she needs him. And she would never've needed him in the first place if she'd been brought up right."

"You seem angrier about what Bernard Bailey did to Nicola than what he did to you," said Lloyd.

Rachel turned to him, and nodded. "Bernard and me understood each other," she said. "I wanted money, and once I knew I could get it without givin' him babies, that's what I tried to do. His son had to be legitimate, so he had to try and *make* me start givin' him babies, and that's what he did. But I could've walked out of here anytime I wanted, like I said. Nicola couldn't. She was just a baby when he started on her. And she couldn't even stand up to him when she was a grown woman." She looked back at Lloyd. "That's why I stopped tryin'," she said. "When I saw that. I wasn't givin' Bernard Bailey no baby of mine to damage like he damaged Nicola."

They left. Rachel went over to the window, kneeling one knee on the safe as she watched them make their way across the courtyard to where the other policemen stood. They were close. Closer than colleagues, certainly. Closer even than lovers, she thought, though she was certain that they *were* lovers. But she and Curtis were lovers, and that didn't mean anything. That was just sex. Good sex. Sex that had taken her mind off the near-nightly matings with Bernard, reminded her that it could be fun. But just sex.

Judy Hill and her chief inspector were much closer than sex could ever make people. They were friends.

"OK, can you hear me?"

Curtis was about to send down the line to Barton his voiceover for the pictures Gary had shot that morning, and the handful of interviews with neighbours that he had managed to get. He rubbed his eyes as his sleepless night began to catch up with him.

"Voiceover for murder at Bailey's Farm. There are four

128

sections—an introduction and history, a lead-in to interviews with villagers, a lead-in to the interview with Chief Inspector Lloyd, and an endpiece. Ready?"

It would get edited in Barton, of course. One of the irritations about being in a regional office was that there was no editing suite; Curtis had no control over what was shown in the end. He just had to hope they kept in the right pieces.

He began. "Section One. In a bizarre and tragic twist to the saga of Bailey's Farm, Bernard Bailey was found dead in his own home this morning when his wife returned from a weekend shopping trip to London. Police say he had been stabbed several times, and that they have no leads yet to the killer, though they are pursuing a number of lines of inquiry.

"Bernard Bailey had been in the news almost constantly over the last six months because of his stand against MM Developments, who hoped to purchase his land to build a road to the Rookery, an ambitious development just north of the Harmston farm that Bernard Bailey had worked for over twenty-five years, and which his grandfather and great-grandfather had worked before him. The alternative route would take the road through picturesque woodland, and Mr. Bailey's stand, being made over largely fallow fields, met with considerable hostility. Hostility that spawned vandalism, and even brought death threats, which began appearing despite the fact that Mr. Bailey had ringed his farm with alarms, and installed closed-circuit television on the advice of the police.

"Section Two. Now, he has been murdered. Despite the alarms, despite the cameras which kept an ever-vigilant eye on his property, Bernard Bailey has died the violent death promised by those death threats. I asked some of the villagers for their reactions to that."

Curtis paused. "Section Three," he said. "The police are anxious to speak to anyone who was in the vicinity of Bailey's Farm between the hours of eight P.M. on Sunday, and ten A.M. on Monday. The area is known to be something of a lovers' lane, and the police stress that all information will be treated in strictest confidence. I spoke to Detective Chief Inspector Lloyd, the man leading the murder hunt, and asked him if he thought that there was a link between the murder and the death threats which Mr. Bailey had been receiving."

He took a deep breath. Almost there. "Section Four. I was at the murder house this morning, and I saw the security for myself. Windows locked, shuttered. Alarms set, cameras on. Documents and cash sat in Mr. Bailey's open safe, so certain was he of his security systems.

"But those systems were breached, and, at forty-seven, Bernard Bailey, who lived what many thought to be an eccentric life, died a shocking and puzzling death. How someone got in past the high-level security remains, for the moment, a mystery, and Bernard Bailey's death could turn out to be as much of an enigma as the man himself."

He paused again. "Curtis Law, *Aquarius 1830*, at Bailey's Farm, Harmston, Bartonshire," he said. "Voiceover ends." Then he lit a cigarette, inhaled deeply, and blew out the match with a stream of smoke directed at the no-smoking sign.

He'd done it. But he had a long night ahead of him still. He had to collect his car, and *Mr. Big* went out tonight; he had to go in for the final editing, and they wanted him to stay until after the programme had gone out, to deal with reaction. Then, with any luck, he'd get some sleep.

Lloyd was in Judy's car, waiting for a call on his newest gadget. It still tickled him to death that he could make and take phone calls almost anywhere he chose. He had asked Stansfield to check out Mrs. Bailey's story about the hotel, and Sandwell was going to ring him back. In Judy's car. It was unbearably hot, even with the windows and the sunroof open, but it was the only place they could find to talk without interruption.

"I think I'd like to have another word with Nicola Hutchins," said Judy, as she checked through her notebook. "Rachel stopped her just when she was going to tell me something. I think I ought to find out what, without Rachel in attendance."

Lloyd nodded.

"But I suspect that Nicola and her husband will have a lot to discuss," Judy added. "Maybe I should leave it until tomorrow. What do you think?"

"It's up to you," said Lloyd.

Judy frowned a little. "I think I'll leave it till tomorrow," she decided. "And I'd better have a word with Mr. and Mrs. Melville. I can't pretend the death threats didn't exist—and their committee might have the resident psychopath on it for all we know."

"If you ask me," Lloyd said, "the resident psychopath's the victim." He thought of those photographs of what Bailey had done to Rachel, of his treatment of Nicola, of what he had been hearing from the villagers about his first wife's constant, dangerous pregnancies. "The man was a monster."

"Yes," said Judy.

There was a little silence then, which Lloyd broke. "Well," he said, "if you want to see the Melvilles, I'd better let you do that." He made to get out of the car.

"Why does Curtis Law make you nervous?" she asked, just when he least expected it.

He closed the door again. How like her. No preamble, no working up to it. Let him believe he had escaped interrogation, then ask the direct, unequivocal question. It had taken him several minutes to steel himself to go out and give Mr. Law his interview, and of course Judy hadn't missed a thing.

He thought about the question. Did Law make him nervous? Yes, he supposed he did. Not so much because of what Curtis Law had done to *him*, though the thought of that programme going out tonight did fill him with dread, but because of what he wanted to do to Curtis Law. He wanted, quite simply, to get him back. He really was thirteen again, wanting to strike back at those who mocked him. He had never resorted to physical violence unless he had had to in the line of duty, and then only

131

very rarely, and purely in self-defence. His form of revenge for a hurt was more subtle, and less easily understood by either him or his victims.

With Judy, it was instant; he would say something to hurt her, and it didn't matter how unfair, how untrue it was, as long as she believed that *he* believed it, if only for a moment. With someone like Curtis Law, it was different. The resentment lodged itself inside him; he would seek an opportunity to avenge himself, and there would still be no room for moral principles. He knew what he was like, and he was afraid he would try to get Law up a metaphorical dark alley.

And now, he might even have begun to do it. Had Curtis Law really resembled the figure on Bailey's security video when he had seen him in the courtyard? Or had he just made himself believe that, in the hope that he could turn the tables on him? Was he capable of that sort of distortion of judgement, that amount of self-deception, in order to get his own back? Judy was the only one who would tell him the truth if he was. But he didn't want to know the truth.

"I just don't like him," he said, eventually, not looking at her. Looking instead out of the window at the courtyard, at the fields, at the people looking for evidence, stopping to flex their backs and mop their brows, then stooping and carrying on. That was a thought. Just who did that land belong to, now that Bailey was dead? He'd have to have a word with Rachel Bailey about that.

Judy repeated the question, just as she did with those from whom it was her job to get answers. No hint of its just having been asked. The same wording. No impatience. No slight raising of the voice. It was absolutely infuriating, and unless he told her, she would ask again. But his call came through, and rescued him.

Rachel Bailey had checked out of the hotel at eight o'clock this morning, Sandwell told him. But she had been staying there with someone calling himself Mr. Bailey, who had left last night, having ordered a taxi for eleven P.M. to take him to

132

St. Pancras. Staff couldn't give him much of a description, but it certainly wasn't her husband. Thirtyish. Well dressed. Maybe fair, maybe dark, depending on who you talked to. Maybe tall, maybe average. Slim. They were all agreed on that. Mrs. Bailey had rung for room service at around half past three in the morning; the night porter had taken her a pot of tea. She had given him a large tip, though it seemed that seeing her in her negligée would have been tip enough.

So it hadn't been Rachel on the security video. London was at minimum two hours away from Harmston, even the way Judy drove. "The plot thickens," said Lloyd, and opened the car door again. "See you later," he said, and escaped.

Judy drove off to go and talk to the Melvilles, and Lloyd went back up the steps to the house, knocking quietly on the open door. When no one came, he went inside, back into the office, where he and Judy had left the unrepentantly non-grieving widow, but there was no one there. There was, however, a voice. A voice as devastating as ever, even when it was travelling, as Lloyd eventually realized, down a chimney breast.

". . . this morning. Just wondered if anyone had found a gold pendant, maybe?

"Gold. Looks sort of like a coin. Not too big, but thick. Thick chain, too. Heavy. It's a man's, really. It's got some writin' on the back, but it's in Swedish, I think. Don't know what it means.

"Maybe you could take another look? Don't suppose you clean everythin' every time, do you?

"Well . . . no, didn't mean no offence. Just didn't think things would *need* cleanin' every time. Yes. If you wouldn't mind takin' another look. Yes. I'll be here. Thank you. Bye."

Lloyd looked at the chimney which had conveyed so much of Bernard Bailey's business to his wife, and tried to recall exactly what they had said in the office that morning, because Rachel Bailey would have heard every word, he was sure of that. He wandered back out, and stood just inside the front doorway, waiting for her to come downstairs.

133

When she did, she smiled her slow smile at him, and he felt that if anyone should make him nervous as to the suitability of his conduct in this case, it was Rachel Bailey. But they were already engaged in a sparring match; she knew he suspected her, and she didn't care. Because she was innocent? Or because she believed she could win?

"I've tidied up in here," she said, leading the way into the sitting room.

Tidied up was hardly how he would have described it. In the hour or so since the sofa had left, she had rearranged the room; it was as if the sofa and Bernard Bailey's body had never been there. The windows were open to admit fresh air; the vertical blinds were also open, and slatted sunlight fell across the room, highlighting the damp patch on the carpet, drying it out. Even the sun was prepared to help. A fan whirred quietly in the corner where an armchair had been, and the armchair and coffee table were where the sofa had been. She sat down, and looked up at him. It was, Lloyd thought, sitting down in another armchair, as if Bernard Bailey himself had never been there.

"Mrs. Bailey," he began.

"Why don't you call me Rachel?" she asked, and there was pure mischief in the blue eyes. "Your lady inspector does."

He smiled. "I think we'll keep it formal, Mrs. Bailey."

"So what do I call you?" she asked, her voice lazy and quiet. "Chief Inspector? Mr. Lloyd?"

"Whichever you feel comfortable with," Lloyd said.

She smiled again, the long, long dimple appearing. "Reckon I like Mr. Lloyd best," she said. "It's more friendly. Your lady inspector calls you Lloyd, don't she? You got no first name?"

"No."

She stood up. "Would you like a cold drink, Mr. Lloyd? Lemonade all right?"

"That would be very nice," he said. "Thank you."

She went down the hallway to the kitchen, coming back after a few minutes with long misted glasses in which the ice rattled, handing him his, sitting down again in the big armchair, kicking off her shoes, curling her legs underneath her. "You wanted to talk to me about somethin'," she said.

Lloyd sipped his drink, and smiled. "Is this homemade?" he asked.

She nodded.

It was delicious. "Did your husband make a will, Mrs. Bailey?"

"Left everythin' to me," she said. "Part of the deal."

"What about his daughter?"

"Said he'd set her up in the practice, and that was enough. Reckon he only agreed to me havin' it 'cos he knew it wasn't worth nothin' then."

Lloyd couldn't help but admire her cool detachment from it all. "But it is worth something now," he said. "You will be selling to Mr. McQueen, I take it?"

"If I don't, the loan company'll take it off me," she said. "No way I can pay them."

"And at four times its market value, you will have more than enough to pay off the debts, and come out of this with even more money than you would have got by giving your husband his son, won't you?"

She took a sip of her lemonade, looking at him over the rim of the glass. "Reckon that makes me suspect number one squared, don't it?" she said.

Lloyd smiled back, and his eyes held hers for a moment. "Reckon it does," he said.

There was a silence then, broken only by the whirring of the fan as it attempted to bring the temperature down to a more comfortable level. Lloyd stood up and toured the room, looking at the paintings, big and bright and flamboyant. And good. They must have cost a great many of the pretty pennies that Bernard Bailey hadn't really had. She patronized an artist from her own neck of the woods, he realized, as he put on his glasses and read the signature, a bold, black "Trelawny." He liked the paintings. He liked the lady who had chosen them. He liked her directness, if that was what it was. He liked her philosophy. He liked her speech rhythms, which seemed almost as though she was counting out the syllables, keeping to a complex metre that didn't allow for interruption.

He had always held very firmly to the view that no one had an excuse for committing murder in cold blood, whatever their reason. And that was precisely what he thought Rachel Bailey might well have done, and not because her husband was sadistically violent towards her, but because she would come into property worth a great deal of money to a third party if he were to die. The problem was that he was finding it difficult to care.

He sat down again. "You weren't in London alone, Mrs. Bailey."

"Who I was with in London don't have nothin' to do with what happened here," she said.

He didn't want to throw Curtis Law's name in just yet, not even to see her reaction. Not until he was sure of his own motives. "Your friend left the hotel yesterday," he said.

"He had to get back."

"But you stayed until this morning. Why was that?"

She sipped her drink. "Bernard didn't want me comin' back on Sunday. They said there was going to be a demonstration here. He didn't want me gettin' hurt." Again the smile. "Wasn't me he was bothered about."

"Someone tampered with your security video in the early hours of this morning," he said.

"I heard. And you think I did it. I heard that, too."

"I theorize, Mrs. Bailey. I do it all the time. You overheard one theory. But I do have another."

"What's that, then?" she asked, as the phone rang.

Lloyd smiled. He had no intention of telling her his other theory. He just wanted her to know that he had one, just as she had wanted him to know that his private conversations had been overheard. His first theory, as ever, had bitten the dust. His other theory, if it could be dignified by the name of theory, was that her boyfriend had come back on Sunday night in order to kill her husband, while she was establishing an alibi for herself by ringing room service at a time which made it impossible for her to have been the figure on the video. And *was* that boyfriend Curtis Law? That was a huge conclusion to jump to without any evidence of a liaison, and a description of her boyfriend that fitted half the men in the country.

And whoever her boyfriend was, she might genuinely be unaware of what he had done, even if that was what had happened. It needn't have been a conspiracy, despite the neat alibi. It certainly needn't have been Curtis Law. No. This theory, not even tested on Judy yet, was quite possibly the product of a desire for revenge, and he wasn't going to air it just yet. Besides, Finch had said that McQueen had clearly not been telling him everything he knew about it all. But it wasn't the sixty-year-old McQueen who had let himself out of that gate at two-forty this morning; that much, at least, was certain.

The phone rang and rang and rang. "Aren't you going to answer it?" Lloyd asked.

She uncurled herself slowly from the chair, and walked towards the hallway. Lloyd watched her, then blew out his cheeks, finished his lemonade, and followed her out.

"I'll be off, Mrs. Bailey," he said, as she got to the phone. "Thank you for the drink."

Mike waited impatiently for the phone to be picked up. He had spent hours checking the computer files, even system files. Every single inch had been checked through for any trace of the death threats, then checked again, until he had been absolutely certain that nothing remained on the computer that could tie him in to them. But he was sure that there were people who could get files that had been discarded. Somewhere, in that thing's brain, it probably still had the bloody death threats that he had so obediently written for her. Rachel Bailey was going to pick up that phone, and he wouldn't stop ringing her until she did.

"Hello?"

He jumped slightly, having long since given up on her answering this time round. "I've got to see you," he said. "And you'll have to come here—I can't be seen at your place. It'll be crawling with police. So you come here. Now."

"Can't, Mr. McQueen," she said, her tone as unruffled as ever. "Not right now."

"I've got to talk to you," he repeated. "And I don't want the police knowing. If you could get here without Bailey seeing you, you can avoid a few policemen, I'm sure. Just get yourself over here."

"I can't," she said again. "Don't know when I'll be able to get over. Might not be until tomorrow. And when I do, Mr. McQueen, I'm walkin' up your front driveway, 'cos I don't have to sneak through hedges and cross folks' fields no more."

Mike stared at the phone. She was proud of herself. Oh, what did it matter if the police did see her? He was in it up to his neck anyway, as Finch had indicated. "Just get here!" he said, and hung up.

Inspector Hill was very fanciable, Jack Melville had thought automatically as he had asked her in, his heart beating a little too fast. He always gave women a desirability quotient; he did it without even thinking. Rachel Bailey had gone off the scale, of course, and the inspector got a high rating, but it was her calling rather than her sex appeal that had increased his pulse rate. He had thought out a sort of a strategy, but it wasn't good; he had had very little time. Inspector Hill had gone in, and he had introduced her to Terri.

"You surely don't suspect a member of my committee of murdering the man, do you?" had been Terri's greeting. "Wasn't it bad enough accusing us of sending death threats?"

The inspector had explained that with regard to the death threats, they had interviewed everyone who had taken a hostile view of Bailey's stand over his farm, and had said that her interest in the committee was not because anyone was being accused of anything, but because elimination was ninety per cent of the battle in any investigation. And they had a lot of people to eliminate from this particular inquiry. Mr. Bailey's death did seem, she had pointed out, the answer to a great many prayers.

"Well, yes, it is, rather," Terri had said, combative as ever. "I'll be perfectly honest about that. If prayer constitutes a murder weapon, then I expect you should arrest the entire village."

And so it had gone on, with Terri dredging up every grievance she had ever had against the police, and she had a lot of grievances. In her time she had been dragged away from sit-downs, forcibly ejected from buildings, locked in a cell after being arrested at a demo for assaulting a police officer. She had been given a caution for that. The next time she had been charged with disturbing the peace, but had been found not guilty by magistrates who had seen her on her best behaviour, unlike the police. Her friends, and by extension, his friends, included all manner of offenders; she had been involved in a drugs raid on one of their houses, and while there hadn't been any charges against her, she had regarded the whole thing as an invasion of privacy, an affront to civil liberty.

All her resentment of the police was directed at the quite astonishingly patient Inspector Hill, and Jack wondered if the poor woman would ever get round to the real purpose of her visit. She had been here for over half an hour.

"The inspector isn't here about the committee," he said, eventually, before she talked herself into a charge of boring a police officer to death.

Inspector Hill looked over at him, her eyebrows raised.

"Isn't she?" said Terri, and turned back to Inspector Hill. "Then why *are* you here?"

"I think I'll let Mr. Melville tell you himself," she said.

"I don't understand," Terri said.

Jack looked at her, and smiled, shrugged a little. "I imagine I was caught on camera, so to speak," he said. "At the scene of the crime." He tried to make it sound jovial; it just sounded a little desperate. He turned to the inspector, holding up his hands. "But I'm not guilty, officer," he said.

"*You* were there?" said Terri, her eyes wide. "At Bailey's Farm? When? Why?"

"It was at about ten o'clock last night," he said, in a truthful answer to her first question. "I was his financial adviser," he added, in an inadequate, semi-truthful reply to her second. "I had to see him sometimes."

He saw the look that suddenly crossed Terri's face as he spoke, a sort of helpless, hurt look, as she thought of a better reason why he might have visited Bailey's Farm than the one he'd given. "Financial adviser!" she shouted. "Your wonderful scheme practically bankrupted him! He had nothing left for you to advise him about! Besides, you were the enemy over this road business. He wouldn't have let you in." There was a slight stress on the gender.

Jack hadn't expected that sort of furious reaction, and certainly not in public. He turned, a little embarrassed, to the inspector. "A couple of years ago I suggested that he might like to come in with me on something that I thought could make us both a tidy profit," he said. "But it was a risk. He went *against* my advice." He looked at Terri as he said that, then turned back to the inspector. "He thought he'd inherited his grandfather's skill with investments as well as his farm," he said. "He wouldn't listen to me, and he went—quite literally—for broke. My previous tips had been successful, and he . . . well, he was greedy. He lost a huge amount of money. But I—I kept him abreast of what was happening with what shares he still had invested."

Terri got up and left the room. It had seemed all right, when he had rehearsed it. Now, with Terri's total disbelief, and the inspector's astute brown eyes looking sceptically into his, it seemed pathetic.

Inspector Hill looked at the door which Terri had closed firmly behind her. "Your wife doesn't seem to think that you were giving Mr. Bailey financial advice," she said.

"I know what my wife thinks," said Jack. "But she's wrong.

Rachel Bailey wasn't even there last night! She was away for the weekend."

"Yes," said the inspector. "Can I ask where *you* were over the weekend, Mr. Melville?"

Jack stared at her. "Just because my wife seems to have jumped to conclusions doesn't mean that you have to, Inspector."

"You seem to be the one who jumped to that particular conclusion, Mr. Melville. I didn't mention Mrs. Bailey."

"Yes, I suppose I did," Jack conceded, with a sigh. "But I imagine that is the construction that my wife has put on the visit." He knew damn well it was, with good reason. And while he didn't really want his fondness for the opposite sex to be dragged into this, at least it had sidetracked the inspector; he didn't think he would have coped very well if she had questioned him about the small investments he had invented for Bailey. "But I barely know Rachel Bailey," he added, "and I was here all weekend. With my wife."

"Thank you." She jotted something down in her notebook, then looked up. "Surely Bernard Bailey had liquidated all his assets?" she said.

Jack swallowed. She wasn't that easily sidetracked after all. "It wasn't worth his while," he said. "A few hundred pounds, that's all."

She raised her eyebrows again. "Perhaps you have the share certificates," she said. "Mr. Bailey doesn't seem to have them."

"He didn't have the shares anymore," said Jack uncomfortably. Wise saws about tangled webs came into his mind; he was now having to invent a transaction. "He sold them a few days ago."

"I thought it wasn't worth his while?"

Oh, hell. "It wasn't! Not until recently." He was digging himself in deeper with every word. "He needed money quickly for some reason," he said, seizing on a partial truth once again. "So he sold the shares. It was peanuts. Enough for his wife to have a weekend at a good hotel in London, which is what I gather he spent it on."

141

"Thank you," she said, clearly not believing a word of it. "But if he had sold them before the weekend, why were you there last night, Mr. Melville?"

"Oh, that," he said. No more clever touches. Just a nice, straightforward lie. "I just went to try to make him see sense. A sort of eleventh-hour appeal to his better nature. But I don't think he had a better nature."

She accepted that at face value, or at least pretended that she had. "Perhaps you can tell me how Mr. Bailey seemed to you?" she asked.

"He . . . he was a little under the weather," he said. "He'd been drinking."

"Was he drunk?"

"Yes, not to put too fine a point on it."

Bailey had been drinking, and, for the first time Jack could ever remember, garrulous. Last night, his tongue loosened by alcohol, Bailey had talked. More than that; he had made threats. Terrible threats.

"I suppose it might just have been reaction to the business about the demonstration," he went on, since she had said nothing. "If you spend all day expecting hostile hordes to descend on you, and then they don't . . ." He shrugged again. "But he . . ." He sighed, knowing what her reaction would be to what he was about to say. "He was threatening to kill his wife." He looked down, away from the steady brown gaze. "He said he would break every bone in her body. From what I could gather, he'd beaten her up quite regularly. And he said he thought he'd kicked some sense into her last time, but he hadn't. And that he would kill her this time, because he might as well go to prison if he was going to lose everything."

"Did he say why he intended doing this?"

"No." A lie.

She looked at him enquiringly. "Were you thinking of mentioning this at all, Mr. Melville?" she asked. "If I hadn't come here?"

"Well . . . I wasn't sure of its relevance," he said. "I mean, if *she* had been found stabbed, of course I would have told you. But . . . well, she wasn't, was she? *He* was."

And she might have stabbed him to death in preference to having every bone in her body broken. He knew that. He just hadn't felt obliged to tell the police, that was all; he hadn't wanted Terri to know he'd been there, and he hadn't wanted to get Rachel Bailey suspected of murdering her husband.

Inspector Hill nodded. "If you have any other information," she said, "perhaps you'll let *me* decide its relevance to this inquiry?"

"That's all I know." All that he was going to tell her, at any rate.

"There is something you may *really* not have thought relevant," she said. "Were the radiators on in the sitting room?"

"I wouldn't know. I was in his office."

"Thank you," she said. "We may wish to talk to you again."

He showed her out, and turned to look at the staircase. Terri was up there, and he had to go and face her. More lies, more tangled webs.

"She thinks I just stood by and let him—" Gus's lips came together, and he couldn't find the words to finish the sentence.

"She doesn't," said Nicola.

"Of course she does! You heard her!" He shook his head disbelievingly. "All those times," he said. "All those times that you told me you'd slipped, or some animal had kicked you! It was an animal all right! How often?" he demanded. "How often, since we've been married?"

Nicola sighed. "I don't know," she said. "And he never kicked me. He saved that for Rachel."

"But why did he do anything to you? What had you done? Give me for instances."

She arrested her hand as it went to push her hair behind her ears. She didn't want to talk about it. She didn't want to tell him. But she would. Why couldn't she be more like Rachel?

143

Rachel, who had defied Bernard Bailey at every turn, regardless of the painful, bruising consequences, even after he'd half killed her. She had been the unwitting cause of it, one time.

"Once was when he told me he was marrying Rachel," she said. "I said it was too soon and she was too young. He . . . he took exception to that."

"And?"

"Gus, I don't want to—"

"Tell me! What else?"

"Lots of things. You never knew what it would be. The last time was when I tried to trace Bailey's Farm in Yorkshire," she said. "Remember? Last spring?"

He frowned. "Yes," he said. "What of it?"

"When I couldn't find anyone who'd heard of it, I asked him about it." She shrugged. "I didn't know I'd done anything wrong. He just . . . started punching me. Said it was for prying into his business."

"And did you tell Rachel that he hit you?"

"No. She must have seen him one time."

Gus stared at her. "I stuck up for him when people called him names!" He jumped up. "How could you let me do that? Why didn't you *tell* me? I could have put a stop to it!"

"How?" said Nicola, helplessly. "By beating *him* up? By going to the police? I didn't want any of that! I didn't want you to know."

"Because you think I'm as useless as she does!" he said, and went out, slamming the door.

Nicola felt sick. She should have told Gus. Rachel probably did think that he already knew, that he had been too spineless to do anything about it. And was that why she *hadn't* told him? Because he would have wrung his hands, and done nothing? Easy enough to say he would have put a stop to it now that the threat had gone. And what when he found out what she had done to avenge herself for all the hammerings? What then?

\* \* \*

144

Judy got back to the farm as Steve Paxton was getting into his pick-up.

"You've had a long day," she said.

"Last bloody day," said Paxton, starting up the truck, which shuddered and rattled as he pulled the door shut. "This place'll be sold by tomorrow lunchtime, you see if it isn't," he shouted, as he drove off.

"Guv?" Tom Finch came over to her as the pick-up rumbled away, leaving a trail of diesel exhaust in its path, brandishing a plastic bag in which was enclosed a vegetable knife. "It was found in the bushes directly behind the barn," he said. "It's got what looks like blood on it. And it matches the ones in the kitchen. There are five in there, all the kind of knives you'd expect, except a vegetable knife. And this, I am reliably informed, is a vegetable knife."

"Who found it?"

"One of the farmworkers. He was working on the hedging. But he didn't touch it. Just called our lad over."

Judy smiled. "Is God on our side for once?" she asked.

"You never know. It must be our turn sometimes."

Judy got into her car, and drove back to the station. There, she looked at the pathetic collection of stuff the search team had picked up from the farm, and the lonely road leading up to it. You deploy God knows how many men all day, she thought, and a farmworker just doing his job finds the murder weapon. If that was what it was. They would still check out the other stuff. It was litter, mostly, and highly unlikely to yield anything of any interest, but even if the knife did prove to be the murder weapon, they might not get prints from it, so something else might be useful. There was a syringe; not as usual in the countryside as in the towns, but not so unusual either, these days. A condom. A couple of cans of Coke, found on the road at the rear of the farm, along with the contents of a car ashtray. That seemed more hopeful—someone might have been watching the house. Or a clandestine, drug-taking, smoking,

145

Coke-drinking couple might have had a clear-out before driving home. Whatever, it would all go to forensic.

She wrote up her official notebook, and called in on Lloyd, but he wasn't in his office. He was probably stuck at that awful place, interviewing people.

She left the station, telling herself sternly that she could not go on ignoring what was happening to her, drove on to the shopping-centre car park, and went to the chemist, being reminded of Rachel Bailey as she nervously checked to see if there was anyone she knew in there. She stuffed her purchase in her shoulder bag, and went back to the car, switching on the radio as she drove home, letting the sixties pop songs favoured by Radio Barton wash over her as she thought about Bailey's murder rather than her own problems.

Melville? He had been worried, clearly, about having been at the farm. But he thought that the video would have a record of his visit, so unless he was being very cunning, he presumably had not tampered with it later on. But he could be the man who had been with Rachel in London, whatever he said about where he spent the weekend. He might even now be sweet-talking his wife into giving him an alibi, though Judy thought that might be a bit of a tall order in view of her reaction. He probably had been at home with her, as he had said.

Nicola? Physically abused from childhood. Had she gone back that night to kill her father? Why? Why now?

Gutless Gus? Could be. Perhaps he found out about Bailey's treatment of his wife, and wasn't so gutless after all.

But not Rachel, who was ordering tea in a hotel in London less than an hour after that figure slipped through the gate. And that seemed much too handy to be a coincidence. Rachel seemed much too aware of what she was doing to have gone home to certain retribution sooner or later. Rachel was as difficult to work out as she had been the day she met her.

Judy parked in the nearest street in which she was allowed to park, which was some way away from the flat since all the people who worked nice set hours had parked in the closer

146

ones, locked up the car, and walked through the hot, still evening to her flat, letting herself in with a sigh of relief. This was a town. With traffic. And people. And this was her flat. With no enigmatic young women or smelly dead bodies in it. It did, however, have Lloyd in it, which startled her, as she opened the sitting-room door.

"What are you doing here?" she said, horribly aware of the package in her bag.

"I have had more enthusiastic welcomes."

"You never come here."

"I do," he said. "Sometimes. This is one of the times. I thought I'd make us a meal."

"Why?" she asked. He didn't know, did he? He couldn't. Even Lloyd couldn't have guessed, for God's sake. She didn't even know herself for sure; that was why she had bought the damn thing that was burning a hole in her bag, which she now tossed on to the sofa. But she was pretty sure she didn't *want* to know. Which was why she hadn't told Lloyd yet.

"Do I have to have a reason to be here? I thought my having a key meant I could come when I pleased."

She laughed, a little uncertainly. "It was just when you weren't at the station, I thought you must be off chasing up leads," she said. "This was the last place I expected to find you."

"We do have to eat, murder inquiry or not." His voice was sharp, the smile gone. "Are you going to report me for dereliction of duty?" He walked past her, out into the hall, and went into the kitchen.

She followed him. "I'm not complaining," she said. "It's just that when we've got a serious crime to investigate, it's usually all I can do to get you to stop work by midnight."

"Yes, well, it's a major inquiry, isn't it? And I'm not really all that good at them, according to the infant who gave me a dressing-down this morning," he said. "So I'll stick to minor ones. What do you want to eat?"

"Nothing. I want to know what's wrong." It couldn't possibly be getting chewed out by the ACC. Lloyd spent half his life being told off by senior officers, and it had never bothered him before. This wasn't like him. It wasn't like him at all. He had been behaving oddly all day, and it had something to do with Curtis Law. "So tell me," she said.

"Nothing's wrong! For God's sake, can't I knock off work early without starting a nationwide scare about my state of mind?"

He had hardly looked at her. He was standing staring into the fridge, and she knew he wasn't even seeing what was in there. "Lloyd," she began, but she got no further.

"Aquarius news will be on in a minute," he said, closing the fridge, putting on the portable. He sat down at the table, and watched the end of the Australian soap that preceded it as though every deathless word of dialogue was of intense interest to him, and the weather forecast and advertisements likewise. Then *Aquarius 1830* came on, leading, of course, with the murder.

Over pictures of the farm, the newsreader's voice, barely able to contain its excitement, intoned: *"Bernard Bailey, the man at the centre of the Rookery development row, is found murdered at his Harmston farmhouse. That report coming up in a moment. Also on tonight's programme: Local Council says, dispose of your own rubbish. We get the reaction of townspeople to the Lunston District Council's proposal to axe collection services and set up neighbourhood tips. And we meet the guard-cat who saw off would-be raiders at this Welchester sub–post office."*

The newsreader came on screen. *"Good evening. Bernard Bailey, the farmer who refused to sell his land to make way for a road, was today found dead from knife-wounds at the farm which earlier in the year became the centre of a dispute which united the Bartonshire village of Harmston against him. Police say a murder inquiry has been launched. This report from Curtis Law."*

Over more pictures of the farm, Curtis Law's report began.

*"In a bizarre and tragic twist to the saga of Bailey's Farm, Bernard Bailey was found dead in his own home this morning when his wife returned from a weekend shopping trip to London. Police say he . . ."*

Judy frowned a little, then stopped listening; something was worrying Lloyd, bothering him so much that he couldn't even slip into another mode for her benefit. He had temporarily lost that facility, and she wanted to know why.

*"Bernard Bailey had been in the news almost constantly over the last six months, because of his stand against . . ."*

She sat down at the table, and tried to work out if *she* could have done something to upset him. She constantly did things which annoyed him, and sometimes did things that made him angry. But she had never done anything, not even inadvertently, that had made him unhappy, and Lloyd *was* unhappy, something she wasn't sure she had ever seen before. She looked back at the television. The pictures were now of the slashed tractor tyres, from last December. "Tom thinks McQueen was behind the vandalism," she said.

"Does he?"

Pictures of the alarmed fence, the cameras, the electronic gate and its high camera tower. *"I was at the murder house this morning, and I saw the security for myself. Windows locked, shuttered. Alarms set, cameras on. Documents and cash sat in Mr. Bailey's open safe, so certain was he of his security systems. But those—"*

"Cash?" said Lloyd.

Judy shook her head. "No cash," she said. "Just documents and correspondence."

"And his daughter says the alarms were switched off when she arrived at the house?"

"Says," said Judy. There was something about Nicola Hutchins's account of that visit that didn't ring true.

"If she's right, it could have been a burglary."

"*If* she's right. And if Law's right that there was money there."

149

"Yes," said Lloyd. "Perhaps he just assumed a safe would have cash in it."

"Perhaps," said Judy. "We'll be seeing him in the morning anyway, to look at the videos. We can ask him then."

"*You're* seeing him in the morning." Lloyd got up, and opened the fridge again. "Did you say what you wanted to eat?" he asked, the brief discussion at an end.

"Whatever you fancy," she said.

She couldn't remember ever having eaten a meal with Lloyd in silence, and she wasn't eating one now. Neither of them was. They were shifting the food about the plates while Lloyd watched the cat who had launched herself, all claws and teeth, at the youths who had demanded money from the post-office till, and everything else that came on. They had sat through a whole episode of another soap opera, and now it was some game show that she would normally have run a mile from, but tonight she was grateful for it, grateful *to* it, for filling up the spaces. She made coffee. Real coffee, which she ground up in the real coffee grinder, and made in the real percolator that Lloyd had given her, taking great care to do it right.

"Shall we take it through?" she asked, and her voice sounded odd, and unnatural, as though she were a bit-part player in an amateur production.

"Sure," he said.

In the living room, Judy put on the television again, going on with the pretence that Lloyd was actually watching it. When the programme finished, a trailer came on, and it was suddenly snapped off. She looked at Lloyd, who put down the remote control, and looked back at her, taking a breath, opening his mouth, then saying nothing.

A terrible storm of possibilities came into her mind. Her mother had died. He had some incurable, fatal disease. He'd been sacked. She had been sacked. He had run over a child.

"I'm going to be a laughing-stock tomorrow," he said.

Judy checked her huge sigh of relief, smothered her instinctive "Is that all?" and reordered her thoughts. As far as Lloyd was concerned, this was serious. He would sooner no one ever spoke to him again than be laughed at. "Why?" she asked.

"That programme is on tonight," he said. "I'd ..." He paused. "I'd much rather you didn't watch it."

"Why not?"

"Because ..." He put down his coffee again. "Because he's made a fool of me," he said, the words coming out in a rush. "It's bad enough knowing it'll be watched by people whose opinion of me doesn't matter a damn, but—" He broke off. "Don't watch it," he said. "Please."

Judy considered her reply carefully before she spoke. "Don't you think it would be better if I did?" she said. "Everyone else will have seen it. It's going to look a bit odd if I haven't."

Lloyd's ego was usually fairly robust, and it needed to be dented now and then. But it had to remain intact; it was essential to him, because without it he just wasn't Lloyd. It had clearly been given a very severe knock, and she was trying hard to find words that wouldn't damage it further, because the truth was that she doubted very much that the programme revolved round him, as he seemed to imagine it did.

"It might not be as bad as you think," she said gently. "Maybe you need a second opinion. You don't have to be here. There's a nice pub just down the road."

"They have televisions in pubs," he said miserably.

Judy smiled. "When was the last time you saw a documentary in a pub?" she asked. "It'll be on some sports channel, showing foreign women playing some obscure sport. Or on some interminable pop programme."

"It'll close at eleven," he said.

"There's drinking-up time. And you can walk back slowly. But you do have to come back," she warned him. "Don't go sloping off home."

He smiled a little. "All right," he said.

So, in the fullness of time, he went out, and Judy watched the programme that she found to her surprise and mounting

151

anger did indeed revolve around Lloyd, did indeed try to make a fool of him. She allowed his echoed voice to die away, switched off the television, and Lloyd's key turned in the lock. He had been hanging about on the landing, waiting for it to finish.

She got up when he came in, put her arms round his neck, and touched his forehead with her own. "No one will be laughing," she said firmly.

"Huh."

"They won't, Lloyd. Everyone who's ever walked a beat knows perfectly well why that happened. If you had his budget, and all the people he had at his disposal, and nothing at all to work on but one problem, and no need whatever to observe the Police and Criminal Evidence Act, you'd have not just got Mr. Big, you'd have worked out who Jack the Ripper was and what happened to the *Marie Celeste* while you were at it."

He smiled. "The *Mary Celeste*," he said. " 'Marie' is a popular misconception."

She smiled back. That was more like it, even if it was an act.

"But he did make a fool of me, didn't he? You thought I was just being over-sensitive."

"Yes, I did," she admitted.

"And why me?" he asked. "There were three forces involved in the end. Two other heads of CID who missed the connection. He didn't even mention the others."

She thought perhaps she knew. Lloyd could be infuriatingly patronizing. She was used to it; Curtis Law wasn't, and he had done it for nothing more than spite, as far as she could see. But she didn't say that. She just shrugged.

"It's going out on the network," Lloyd said, in a small voice. "Everyone will see it."

"Lloyd," she said. "It will be watched by about five per cent of the population if he's lucky. Half of them will fall asleep, and the other half will all have forgotten what it was about the next morning."

"Yes," he said, with a little smile. "You're right."

"And you are going to come with me tomorrow to Aquarius?"

He looked at her from under his lashes. "Do I have to?"

"The sooner you see him the better. You can act as though nothing's happened, you *know* you can." She had restored some of his self-esteem, but that wasn't what was worrying him. She led him to the sofa, and sat down with him. "Tell me what's really wrong," she said.

He put his arm round her. "How much do you love me?" he asked.

She smiled, not sure of the connection. "I don't think love's something you can quantify," she said. "You either love someone or you don't. I love you. That's it."

"It's just that I keep seeing this scenario," he said. "Where Curtis Law goes off to London with Rachel Bailey, leaves her there on Sunday night and Monday morning to establish a watertight alibi for herself, then either with or without her knowledge, comes back, goes to Bailey's Farm, gets in on some pretext or other, and stabs him to death."

"And?"

"And I think I'm being dangerously less than objective. That figure going through the gate could be one of at least three people I met today, all of whom loathed Bernard Bailey, but it wasn't when I was talking to any of them that I actually thought about it. It was when I saw Curtis Law, and he was just there to *report* on the murder. That's crazy, isn't it?"

"No," she said.

"It is! I'm trying to *pin* it on him, for God's sake, Judy! I doubt if he has any feelings about Bernard Bailey at all, and I have no evidence whatever that he and Rachel Bailey are anything more than acquaintances." He took a breath. "I just wondered if you loved me enough to tell me if you thought I was paranoid."

Judy smiled. Lloyd's scenario might be quite wrong, but it wasn't one conjured up out of thin air and injured pride. She too had met people who *could* have been the figure at the gate, but it was when she had seen Curtis Law that she had involuntarily *thought* of that figure, and only then. She hadn't known Lloyd had, and he hadn't known she had. They had each independently thought of it because it *looked* like him, it was as simple as that. And crime reporters knew how the police operated; when one half of a marriage was found murdered, the other half came under immediate and detailed investigation. She had never known a reporter not to ask, off the record, if the spouse had an alibi, because if not, suspicion was automatic, and if so, that alibi was subjected to scrutiny. Curtis Law hadn't asked, which was odd. But odder still was the fact that, on that report, he had *given* her an alibi, one that no one on their side of the fence had mentioned to him.

"I do love you enough," she said. "And I don't think you're paranoid."

"Good," he said, kissing the top of her head. "Now you can tell me why I'm not, and bring me up to date with your inquiries." He stood up. "Do you fancy a sandwich? I'm starving."

It was after midnight, and he was all set to work. Judy yawned. "If I'm going to be up all night, you have to come with me to see Curtis Law tomorrow," she said. "Is it a deal?"

"Done!" he shouted from the kitchen.

# CHAPTER SIX

CURTIS LOOKED UP FROM THE DRAFT OF HIS lunchtime bulletin on the murder as Chief Inspector Lloyd and Inspector Hill were shown in, and got to his feet, stubbing out his cigarette. He tried to gauge Lloyd's mood, but he couldn't; he thought it best if he mentioned *Law on the Law* first.

"I don't suppose this is a social call," he said. "Not after last night's programme. I'm sorry if it—well, you know. But . . ." He shrugged. "That's show business."

"Oh, I quite understand that, Mr. Curtis," said Lloyd. "Don't give it another thought."

He looked as though he really didn't mind, but Curtis doubted that.

"We're here to see the videos," Lloyd went on, handing him the one that Sergeant Finch had confiscated. "But first I would like to ask you some questions about your report on the murder, if I may."

Curtis smiled, despite feeling a touch apprehensive. He had been expecting this, and he had his answers ready. "Of course," he said, waving a hand at the two vacant chairs. "What did you want to know?"

"When you used the expression 'documents and cash' about the contents of Mr. Bailey's safe, was that just poetic licence?"

Curtis frowned. That had not been the question he had anticipated. "No," he said. "Journalists don't use poetic licence." He saw the raising of Lloyd's eyebrows, and ducked his head a little in acknowledgement of his naive answer. "I don't, anyway," he said.

"You actually saw cash in Bernard Bailey's safe?"

"Yes. Quite a lot, I think. Notes. In bundles. Why?"

"We didn't find any cash."

Curtis stared at him. "You must have done," he said. "It was there, on the top shelf."

Lloyd shook his head.

"Well," Curtis said. "Perhaps Rach—Mrs. Bailey removed it." But that made no sense, he thought, even as he spoke the words. Rachel had been half out of her mind; she wouldn't have been able to think straight enough to remove money from the safe, unless she'd done it before she'd found Bailey. But why would she remove it at all? She wouldn't, was the answer. Paxton seemed the only possible explanation for its disappearance. "Perhaps that foreman bloke helped himself to it," he said.

"Unlikely," said Lloyd. "Our officers arrived to find him coming to blows with your cameraman, and they were on the premises from then on."

"Yes, but one of them was attending to Mrs. Bailey, and the other was throwing us out. Where was the foreman while all that was going on?" That had to be the explanation, Curtis decided. Perhaps Paxton had already known the money was there, and had realized that in all the confusion, he could take it without anyone noticing.

"We'll make inquiries," said Lloyd. "And . . . how did you know that Rachel Bailey had spent the weekend in London?"

That *was* one of the questions Curtis had been waiting for; he had realized that Lloyd would jump on it as soon as he heard it. "Your sergeant must have told me," he said to Inspector Hill.

"He didn't know himself when he spoke to you," she said.

He'd thought of that, too. "Someone else, then. One of Bailey's employees, probably. I spoke to a lot of people."

"Thank you, Mr. Law," said Lloyd. "Now we would like to see the videos."

"Yes, sure. Just . . . take a seat." Curtis put the video in, pressed the play button, and they watched the soundless film.

Arriving at the farm. Curtis himself getting out, using the phone. The road ahead as they drove through the opening gate, up to the farmhouse. Then a mishmash of sweeps as Gary got out, running with the camera. The open front door, the hallway, lit only by the light from the sitting room, rendering the picture non-existent until the camera made an adjustment for the light and the closed box of the alarm-control panel and Bailey's office door came into focus; the camera swivelling round as Gary went into the sitting room. What looked like a blank screen until the camera adjusted again, then Bailey's body in long shot, followed by an unsteady zoom in. The camera moved round to Rachel, frightened out of her wits, saying something, looking bewildered and hurt, before the picture went haywire again.

"That's it," Curtis said. "And you wanted to see Gary's shots of people going to the house on Sunday, is that right?" He reached behind him for the video, and put that one in, watching as various people tried to effect an entry to the farm. "What's he doing there?" he asked, as he saw one visitor he recognized. "He's a debt collector." He ran it through to the next visitor. "She's a member of SOWS," he said. The next startled him even more than the debt collector had. "That one . . . he's a repo man. Collects cars. I did a piece on him."

He looked at his visitors. "Was Bailey in financial difficulties?" he asked, but he hadn't expected them to answer, and they didn't. He was already mentally rewriting his lunchtime bulletin. "If he was," he said, "why on earth didn't he just sell the place?" He ran the tape further on; a couple more people came and went, but there was nothing of interest, until Mike McQueen, who spoke briefly on the gate phone, and was allowed in.

"Can I get you anything?" he asked. "We've got some cans of Coke in the fridge."

"Thank you," said Inspector Hill.

"I don't suppose I could beg a cup of tea, could I?" said Lloyd. "I overslept, and I can't function without one."

"Sure."

Curtis went into the little kitchen, and put the kettle on. Why hadn't Rachel told him that Bailey was in debt? He had to be, with these two calling on him on a Sunday. He was meeting her at the flat at lunchtime; they had decided that would be best, rather than his going to the farm, because the police wouldn't be crawling all over it. He'd ask her. Maybe she hadn't known about it. He threw a teabag into a mug, and drummed his fingers on the worktop, waiting for the kettle to boil.

"Why are you having diplomatic tea?"

Lloyd didn't drink other people's tea; he maintained that no one knew how to make a decent cup of tea except him. And he hadn't overslept; *she* had. She always liked to give herself time in the morning, but Lloyd got up at the last minute. This morning, they had both done it, causing her to miss breakfast, which hadn't bothered her as much as it might. She had been feeling a little queasy in the mornings, and had given it a miss once or twice lately.

She had waited until Lloyd was safely out of the flat before returning for something she had deliberately forgotten. Then she had put the testing kit safely in the bathroom cabinet, and had caught Lloyd up, promising herself that she really would do it. Tonight.

When she had arrived at the station, she had switched off her engine just as the local news had come on; she had put the radio back on and had listened to the reaction to *Law on the Law*. Mostly people complaining about the programme, rather than the policing, she had been gratified to hear. She had got out of her car quickly as she had seen Lloyd leave his, so that they would meet whatever reception Lloyd was going to get together, because he had still been convinced that everyone would be sniggering behind his back. But Law's over-kill approach, his singling out of Lloyd for blame, had turned the whole thing into a them-and-us situation in which there were no shades of grey; Law was a bastard, and Lloyd was a hero.

He had come with her to talk to Curtis Law without giving her an argument, saying he was only too glad to get away from people popping their heads round his door to tell him what they'd like to do to Law if they got their hands on him. But she knew that the show of support had meant a lot more to him than he was saying, and that Lloyd was ready for Law now. Which she wasn't sure was altogether a good thing.

"I'd sooner have a Coke, but tea takes longer, and I wanted to talk to you," he said, his voice as quiet as hers had been. "He smokes and drinks Coca-Cola, you'll notice," he added.

"So do I," said Judy.

"And did you notice that his instinct is to call Mrs. Bailey Rachel?"

"So do I," she said again.

"And there's this." Lloyd picked up a copy of *The Times*, the crossword almost complete.

Judy found her father and London coming into her mind again, and tried to push the thoughts away. She must have been born with some sort of homing instinct, like salmon; she was being compelled to return to her spawning grounds to reproduce.

"Yoo-hoo," Lloyd was saying. "Ground control to DI Hill."

"What?" She focused on Lloyd. "Oh, sorry. I was thinking about something else."

He smiled. "That's most unlike you, Inspector. Penny for them."

She would have to be careful. Now that he was no longer preoccupied himself, he would start noticing if she was. "I was thinking about my father," she said. "I'm not sure why. Maybe just because it's a long time since I've been to see my parents." She smiled. "Linda sees more of them than I do," she said guiltily. Lloyd's daughter had lodged with her parents for a while when she was in London, and still visited them practically every week. Judy sighed, acutely aware of her inadequacies as a daughter, as a life-partner, as a potential mother. "I'm sorry," she said. "What were you saying?"

"I was saying—did you get a close enough look to know if these are the same block capitals?"

Judy looked at today's crossword, and realized why she had thought of her father every time she had looked at yesterday's. She pointed at it. "They're crossed out left-handed," she said. "The clues."

Lloyd frowned. "How do you know?"

"Right-handed people do it the other way. Bottom left to top right. Left-handed people do it like that. Bottom right to top left. When I was in that room yesterday I kept thinking about home, and I didn't know why. But it was because of the crossword clues being crossed out like that. My father crosses out the clues as he goes along—and he's left-handed. It must have registered at the back of my mind."

"Have you noticed whether or not Mr. Law is left-handed?"

"No," she said. "But it won't be difficult to find out."

"And," he said, "there is one other reason."

But Judy had to wait to find out what that other reason was as Law came back in.

"Anything else I can show you?" he asked.

"I'd like to see the first tape again, please," said Lloyd. "From the top."

Law obliged, removing the tape that was in, and putting in the first one again. With his left hand, Judy noted. It was presumably *his* crossword.

The gate, Law using the phone, the front door, the screen going dark, Bailey's office door . . .

"Pause it, please." The picture froze on the door, and Lloyd looked at Law. "How did you see cash or anything else in Mr. Bailey's safe when—as is quite evident on the still displayed on your video—his office door was closed when you arrived at the farmhouse?"

Law stared at the screen, then looked back at Lloyd. "Someone must have opened it after that," he said.

"When? Who? According to you, one officer was calming Mrs. Bailey down, and the other was ejecting you and your cameraman."

"You don't think *I* took the money, do you?" asked Law incredulously. "I know I'm not likely to be at the top of your Christmas-card list, but accusing me of theft seems a little—"

"No," said Lloyd, interrupting him. "You would hardly have mentioned it in your report if you had stolen it. But someone took it, and I'm trying to get an idea of when."

Law shrugged. "I've already told you what I think happened to it, and that seems to bear me out. The foreman must have gone into the office after the scuffle and left the door open. I must have seen the money as I left."

"Perhaps." Lloyd picked up the newspaper. "I see you do the crossword," he said.

"Yes," said Law, looking a little confused by the abrupt change of subject.

"Do you always do it?"

"Yes." His tone was a touch wary. "I'm not one of those three-minute, forty-two-seconds men, though," he added.

"No," said Lloyd. "In fact, you didn't finish yesterday's at all, did you?"

Law frowned. "Yesterday's?" he repeated.

"Yesterday morning's *Times* was found beside Bernard Bailey's body," said Lloyd. "With the crossword half-done. By someone left-handed. Mr. Bailey didn't take *The Times*, he didn't do crosswords, and while I don't know which hand *he* favoured, I know which one you do. I think it was *your* newspaper, Mr. Law."

Law's eyes widened, and he hit his forehead. "I *knew* I'd mislaid it," he said. "I was going to finish the crossword when I got home, and it wasn't in my pocket. It must have dropped out. I'm sorry."

"Where were you at half past two yesterday morning?"

"I was in bed."

"Can anyone confirm that?"

"No," Law said. "I live alone. But don't you think it's more likely that I dropped it during the scuffle with Bailey's foreman?"

"Is it?"

"Of course it is," said Law. "I was doing the crossword when he got the call about Bailey having been murdered. I thought I'd left it in the café, but obviously *that's* what happened to it."

Lloyd smiled. "Let's watch the next bit, Mr. Law."

Law looked less than enthusiastic as he played the video again. The camera swept round, the screen went almost white, then Bailey's body and the coffee table appeared. Under it was the newspaper.

"Pause it." Lloyd looked at Law, his eyebrows raised. "The paper seems already to be there, Mr. Law."

Law swallowed. "So was I," he said quickly. "I went in first."

"Gary will confirm that, will he?"

"I doubt it. He was trying to keep the camera functioning, as you can see. I doubt if he knows where I was."

"But you didn't lose it in the scuffle, did you?" said Judy.

"Obviously not. It must have fallen out of my pocket when I bent down to look at Bailey." He looked from Judy to Lloyd. "I've confirmed that it was my paper," he said. "I've apologized. Why all the questions?"

"Oh, just little puzzles, Mr. Law."

"Well, I hope I've cleared them up for you."

"Perhaps." Lloyd stood up. "Good morning, Mr. Law. Thank you for your time. But I think we may be having another chat quite soon."

Judy smiled, when they got back out. "You really enjoyed that, didn't you?" she said.

"Yes." He smiled back. "Do you think he is Rachel's boyfriend?"

"I don't know. Which is why," she said, as she got to her car, "I'm going to have another word with Nicola Hutchins, because I'm pretty sure she knows who is." She shrugged. "She won't be difficult to crack," she said, a little guiltily.

Someone who was perfectly prepared, just to get her hands on some money, to live with a man capable of calculated, sadistic violence towards her, was able to make her feel guilty, and Judy wasn't sure why. But she *had* walked all over Nicola Hutchins, and she was about to do it again; she didn't exactly feel proud of her ability to do that. Rachel had spoken of her in the same breath as Bernard Bailey more than once, and Judy hadn't liked that at all.

"And I'm going to check out Mr. Law's story," said Lloyd grimly. "He's no innocent bystander. He's no mere reporter of the facts. He didn't ask me why half past two in the morning was important—he just went straight into his explanation for the paper being there."

"But it probably *is* what happened," Judy pointed out.

"Is it? Would blood have come off the sofa and on to the paper if he'd dropped it when he said he did? Wouldn't it have been too dry by then? It was certainly dry by the time I got there."

Judy wasn't sure. It had been more or less dry when she had seen it, but some might still have got smeared on to the paper.

"And he didn't ask me why he would *want* to kill Bernard Bailey. A disinterested observer would surely have found the suggestion a little odd."

"Yes," said Judy, thoughtfully. "I expect he would." And she headed off to speak to Nicola Hutchins.

"At last."

"Sorry, Mr. McQueen. Couldn't get here no sooner," she said.

She was wearing a sundress so light and fine and soft that it barely seemed to exist at all. It was short. It was sleeveless. It had probably cost more than Shirley's entire wardrobe. Mike had never seen her like that; she had always worn modest, if expensive, clothes on her visits to him before.

He held open the study door, and she went in, sitting down at the desk, looking up at him expectantly. "What did you want to see me about?" she asked.

He shook his head. "I really fell for it, didn't I?" he said, taking a cigar from the box, and walking over to the open French window, his back to her. "Hook, line, and sinker."

"Fell for what?"

He turned back, picked up the matches, and removed the unlit cigar from his mouth. "Such innocence," he said. "You're good. You're very good." He walked out on to the terrace, and didn't turn round when he heard her follow him out. She moved into his line of vision.

"I don't know what you're talkin' about," she said.

She had been sunbathing during the heat wave; her skin had tanned, rather than reddened, as you might expect it to, with her colouring. But there were those dark lashes that fringed her eyes, and those dark brown, almost black eyebrows, and Mike supposed that was the explanation; her genes had naturally produced the look that other women used hair dye and eyebrow pencil and mascara to achieve, and they allowed her skin to tan.

He had thought that her attraction would have waned, now that he knew what she was really like. The woman was trying to implicate him in her husband's murder, and he still wanted her. Her legs were bare and brown, and Mike couldn't take his eyes off them, as she leant back against the hideous fake-rustic garden table that Shirley had installed, its honest wood turned and varnished and polished, its rough edges smoothed. She had done much the same to him, he supposed, now that he came to think of it.

"I'm talking about death threats," he said. "It never crossed my mind that I was being set up to carry the can for a murder."

She stared at him, her eyes widening. "You don't really think I did that, do you?" she said. "I wouldn't do that to you,

Mr. McQueen. You and Mrs. McQueen have been good to me." She shook her head. "I didn't do that," she said slowly, seriously. "I didn't. And I didn't stab Bernard, neither. I wasn't even there."

"So it was a stroke of good fortune that someone came and stabbed your husband to death just when I was going to take the other route and you were going to lose out?"

She shrugged a little. "Reckon so."

Mike shook his head. "I'm afraid not, pet," he said. "Because I won't be buying your land." He lit his cigar to give himself something less heady than her perfume to smell. He shook the match out. "The police will see I had no motive."

"You think if you don't buy my land the cops'll just forget 'bout how much you wanted it?" she said, her voice low and sweet. "They might start rememberin' if I tell them 'bout the abortion."

Mike stepped forward in what was intended to be a threatening manner. "Are you trying to *blackmail* me now?" he asked.

As threats went, it was less than effective. The slow smile began to appear, and her blue eyes twinkled at him. She stepped forward, too, her face close to his. "Reckon I am," she whispered.

He moved away from her again. "Well, it won't work. I'm not buying your land. Tell the police what you like."

Still she smiled. Nodded her head a little to acknowledge her failure as a blackmailer. "All right," she said. "But I didn't stab Bernard. And I didn't get you to do them death threats so you'd get into trouble. The death threats didn't have nothin' to do with you. I just needed them, that's all."

Mike was intrigued, if a little sceptical. "*Needed* them?" he said.

She leant back on the table again. "You know Curtis Law?" she asked.

"The young man from Aquarius? Yes."

"Well, him and me—we've been . . . you know."

Mike couldn't remember the last time he had felt a stab of real, green-eyed jealousy. He thought perhaps he never had. He puffed his cigar. Once, he would have thought she was telling him in all innocence, with her "Mr. McQueen" act. Now he knew better. She knew exactly the effect she had on him, had played on it ever since he'd met her.

"It's been goin' on ever since he came here 'bout the vandalism," she was saying. "Only—there wasn't no way I could get away to see him. Bernard never let me out of his sight that long. Curtis don't even live in Bartonshire, and couldn't neither of us afford to go to hotels or get a flat or nothin'. Only time I saw him was when he come to the farm. But after the alarms went in, there wasn't nothin' bringin' him here. And I thought up the death threats. That was all," she said. "It was just to get Curtis here."

The thought of assisting her to make assignations with her lover was worse, much worse, than assisting her to do away with her repulsive husband. A voice at the back of his head was pointing out that Curtis Law was her contemporary, not old enough to be her father, but it made no difference to how he felt. She had used him, used every trick in the book to ensnare him, knowing he would do exactly what she wanted.

"That's all there was to it," she said. "Nothin' to do with you."

No. Nothing to do with him. He'd risked prison so that Curtis Law could get his leg over, while all he could do was fantasize about it. But tables could be turned; that fantasy could become reality. He breathed in her perfume, instead of trying to ignore it. It would become reality.

She gave him a little smile. "You goin' to buy the land now?" she asked. "Now you know I wasn't tryin' to set you up?"

"No," he said.

"I'll go, then." She walked past him, back into the house.

She thought he would call her back, but he let her go, because she was desperate for that money, and she would be back. And next time she would do what he wanted, for a change.

Nicola came home to find Inspector Hill waiting for her.

"Sorry," she said. "Gus keeps saying I should get a mobile phone."

"That's all right," said the inspector. "I'd just like to ask you a few more questions."

She had been expecting this, had resigned herself to it, steeled herself against it. She hoped.

Inspector Hill got straight down to the reason for her visit, with what Nicola already recognized as typical directness. "Yesterday," she said, "you were going to tell me something about Rachel. What was it?"

"Nothing," said Nicola, pushing her hair behind her ear, and wishing she hadn't. It wasn't a good start.

"Something that you thought had caused him to get violent. Not the baby business—something Rachel had been doing, rather than not doing. What was that, Mrs. Hutchins?"

"It's none of my *business*," Nicola said fiercely. "And Rachel wasn't there. She was in London."

"But you think she *had* been there, don't you? You think he might have assaulted her, so you must think she had been there to be assaulted."

"I just assumed she was there!" She wasn't going to say what she saw. If he had been going to do that to her again, he deserved everything he'd got, and anyway, she still didn't understand what had happened. "And I assumed he'd been hitting her, because he was always hitting her. She didn't do as she was told, not like me."

Inspector Hill looked concerned. "Rachel told me your father had been physically abusing you since you were two years old," she said. "Is that true?"

"I don't know," said Nicola. "But I can't remember him not doing it."

"Didn't your mother—?"

167

"Don't start blaming her! She was frightened he'd do something worse if she tried to stop him, and she was right, if what he did to Rachel's anything to go by."

"Why didn't she leave him?"

"She was frightened to. She tried to, once, but . . ." Nicola shook her head. "He stopped her."

In the silence that followed, Nicola could hear the big old-fashioned pendulum clock tick away the seconds in the waiting room next door, and remembered that day. Her mother had never learned to drive; she had waited until the coast was clear, and had ordered a taxi. It had arrived in the courtyard; hooted. She had picked up the cases, shepherding Nicola ahead of her. Nicola had gone out to find the taxi driving away, and her father standing there. She closed her eyes, her fists clenched to her mouth, as the memory claimed her. "He stopped her," she repeated, her voice a whisper.

"Is that what you thought Rachel had done? Tried to leave him? And he had tried to stop her?"

Oh, God. The detour into her personal history had lowered what defences she had managed to build up, sending her right back to her totally defenceless childhood. Nicola had counted thirty-five ticks of the waiting-room clock when she caved in. She had to tell her something. She didn't have the pith to keep this up, so there was no point in trying to. Better just to get it over with, tell her what she wanted to know. Rachel wouldn't do this to *you*, a voice in her head was saying, as she spoke. But she couldn't help it. She couldn't.

"I know she had an affair with someone," she said. "It was weeks ago. It might all be over."

Forgive me. Forgive me, Rachel. I'm not as strong as you, not as brave. I can't do this.

"Let's take this one step at a time," said Inspector Hill.

"You promised."

Jack ran his hands down his face, and looked at Terri. "I

168

swear to you," he said. "I am not and I never have been having an affair with Rachel Bailey."

"You've sworn to me before, Jack Melville!"

He knew that. That was the thing about being a liar. No one believed you when you were telling the truth. His web was even more tangled than most; the more he protested his innocence, the less she would believe him, and that suited him right down to the ground. Did that make the truth a lie?

"I know I have," he said. "Terri—I love you. You know I do. And I know I've been a lousy husband in that respect, but—maybe I make up for it in others?"

She shook her head, sniffed away a tear. "You promised," she repeated.

He had gone up to her yesterday after the inspector had left, but she hadn't spoken to him at all. She hadn't come downstairs again; he had slept in the spare room. That was the pattern, after he had been discovered in an infidelity.

"I knew," she said. "I knew as soon as she came here, as soon as I saw her. You'd never be able to ignore someone like her."

Now, the recriminations had started. He would protest his innocence, and would sleep in the spare room for a few nights, while she went on at him about broken promises and didn't cook for him. And eventually, he would confess, and she would let him sleep with her again. No sex. Then, after a couple of weeks of that, she would forgive him, he would promise never to look at another woman, they would make love, and life would go on peaceably until the next time.

"But she could ignore *me*, and did. She isn't interested in married men."

Terri's eyes blazed. "And how do you know that? How do you know she isn't interested in married men?"

"I may have made a pass."

"May have? Don't you remember?"

"All right, I did make a pass. I'm sorry. But—well, I did it from force of habit, almost. And she turned me down."

"Playing hard to get?"

No, she hadn't played hard to get, thought Jack. She'd played impossible to get. "She turned me down," he repeated. She had told him, politely, and very, very languidly, to get lost. Married men were not, it would appear, Rachel Bailey's cup of tea. He had tried a few times, but always the same answer.

"Oh, I'll bet she did! I'm sure Bernard Bailey was so fascinating she couldn't tear herself away from him!"

"It was before she was married, and she turned me *down*. She told me to behave myself and go home to my wife, and that was what I did. I haven't even seen her to speak to since she married Bailey."

"Then why did you go there on Sunday night?"

"To see Bailey. I told you, he had some investments."

"Will you stop *lying* to me! No one believes your ridiculous story about investments! Not me and not the police. And if you *are* seeing Rachel Bailey, you had better come up with a better lie than that!"

He would. Just give him time.

She stood up. "I'm going out," she said. "You can get your own lunch."

He sat down at the computer, switching it on, his mind not on his job, but on how he was going to weather this. "If" had crept in to the accusations, he'd noticed, and that was a little worrying. Perhaps the truth wasn't as convincing a lie as he had thought.

He might have to confess. To having an affair with Rachel, of course. Not to what he'd really done.

Rachel got into her car as soon as Inspector Hill had gone, and drove to the flat. She had had a difficult day; firstly, she had had to explain to Steve Paxton and the other three men that there was no money for their wages, and had promptly lost three-quarters of her work force. Steve had said that he would help her out until something got sorted. Then McQueen had turned awkward on her, and explaining about the death threats had just made matters worse. He had been jealous. She could use that, though. She could handle him, she was sure of that.

She wasn't so sure about Inspector Hill. Nicola had told her about finding her with Curtis, of course, and Rachel had admitted it, though she had still denied that he was with her at the hotel. Whatever happens, just deny it, Curtis had said, though she couldn't see the point. But what was bothering her was that the inspector had been going on about some money that was supposed to have been in the safe; Rachel had told her she knew nothing about any money, that as far as she knew, Bernard had had none.

What else could she say? He had scraped together some cash for her to go to London, accepting how much it cost without a murmur, happy to stick to his side of the bargain now that she was sticking to hers. She had pretended to book herself in, as though places like that could give you suites in the middle of summer at a week's notice. Curtis had booked it in Bernard's name weeks before, and she had just kept her fingers crossed that Bernard knew as little about how hotels conducted their business as she assumed, and he had. And as far as she had known, that was the only cash Bernard had had; she certainly didn't know about any more. She had thought that Bernard had just juggled figures around, borrowed money from one source to pay back his borrowings from another; that was why she had been so certain that there had to be a limit to how long he could go on doing that. Now it looked as though he had had a supply of cash all the time.

But finding out that she might have been in a no-win situation all along was something a gambler like Rachel could live with; the real worry was that it was Curtis who had told the police about this money, and maybe it had never been there in the first place. Maybe it was part of the plan, something he hadn't told her about. He hadn't told her much, had said it was better for her not to know the details, but she had no idea what was going on. He hadn't come round last night, and she'd stayed in all evening, desperate to see him, her bewilderment of the morning turning to anger when he didn't arrive.

She let herself into the flat, stepping over the letter on the mat, and sank down at the table, suddenly very tired. When she heard his key in the door, she went out to see him stoop and pick the letter up. It was just more junk mail—he wouldn't *get* any real mail here, and that unconcerned, unthinking, reflex action upset her even more.

"What went wrong?" she demanded, but the question came out without warning through sobs as sudden and unexpected as when she had first talked to Inspector Hill.

"Nothing," he said, throwing the letter into the bin with all the others, coming to her, putting his arms round her. "Nothing went wrong. Everything's fine."

"But he'd been stabbed!"

"I know. I know you got a terrible fright. I couldn't tell you, don't you see?" He was holding her close, stroking her hair, kissing her face. "I couldn't. Your reaction had to be real, Rachel. It had to be. I couldn't tell you. I didn't know it would do that to you."

"You told me that he looked like he was asleep!"

"Yes. I know, I know." He led her into the living room, and sat her on the sofa, still holding her, stroking her. "I lied. Firstly, I don't know a thing about chloral hydrate, but I expect he'd have to drink a bucketful before it killed him. And secondly, you had to find something you didn't expect, so that your reaction was right. Someone could have come in with you—Nicola, or anyone."

She pulled away from him. "But I nearly died! I thought it had all gone wrong! Then when the cops came and dragged you away, I thought we were goin' to be arrested!"

"I know. But it hadn't gone wrong. We weren't arrested, and we're not going to be." He smiled at her. "He was drunk," he said. "Really drunk. He made it easy for me."

"Bernard?" Rachel had never seen Bernard drunk. "Why'd he be drunk?"

"I don't know. And I don't care."

Rachel did. Bernard didn't get drunk. "Somethin' must've happened," she said. "If he got drunk."

"So what? We did it," he said again. "We did it, and we're going to get away with it. You said I could run rings round them, and I have."

She sighed. "You sure that newspaper thing's going to work?"

"Oh, don't start that again!" he said, almost laughing at her now. "Of course it's going to work. Chief Inspector Lloyd's off checking my story even now." He grinned. "You were right about Paxton. He blurted it out as soon as I asked."

Rachel still felt worried about that, even in retrospect. "What if he hadn't?" she said.

"I'd have made some excuse to get up to the farm. But he did, so I didn't have to, because Gary was up and off before I was."

"That's another thing! Why did you let him come in filmin' everything?"

"Ah," he said, a little shamefacedly. "Well. It was a scoop, wasn't it?"

She sighed, and hoped his lack of sensitivity meant that he made a good assassin. "Nicola's told them 'bout us," she said. "And she told them 'bout him kickin' me half to death that time."

"We knew she would," said Curtis, then paused. "Rachel. Did you know that Bernard was in financial difficulties?"

"Yes."

"Why didn't you tell me?"

Because, thought Rachel, it's none of your business. You know what I want you to know, Curtis Law, and no more. "What difference would it've made?" she asked.

"None, I don't suppose."

Rachel changed the subject. "Nicola was there," she said. "At the farm. On Sunday night. Somethin' 'bout a sheep. She reckons Bernard was out." She frowned. "I don't get that."

Curtis shrugged. "She probably just didn't see him."

Maybe not, thought Rachel. The sitting-room door was closed. But she'd waited for him for over an hour. Wouldn't she have checked to see if he was in the sitting room? She would, of course she would. Her heart dipped a little as she realized why Nicola had been having such a hard time with the inspector. "I think she did see him," she said. "But she's trying not to say, because she thinks *I* stabbed him."

"Well, we knew he might have callers. And she might have been there, and she might have seen him, and if she says so, then she says so. But *you* weren't there, were you? It's called the burden of proof, Rachel. And it means that it doesn't matter what they think. They have to prove it."

He was always telling her what things meant. Mike McQueen didn't. Chief Inspector Lloyd didn't. And that was another thing. "I saw your programme," she said. "You tried to make Chief Inspector Lloyd look stupid, but he's not."

"Yes, he is." Curtis smiled, hugged her. "Come to bed," he said. "We should celebrate."

Rachel groaned. "Curtis. Didn't you get enough at the weekend?"

"No. I can never get enough of you. Come to bed, Rachel. Stop worrying. This wouldn't be happening if you hadn't been so desperate to get your hands on that money."

She couldn't help worrying. "That's another thing," she said. "What's all this 'bout some money in the safe?"

"Oh, yes, that. I saw a lot of cash in the safe. They say it wasn't there when they checked it. Probably took it themselves," he said, with a grin.

"Don't joke about it! Someone took it. Maybe someone was *there*, maybe they saw you—"

"No one was there. No one saw me. I think your foreman helped himself to it."

"Steve Paxton? When?"

"When the police had their hands full with you and me and Gary." He got up, and held out his hand. "Come to bed."

174

That might explain why he didn't mind helping her out for nothing, Rachel thought. She looked at Curtis's outstretched hand, and sighed. She was tired. She had been living on a knife edge since Sunday evening. And he hadn't even come to see her. "That's another thing!" she said. "Why didn't you come over last night?"

"I had to collect the car."

"You could've come after! You must've known I'd be worried 'bout Bernard bein' stabbed and everythin'."

"I had to go into Barton. They had a run-through of the programme before it went out, and they wanted me there to answer questions from the newspapers once it had been shown. And that went on for ages afterwards. I was whacked, Rachel. I hadn't had any sleep. I just went home. Anyway—we'd agreed I shouldn't go to the farm."

"You could've rung," she said.

"It was too late. And I knew I'd be seeing you today." He grinned. "If you've finished grumbling, come to bed."

She had slept on her own two nights running now, and she had enjoyed that. Sex at lunchtime hadn't been on her agenda.

"I got rid of him for you," Curtis said. "Don't I deserve some reward?"

He had. He had got rid of Bernard Bailey, once and for all. She smiled, and took his hand. "Yes," she said, allowing him to pull her up, lead her into the bedroom. But she was still worrying. She didn't like the bit about Bernard being drunk, and she didn't like this money that had gone missing from the safe.

Two things had happened that they had not anticipated, and Rachel was gypsy enough to believe that the third was just around the corner.

Lloyd had come back to the intelligence that the knife that had been found had blood matching Bernard Bailey's on it, but no fingerprints. The Coke cans had fingerprints on them, but several sets, so they would take a while to sort out. They hadn't got round to the rest of the stuff, but Lloyd had told them that it might not be necessary. His paranoid theory was almost certainly right.

He had checked the business of the missing money with the officers at the scene, and the office door had been closed when they arrived, and had remained closed until they had cleared the house of all interlopers and called the doctor for Mrs. Bailey. The room had then been checked to see if it was harbouring Bailey's assailant, and the safe had been found open. The first thing they had done was to see if there was money in it, which there wasn't, which was why they had cordoned it off, thinking that there might have been a burglary. And now it looked as though there had been.

The videos indicated that none of Bailey's employees could have got into the house, with the exception of Steve Paxton, who wasn't within range of any of the cameras for a few minutes before he went off for breakfast; Lloyd had suggested that Tom Finch have a word with Paxton, his no-nonsense, to-hell-with-diplomacy approach being called for in the matter of opportunist thefts. Because that was all it was, Lloyd was certain. Bailey had not been killed for the contents of his safe.

But there was no way that Law saw that money on his dash after the story; therefore, he had been in the house at some point *before* the money went missing, and had become confused about exactly when he had seen it. Understandable, if he had just murdered someone, which seemed the most likely explanation for his presence, if they were right about him and Rachel Bailey.

When Judy came back to tell him that Curtis Law had been caught in the cowshed with Rachel, he immediately telephoned the ACC to let him know that the tide might be turning, but he was off sick, apparently.

"I thought he looked a bit pale and wan yesterday," he said to Judy, heaping the packets of sandwiches and cans of soft drinks he had got for their working lunch on to his desk. "He just would be away, when I've got some good news for once."

Case came in then, to check on progress, so Lloyd passed

the good news on to him. He didn't seem as pleased as he might be.

"You don't make a move—not a single move—without rock-solid evidence," he said. "Do you hear? I don't want the ACC coming back off his sickbed to find that this case is resting on the word of a couple of bobbies about whether or not there was money in that safe yesterday morning. Not after that programme. I can hear Law shouting 'fit-up' already."

"I'll get evidence," said Lloyd. "Don't worry."

"Rock solid," Case repeated, and looked at Judy as he got to the door. "I'm trusting you to make sure it is rock solid," he said. "Your boyfriend has an axe to grind."

Lloyd didn't like Case knowing about him and Judy; he never lost an opportunity to remind them that he did, and that made Lloyd uncomfortable. It didn't seem to bother Judy in the slightest. She waited until Case had gone before carrying on with her report, though.

"Rachel is still denying that he was with her in London," she said. "I couldn't shake her."

Lloyd opened a can of lemonade and drank thirstily, even though it bore no relation to the real thing as supplied by Rachel Bailey. "I'm sure there's a nice publicity photograph of Mr. Law that we can show the staff," he said, and listened to the rest of her interview with Nicola, frowning slightly. "What makes her think Rachel was there on Sunday night?" he asked.

Judy shrugged a little. "I think perhaps it was just that her father was drunk, and she thought Rachel's affair must have been the cause," she said. "That the likely scenario was that he had started in on her, Rachel had fled, and he'd gone after her, brought her back. Not that she's saying any of that in words of one syllable—I think she's pretty loyal to Rachel. And she isn't telling me everything, I'm sure of that. She might be covering up for her."

Lloyd nodded. "Rachel Bailey said this was the first time in eighteen months she had no bruises," he said. "If bruises are an issue, someone's going to have to check."

"Are you volunteering?"

"Really, Inspector!" he said, in mock horror.

But he did very much hope that she didn't have bruises. Partly because he hoped she hadn't been there at any time that night, and partly because he didn't *want* her to have bruises. How *could* Bailey have constantly abused her like that, never mind doing what he had ended up doing to her? He became aware that Judy was looking at him. "What?" he said suspiciously.

"Tell me something," she said. "If she offered to go to bed with you, what would you do?"

He stared at her. He had grown used to her direct approach, but he had made a rule long ago that they mustn't let their private relationship intrude in the office, and while he very rarely kept it, Judy almost always did. And in any circumstances her inquiry would have startled him. "What sort of question's that?" he said.

"One I want you to answer seriously, and truthfully, if that's not too tall an order."

He and Judy held differing opinions on the matter of sexual relations. She thought sex was over-rated as a measure of fidelity; it was the emotional commitment that counted, she said, not a physical activity most of which was sheer animal reflex to certain stimuli. But he thought it was a commitment in itself, something not to be indulged in on a whim.

He did what she asked, and gave his answer serious consideration. He had been attracted to other women, but he had never truly been tempted to be unfaithful to Judy. Rachel Bailey, as Judy clearly knew, *would* be a temptation. But Judy had never been unfaithful to him, and even if that was because of his principles rather than hers, it came to the same thing in the end. If he strayed, it would be a betrayal of her loyalty, and she would find that just as hard to handle as the next person, whatever her beliefs. He wouldn't hurt her like that. But then, if he knew that she would never know anything about it . . .

He smiled at the very idea. He didn't suppose Rachel went

178

for balding, middle-aged policemen unless they could buy her sports cars, and if there was such a being, he wasn't it. There was little likelihood of their opposing principles being put to the test, so he would give her the truthful answer she had requested. "I honestly don't know," he said, opening another can. "It might depend on whether or not I thought I could get away with it."

Judy nodded. "Anyway," she said, disconcertingly behaving as though the strange little conversation had never happened. "How did you get on checking Law's story?"

Lloyd had made one very small inquiry which had set his imagination off on its usual trip round the houses, but basically, the second part of his theory seemed to have gone the way of all theories. "His story checks out," he said. "Mrs. Archer, who owns the newsagent-café place, says that Law and his cameraman arrived just after nine. The cameraman had breakfast, Law had coffee. Law bought a *Times*, and sat there doing the crossword." He sighed. "She even saw him put it in his pocket," he said. "And I had another look at the tapes from Bailey's closed-circuit TV. You can see the paper in his pocket when he's on the phone at the gate. And it wasn't in his pocket when we saw him later on."

Judy smiled. "No conspiracy theories? Mrs. Archer is in on it with him, for instance?"

"Very funny." He looked at her for a moment, then tipped his chair back. "A mini-theory," he said. "Anything strike you as odd about Mrs. Archer's story?"

Judy frowned as she mentally checked off what he had just told her. "No," she said. "It's a very small shop in a very small community. Mrs. Archer is quite likely to notice what two media folk are doing. Especially if they're haring off after a story."

Lloyd nodded, and rocked gently backwards and forwards. "But Law said he was a *Times* crossword man," he pointed out. "Did it every day."

179

Judy gave him a look. "If you're going to say he got seven down wrong, I'm going to the canteen," she said.

"No, no—listen. I wondered about that, because if he does the crossword every day, and he's never sure where he's going to be, then—well, *The Times* isn't like the *Sun*, is it? You can't be certain there'll be one left if you just buy it wherever you happen to be, because newsagents don't get in vast numbers of it. So I got someone to ring all the newsagents close to where he lives." He rocked for a moment. "And he gets it delivered."

"So?"

"So why did he buy one from Mrs. Archer? Why didn't he just bring his own paper from home?"

"There could be a dozen reasons," she said. "Maybe it was put through the wrong door. Maybe the back page got ripped when he took it out of the letterbox, and he couldn't do the crossword in that one, so he bought another one. Maybe he just forgot it."

"Mm," said Lloyd. "Just seems odd, that's all."

She frowned. "Supposing he did get one delivered, and then buy another one?" she asked. "What would he gain by that?"

"Well," said Lloyd. "If he had left one paper inadvertently at the scene of the crime, a second one could just possibly give him an alibi."

"He killed Bailey before breakfast, then went to the café and bought one specially so he could pretend to have dropped it in the farmhouse when he went up there an hour later?" Judy looked sceptical, but she wasn't just dismissing it, Lloyd noticed. "He'd have had to have known that Paxton was going to get that call," she said.

"Yes," Lloyd said. "He would. Wouldn't he?"

Judy looked interested. "I did get a slight reaction from Rachel Bailey when I asked her about *The Times*," she said, then shook her head. "The person on the video left the farm at twenty to three in the morning," she said. "Law's paper hadn't left the wholesalers."

It had taken her longer than usual to spot the rather large

180

flaw in his reasoning, he thought. In fact, she seemed not to be giving any of this case a hundred per cent of her attention. But ninety-five per cent of Judy's attention was worth a hundred of anyone else's, so it hardly mattered. He smiled to himself. Was she *that* worried about Rachel Bailey's influence? He'd like to think that she was. She had never seemed one jot jealous of him before. But she wouldn't have asked that question at all, never mind in the middle of the working day, if Rachel Bailey's potent charm wasn't worrying her, however slightly.

Judy bit into her next sandwich, then her eyes widened, and she spoke in an unladylike fashion, with her mouth full. "But if he'd been in London the night before," she said, "and caught the eleven-thirty train, he could have bought it there."

"Yes!" Lloyd said, bringing the chair down with a thump. Judy looked relieved, as she always did when he made a safe landing. He smiled broadly at her. He had known if he ran it past Judy, she'd home in on what was eluding him, even if she wasn't her usual alert self.

"Can we find out where it was bought?" she asked.

He wasn't sure. "In old British movies," he said, "the detective could always trace a paper back to *exactly* where it was purchased. There was a code on them. Is there still? Or did that go with hot-metal type?"

"I don't know," said Judy. "But we've still got the paper."

Lloyd frowned. "Didn't it go to forensic?"

"No. There didn't seem much point, because so many people handle newspapers before they ever go to whoever actually buys them. I thought I'd leave it as a last resort."

"Good." Lloyd picked up the phone, and demanded that it be brought to him immediately if not sooner. It arrived in commendably quick time, folded into a plastic bag; he could see the whole of the top of the front page, and there was no code. But it might be on the back page, which he couldn't see, so he rang the press officer, and asked her to check her copy for codes.

"Nothing on the back," she said, after a moment. "But are

you sure there *isn't* one on yours? There's a number and a letter just under the masthead on this one."

Lloyd rang *The Times*. It was distribution he wanted, according to the switchboard, and distribution he got. He introduced himself. "What does it mean," he asked, "if one of your editions has no code number on it? Is it worth a fortune?"

The man at the other end laughed. "I'm afraid not," he said. "It just means it's a London first edition."

"You mean the edition that's on the streets at eleven o'clock the night before?"

"That's it."

"The edition that you would buy at a stall, like ... say ... the one at King's Cross Station?"

"Yes."

"And *only* that edition?"

"Only that edition," he said. "The London first edition. All the others have a letter and number code on them."

Lloyd beamed. "Thank you," he said. "You have made me a very happy man."

"Glad I could be of help," he said.

It was good, but, obeying Case's orders, Judy pointed out that it was a bit airy-fairy for arrests and search warrants and all the rest of it. What they really wanted was proof that it was Law who had been on that train, and Barton station had security cameras.

He stood up. "Barton railway station, then," he said, polishing off his drink. "Hard evidence. Let's go."

Barton station was big and busy and had been a hunting ground for pickpockets and flashers and even the odd mugger until it had got the surveillance equipment in. It had cameras everywhere. Except on the trains themselves.

"They watch the people, not the trains," said the chief security officer. "I mean, one or two might take in a part of a train while it's in the station, but you couldn't guarantee it."

"What about the concourse?"

"Yes, there's plenty there. You can't enter or leave the station without a camera picking you up. What time was this train?"

"It would arrive in Barton at about twelve-thirty A.M.," said Lloyd.

"Oh, well, it would be quiet then. It's pandemonium an hour earlier than that, but it's pretty dead after midnight. Shouldn't be too difficult to spot your man. Most people on that train are going further north than this."

He and Judy settled down to look at more videos. A trickle of people came through the automatic doors. A man in his fifties. A couple with small, fractious children. Two women on their own, one carrying luggage, the other not. It was fascinating, watching people, thought Lloyd. Maybe he *would* become a security man when he retired, after years of saying that he would sooner nail his head to the floor. The man used the phone. The family and one of the women waited just inside the exit doors, presumably for whoever was coming to pick them up. A member of staff came through, carrying an anorak, and handed it in to Lost Property. Lloyd observed that some absent-minded trainspotter must have found it a bit too hot for the uniform. Judy smiled. The security officer did not. The other woman, the one with the bag, went out, probably to the taxis. The children sat on the suitcases, and were given small chocolate bars to cheer them up a bit. Another person came through, a youth with a backpack. He too went straight out. They watched until everyone had been picked up by their various cars. Even watched the cars arrive, from the camera on the road outside. No Law.

They knew he must have bought his paper in London, and surely he *had* to be the man who had been with Rachel. That man had left to get that train, so where the hell was he? Had he changed his mind?

"Course you don't have to leave the platforms that way," said the security chief. "There's an exit on platform three direct into the car park."

Lloyd and Judy looked at one another, then at him. "And

you have cameras in the car park?" said Lloyd, his voice light and dangerous.

"Oh, yes. Like I said. You can't enter or leave this place without being seen by at least one camera."

Lloyd rubbed his forehead, feeling an incipient and rare headache forming. Staring at bloody videos, that's what was giving him a headache, but he was going to have to stare at some more, thanks to this prat not telling them that in the first place.

It was late afternoon by the time the videos had been located, but the wait had been worth it. From the output of three cameras, Law, large as life, could be tracked walking across the car park from platform three, past the exit, going towards his car, driving back the way he had walked, and out. Both he and his car were beautifully photographed, and entirely unmistakable. On one of the shots Lloyd saw the woman with the bag walking past the taxis, past the car-park exit, and smiled. She hadn't taken a taxi, then, he thought. Not afraid of being mugged or raped or any of the other things of which women were, in his opinion, overly afraid. Good for her. Yes, he might not find this sort of job too awful. He'd think about it.

"We've got him," he said. This was enough for a search warrant, enough on which to arrest him. Even by Judy's exacting Case-hardened standards. He never thought he'd see the day when Judy was telling *him* not to cut corners.

The Barton office of Aquarius Television produced Law's home number, but there was no reply, and at the Stansfield regional office they found only a girl called Samantha who had no idea where Curtis Law was. On arrival at Bailey's Farm they saw a rather angry Paxton storming off, leaving Tom Finch, who came over to the car. Of course, thought Lloyd, he was there making inquiries about the missing money.

He bent down and spoke through the open window. "Paxton doesn't seem to know anything about any money, and I've just been given GBH of the earhole for calling him a thief," he said.

"Did you call him a thief?" enquired Judy.

"No, guv! Just . . . leant on him a bit. Who else could have nicked it?"

"If Mrs. Hutchins is right that the alarms were off, anyone agile enough could have got in over the fence and taken it," Lloyd said.

"I've been thinking about that," said Finch. "Law helped Bailey set up the closed-circuit television, didn't he? So he'd know where all the cameras were, and all that, wouldn't he?"

"Yes."

"Well . . . if the alarms had been off like Mrs. Hutchins says they were, he could have got out the back, couldn't he? Dodged the cameras, and gone over the fence, like you said. Without being seen at all. He wouldn't have had to use the gate, and get himself on the video."

"What are you saying, Tom?" Lloyd asked testily. "That it *isn't* Law on that video? That we're on a wild-goose chase? He left his paper here!"

"No," said Tom. "I'm saying that I don't think the alarms could have been off when he *was* here. And from what Paxton says, Bailey seems to have been scared to death someone was going to get him, so I can't see why he'd have them off at all."

"You think Mrs. Hutchins is lying?"

"Well, I'm not convinced she came here about a sheep, guv. No one knows anything about a sheep getting out. Not here or anywhere else, according to Paxton. I reckon something went on here on Sunday night, and I don't think it had anything to do with a sheep."

"OK," said Lloyd. "Have a word with Mrs. Hutchins, Tom—see what you can get."

"Meanwhile," said Judy. "Have you seen anything of Mrs. Bailey while you've been here?"

"She went out while I was talking to Paxton."

"Was Curtis Law with her?" asked Lloyd.

"No. She was on her own."

Lloyd hit the steering wheel in annoyance. "Where the hell is the man?" he said.

"Off somewhere on a story?" suggested Tom.

"No. He's been told to mark time at Stansfield and await developments on Bailey," said Lloyd. "He's somewhere with Mrs. Bailey." Then he smiled, as a thought occurred to him. It meant driving all the way back to Barton, but it would be worth it. "And I know where," he said. "Have to love you and leave you, Tom. Good luck with Mrs. Hutchins."

He drove out of Bailey's Farm, and on to the open road, heading back the way he had just come. "A very nice service flat," he said, in reply to Judy's query about where they were going. "Where I had to endure young Mr. Law's even younger producer being smug and self-satisfied while he showed me all the gadgets and gizmos they'd set up there. While he told me what lengths they'd gone to to make Roger Wheeler's identity rock solid. Like taking the flat on a six-month rent. I expect Rachel Bailey and Curtis Law have made use of it, don't you?"

He used his mobile to ask for back-up from Barton when they got there to discover both Law's car and the BMW parked outside. Complete with uniformed colleagues, they effected entry by means of keys obtained from the caretaker, when their knocks had gone unheeded. Curtis Law was apprehended in bed with Rachel, having clearly decided that there *would* be no developments on the Bailey murder that day. But he was wrong. Lloyd arrested him, then left the uniforms with him while he got dressed, to find Judy looking round the flat, automatically poking and prying, noting down what she found.

She smiled at him as he came into the room. "I often wonder if I would have done this sort of thing anyway, whether or not I'd joined the police," she said. "It's fun."

Like watching unsuspecting people on videos, Lloyd thought. They had long ago accepted that they were chalk and cheese, but perhaps they did have something in common after all. They were both exceedingly nosy. And he had done a bit of poking and prying himself. The wardrobe still held the padded-waistcoat affair that Law had worn to help bring off his coup, but nothing else. The flat was clearly just somewhere to meet.

186

What Judy at first thought, with a squeal, was a small furry animal in a cupboard turned out to be Law's wig; she put it back where she had found it, then took out his beard, and a mobile phone. "More of his disguise," she said.

Lloyd took the phone from her and looked at it. He was an expert on these things now. "It's charged up," he said, puzzled.

Judy looked thoughtful, and noted that down. Then she went out into the corridor, and picked up the letters that lay unopened in the bin.

Lloyd frowned, following her out. "And why doesn't he open his mail?" he asked.

"It isn't his mail," Judy said, sorting through it. "It's addressed to Roger Wheeler. Mail shots from car-hire places, mostly. A couple from credit-card companies." She smiled at him, looking grimly pleased. "*Law on the Law* will have an interesting programme to make this time round, won't they?"

Curtis Law was led away while Rachel, wrapped in a bathrobe, stood watching, her face pale. They couldn't arrest her on what they had, not yet, and one thing Lloyd had discovered while he was in Law's bedroom was that Rachel had told the truth. She had no bruises. And he had been angry, when he'd seen her there with Law. She was worth much more than this sordid set-up. He felt guilty now about how he'd behaved; he would have apologized, but she ran into the bathroom, locking the door, and they could hear her being sick.

And he felt guiltier than ever.

# CHAPTER SEVEN

"THIS IS A LITTLE EARLY IN THE RITUAL FOR THE confession, isn't it, Jack?"

Terri was in the garden, painting in the late evening sun, trying to capture the long shadows. She was a good artist. Not great. Not like whoever had done those wonderful paintings in Bailey's hallway. He had made a mental note to ask Rachel Bailey who had done them, if ever he got the chance, but he very rarely bumped into her. He truly *hadn't* seen her to speak to since the day she was married.

Everyone had seen her that day. Bailey had spent a fortune that he didn't have on a wedding that did justice to his stunning bride. It had been the most incongruous thing Jack or any of the other guests had ever seen, especially in the church, as they had turned to see this amazing creature walk down the aisle towards Bernard Bailey, of all people. And when he had been told he might kiss the bride, he hadn't.

Rising up from the pews like a murmured response had been comments to the predictable effect, and now, he thought, if they were lucky, the congregation might get to see her in her widow's weeds; there would be even more scope for fantasy when Bernard was laid to rest among the tombstones and slabs of Harmston cemetery, scene of many a youthful indiscretion of his own.

So, he thought, dragging his thoughts back to his present predicament, Terri knew it was a ritual. He hadn't realized that.

188

"Their husbands have never been murdered before," he said. "I thought you might start thinking I'd done it."

She looked up from her delicate watercolour of the wild honeysuckle as it trailed down the rough, local-stone wall. It looked like a painting of honeysuckle trailing down a wall. His attempt would look like pink and green paint dripping down grey and beige paint, so he had no right to criticize. But in the hands of whoever had done *those* paintings, it would look like an untamed creature tumbling onto a lover; it would be alive. Even the wall would be alive.

The ones in Bailey's house were impressions of the seasons; there were more pictures in the sitting room, but he hadn't had the chance to see them properly. Just enough to recognize the style, the bold statement, the deep, vibrant warmth of autumn colours. The hallway was shimmering spring, the greens and yellows of daffodils joyfully overtaking the white of melting snow, the pink and white of sunlit, wind-tossed blossom against the rough browns and greys of bark. The silver and blue and black of a rain-pocked stream that filled the canvas, rushing, dancing water that you could feel and taste and hear and smell. Just colour. Just colour on canvas, and you could drown in it.

"Murdered him?" she said. "Why in the world would I have thought that you had murdered him?"

"Because I was there. Because I find him—found him—as repellent as you do. Because I couldn't think of a better lie to explain my presence in his house than the one which was so obviously disbelieved by you and the inspector. The truth is that there was an emergency Lodge meeting on Sunday evening, and I thought he'd be at it, and I could see Rachel."

Now, he was telling a black lie. He had no more notion of Lodge meetings than she had. But she would believe him. Did that make a lie the truth?

"But he was there," he went on, when she didn't speak. "I had to think of some reason for calling on him, so I told him I wanted to talk to him about the woodland."

She was looking disbelieving again. "And he let you in?"

"Yes. I went in, all ready to give my speech about the woodland, but he was too busy threatening to kill Rachel to listen to anything I had to say."

Terri went back to her careful, dead watercolour, with its perfectly formed and shaded blooms, its evening-class correctness. She had been taught how to use her talent; she had never learned how to let it use her.

"Was he threatening to kill her because of you?" she asked.

"I suppose so," he said, seizing on the explanation for Bailey allowing him to pass. "That must be why he let me in. To tell me to my face. But he was so drunk I didn't understand most of it. I find his ridiculous accent impenetrable at the best of times."

"Has it been going on since before she was married?" she asked, her voice shaking a little. She put down the brush again, but she didn't look at him. "Has it?"

His talent was for telling lies, and he had been using it and letting it use him for years. Now, he had to decide how long this fictitious affair had lasted. If he said yes, the thought of a two-year affair might be more than Terri was prepared to take; if he said no, she would want details. He shook his head, preferring to err on the side of caution. "No," he said. "That bit wasn't true."

"So when *did* it start? *How* did it start?"

He sat down, and made a full and frank confession about something which had never happened, lacing it with dates and events, and he knew it was utterly convincing. But he would lose track if he wasn't careful.

"Arrested?" McQueen repeated.

"Yeah." Rachel looked up at him, trying to judge his mood. Certainly more receptive than it had been the last time. "So can I come in?" she asked.

"What's he been arrested for?" he asked, then turned and walked towards the study. "I'm out on the terrace," he said. "I was just having a beer. Can I get you something?"

190

She shook her head, following him out through the French windows as she had done that morning, on to his terrace, now bathed in rays from the setting sun. He slid into the bench attached to the table, and indicated that she should take the bench opposite.

She smiled, and sat down, watched as he took a long draught of beer, then answered his original question. "For killin' Bernard."

He didn't quite choke. "My God," he said, setting the can down, and his face broke into a smile as he looked at her. "You got someone else to do that for you, too. I should have guessed."

Naturally. And she might be in terrible trouble, but her philosophy was never to meet any sort of trouble half way. "I didn't have nothin' to do with it, Mr. McQueen," she said.

McQueen took another sip of beer to help down the one he'd almost choked on, and shook his head, still smiling at her. "Of course you didn't, pet," he said.

She shrugged. "Don't know nothin' about it," she said lazily. "Just know they arrested him this afternoon. And if they've got Curtis for murderin' Bernard, they're not goin' to think nothin' about you buyin' my land, are they?"

He shook his head. "No," he said.

"You still think I killed him?"

"No, pet," he said. "I don't think you were anywhere near him. Or what would be the point of getting your boyfriend to kill him for you?"

Rachel smiled. "Never asked him to," she said. "Not my fault if he's hot-headed."

"You don't seem too bothered about him being arrested."

She was terrified, if he really wanted to know. She had known that Curtis had underestimated Lloyd when she had watched that programme, had known that they should have been making contingency plans, not celebrating anything. They had been lying on the bed, sleeping off the exertions of the afternoon, when the police had walked in on them, and Curtis hadn't liked it any better

191

than he had when Nicola had found them in the cowshed. He had complained about it, once he'd got his clothes on and hadn't felt so vulnerable.

They said they'd knocked, but if they had, it hadn't penetrated. And, she supposed, knocking on the door of a luxury flat didn't have quite the same effect as banging on the side of a VW camper. That shook the van, echoed. That woke you up, all right. Travellers got the blame for everything, and the scene was one she knew well, with cops invading your privacy, giving orders, silencing protests, acting as though they owned the place. Curtis had looked as bewildered as Lloyd had looked angry, and when one of the uniformed ones had made a remark about her desirability, Lloyd had just told her to cover herself up. And she had thought he was different.

But then, she had been convinced that Curtis really could run rings round the police. Maybe she was losing her touch. The whole thing might be falling apart right now, if they had enough evidence against him. And if they had, how long would she stay out of prison? But she had to take care of her future on the assumption that she had one, and that was just what she was going to do, because McQueen had been panting for it for months. "You really not goin' to buy the land from me, Mr. McQueen?" she asked.

"I'm really not. And you can drop the Mr. McQueen act, because it's fooling no one, pet."

She knew that. She eased off a sandal, and smiled, running her bare foot slowly up his leg. "You maybe don't want my land," she said. "But you want somethin' of mine pretty bad." He closed his eyes and groaned as soon as she touched him; after a few moments, she withdrew her foot and sat back, her arms along the back of the bench.

"Can I have a beer now?" she asked.

He opened his eyes, and looked at her for a long time. Then he nodded, got up, and went into the house.

* * *

Nicola was entertaining another policeman. Sergeant Finch's angelic looks belied his tough nature, but she found that easier to cope with than Inspector Hill's unruffled calm. He had wanted to know if she had seen any money in her father's safe, and she had said no, she hadn't. He had asked if she had noticed any signs of a disturbance, and she had said no, she hadn't. He had asked her if she had *left* any money in her father's safe, and she had laughed.

Then he had got on to the reason for her visit to her father. She had told him that she had gone to the farm to try to find out about the sheep, that her father hadn't been there, that she had waited for over an hour, then she had left. She was certain he knew she wasn't telling the truth, but she felt reasonably confident that she could keep him at arm's length, and out of her psyche, unlike Inspector Hill.

He had come during evening surgery; Gus had sent the last two patients away, having established that the animals weren't ill, but merely there for annual inoculations. Now he was sitting listening, his eyes going from Finch to her, as though he were watching a tennis match.

"Why did your father go out, do you think?"

"I thought he might have gone to look for the sheep."

"Why do you suppose the alarms were off?"

"I can only think that he went across the fields rather than take the Land Rover. He'd have to put the alarms off. He'd be crossing the beams."

"Makes sense."

She knew that. It was what had really happened that didn't make sense, not what she was telling Finch might have happened.

"Problem is, your father's sheep are all accounted for."

"I know."

"No one else has had a sheep go missing either."

Oh, God, she wished they would forget about the bloody sheep. There was no sheep. There never had been any sheep. "Maybe my father imagined it," she said. "He was very drunk when he rang me."

193

"There's a bit of a problem about that, too," said Finch. "You see, there's no record of him having telephoned you."

"Then presumably he wasn't at home when he rang me."

"Everyone I've spoken to says your father had no intention of leaving the farmhouse on Sunday."

"I don't know anything about that," Nicola said, surprising herself with the assurance with which she was coping with Finch. She could do this. She really could. She didn't have to cave in. "If he didn't ring from his own phone, he must have rung from a call box or something, which means he must have left the farm."

"And then found the sheep."

"Yes," she said. "And then found the sheep."

"And the sheep was on the road, so presumably he must have been on the road when he found it."

"Yes," said Nicola, tiredly.

"So he hadn't crossed the fields to look for it? He'd gone out for some other reason, and just . . . found it?"

"Yes. Is that so unlikely?"

"No," said Finch. "But according to you, he left the house unlocked and the alarms off, and that seems very unlikely."

With that, Gus got up and left the room. Again. And now she had to answer Sergeant Finch's questions with no moral support at all. But then, she thought, wasn't that precisely what she had been doing all along?

"He was drunk. I told you."

"Then why do you think he went out?"

"Perhaps he finished the whisky he had in the house, and went to get another bottle." Nicola was rather enjoying this fiction. "And the quickest way to walk to the village is by crossing the fields. So that might be why he had to leave the alarms off."

"Well," said Finch. "That would be an explanation. Except that no one saw him at the pub or anywhere else on Sunday night."

"Then I've no idea," said Nicola. There was, after all, no reason why she should have.

When Mike had returned with her beer, she had been as she was now, sitting on the edge of the table, her long legs crossed at the ankles, her bare feet on the bench. He had put the can and a glass on the table and had sat down, his hand resting on her feet, absently stroking them in an unconscious gesture of ownership as she told him why the money that the land represented was so important to her.

He had thought that he had been poor, because his parents had struggled, like so many people in the north-east, in the depression. He had been three years old when the war had widowed his mother; she had had to bring him and his sisters up as best she could until they could leave school and get jobs. But poor though they were, he had always had shoes on his feet, and a roof over his head; Rachel had been born into a peaceful, affluent society, and she had begged in the streets. The world made very little sense to him.

She was playing with him, of course. Not literally, as she had done ten minutes ago, briefly and agonizingly, but just as she had for the last twelve months. And he let her talk until the sun was all but gone, until she leant over to drop the can into his refuse bin, and the expanse of sun-tanned thigh exposed by the movement was too much for him.

"I'll buy your land," he said, his voice thick, and stood up. "Can we go to bed now, for God's sake?"

She uncrossed her legs, placing them one either side of him on the bench, inviting him to take her there and then, in the dark privacy of his walled terrace.

Her unused beer glass swayed and toppled, rolling slowly over the polished, varnished timbers of Shirley's rustic monstrosity, and in as many moments as it took for it to reach the edge and shatter on the paving, years of denial and months of sheer lust were emptied into that golden body.

Rachel kicked off the pants he had dragged down out of his

195

way, and slid off the table, smiling at him. "Now let's go to bed and do it right," she said.

Rachel would be frantic with worry by now. The police had frightened her, barging into the bedroom like that; they'd frightened him, too, looking as though they wouldn't think twice about putting the boot in. But they had merely escorted him to Barton's main police station, and then he had been taken to his own house while a couple of DCs searched it, then he had finally been brought here. But this wasn't supposed to be happening.

He smoked quickly, stubbing cigarettes out half smoked, lighting new ones. So far, he had denied ever seeing the knife in his life before, denied that he had bought the paper in London, denied that he had been on a train on Sunday night.

Lloyd tipped his chair back, and Curtis watched as it balanced precariously on its hind legs.

"You helped Mr. Bailey install his closed-circuit television system?" he asked. "Is that right?"

"Yes."

"So you'll know where all the cameras are, I suppose."

"I didn't put them up personally," said Curtis. "I helped him decide how best to employ them."

"Which included where to site them."

"Yes."

"Why did you do that? Aren't there professionals who do that sort of thing?"

"Mr. Bailey was a very prudent man. He preferred to have my advice for nothing."

"Why did you offer to help him?"

"I would have thought that was obvious," Curtis said. "I wanted to be near Rachel."

"I think you wanted to get to know his security systems," said Lloyd.

"Why would I want to do that?"

"Because you wanted his wife. And doing away with Bailey

196

would clear the field, wouldn't it? Apart from anything else, she's going to come into a tidy bit of money when she sells."

"I don't give a fuck about the money!" Curtis shouted, stung into a genuine response.

"Mr. Law," Lloyd said, in a sing-song tone both bored and disapproving.

"I'm sorry," Curtis said, and looked at Inspector Hill. "I'm sorry," he repeated. "But the money doesn't come into it."

Lloyd let the chair down suddenly, making him jump. "Doesn't come into what?"

"My feelings for Rachel." Nice try, thought Curtis, but it didn't work.

"We know the paper was purchased in London on Sunday night," Lloyd said. "We have a security video which shows that you left Barton station at around half past twelve on Monday morning. And this was found in your house, Mr. Law. I am showing Mr. Law the cancelled return ticket from St. Pancras to Barton," he told the tape, and placed a plastic bag marked AM2 on the table. "The seat was reserved," he said. "Smoking, facing, on the eleven-thirty train. Which arrives in Barton at twelve-thirty in the morning," he added. "Give or take the odd cow on the line."

Curtis looked at it, then at Lloyd.

"It was in your expenses folder," he said.

"Perks," said Curtis.

"The person calling himself Mr. Bailey left the hotel to catch an eleven-thirty train from St. Pancras," Lloyd said. "Was that you?"

"Yes, it was me."

"Then are you trying to tell us that it isn't your paper? That this is not your crossword?"

They knew it was his paper, and it would take a handwriting expert two seconds to confirm that it was his printing in the crossword grid, his scribbled workings-out in the margins. "Yes," he said. "It's my paper. And I did buy it at King's Cross station on Sunday night. But I dropped it at the farm when I went up there on Monday morning, that's all." It was a lie, and it was barely spoken before it was spotted by Lloyd.

"If you already had the paper, why did you buy another one?"

"I hadn't got mine with me."

"Either of them?"

Curtis looked at him. "What?"

"You get it delivered to your home. And you'd bought one at King's Cross. Two newspapers. And yet you bought a third."

"I had to take my car in for a service," he said. "I had to meet Gary because he was giving me a lift into Harmston, and I knew I'd be leaving before the paper came. That's why I bought one in London. Because I like having it with me at work. There's a lot of hanging about."

"But then you didn't take it with you to work? Why not?"

Curtis shrugged.

"I think you didn't have it with you because you'd dropped it while you were stabbing Bernard Bailey," Lloyd said.

Inspector Hill took over then. "Someone tampered with the CCTV at Bailey's Farm," she said. "Someone ran the tape back thirteen minutes, and shortly afterwards, someone left. Someone who knew how to avoid the camera on the roadway. Someone who looked very like you."

Curtis shrugged again, and tapped his fingers quickly on the table for a moment or two, before taking another cigarette from the packet. They couldn't be certain it was him, not from the view he'd presented to the camera. They had to have more on him than that.

"We know you made an earlier visit to Bailey's farmhouse than the one you made at ten-thirty on Monday morning," Lloyd said. "Because you saw money in the safe, and that door was closed while you and your cameraman were in the house."

Curtis smiled. "You wouldn't dare use that," he said. "Your mates would swear black was white if it meant they could get back at me for *Mr. Big*."

198

Lloyd looked surprised. "You have a very high opinion of my popularity rating."

"No," said Curtis. "I have a very low opinion of your colleagues."

"There were Coca-Cola cans and cigarette ends found on the road outside Bernard Bailey's property," Inspector Hill said. "You know if they were yours, and we can find out. The cans have fingerprints on them, and we can have the cigarette ends tested. We can get a DNA profile from saliva."

"Then maybe you'd better do that," said Curtis.

"I think we'll leave you to think about the wisdom of that," Lloyd said, getting up. "Interview suspended, 20.55 hours."

Curtis was taken to the cells, and asked if he wanted a meal. He did; he hadn't had any lunch, and he was starving. This wasn't supposed to be happening, he thought, as his meal came, and he forced it down to give himself strength for the next session. But it was, and all he could do was try to keep Rachel out of it.

He sat back on the bunk when he had finished eating, and did what Chief Inspector Lloyd had suggested. He thought about it, thought about it hard, until they came for him again.

Lloyd listened and watched as Judy briskly reconvened. "Interview with Curtis Law resumed at 21.30 hours, Tuesday, twenty-ninth July," she said. "Present are . . ."

Curtis Law had been fed and watered, and given a rest from questioning. The book was being observed, page by page, paragraph by paragraph. There would be no suspicion of Law's treatment being other than exemplary. Now he was back, he was reminded of his rights, and he still didn't want a solicitor. Judy even advised him that he should reconsider that, but he refused.

Then she asked him if he had anything to tell them about Bernard Bailey's death, and he nodded, taking a moment before he spoke. When he did, his voice was quiet, and resigned.

"I spent the weekend with Rachel in London," he said. "The

199

last time I had been with her, she had had bruises, like she always did, because that bastard used his fists on her all the time, and that was bad enough. But there were other bruises. Old ones. All over her body. None on her face, or her neck, or her legs. Just her body, so that when she was clothed, nothing would show." He looked away from them, blinking away the tears that had sprung into his eyes. "Uncontrollable temper is one thing, but *that*—that was like some sort of torture, like the Gestapo or something."

That was exactly how Judy had described it, Lloyd thought.

Law got himself together before he carried on. "He had been going to do that to her again, and she had told him she was pregnant in order to stop him. When I left her on Sunday, I kept thinking what was going to happen when she went home. The baby should have begun to show, and it wasn't going to, was it? Bailey was certifiable, but he wasn't stupid. I bought a paper, caught the train, and tried to do the crossword to take my mind off it, but I couldn't, because I kept thinking about what he would *do* to her when he found out she wasn't pregnant."

Law had been directing his statement at Judy, but now he looked at Lloyd. "I just went there to tell him that I was in love with Rachel, and I was taking her away," he said. "I didn't mean to kill him. I didn't mean to do anything. I just wanted to tell him, so that she *couldn't* go home. She was determined to hang on, to divorce him, and get the money he owed her, but I couldn't let her do that. I had to make her leave him. Do you understand?"

"Yes," Lloyd said. "But you did kill him, didn't you?"

Law nodded.

"For the tape, please," said Judy.

"Yes," said Law. "I did kill him."

Lloyd wasn't doing his usual thing of taking a turn round the room, reading notices, standing on tip-toe to look out of the high window, wandering off to get coffee. He did that when he wanted to catch them out. But this was a confession. And a kind of hollow victory, because it had been so easy. He just

200

wanted it to be over. He still had a bit of a headache; he was tired, and thirsty, and fed up.

"When I got there, he was drunk. I mean, really, really drunk. I don't know how he made it to the phone. I said it was me, and he let me in, but I'm not convinced he really knew who I was. And I told him about me and Rachel. I told him everything. I told him I loved her, I told him I knew what he'd done to her, I told him I was taking her away—and do you know what he did?"

His mastery of the pause was almost up to Lloyd's own standard.

"He fell asleep on me. Just lay down on the sofa, and fell asleep. And I couldn't believe it. He hadn't even taken any of it in. That bastard had—"

Lloyd saw the tear fall before Law felt it; he flicked it away, and tried to go on, but he couldn't, not for a moment.

"Would you like a glass of water or something?" Lloyd said.

Law shook his head.

Pity. Lloyd did.

"I looked at him lying there, and . . . and I thought of what he'd done to her, and there was a knife on the table, so I picked it up and . . . and—I stuck it into him." He had mimed the action, and the tears came again, unchecked. "I don't know how often," he said. "Three, four times. Then I tried to cover up the fact that I'd been there."

Lloyd asked again if Law would like some water, and this time he nodded, thank God. He stood up. "I'll get us all some," he said.

"Chief Inspector Lloyd leaves the room, 21.43 hours," said Judy.

Lloyd went along to the water dispenser that thankfully they had had put in, though he had thought it a complete waste of money at the time. There was nothing wrong with the water out of the taps, he had said, he had yet to hear of a policeman dying because he'd drunk unfiltered water, they had much better things to spend their money on than quite unnecessary pieces of equipment, and so on. But the dispenser was much closer than the taps, the water was chilled, and tonight it tasted like wine, like the water from the streams at home had tasted. He smiled tiredly. He hadn't thought of that for years. He drank two cupfuls, wishing that they had put in an aspirin dispenser while they were at it, then filled three more, and made his way back to the interview room.

"You doctored the tape," Judy said. "Then what did you do?"

Law rubbed his eyes. "I let myself out of the house, threw the knife into the bushes, and I left the farm. I dodged the camera on the roadway—it's not difficult. But then I realized that I'd lost the newspaper, and I couldn't get back in to get it."

"Does that mean the alarms were on?" asked Judy.

"Yes," said Law. "Why wouldn't they have been?"

"No reason," she said, wondering if Finch had got to the bottom of Nicola Hutchins's strange story yet, as the door opened slowly, and she turned to see Lloyd carrying three paper cups of water, easing his elbow off the handle.

"Chief Inspector Lloyd returns, 21.50 hours," she said, getting up and relieving him of two of the cups, handing one to Law. "Go on," she said.

"Well, I had the idea about doing the crossword in my own newspaper where people could see me, and getting up to the farm somehow so it would look as though it was the one I'd dropped. But I realized I *couldn't* use my own paper, because Gary was picking me up. But he always goes to the café for breakfast when we're in Harmston, so I thought that if I could get another paper there, and if I could get to the farm once the news broke, I could try to make it look like I'd dropped it then."

Judy sipped her water, and made a note.

"When Paxton told us what had happened, I put the paper in my pocket, and when we got to the farm, I waited until Gary had got out of the car, and I hid it under the seat." He looked at Lloyd. "I went into the house after Gary, not before," he said.

"You were right. He went in there and pointed his camera straight at Bailey, and the newspaper. I didn't know he'd be filming everything."

Judy looked back through her notebook, at the places where she had put query marks.

"Why did you go to see Bernard Bailey at a time when you had every reason to suppose he would be in bed?" she asked.

"I . . . I wasn't thinking straight. I just wanted to stop Rachel going back to him. I wanted to get it over with."

"You wanted to get it over with? So why didn't you get there until twenty past two? It takes less than half an hour from Barton station to Harmston at that time of night."

"I got there at about one," Curtis said. "I sat in the car."

"Why? I thought you wanted to get it over with?"

He looked at her for a long time, then nodded. "All right," he said. "I meant just to talk to him. When I left Rachel, I didn't tell her what I was going to do, but I meant just to talk to him, maybe early in the morning, when Gary and I got there. But then I realized that I couldn't do that. She couldn't have gone home, and she would have lost her money. She would never have forgiven me."

"So you decided to kill him?"

"I don't know what I decided. Yes. Yes, I did. I thought if I could get him to let me in—I knew he had a shotgun somewhere, thought maybe I could get hold of it. So I drove out to the farm, and then I sat in the car trying to work up the courage to do it. And I emptied my ashtray because I smoked so much I couldn't get any more cigarette ends in there, and I didn't want to throw them out lit. It was so dry—I didn't want to be responsible for starting a forest fire or anything. And when I did finally get out and use his entry phone, I don't know how he managed to answer it. He let me in, but he was so drunk he couldn't stand up. He'd thrown up on the carpet and all over himself. I don't think he even knew who I was. He fell onto the sofa, and passed out. I saw the knife just sitting there, and I just—stabbed him with it."

"And you did intend killing him when you stabbed him?"

He nodded.

"For the tape, please, Mr. Law. Did you intend killing Bernard Bailey when you stabbed him?"

"Yes."

"Can you tell me why you left the hotel a day before Mrs. Bailey?" Judy asked.

"I had to. The first train on Monday morning wouldn't have got me back early enough to take my car in and be in time for Gary picking me up. So I got the last train on Sunday evening. She knew nothing about it. Nothing at all. The whole thing was my idea from the start."

"From the start?"

He closed his eyes, letting his head fall back.

"You didn't get this idea on the train, did you?"

"No," he said, his voice flat.

"This demonstration that was supposed to be taking place in Harmston on Sunday—you invented that, didn't you? So you and Rachel could go away for the weekend?"

"Yes." There was a pause, then he carried on. "I had to get Rachel away, so I could kill that bastard before he killed her." He brought his head up again, and sat forward. "I had to do it!" he shouted. "She wouldn't *leave* him. She couldn't take any more punishment like that, but she *would* have done. I swear, she thinks she's indestructible. She *knew* he was in financial difficulties, that he might have to sell before he realized she wasn't pregnant—*I* didn't! All I could see was someone who had no intention of selling, and who would beat her to a pulp when he found out she'd been lying to him! I had to do it. I *had* to!"

"And that's why you left the hotel and she stayed," said Judy. "So that you could kill him while she established an alibi by ringing room service in the middle of the night."

"No," he said. "Rachel knew nothing about it. Nothing at all."

Judy glanced at Lloyd, but he was deliberately staying out of

204

it, leaving it to her. He didn't want Rachel Bailey to be involved. He wanted her to do his dirty work. He'd done hers before now, and she didn't begrudge him the favour, but she hadn't much heart for it. Curtis Law and Rachel Bailey seemed to have done everyone something of a service.

"But you dropped your newspaper at the scene," she said. "And thought up the business with the other one. So you were in the café, conspicuously doing your crossword, when Steve Paxton got that call. How did you know Mrs. Bailey would call there?"

"I didn't," said Law.

Judy glanced through her notebook, saw the list of the contents of what the papers would undoubtedly call their love nest in Barton, and saw Lloyd's little puzzle about the mobile phone.

"Why did Mrs. Bailey ring room service at half past three in the morning?" she asked. "Was it because you had wakened her up? Because you phoned her to tell her what had happened?"

Judy was taking a Lloyd-like leap at this one. There had been no record of a phone call to Rachel Bailey at the hotel, but the mobile phone had been charged up, and there had to be some reason for that. Being apparently omniscient was sometimes all you needed for a confession, and it wouldn't hurt to try.

"You had left her the mobile phone in case you had to contact her, hadn't you?" she said.

Law covered his face with his hands, and there was a long silence. Judy prayed that the tape wouldn't give its audible warning that it was running out; it must be pretty nearly there by now. Hang on, she told it silently. Hang on. I've got him, I know I have.

"I rang her," he said eventually, from behind his hands. "I told her I'd killed him. I knew she'd told Bernard she'd be home by ten, and I knew Steve Paxton would be in the café then. I asked her to ring him. I know what he's like—I knew he would say what the call was about if I asked him, and that would give me the excuse to go up there."

"And she had the phone in case something went wrong, and you had to get in touch with her, didn't she?"

"Yes, but not the way you think. I told her that I was giving it to her because I wanted to be able to ring her whenever I liked without Bailey getting suspicious. But it was really because I didn't know what was going to happen once I got into the farmhouse. I didn't know if I'd be able to find his gun, or even if I could do it once I had. I gave it to her so I could be sure of getting hold of her. If Bailey knew about us I had to be able to tell her not to go home." He pulled his hands down his face, and looked at Judy. "But I did kill him, and she wouldn't have known anything about it at all, if I hadn't had to ring her about the paper."

"Planned murders really only work in books," Judy said. "Real life has a habit of getting in the way."

Lloyd terminated the interview as the warning sounded, and Law was led away to be charged with murder. Judy felt rather sorry for him, though Lloyd, not unnaturally, did not. And when they tried to pick up Rachel herself, who was, at the very least, an accessory after the fact, she had gone to ground. Now, why didn't that surprise her?

She felt a little weary as she and Lloyd said good-night, and got into their respective cars. She turned the key, and felt even wearier when she saw the petrol gauge; she had meant to fill up that morning on her way to work, but what with one thing and another . . .

She didn't even dare to try making for the nearest all-night petrol station; she must have been driving on the vapour as it was. She flagged Lloyd down as he tried to make good his escape.

"Leave it," he said. "We can sort it out in the morning."

"Do you believe Rachel Bailey had nothing to do with it until afterwards?" she asked, as he drove her home.

He sighed. "I don't know." Then he smiled tiredly. "But if that's her story, you can be sure she will stick to it."

Yes. She couldn't walk all over Rachel. Not even Bernard Bailey had been able to do that, because Rachel was as tough as the old boots in which she had spent her childhood. And she might be very good at summing up the flaws in her fellow man, but she was as paralysed with fear at the idea of returning to the poverty in which she had grown up as Nicola was of returning to the violence in which she had; Nicola had chosen Gutless Gus as insurance against it, and Rachel had chosen the pursuit of money.

"Where do you think she's gone?" she asked.

"Who knows?" said Lloyd. "But she'll turn up. She has to, if she wants to collect."

Judy frowned. "Will she collect?" she said. "If she's involved?"

"I'm not sure. I think she might. I'm sure she persuaded Law to do it, but possibly not overtly. I doubt if we could prove she helped plan it."

He was parking in the restricted zone. "You'll have to get up and move the car before eight if you're thinking of staying the night," she said.

He smiled. "I wasn't," he said. "For one thing, I have to change my clothes now and again, and for another, I've got a bit of a headache. I think I'll just go home, if you don't mind— I'll pick you up in the morning."

She smiled, too. "You don't have to make excuses," she said. "I wasn't thinking of jumping on your bones."

"I'm not making excuses! I've got a headache. But I would like to use your loo. I don't know how many cans of drink I've got through today. This weather gives me a thirst."

They were in the flat, in the hallway, and Lloyd was on his way to the bathroom, before she remembered. She went into the sitting room, telling herself that he had absolutely no reason whatever to open her bathroom cabinet, when she heard the loo flush, heard the question that followed a moment later.

"Have you got any aspirin in here?" he called. "I don't think I've got any at home. I can't remember the last time I had a—"

The unfinished sentence said it all. She sat down, and waited.

He appeared in the doorway, the box in his hand. "And are you?" he asked, his voice like ice.

"I don't know," she said. "I haven't done it yet."

"But you do know," he said. "Or you wouldn't have bought it." He came into the room.

She couldn't look at him. "I have all the symptoms."

"How long?"

"This is the second month I've missed."

"Then you really don't need this, do you? And when was I going to be let in on your little secret?"

"I was going to tell you!" she said. "I just—I just wanted to be sure."

"You *are* sure!" He sat down on her coffee table, and made her look at him. "Why didn't you tell me?" he asked.

She was so confused about the whole thing she hardly knew anymore why she had kept it secret. Because she had hoped she was mistaken, and she had known she wasn't, and she didn't know what she wanted to do about it.

"I wanted to be sure of how I felt," she said.

"How you felt," he said. "Of course, how *you* feel is so much more important, isn't it, than how *I* might feel."

"That's not fair."

"It's always you!" he said, his voice rising. "What *you* want to do, how *you* want to live, what *you* need, what *you* want. So *you* were going to decide what *you* wanted to do with *our* baby! Do you *ever* think of us as a couple?"

"Of course I do!"

"Well, you've a bloody funny way of showing it! And when you had decided you didn't want to keep it? What were you going to do then? I'd never have known, would I?"

"Yes! I didn't mean I wanted to—" She broke off, and

208

started again. "I just wanted to work out how I felt about it before I spoke to you, that's all!"

"Don't kid yourself, Judy! I'd have known nothing about it. That's why you didn't tell me. Because I've got no say in the matter."

"No!" she said. She had been trying to pretend that she wasn't pregnant, in the hope that it would all just go away, and she would never have to decide where she stood, but she had always been going to tell him, once she understood her own feelings. "This is what I was trying to avoid!" she said. "The last thing I need is you giving me a hard time before I even know what I want!"

"The last thing *you* need. Before you know what *you* want. To hell with what *I* need or want. Don't you think perhaps I need to know whether or not you want my baby?"

"Oh, Lloyd! It's not *like* that!" She certainly didn't want anyone else's. She just wasn't sure she could face having any baby. "Is it important to you that I do have it?" she asked.

"Oh, who cares? Certainly not you! Why break the habit of a lifetime and start worrying about what's important to me now?" He put the package down on the table, and stood up. "There you are," he said. "There seems very little point in doing it, but go ahead, if it makes you feel better. Let me know if you need any time off work."

The flat door slammed, and she heard his feet rattle down the stairs, heard the front door slam. Heard his car door slam. Heard the engine start up, heard it roar off, much faster than usual.

She walked out on rows, not him. She drove fast, not him. She had really hurt him this time, and that was the last thing she had meant to do.

# CHAPTER EIGHT

DETECTIVE CONSTABLE MARSHALL WAS A PLEAS-
ant, friendly Scot, with a delivery almost as slow as Rachel's,
and a face almost as anxious as Nell's, but every time a policeman, however unthreatening, walked up the path, Nicola was
certain that he had come for her. DC Marshall had come to tell
her that Curtis Law had been charged with her father's murder,
and it had taken her a moment to adjust to what he had said.

"Just Curtis Law?" she said, her heart beating a little too fast.

"We would like to interview one other person in connection
with the incident," he said, clearly being careful not to deviate
from the press release.

Rachel. It had to be.

Gus was hovering, as he always was at the start of the police
interviews; if events were to take a turn he didn't like, he would
be off like a shot. If she *had* told him about her father, he
would probably have left her sooner than actually do anything
about it.

"And we thought you ought to know that the post mortem
will be carried out on your father's body this morning," he said.

Nicola nodded briefly, then realized that the funeral hadn't
even crossed her mind. "Will his body be released after that?"
she asked. "For the funeral arrangements to be made?"

"It might be," said Marshall. "But there's a possibility that it
won't, now that charges have been brought. The defence might
want the chance to carry out their own post mortem."

He left, and she turned to go back into the surgery.

"Don't you think the funeral arrangements are Rachel's business?" Gus said.

"I don't know whose business they are," she said. "Rachel's boyfriend's been charged with his murder, and I don't think she'll be far behind. Even if she isn't, I doubt very much if she'll *attend* his funeral, far less arrange it."

Gus looked startled, as well he might. She had never snapped at him in her life. And she didn't even really mean all that. She was sure Rachel would discuss it all with her, if appropriate. But right now, it seemed singularly inappropriate.

"Nicky," Gus said slowly, almost unwillingly. "On Sunday your dad wouldn't leave the house, not for five minutes."

"What about it?"

"Well . . . Finch said yesterday, didn't he? That there was no record of him calling this number." He looked down.

Nicola had no urge to kiss the top of his head. "So?"

His head came up again. "Did he really ring you about a sheep?" he asked.

Nicola went through to the surgery. There was no need to answer; it didn't matter whether her father had or hadn't rung her about a sheep. What mattered was that Gus had asked.


"At last," Freddie said.

"Sorry I'm a bit late. I presumed you'd start without me." Lloyd always contrived to be a bit late. The actual opening ceremony was the one that got to him. Once Freddie was diving about with bits of body, he could just about take it. This morning, he wasn't sure he could take any of it.

"No, no, no!" said Freddie. "Not that! At last you have brought me one that Spilsbury himself would have smacked his lips over."

Freddie was happier than Lloyd had ever seen him, and Freddie was a man who was immensely happy in his work. That did not make Lloyd feel one jot better.

"Go on," he groaned.

211

"Well, the stab wounds didn't kill him. Neither did the barbiturates."

Barbiturates? Lloyd blinked at Freddie, beaming with pride and pleasure, enjoying every macabre moment, and he still hadn't got to the punch line.

"No," he went on, "what did for him was respiratory failure due to a massive overdose of morphine." He smiled even more happily. "Enough to see off a horse."

A lot of questions came into Lloyd's mind, but one more than any other. "How late for this post mortem am I?" he asked.

"Very late. I opened him up last night. Couldn't wait any longer."

"You mean," Lloyd said slowly, "like a child sneaking down to open his Christmas presents?"

"Yes," said Freddie, gloriously unaware of Lloyd's horrified reaction to what he had said. "Exactly. I knew he couldn't have died from loss of blood—well, I said so at the scene. And I thought maybe respiratory failure at the time, if you remember. But I said I thought it was odd. I asked if he was on medication, because he'd had the radiators on, which suggested that he had felt cold, and some morphine-based drugs will do that to you, if you've taken too much, and there were signs which suggested it might be that. But Judy said he wasn't on medication. Then when I had a good look at him back here, I saw the bruising on his jugular. I wondered about that, obviously, but I had to put him away. Then last night when I got back, I came here and opened him up, and that was when I found all the—"

"Don't," said Lloyd. Details he could not take, not after drinking so long and so late after he had reached home last night that he had got Tom Finch to pick him up this morning rather than drive into work. All he'd need would be to get breathalysed and lose his job before he was made redundant. It was only at the police station that he had remembered about Judy. She had arrived late; they hadn't spoken. He had picked up his car before coming here, on the grounds that the alcohol had had more than enough time to leave his system; he really hadn't had all that much. He had drunk long and late, but not particularly to excess. However, his head still ached, and his stomach was still just a little fragile, so perhaps his system knew better than he did just how much counted as excess.

Freddie smiled. "All right," he said. "No gory details. You look a bit rough, do you know that? Anyway, I know I should have told you I was doing it, but we've got this equipment now," he said, pointing above his head. "Videos the whole operation, so I thought—why bother Lloyd? He can watch it at his leisure and fast-forward through the really nasty bits."

Another bloody video. Literally bloody, this time. Lloyd felt as though he had spent his entire life watching videos. And indeed, that had, until this week, been his relaxation. Old films, old TV series, that sort of thing. But he thought that this case might spoil that innocent pleasure for life. Had it really only been yesterday that he had thought he might want to do it for a living?

He felt like death himself as he looked at Freddie, who was labelling some unspeakable specimen, and sighed. "And now that you *have* the pathologist's equivalent of a mountain bike with thirty-six gears, where does that leave the man we charged yesterday evening with murder?" he said.

Freddie sucked in his breath. "Stab wounds didn't kill him," he repeated. "I told you it was an odd one—you should have waited."

"Did they hasten his death?" asked Lloyd. "They must have, surely."

"No. Wounds like that, inflicted on someone in as robust good health as Mr. Bailey, not only wouldn't have killed him, they wouldn't have kept him in hospital. A pub brawl injury. He'd have been patched up and sent home. The worst one wasn't remotely life-threatening."

Lloyd rubbed his forehead. "But he wasn't in robust good health when he was stabbed," he said. "He had been pumped full of barbiturates and morphine and had been throwing up

213

and God knows what all. What happens if you stab someone in *that* condition?"

Freddie signalled for the singularly unfortunate Mr. Bailey to be wheeled away, and the hosing-down and cleaning-up operation began. "What happens," he said, "is that you make a number of unnecessary holes in his chest. The stabbing didn't make a blind bit of difference."

Lloyd didn't want to hear this. He really, really didn't want to hear this.

Freddie peeled off his gloves, and threw them in the bin. "If these wounds had been inflicted on someone who had not subsequently died, you'd have been looking at a charge of malicious wounding, at best, I'd say. Maybe attempted murder, in that I understand that to have been the intention, but the knife didn't go in far enough to do any real damage."

"You mean we're going to have to let him go?"

"I'm just the pathologist—I don't make the rules. I'm saying that your man stuck a not very sharp knife into his victim with a fair degree of force, but it didn't go in very far, largely because it was a very short knife, and the deepest wound, the one I thought might be serious when I examined him at the scene, was in no way life-threatening, because he didn't hit any vital functions, and the wound was not of itself serious. The stabbing did not contribute to Mr. Bailey's death, Lloyd. So unless he poisoned him as well . . ." He grinned. "I'd say Mr. Law's actions had nothing whatever to do with Mr. Bailey's demise."

Lloyd had rarely heard Freddie so definite about anything. He'd had Curtis Law up a dark alley quite legitimately, and now he was going to wriggle out of his grasp before he could deal with him, or his feelings about him. "So what did happen, and when?" he asked.

"Well," said Freddie. "The victim had consumed a considerable amount of alcohol. Then he was given a fast-acting barbiturate, and an overdose of morphine. I would suggest that the first was to facilitate the administering of the second—it was

214

the sort of dosage that your dentist might use for a tricky wisdom tooth. Put you out for twenty minutes or so. I imagine it was the one injected in the jugular, in order to induce immediate unconsciousness."

Lloyd nodded.

"It was done clumsily," Freddie went on, "thus producing the bruising that became evident when we were doing the preliminaries. He was injected subcutaneously with the morphine. The puncture mark is quite close to a vein, but if that was the intended target, it missed." He smiled broadly. "Then Mr. Law came and stabbed him," he said. "Not exactly a popular chap, I take it?"

"Does that make sense with what people have told us about his condition?"

"I don't know what everyone's told you. He would come round from the first injection, still far from sober, obviously, and fairly relaxed from the drug. Probably just lie wherever he was for ten or fifteen minutes, enjoying the sensation. As soon as that was wearing off, the morphine would begin to kick in, and he would appear to be very drunk indeed. He may have had a few minutes, no more, of something approaching whatever lucidity he had had to start with, given that he was drunk, but for the most part I don't suppose he knew what had hit him."

"Can you tell me when these injections would have been given, taking the time of death as, say, four o'clock?" asked Lloyd, and gave Freddie a run-down on the picture that had emerged.

Between eight-fifteen, when McQueen left him, and half past nine, when Melville saw him, Bailey had had a great deal to drink. He had then apparently rung his daughter at ten-thirty or so, and had sounded very drunk. She had called on him twenty minutes after that, but he had apparently gone out, and had not returned when she left an hour and ten minutes later. Curtis Law had called on him around two and a half hours after

215

that, had found him falling-down drunk, and had stabbed him after he had passed out on the sofa.

"Assuming the accounts are all accurate, and truthful," said Freddie, "then I'd say he'd been given the drugs between eleven o'clock and midnight, and went into a coma about three hours later, and died about two hours after that. If someone else isn't telling the gospel truth, which seems possible if one of them killed him, then it could well be, say, a couple of hours or so earlier than that, but not later, I don't think."

In other words, it happened when Curtis Law was on a train. They had issued a press release; Law was a media man, however obscurely regional, and the media had leapt on it. The press officer hadn't had time to blink. She had done interviews with all the news channels, issued statements to all the nationals. The idea of someone who had been reporting on a murder being charged with it had had considerable charm for the media.

Now, it would be POLICE IN MURDER CHARGE U-TURN, and they would waste no time in pointing out that the policeman in question had been the subject of a hard-hitting documentary made by none other than Curtis Law. He would have the top brass demanding explanations, he would have more embarrassing encounters with the press, if he was allowed to speak to them at all, and no chance of keeping his job come Judy's triumphant return to Stansfield as a DCI.

And he wondered if that was why, deep down inside, he had been so horrible to her last night. He had wondered that as he had sat up drinking, telling himself how selfish she was. She *was*, but he wasn't sure that was what had made him say those things. He wished he'd stayed in bed this morning. He wished he hadn't been so eager to charge Law and get home last night. He stepped out into the corridor, and used his new toy to tell Case the current situation prior to Law's intended magistrates' court appearance, and to cancel the warrant for Rachel Bailey's arrest. Then, his ears still ringing with Case's colourful reaction to the news, he went back in to Freddie.

"If Mr. Bailey was given these injections somewhere other than his own house, it surprises me that he found his way back again," said Freddie.

One of these people was there between eleven o'clock and midnight, and would have had the means, Lloyd supposed, though he knew very little about animal doctoring, the opportunity, if Bailey *had* been there, and a motive going back to infancy. And she was the only one who said he hadn't been at home, which Freddie was now indicating in a Freddie-like fashion was probably untrue. She was the one who had told a story about an injured sheep that no one knew anything about.

"Would someone used to handling a hypodermic have made a botch of giving the injections?" he asked.

"It's possible. I don't imagine Mr. Bailey wanted to be knocked unconscious, so he may well have caused the bruising to the vein himself with his reaction to what was happening. And just a shaking hand could have caused the needle to miss the vein with the next one. Or someone could have wanted it to look amateurish, of course. Or possibly it just *was* an amateur."

Very good. Very decisive. Thank you, Freddie. But Nicola Hutchins had some questions to answer. Her father had not called her from the farm, and according to everyone they had spoken to, he didn't seem likely to have called her from anywhere else, because he had refused to leave the house on Sunday, for fear that someone would be waiting to get him. Which didn't sit well with her contention that he was out and the alarms were off when she went there. Why would he have gone out? Why would he have put the alarms off if he was leaving the house unattended, even if he was drunk? And when would he have put them on again if he was drugged up to the eyeballs into the bargain? He asked Freddie his opinion on that.

"I can't see him having much interest in alarms," said Freddie. "But what I can tell you is that his keys were in his shirt pocket when he was stabbed, and stayed there. The blood was entirely undisturbed. Since the alarms were set when we got there, then they were set when Bailey was stabbed."

"Doesn't that mean they must have been set all along?" asked Lloyd.

"Well, in theory, what his daughter says is possible. That he switched the alarms off, went looking for the sheep, came back, switched them on again, and only then was given the overdose. Or his assailant switched them on again before he or she left. But whoever killed him would have had to get in without either Bailey or his daughter or any of the cameras seeing them."

"And once the alarms were on, would have had to leave by the gate and would have been recorded doing so on the video," said Lloyd. "And she's the one we've got doing that at the material time. I don't think the alarms were ever off. That was just to explain how this sheep had got out without waking everyone in northern Europe. And if it did, the alarms would have had to be off in the first place, which I'm sure they weren't."

They had been looking at all the wrong things. Checking on all the wrong times. They were going to have to start all over again, and Lloyd didn't think he could, in his hungover condition.

Freddie cleaned up, removed his protective clothing. "It's almost lunchtime," he said. "Fancy a hair of the dog at the Dog and Hare?"

"The Dog and Hare?" Lloyd said. "Is that for real?"

"One of these new-fangled pubs with pseudo, would-be witty old-fashioned names," Freddie said. "I'll bet it took them months to decide which way to spell hare. They settled for the animal in the end—makes for easier graphics on the pub sign. But they do reasonable bar snacks."

Lloyd didn't think he could face a bar snack, however reasonable it was. Or a hair of the dog. But he didn't want to go back to the station either. He still didn't want to speak to Judy and he wasn't sure if it was because he was still angry with her, or because he felt ashamed. And if he felt ashamed, that was just her all over, wasn't it? It was always his fault. He always

218

ended up apologizing, and why should he? She had had no right not to tell him. None.

"Yes, why not?" he said, and rubbed his temple. "Any chance of some aspirin?" he asked.

"Oh, God, there's a six-week waiting list for aspirin in hospitals," said Freddie. "Have a snifter. Much better for you."

The walk to the Dog and Hare cleared his head a little; he ordered lager for Freddie, and a malt whisky, which he stared into while Freddie ate his reasonable bar snack.

"It's not this investigation that's got you like this," said Freddie. "Or that ridiculous programme the other night. Or your hangover. My guess—wild though it might be—is that poor Judy's in the doghouse again, and you feel guilty for putting her there."

Lloyd looked at him coldly, unable to admire the accuracy of his diagnosis. "I know you think the sun rises and sets on her," he said. "But she—"

"So do you," Freddie pointed out, interrupting him.

"Yes, all right! But she is the most monumentally selfish—" He broke off when he saw Freddie smile. "What's funny?"

"I trained as an ordinary, regular, everyday physician, you know," said Freddie. "I was even in general practice for a while."

Lloyd was a little surprised at the sudden apparent change of subject, which wouldn't, of course, be a change of subject at all. "So I believe," he said. "Until you discovered the joys of forensic medicine. What's that got to do with the price of fish?"

Freddie smiled. "And at one point I went on a psychology course," he said. "Designed to make us better GPs."

Lloyd grunted, unsure of where this conversation was going.

"I've forgotten most of it," Freddie said. "My patients these days tend to need very little psychoanalysis." He smiled again. "But part of it was about two-person relationships. Father-son, mother-daughter, brother-sister . . ." He paused. "Couples," he said.

219

"I hope you're not thinking of psychoanalysing *me*," said Lloyd.

"No. Couldn't if I wanted to. But—one thing they told us stuck in my mind. They said that in every close relationship there was the lover, and the beloved."

Lloyd looked at him suspiciously, not sure if he was being serious.

"The lovers," Freddie said, "pack their bags and go to Australia whether they want to or not, because their beloveds want to go." He drained his glass. "The lovers turn down fantastic jobs in Australia because the beloved *doesn't* want to go."

That sounded familiar enough. He *was* being psychoanalysed. Or being set up for some unfunny Freddie-type humour. Lloyd looked away.

"You're the lover, Lloyd," said Freddie. "Judy is the beloved. You fall in with her wishes, just like Anthea falls in with mine."

Lloyd had never heard Freddie utter his wife's name before. My wife, the wife, the missus, my better half, 'er indoors—that was how he had always referred to Anthea as long as Lloyd had known him. Freddie *was* being serious. He looked back, a little reluctantly.

"She's put up with me doing this job for twenty years," Freddie said. "And she hates it. Oh, she grumbles, like you. Says I'm selfish, I only think about myself—all that. Says she's got a good mind to leave me—nearly did, last year. Well, you know that."

"But she didn't," said Lloyd, picking up his whisky, tossing it back, in true hair-of-the-dog style. "Did she?"

"No." Freddie stood up, picked up the empty glasses, and went to the bar, getting a second round.

"Not for me. To tell you the truth, I'm a bit thirsty. I'll have a mineral water." Lloyd thought about what Freddie had said as he watched him automatically flirt with the barmaid. That, presumably, was something else Anthea put up with, he thought, as Freddie returned with the drinks. "And you *knew* she wouldn't leave you," he said, taking a deep, refreshing draught.

Freddie shook his head as he sat down. "I didn't know any—thing of the sort," he said. "That's the problem. I don't know where the line's drawn."

"What makes you think she does?" asked Lloyd. He had no idea what Judy would have to do to make him sever the relationship.

"I *don't* think she does. I think she'll only know if I ever overstep it. And by then, it'll be too late." He smiled. "We beloveds don't really have it all our own way. We spend a great deal of time worrying about whether what we've just done, more often than not in all innocence, is going to spell the end."

Judy had said once that she felt as if she were walking a tightrope, Lloyd reflected, then smiled at himself for taking Freddie's bargain-basement psychology seriously. "What happens if you get two lovers?" he asked. "Or two beloveds?" Freddie was always chatting up Judy—where did that fit in to his theory?

"You don't," he said. "It's not like star signs. The beloved in one relationship might be the lover in another. Or it changes as we develop. Children tend to be beloveds, the parents lovers. Then that can turn on its head as the children become adults and the parents become old." He picked up his drink. "Lover and beloved," he said, and grinned. "That's what leads to granny flats and golden weddings." His face became serious again. "Or old-folks' homes and murder," he added. "It depends where the lover draws the line."

He was talking about Curtis Law. And he *had* murdered for Rachel Bailey, or thought he had, which was the same thing. Lloyd thought about that. Would he murder for Judy? Where *did* he draw the line? Freddie was right. He had no idea, so how could she? He supposed he would draw the line at murder, un-like Law. But not because she hadn't told him she was preg-nant, certainly not. That wouldn't make him *leave* her. She

221

wouldn't be thinking that, would she? That he would end it because of that?

He was beginning to think that it had perhaps not been entirely selfish anyway. She was worried. Frightened. She hated anything being different from the way she was used to. She was just being Judy, and he had overreacted. He always did. But he didn't want her doing anything rash because she thought he had taken terminal offence.

He stood up, and finished his water. "Thanks," he said, putting down the empty glass. "For everything."

He had thanked Freddie for giving him unasked-for advice on his relationship with Judy. This had to be the weirdest week he had ever lived through.

Mike had done it right second time around. Then he had slept for twelve solid hours, opening his eyes to discover Rachel looking down at him, smiling. He smiled back, and reached out a hand, touched her golden hair.

"We got to talk," she said.

"You were talking, pet. All the time."

"What was I sayin'?"

"As if you didn't know." He had been a young man again with her. He had wondered, during the months of longing for her, if Rachel could really deliver all that she promised. And when he had decided to find out, it had been going to be a one-night stand. But now that she had fulfilled that promise and more, he fully intended taking her up on her huskily whispered offers to make it a more permanent arrangement if that was what he wanted. "You suggested I might want more of this," he said.

"And do you?" She knelt astride him, smiled down at him.

"Yes."

"Good."

"But I think you hope you can up the price," he said.

She shook her head. "I'll settle for what you were offerin' Bernard."

222

"You'll settle for the market value."

"You were offerin' Bernard four times that much for it," she said, bending to kiss his lips briefly, tantalizingly.

He put his hands on her thighs. "That was when it was Bernard's land," he said. "It's yours now."

She nodded. "Reckon it's a seller's market now," she said, her mouth on his again. "You want to haggle, is that it? Gypsies are good at hagglin'. Start me off."

"The market value," he repeated.

"If you had to go through that wood it'd cost you a lot more'n that." She pulled her head back, and smiled at him. "You'll have to up your offer," she said. "Or how can we bargain?"

He shook his head.

She sat back. "You go through that wood and you'd get protestors and I don't know what-all down here. Lyin' down in front of the excavators. Vandalizin' the equipment, holdin' up the work. Whole village'd turn on you. Wouldn't've been so bad when you'd no option, but now . . ." She shrugged. "The protestors might even get the road stopped, if I'm willin' to sell my land for the same price you were offerin' Bernard," she said, smiling. "Not like I've doubled the stakes nor nothin'. So you goin' to make me an offer?"

He shook his head again.

The smile grew a little uncertain. "Aren't you supposed to haggle too?" she asked. "You're not offerin' nothin'. So how can I?"

"I've *made* my offer."

"But the market value's no good to me. Loan company'd have it all, and I'd still owe them money. Wouldn't be able to pay off nothin' else. I'd lose everythin' I got." She looked thoughtful. "I'll settle for three-quarters of what you were offerin' Bernard."

"No deal."

"Two-thirds."

"No deal."

223

"Can't go no lower than that. Lower'n that, and you can't have no more of this."

"Oh, I think I can have more," Mike said. "But you can't. It's the market value, take it or leave it."

He watched her realize that this wasn't some teasing game, watched her face grow serious. "How much do you reckon it'd cost you to go through the wood?" she asked. "I'll settle for that."

"I won't have to go through the wood."

"You will if I won't sell."

"If you won't sell, the land will be repossessed."

"The loan company'll know how bad you need it," she said. "They won't settle for the market price. Pay me what you'd pay them. That way you don't lose nothin', and I get to keep somethin'. And you'd get me into the bargain," she said, and smiled, her eyes mischievously bright. "Loan company won't cap that."

"It would indeed be a bargain," said Mike. "Except that I *am* the loan company."

And for once, Rachel Bailey had nothing to say.

He smiled at her. "If someone's offering a free gift, I take it. I'm a businessman, pet."

"You're a bastard," she said quietly.

"That too." He sighed, stroked her thighs. "You worked hard for months making me desperate to screw you," he said. "And now I have."

She looked at him, nodding slightly. "Reckon you have," she said, her voice slow and easy and gentle. She made to get off him, but he kept his hands where they were, and she sat back down again.

"And if you want a roof over your head, you'll let me go on screwing you," he said. "Because if you don't, by the end of the week I guarantee you'll be homeless and penniless."

She was listening.

"I'm prepared to let you keep the house. And a bit of land. From what you were telling me last night, you should be able

224

to run a smallholding. It won't be much of a one, with an access road going right past it, but maybe you can do pick-your-own strawberries or something. How you make your living isn't my concern. How you pay the rent is."

"I want it done legal," she said, "So you can't throw me out when your wife catches on."

He smiled. "I'll arrange for us to see my solicitor this afternoon," he said. "And you'd better hope that my wife doesn't catch on, pet, or you'll have to start finding money for the rent. I'll throw you out quickly enough if you get behind on that. But then, you know that. I'm a bastard, remember?"

She nodded again, and got out of bed, pulled on her non-existent dress, and left. He watched her walk barefoot down his driveway, then break into a run.

He had Bailey's land, but he had lost his gamble just as surely as Rachel had lost hers. Still, he had got what he wanted out of her, if not her husband, and he had kicked over the domestic traces for the first time in his life. He'd be smoking cigars in the lounge next. He smiled. Rachel Bailey's lounge, at any rate. *And* he could call it a lounge without being corrected, into the bargain.

Curtis left court relieved and thankful to be no longer facing a murder charge, but thinking angrily of what a fool he'd made of himself in front of Lloyd. He'd almost cried when he had described Rachel's bruises; he had broken down altogether when he'd told them about how he'd felt, standing over Bailey, the knife in his hand. All the emotion had come rushing back, and had overwhelmed him. Because he had enjoyed sticking a knife into Bernard Bailey, and that had disturbed him more than he liked to admit, even to himself, never mind to them. The physical contact, the feeling that he was hurting him, the little shivers his body had made as the blade had gone in. He'd enjoyed that. He had wanted to hurt Bailey for all the hurt he'd done Rachel.

He hadn't enjoyed being told how foolish he had been, and

how lucky he was not to be facing prison, by Finch, of all people. And he wasn't going to enjoy the next thing he had to do either. He didn't suppose it mattered to Rachel who had killed Bailey, but it mattered to him.

And now he was going to have to tell her that he hadn't killed him after all.


"McQueen's just confirmed that the road to the so-called Rookery won't be going through the so-called Bluebell Wood," Jack told Terri as she came into the sitting room, rather surprised that she had chosen to join him at all.

"Good," she said, shortly. "Have you heard the news?"

"Real news or village news?" he asked.

"Both. They've arrested the TV reporter for Bailey's murder."

Jack blinked. "The *TV* reporter?" he repeated. "Why on earth would he want to kill Bailey?"

"Well, rumour has it that he was getting rather more out of his visits to Bailey's Farm than just a good story."

Oh, God. Now how was he supposed to react? The jealous lover? The indifferent philanderer? His reaction was that of the totally confused liar who had finally run out of ingenuity. "People are bound to assume that, I suppose," was what he eventually came up with. It was true. For all they knew the TV reporter was a homicidal maniac, and had had nothing whatever to do with Rachel Bailey. But he doubted it.

"And there's something else," she said. "Mrs. Day had a bit of news as well that might concern you."

She was enjoying this, whatever it was.

"Jim Day does Mike McQueen's garden," she said. "And when he came home for lunch, he told Mrs. Day that he'd found frilly panties and a pair of women's sandals under McQueen's garden table."

Jack smiled. "Well, well, well," he said. "Who needs the fleshpots of Soho when they can have Harmston?"

"Who needs the fleshpots of Soho when they can have Rachel Bailey, you mean," said Terri. "Guess who he saw

226

leaving the house before McQueen had come down for breakfast? With nothing on her feet. I don't know if he was in a position to check up on what other items of her wardrobe were missing."

She had been with Mike McQueen as well? She had been quite explicit. Married men were out, she had said, and he had believed her. But that had been for his benefit alone, presumably, because no one was more married than Mike McQueen, and he was more than thirty years older than Rachel, for God's sake. And was he, who had only yesterday concocted an entire history for his love affair with Rachel Bailey, the only man in the county who hadn't actually slept with her?

"And there's some story about money that's supposed to have gone missing from Bailey's safe," Terri went on. "The police practically accused Steve Paxton of stealing it, and he walked out on her, saying she'd put the idea into their heads. So your girlfriend's lost her foreman. She can't have offered *him* her favours, presumably, so that might be some consolation to you."

Jack wasn't listening. If the money in the safe was an issue in Bailey's murder, then it was relevant, and he wasn't going to get away with this for very much longer.

"I don't imagine for a moment there ever was any money in the safe," said Terri. "It's probably something she and her TV reporter cooked up between them to try to make it look like a burglary, or whatever. Bailey was completely broke, wasn't he?"

"Mm," said Jack.

"And she was spending money he didn't have and sleeping with everyone who crossed her path," Terri said. "I'm not surprised he was threatening to kill her. But it looks as though she had other ideas."

Things were going from intolerable to impossible, and his tangled web was unravelling itself faster than he could keep weaving it.

\* \* \*

227

"You look terrible."

"Thanks. I had a drop too much consolation last night."

Judy felt guilty. Lloyd obviously hadn't had any more sleep than she had; for once, her ability to crash out and let the world take care of itself had deserted her. But he was used to sleepless nights, and to the odd bit of over-enthusiasm for malt whisky. It didn't usually make him look like that. *She'd* done that to him, and she felt awful about that.

He hadn't picked her up that morning, and had avoided her when she had finally arrived. He was here now only because he had to be, because they had to discuss the now complicated Bailey business. She had to grab her chance, in the hope that it hadn't gone for good. "I know we don't discuss these things at work," she said. "But I really didn't mean to upset you. And I *was* going to tell you."

He nodded. "I know," he said. "I just let rip as usual. Ignore me."

She couldn't, and he knew it. Because she never knew which bits were true. But the row, if that was what it had been, was over, and she felt a huge wave of relief wash over her.

He massaged his forehead. "You don't have any aspirin, do you?" he asked.

"No, sorry."

"Oh, well," he said. "I suppose that'll teach me to wrap myself round a whisky bottle."

Judy frowned a little. "You had a headache before you did that," she said.

"Well, it didn't make it any better." He sat on her desk. "I suppose you and I should go and have a chat with Nicola Hutchins," he said. "Enough morphine to kill a horse, was Freddie's expression, and I don't think that was just a figure of speech."

Judy agreed that they certainly should, having regard to all the strange circumstances. "Though we do know that two other people were there before her," she said. "And Freddie says it

228

could have happened earlier. I have to say I can't see Nicola Hutchins having the guts to do it."

"I can't see her immediate motive," said Lloyd.

They had now seen Bernard Bailey's will, and, as Rachel had told Lloyd, Nicola was specifically excluded. There were some bequests to animal charities which wouldn't now be paid out, and the residue went to his wife in its entirety. That may have upset Nicola at the time, but it seemed unlikely that she would murder the man twenty months later as a result of that slight. And it meant that belief of monetary gain was out. Still, life-long abuse had to be regarded as a motive, even if they didn't know what had lit the touchpaper.

"You know what?" Lloyd said, as they got into his car, though hers had been refuelled and she had offered to chauffeur him. "I can't help feeling as though someone's pulling our strings."

"Who?"

"You'll only say I'm paranoid."

"Curtis Law was on a train," said Judy.

"But Rachel Bailey wasn't. Where was she between eleven and twelve? Nicola Hutchins said she thought Rachel was there with her husband. And perhaps she was. Perhaps Law was at the hotel on his own when he took his taxi to St. Pancras."

"She also said that she thought Bailey had been hitting Rachel, and I seem to remember that according to you, she has no bruises."

"Nicola was guessing about that!"

"She was guessing about the whole thing. Or lying." Judy looked at him seriously. He'd asked her if she loved him enough to tell him, and she did. "Have you really not crossed Rachel Bailey off?" she asked. "And if not, why not? Because you fancy her and you're overcompensating, because you're being paranoid about her boyfriend, or because you seriously think she poisoned her husband?"

Lloyd sighed. "Because I'm quite certain that she was involved right from the start in her boyfriend's attempt to murder

229

her husband. And because I don't believe Law just happened to pick a night when someone else chose to murder him."

"It was the first time he had been alone in the house for months," Judy said. "The wonder is that more people weren't trying to kill him, if you ask me."

"True," he said, and smiled. "But young Mr. Law did have access to drugs of the kind used."

"Not as ready access as Nicola Hutchins," said Judy. "And you're not telling me that McQueen couldn't lay his hands on drugs any time he wanted. Come to that, Mrs. Melville is a known associate of a convicted drug dealer, so her husband has a contact."

"Quite," said Lloyd. "Which is why I'm not leaping to the conclusion that Mrs. Hutchins murdered her father. And as to your other points," he went on, "I'm glad that Rachel Bailey isn't on a murder charge. *That's* because I fancy her, and I am possibly overcompensating by still including her on my list of suspects." He sighed. "And yes, I wish her boyfriend still was on a murder charge. That's because I'm paranoid. And I'm not crossing anyone at all off. That's because I'm a very, very good detective."

She smiled. "You'll do," she said.

This time, Lloyd did the talking, while she took notes, and watched Nicola Hutchins as she and her husband were told that Curtis Law had been released and the charges withdrawn.

"What about Rachel?" she said.

"I can't discuss any other aspect of this inquiry with you," said Lloyd. "But I can tell you that I have a search warrant." He took it out, and gave her a copy. "I am going to instruct my officers to check your drug supply, and your treatment records. I understand that you do have to keep a book with regard to certain of your drugs."

Nicola at last realized that Lloyd was questioning her as a suspect, and her eyebrows rose high on her forehead. "And you think *I* drugged him?"

Judy was making notes. She indicated the stress, which seemed to her to be on the wrong word.

"Well," said Lloyd, "it's much too early to say that we think anything that positive. But your father died as a result of an overdose of drugs. You were at the farm at the material time, and you do have access to the drugs involved, which were a fast-acting barbiturate and morphine or a morphine-derivative. A hypodermic needle was found on the road outside your father's property, and contains the residue of the drugs used. It is one which is just as likely to be used by vets as by anyone else. You do see, don't you, that you are rather bound to come under suspicion?"

"You think I murdered him."

Gus Hutchins got up and walked out. Nicola hardly seemed to notice, as she launched into her story once again. "My father rang me about a sheep," she said, "and I went there to ask him where it was. He wasn't there. I waited for him, and when he didn't come back, I left."

Judy noticed it again. Always, always, that slight hesitation before her repeated declaration that she had waited for him, and then she had left. If you listened to lies for a living, you got pretty good at spotting them, and Judy would swear that that was a lie.

"If I'd been going to murder my father, I'd have done it years ago," Nicola went on. "And why would I have used morphine *and* barbiturates? Why wouldn't I just use the barbiturates? They don't have to go in the book. Besides, I'm not the only one with access to drugs, am I? Rachel's boyfriend was showing his haul off on television on Monday night. He seems to be able to get whatever he wants whenever he wants it."

Judy saw Lloyd colour slightly. There was a strange bravado about Nicola Hutchins this morning that she hadn't seen before.

"But he wasn't there at the material time, Mrs. Hutchins," Lloyd said. "You were."

"But I thought *she* was," said Nicola. "Rachel. That's why I thought he'd been hitting her, and she'd got away from him.

231

I . . . I thought he'd gone after her." She looked puzzled. "But he hadn't," she said. "And she was in London, wasn't she? I don't understand. I didn't murder him."

"What made you think Mrs. Bailey was there?" Lloyd asked.

Nicola had a visible argument with herself before she answered Lloyd's question. "Because I saw her car," she said eventually. "I saw it driving away as I was coming up to the farm gate."

Rachel was more bewildered, more confused, more afraid than she had been at any time. "What do you mean?" she said, for the umpteenth time.

"I mean what I said." Curtis sighed. "I didn't kill him."

"But . . . but I saw him! He was dead. You'd stabbed him!"

Curtis put his arm round her, and sat her down in an armchair. "But that isn't what killed him," he said. "Something else did."

"What else?"

"I don't know. They didn't tell me. They just said that I hadn't killed him, and they dropped the charges and let me go."

He held her close, kissing her, telling her everything was all right, explaining it all to her again. She understood, for God's sake. She understood that *he* had been eliminated from their inquiries. But she also understood, which he didn't seem to, that she hadn't.

"I know," he said. "That's why I'm here. I think they'll be asking you more questions, and it's important you know what to say if they do."

"Why?" said Rachel, jumping immediately on the inconsistency. "Why, if we never had nothin' to do with how he died?"

Curtis smiled. "Stop doing this to yourself," he said. "Stop worrying. I just think it's best if we keep things simple. If our stories don't tally, then they *will* keep badgering you, because I don't suppose he died of natural causes. If they're still looking

232

for a murderer, you'll still be the prime suspect, because of the land."

Rachel pulled away from him. "But you said we didn't kill him!"

"We didn't. But I'm sure someone did. And I think the police will ask you more questions. I didn't tell them the whole truth, and I think it's important that you know what I did tell them, so that they don't start suspecting you all over again." He looked at her shamefacedly. "Because the way things have turned out, I've got an alibi, and you haven't."

Oh, great. He'd left her up the creek without an alibi. "You mean I'm going to end up in prison for somethin' someone else did," she said miserably.

"No, I don't. But I thought I was going to get done for murder, and I lied to them about how much you knew. You have to know what I said to them so they don't get suspicious, that's all." He clasped her hands. "Trust me."

How could she? She had thought he could run rings round the police, and he'd got himself arrested within thirty-six hours. Now it turned out he hadn't even done it right. The tears began to fall.

"Don't," Curtis said, squeezing her hands. "I'll tell you what to tell them, and you'll get them off your back, I promise. Will you trust me?"

She didn't have much option. She nodded.

"Good." He let go of her. "Wipe your eyes, and listen carefully."

She listened carefully. She was good at that. She had listened carefully to Bernard as he had explained the simple job she had to do, and the enormous amount of money she would get for doing it. She had listened carefully to every warm-weather word that had been uttered in Bernard's study ever since the day McQueen had walked in here with his offer. She had listened carefully to Curtis's story about Mr. Big, told to her in strictest confidence and in the hope of a quick shag as a result. She had listened carefully to Bernard's threats as he had

233

beaten her half to death, to Curtis's horror when he had seen the faded results of that beating, to his offer to get rid of Bernard for her, to his plan for doing it. She had listened carefully to Curtis making Lloyd look stupid on that programme. But he *wasn't* stupid. She had known then that it would all go wrong, and it had.

"Have you got that?"

She nodded.

"Good girl." He smiled encouragingly. "You shouldn't have to be doing any of this," he said. "But I thought they'd got me, I really did."

They *had* got him. It was just because he hadn't done it right that he had got off, and she was supposed to trust him. Rachel tried to stop her lower lip from trembling as the tears came again. She had refused to cry when Bernard Bailey had been using her as a punchbag what seemed like every other day; she had refused to scream with pain when he had been digging the heel of his shoe into her already swollen and bruised ribs, trying to make her do just that. Why cry now, when she was rid of him, and had done a deal with McQueen which at least kept the roof over her head?

Because prison hadn't been staring her in the face, that was why. She had begged Curtis not to leave on Sunday night; she had known it could never work. He had been too sure of himself, too cocky.

"I've got to go," Curtis said apologetically. "See if I've still got a job." He smiled, his face tired. "I'm famous now, all right," he said.

It had been all over the morning news, even the real news. Pictures of the farm, and of Curtis interviewing her and Bernard. And a voice saying, *"Charged: the man who reported on the stabbing to death of this Bartonshire farmer is accused of his murder."* They liked it being one of their own, the ghouls.

*"Will* they sack you?" she asked.

"Maybe. But I'm not being charged with anything after all,

234

so . . . I don't know." He smiled. "It might even be good for ratings. The police jumped the gun—I can maybe make out Lloyd was out to get me because of *Mr. Big*."

Oh, God. She didn't want him trying to be clever, not with Chief Inspector Lloyd. She didn't want an angry Lloyd on her back. He'd been angry when he came to arrest Curtis, and he'd be angrier still now. "Don't, Curtis," she said, tears spilling down her cheeks. "Just let it be."

"Why? He *did* jump the gun."

"And you *did* stab Bernard!" she sobbed. "Don't push your luck, Curtis, please. It's my luck, too."

She allowed herself to be pecked on the cheek, and went with him to the door, watching him drive away. Then she went back into the sitting room, leaving the door open, sat down on the armchair, and cried. But the tears went when she heard the knock at the door; confident, official. A policeman's knock. And she didn't cry in front of them.

She went to the open door to find Chief Inspector Lloyd and Inspector Hill. "You let him go," she said.

"Yes," said Lloyd. "May we come in, Mrs. Bailey?"

"Sure." She followed them in. "Take a seat," she said, and the inspector sat down, looking elegant and cool as she took out her notebook. He still stood, looking hot and bothered and a bit flushed. But he wasn't angrier than ever. He wasn't angry at all.

"Mrs. Bailey," he said. "I owe you an apology for the remark made by one of the officers yesterday afternoon. There was no excuse for his behaviour, or for mine in failing to reprimand him. I should have asked him to apologize to you in person, but I hope you can accept my apology from both of us."

Rachel smiled at the little speech. She hadn't been wrong about him after all. "Sure," she said. "It's all right. Sit down. Can I get you somethin'?" she asked. "Lemonade again?"

"Oh, yes, please," said Lloyd.

"Thank you," said Inspector Hill.

Rachel looked at Lloyd again. "Lots of ice," she promised him, as she departed for the kitchen.

This was like some sort of dream. They'd arrested Curtis, and Lloyd had behaved like a cop, ordering Curtis about, ordering her about, letting that bastard get away with saying he wouldn't mind giving her one. Now Curtis was out, and they were here, Lloyd back to being polite and courteous and even apologetic. It didn't make any sense.

She returned with a tray of drinks, and the jug, which she left close to Lloyd. "Help yourself to more when you want it," she said, and sat down with her own drink, putting it on the coffee table when she realized her hands were shaking.

"Curtis says I could've got done for murder just 'cos I rang Steve," she said.

"It could have been regarded as aiding and abetting," said Lloyd. "As it is, there won't be any charges. Not as far as the stabbing is concerned."

Rachel frowned. She still couldn't quite work out why. "How come you're not chargin' us with nothin'?"

"Because he didn't die from what Mr. Law did, and we can't charge someone with maliciously wounding someone else who died before he could bring a complaint against anyone," said Inspector Hill.

Rachel nodded. "But that don't make what we did right."

"No," said Lloyd. "But in effect, it never happened at all as far as the law is concerned." He helped himself to more lemonade, and sat back. "Mrs. Bailey, can I ask where you were at ten to eleven on Sunday night?"

That wasn't any of the questions Curtis had said they might ask. "You know where I was," said Rachel. "At the hotel."

"No," said Lloyd. "I know you were there at half past three on Monday morning, when you rang for room service. But I don't know you were there late on Sunday evening. Did anyone see you there?"

That was what Curtis had meant about her not having an

236

alibi. "No," she said. "We ate in the room, and then after Curtis left, I just stayed in the suite. Why do you want to know that?"

"Because," said Lloyd, "Mrs. Hutchins says that when she called here at ten to eleven on Sunday night, she saw your car driving away from the farm."

Rachel frowned. "Nicola said that?"

Lloyd nodded.

Rachel shook her head. "She wouldn't say that. It's not true."

"She seemed very certain."

What was going on? They must have frightened her somehow. "She said what you wanted to hear, that's all," said Rachel. "She's like that."

"We didn't suggest it."

"But it's not true. You don't know her," Rachel said. "You go on at her enough, she'll confess to killin' him herself if she thinks it'll make you stop. She won't argue with no one."

"I think you might be underestimating her," said Lloyd.

No. They didn't know her. Maybe they hadn't meant to frighten her, but they had, and she had said the first thing that came into her head to get rid of them.

"You are denying that your car was here at ten-fifty on Sunday evening?"

"Don't know nothin' 'bout where my car was," Rachel said. "But *I* wasn't here."

Lloyd frowned. "You don't know where your car was?" he said.

"Took it from me at the hotel. Parked it somewhere. Brought it back to me Monday mornin'. Don't even know where the car park is."

Lloyd and Inspector Hill left, and Rachel felt the tears coming again. Curtis was right. They did suspect her all over again. But tears wouldn't help, she told herself sternly. Nicola had said she had seen her car, and that was the important bit. That was what really needed sorting out, and she wouldn't do that if she sat here crying. She looked at the clock; it was half past twelve, so Nicola should be at home for lunch.

And Rachel was going to find out *why* she had lied to the police.

# CHAPTER NINE

**"OH—YOU'D BETTER COME IN," SAID GUS.**

Rachel followed him into the dining room. She'd never been in this room; when Gus had been working it had been a sort of storeroom, full of things belonging to the first Mrs. Bailey. Gus and Nicola had always eaten in the kitchen before. Gus must have done it up since he'd nothing else to do.

Gus sat down again at the table, and Nicola looked guilty.

"Rachel," she said. "Er . . . would you like some lunch? I'm sure there's enough for Rachel, isn't there, Gus?"

"Don't want no lunch, thanks," said Rachel. "I want to know why you told Chief Inspector Lloyd you saw my car on Sunday night."

Gus stopped eating, and looked at Nicola, who had gone pink.

"I had to, Rachel," she said. "I'm really sorry, but I had no choice."

Rachel looked at Gus. "Don't look like she told *you* 'bout seein' my car," she said, and looked back at Nicola. "Just the police. Why, Nicola?"

"I didn't tell anyone about your car, honestly, I didn't. Not until I absolutely had to. I swear, Rachel, I would never have said a word, but they think *I* did it!" She shook her head slightly. "And I didn't," she said. "I didn't murder him."

Now Gus had gone pink.

"Why do they think you did?" asked Rachel slowly.

"He died of a drugs overdose," she said.

A drugs overdose. Bernard had died of a drugs overdose,

and Nicola had told the police she had seen her car when she hadn't. Nicola? Nicola had killed Bernard? She couldn't believe that. What would make her suddenly do a thing like that? But it explained why she had been frightened enough to lie to the police about her. "So you said you saw my car to get you off the hook?" she asked, her voice gentle.

"Well . . . yes, I suppose. I couldn't *not* tell them when they were accusing me of murder, could I? I know you said I should stand up for myself, but I couldn't . . ." She searched for words, then her shoulders went back. "I couldn't," she said, decidedly. "I had to tell them. I'm sorry."

Rachel's frown was growing deeper by the second. "But you *didn't* see my car," she said. "Did you?"

"I did. I thought he must have been hitting you, and you'd got away, driven off somewhere. At first I thought he must have gone after you. And then, when I found out next day that he'd been stabbed, I thought you must have gone back, picked up a knife, and stabbed him. And I didn't say anything, Rachel, not then. But I had to today. They think I *murdered* him. If that is what you did, maybe you should tell them. Because he didn't die from the stabbing."

Rachel nodded slowly. "Right," she said.

"I'm sorry, Rachel."

"Don't worry 'bout it." She would worry enough for both of them, she was sure. "I'll . . . I'll let you get on with your lunch," she said, and turned to leave, catching sight of the photograph on the sideboard. She frowned. "Who's that?" she asked.

"What?" Nicola followed Rachel's gaze, and her face brightened again as she smiled. "That's my mother," she said. "When she was about sixteen. We found it when Gus cleared this room out, so I had it framed. Haven't you seen it before?"

"No," said Rachel, absently, but her answer wasn't entirely accurate. She *had* seen the photograph before. That very morning. On the table between the beds in Mike McQueen's bedroom.

"Money?" said Mike, and shook his head. "No. His safe was open. I think I would have noticed if it had had cash in it. Why?"

"It's just that it seems to have gone missing," said Finch. "It could have a bearing on Mr. Bailey's murder."

Mike frowned. "Surely you've got his murderer in custody? I understood from the news that you'd charged the TV reporter."

"Mr. Law was released earlier today," said Finch. "And the charge has been dropped."

Mike sat down. "Dropped?"

"Yes, sir."

"Why?"

Finch looked back at him without speaking. The sun was glinting off his blond curls, making him look more like an angel than ever. Or Nemesis. Those death threats were still lurking somewhere in his computer's brain, he knew they were. And now Finch was saying that Law wasn't being charged with Bailey's murder after all. Rachel Bailey might be his downfall yet.

"Well, if he didn't kill him, who the hell did? A burglar? With all his security?"

"That's what I'm trying to find out. The money's what my boss calls a little puzzle. He likes to have them cleared up. But if you didn't see any money in his safe, you didn't."

"No, I didn't. And I didn't steal it, either."

"Thank you, Mr. McQueen. Don't get up. I'll see myself out."

Mike got ready for his date with Rachel, and found her waiting at the gate of Bailey's Farm, which now stood permanently open. The vultures would be descending any minute now.

She got into the car. "They let Curtis go," she said.

"So I've just heard."

"Is that goin' to make a difference to what we agreed?"

"No," said Mike, letting in the clutch and driving off. "Not if you're sensible about it." He glanced at her. "You can have as many men friends as you like," he said. "But I don't want that young man hanging round you. He's a television reporter, and I don't want anything I might tell you being passed on to him. Pillow talk's been more than one man's downfall, and it's not going to be mine. So get rid of him."

"All right."

One thing about Rachel Bailey, he thought. She knew which side her bread was buttered.

Lloyd had spent the early part of the afternoon explaining to the ACC, who seemed to be in perfect health, that he had had a body with stab wounds, and someone who had confessed to stabbing the owner of said body when it still functioned, which he, simple soul that he was, had assumed meant that he had found the murderer. He wasn't to know that people had been literally queuing up to murder the man. Though, God knew, if he had known, he'd have joined the queue. He hadn't said that last bit out loud.

It hadn't been that bad an interview; he just hadn't felt up to it, in his less than robust, hungover condition. The ACC did understand that he had had no reason *not* to charge the man, and that he had not been motivated by a desire for revenge. But the papers wouldn't. Even if individual reporters did accept that it had been a genuine mistake, they wouldn't print that.

He didn't feel much like a trip to London, but one was called for, since he was being trusted to continue heading the inquiry on the grounds that removing him from it would made it look as though . . . et cetera, et cetera. And the only way to get the whole nonsense off the news was to get it right the second time round.

"We have to check out the whole business of the hotel," he said to Judy as he went into her office. "I want to see how it works. How its car park works. Whether she took that car out for any length of time. Law could be giving her an alibi for earlier in the evening. And maybe stabbing Bailey was some sort of heroic gesture to save her from herself."

Judy pulled a face.

"And then he landed himself in it by dropping his newspaper," said Lloyd, rather enjoying this surreal version. "So he has to tell her what he's done and she has to start covering up for *him* instead of the other way round. Though it would have been a great deal simpler just to tell her to get rid of the newspaper, if you ask me, but then, I'm not a romantic telly-person with an overdeveloped sense of the dramatic."

"No," said Judy. "You're a romantic *policeman* with an overdeveloped sense of the dramatic. Nicola Hutchins isn't telling us the truth about what went on in that house on Sunday night."

"I thought you didn't think she had the guts to kill her father?"

"I know," said Judy. "But she's changed since I interviewed her before, Lloyd. And circumstances have changed, haven't they? If she *had* given her father an overdose, and went to the farm on Monday morning expecting *that* to be what he'd died of, she would be pretty well thrown by discovering that he'd been stabbed, wouldn't she? And she was. She really was. So I could have got an entirely wrong impression of her, and I think perhaps I did. Because this time round she didn't seem at all thrown to discover that he'd died of a drugs overdose, did she?"

Lloyd sat on her desk and thought about that. No, she hadn't. And he'd read Judy's notes from her original interview, and Nicola Hutchins's apparent belief that her father had committed suicide had seemed very odd to him at the time. But they had to check out her story about Rachel. She might have seen her at the farm. They couldn't just ignore it, especially in view of how much Rachel stood to gain, and the fact that her boyfriend had tried to kill him. And Judy would enjoy a trip to London, even if he didn't.

"And what about the sheep?" said Judy.

Ah, yes. The sheep. The phantom sheep. He believed her about that, too, but it was a bit difficult to maintain that belief in the absence of any sighting of this sheep by anyone at all.

243

The Ghost Sheep of Harmston. He could write about it when he retired. In between people-watching as a security man.

"Still," he said, sliding off her desk again. "We still have no idea what her immediate motive could have been."

"Abused people don't always need an immediate motive," said Judy. "Look at battered wives."

"I'd be a lot happier if we could think of one. Battered wives don't usually make up complex stories about injured sheep and empty houses. And we do have to check out this hotel. I'm just nipping out for half an hour—be ready to go when I get back."

"Yes, sir."

He walked out to his car as fast as he could, given that his head hurt with every step. He had had an idea.


Curtis still had a job. And he'd dropped a tiny hint or two that Lloyd might have had it in for him. Nothing slanderous. Just enough. He had spent all day answering questions from other reporters; newspapers were offering him ridiculous amounts of money for his story; Aquarius TV was already negotiating a deal on repeats of the *Law on the Law* series for a satellite channel, as well as *Mr. Big*, which everyone wanted now. It had taken a great deal of the sting out of having been made to look foolish. Lloyd was going to wonder what had hit him.

His bosses had been curious to know how come he had been suspected, never mind charged, but they knew no more than the press release had told them, which was that the police were now satisfied that Mr. Law's actions on the night in question had in no way contributed to Mr. Bailey's death, and Curtis had, without telling any outright lies, suggested that those actions had been carried out on behalf of Aquarius; that he had been in the vicinity, in the hope of catching the leaver of death threats now that the road was to go through the woodland, and that they had found traces of his presence, and had jumped to a wrong conclusion.

And so far, he had pointed out, the police were apparently ignoring the fact that the man *had* been receiving death threats.

If he, a mere reporter, thought that whoever had been leaving them would be active on Sunday night, shouldn't they have thought of it? Because it looked as though he had been active with a vengeance, didn't it? And all they could do was arrest him for the murder, just because he happened to have been there.

He had watered all that down for the interviews, but he had got substantially the same message across. One of the press boys had mentioned suing Bartonshire Police, but Curtis thought that Rachel would regard that as really pushing his luck, and had said that it was all in the game, and he wouldn't be suing anyone. But he would milk the situation for all it was worth, career-wise, whatever Rachel thought. She worried too much. They were in the clear. Soon, they could go away and find somewhere to live where he could come home to her every day in life, and she could spend her money any way she chose.

He strolled up to the farmhouse, to find her waiting at the door, having seen him on the monitor. He had barely time to get in before she was sitting him in an armchair, curling up at his feet, and telling him that she believed Mike McQueen had killed Bailey.

"Mike McQueen? What on earth makes you think *he* killed him?"

"He knew the first Mrs. Bailey, and he never said nothin' to no one 'bout that. He had somethin' else goin' on with Bernard besides this road—I knew he had. I knew he wanted this land too bad. Don't you see? *He* might've murdered Bernard."

"But he isn't the one who came here on Sunday night with a bag full of drugs, is he?" said Curtis.

Rachel looked at him, then shook her head slowly. "No," she said, her voice quiet, and a little sad. "But if Nicola did it, someone put her up to it. She wouldn't do nothin' like that off her own bat. And I'd still like to know why McQueen's got a photograph of Mrs. Bailey on his bedside table. What d'you think it means?"

245

Curtis stared down at her, his mind blown away, unable to speak, or think, or react, even.

"Curtis," she said. "What d'you think it *means*?"

"I think it means you were in McQueen's bedroom," he said, when he found his voice.

"Never mind that! He knew her, don't you see?"

"What were you doing in his bedroom?"

She sat back. "What do you think I was doin'?" she said.

Curtis blinked, looking at the wonderful creature who sat at his feet, and who was calmly telling him that she had been with another man. "Are you saying you—you slept with McQueen?"

"Had to. Thought it was the only way he was goin' to buy my land. But the bastard cheated me. He lent Bernard the money in the first place—the land's his, and I'm not gettin' nothin' for it." She leant forward again. "That's why the photograph's important," she said. "If he killed Bernard, I can get compensation for that. He's left me without nothin'. If we can prove—"

Curtis shook his head in disbelief. "Do you never think of anything but *money*?" he said. "You were letting McQueen screw you while I was locked up in a cell!"

"I was lettin' Bernard Bailey screw me all the time, and you didn't think nothin' 'bout that."

"That was different!" And he *had* thought about it. Over and over again, ever since she'd told him what it was like.

"No," she said. "It's just the same. Whether it's Bernard or Mike McQueen or you. It's just sex, and sex don't mean nothin'."

"You bitch," said Curtis. "You bitch! I *killed* for you!"

"Well, I'm glad you didn't really, because if Mike McQueen did, he's goin' to pay for it."

Curtis felt sick. He stood up. "I risked everything for you," he said.

She shook her head. "You risked everythin' 'cos you *wanted* me," she said. "That's all." She stood up, too. "And from what

246

I can see, you've not done too bad. Can't put on the news without seein' you. You're famous. That's what you wanted, isn't it?"

Curtis hadn't wanted fame as much as he had wanted her. But he didn't now. Not anymore. He took one long, last look at her, then stumbled out of the room, out of the house, out of Rachel Bailey's life.

DC Marshall thanked her for her cooperation, and left.

Gus was skulking in the background, as ever. As soon as Rachel had left at lunchtime, he had been demanding to know why she had told the police that she had seen Rachel's car. She had told him to mind his own business, and had gone back into the surgery.

Then Marshall had come to check out her drugs, and her books, and she had had to explain that she didn't always charge for treatment, not if it was something serious, and she knew the pet's owner had no money, so yes, she did use quite a lot of drugs for which she received no recompense. And yes, there were a lot of unpaid bills, but the work had been carried out, and the drugs used or supplied, even if the animal's owner hadn't seen fit to pay for the treatment.

"Is it all right?" Gus asked, hovering in the surgery doorway.

She gave him a brittle smile. "Do you mean is there an overdose-sized hole in my supply of morphine-stroke-morphine derivatives?" she asked. "Well, Gus, the answer is that no one's ever likely to know, except me, not without a great deal of painstaking work. I expect DC Marshall is telling his boss that right now."

She waited pointedly until he moved out of her way, and went into the sitting room, with him following behind; then he hovered in that doorway instead.

"Are you *enjoying* this?" he asked.

"Enjoying it?" Nicola thought about that. No, she couldn't in truth say that she was enjoying it. Being suspected of murder

247

by your husband was not an altogether enjoyable experience. But it did release you from so many bonds of gratitude. Because that was what it had been, all along. Not love. Gratitude.

Thank you, Gus, for not taking your fists to me every time I displease you in some way. Thank you, Gus, for being gullible enough to believe that the bruises you saw from time to time had been put there by some strange and persistent animal. Thank you, Gus, for choosing to believe that my mother wanted to have one failed pregnancy after another until it killed her, and for never thinking for one moment there was more to it than that. Thank you, Gus, for never asking me to explain why I was how I was, why I did what I did, because then I might have felt obliged to tell you that my father was a vicious, sadistic phoney with an overriding obsession about an old man's money, and that I lived in such fear of him that I couldn't even run away from him.

But all that's over now, Gus, because he is dead, and his death has released me from fear. And now is not the time to start questioning what I've done, and why I've done it, because your questions have released me from gratitude. And these two things add up to the simple fact that I will only answer your questions if I wish to answer them, and I may not always tell you what you want to hear, or even the truth.

"Yes," she said. "I think I am."

"Did you really see Rachel's car?"

"Does it matter?"

Gus came into the room properly, and sat down on the sofa, patting the seat beside him. Nicola joined him, looked at him expectantly.

"Nicky," he said, taking her hand. "Have you lied to the police?"

She smiled at him. "Yes, Gus," she said. "I have."

Jack switched off the computer, and sat back. Terri was off somewhere celebrating over afternoon tea with her fellow SOWS, and his life was in real danger of crumbling into as many tiny pieces as the scones they were even now spreading liberally with jam and cream.

He didn't have any jam and cream to stick his scone together again. Terri was saying things about Rachel Bailey that could get her into real trouble, all because he had made up lies about her. He had never intended any of this. And she had suggested, rather more acutely than obliquely, that Rachel might have murdered her husband, and had advanced as her reason for this theory the belief that Rachel and her boyfriend had invented a story about money in a safe. Now she would be telling her friends all about it, and eventually, it would reach the ears of the police.

His standard of living was about to take a nose dive, whatever he did. But now, he was going to have to go to the police himself, before they heard the rumour that Terri was so zealously spreading. And that would mean that Terri would have to be told the truth so that she stopped spreading it. And that would mean that his marriage was probably at an end.

Judy, armed with a publicity photograph of Curtis Law, and a still from Rachel Bailey's TV interview, confirmed with staff and guests that the couple had indeed been at the hotel, in person, on Friday, Saturday, and Sunday. An American couple who had met them as they arrived had had a drink and a long chat with them about London; they had been very taken by Rachel, whose accent was so like their own, and who knew so little of London that they had actually taken her for American at first. She had been like a little girl, they said. She'd never stayed anywhere like this in her life.

Neither had Judy, but she tried to look as though being there was second nature to her. She was, after all, a Londoner. Lapsed, perhaps, but a Londoner, all the same. Londoners, of course, did not as a rule stay in five-star hotels, but tourists seemed to think they did, so she had at least to look as though she wasn't just as wide-eyed as Rachel had been. But she was.

Judy had hoped that the mini-cab driver might have seen

Rachel with Curtis, and that it would be possible to trace him, so that they would have a definite sighting of her in the late evening, and she could get Lloyd off his new offensive, but the hall porter had explained that while they would, if the guest so desired, call a mini-cab company—he spoke the words like a particularly unpleasant oath—their usual practice was to light a small beacon at the rear entrance to the hotel, to which the black cabs which passed constantly would respond.

If a cab had been ordered for eleven o'clock, the hall porter had explained, he would have lit the beacon at a couple of minutes to eleven, and by eleven he could guarantee that a black cab would have come into the courtyard at the rear, which was where the entrance to the Executive Wing was. But obviously, there was no way of knowing which cab it had been.

Judy's suggestion that this sounded a little hit-or-miss was met with scorn. They did explain to customers that they should perhaps allow ten minutes at peak periods.

She had then hoped that the porter who had seen Law into the cab might have seen Rachel, but that wasn't to be either. The hotel had decided long ago that porters helping guests into cabs was simply not effective, cost- or otherwise. The moment you had three lots of guests getting into cabs, one lot at least was going to have to open the door themselves, and feel slighted. You couldn't have unlimited porters hanging about on the off-chance. This system meant that guests did not feel obliged to press a pound coin into the hand of someone who had done absolutely nothing, and it worked a treat.

It did unless you wanted some positive evidence in a murder inquiry, thought Judy. Lloyd was looking every inch the busy London executive, talking on his mobile, from which Judy was beginning to think he would have to be surgically removed. He even looked stressed, which was the true stamp of executivedom; she had offered to drive, but he had said that he didn't want to get stopped for speeding. She had enjoyed the journey, especially when they had plunged, as they had, right into the evening rush-hour. She had sat back, window down, letting the sights and smells and noises soothe her as they had moved ten feet and then stopped behind tourist buses and black cabs, as they had been passed by motorbike couriers doing a slalom through the traffic, as they had given way to ambulances trying to get to emergencies before the Grim Reaper, while Lloyd had just got more and more frustrated.

When they had arrived, the car had indeed been whisked away; the executive car park was two streets away, and guests rang for their cars to be brought round to the Executive Wing entrance. Mrs. Bailey hadn't asked for her car until Monday morning, when they had brought it round, and loaded it up for her. She had left the hotel at eight A.M.

"That was Alan Marshall," said Lloyd, joining her. "Apparently, we're not likely to be able to confirm one way or the other about Nicola Hutchins's drugs."

"Handy," said Judy. "If you want to bump Daddy off."

"I suppose so," said Lloyd. "He's getting on with the legwork, so he might turn something up. But I want to talk to someone about this car park. See if there's any way the system can be bypassed, and the car taken out without it going through reception."

Oh, well, thought Judy. He was nothing if not thorough.

"I've asked to see one of the suites as well," said Lloyd, and took a key from the receptionist.

Judy wondered if it was time to mention paranoia again, and unwillingly led the way down a narrow corridor into the Executive Wing. Lloyd slid the key in, awkwardly holding the door open for her, and as she walked in, she knew how Rachel had felt. "Wow," she said.

"Not bad, is it?" said Lloyd. "Bernard Bailey pushed the boat out to the end."

He was opening drawers and cupboards. "Drinks," he said. "Do you fancy one?"

She smiled, thinking he was joking. "Is this the suite Rachel and Curtis Law had?" she asked. "Do you think you're going to find something?"

251

"Nope." He took out a bottle of fruit juice. "Theirs was the one across the way, I think. But they're all pretty much the same. Except this one looks out on to the road." He went to the old-fashioned sash window, and opened it. "There you are," he said. "Fill your lungs with good clean diesel fumes."

She went to the window, and looked out at the bright summer street, and did indeed breathe in the heat-intensified smell of the city. She loved it. It made her feel as safe as that awful farm made her feel unprotected. She still didn't understand why they were here, though. Not so as she could smell the city.

She turned to see Lloyd finish off the bottle of fruit juice. "You are going to pay for that?" she said.

"Of course."

"Do you think there was some hanky-panky with the suites, or what?" she asked.

"Nope," he said again. "I expect there was a fair bit of hanky-panky *in* the suites, but no—I don't think Curtis Law and Rachel Bailey had clones or anything."

"Thank God for that," said Judy. "But if this isn't their suite, why are we here?"

He smiled. "Because it's our suite," he said, and picked up the phone. "Ah, good. Yes, please. Thank you." He hung up.

Judy wasn't sure how that constituted a conversation, but she let it pass. "You've booked us in?"

"Yep."

She smiled. "Why, Chief Inspector Lloyd! Is this sexual harassment?"

"Well, I do hope to fit in a little harassment of a sexual nature later on," he said, "but first we have a dinner date."

Judy looked at him, and herself. They had been travelling for some considerable time in a heat wave, and she could imagine the dining room in this place. "We're not exactly dressed for dinner," she said.

"No matter. It's very informal. It's at your parents' house."

There was a knock at the door, and a youth brought in a

bottle of champagne and two glasses, which he set down on the table, a red rose which he handed to Judy, and a small bag, which he handed to Lloyd. He got a very handsome tip, by the look on his face as he left.

"And I have taken thought for the morrow," Lloyd said. "The usual toiletries, and with advice from your mama, I have packed one pr knicks, one bra, one pr tights, flesh-coloured, and she said that any summer outfit that you usually wore to work would do, providing I knew which shoes went with it, and I think I've done it right, please don't tell me if I haven't."

Judy felt tears coming as they were doing with embarrassing ease at the moment, and briskly sent them packing. She kissed him. "You're lovely," she said.

"I know." He put the champagne in the fridge. "For later," he said. "And there is no hidden agenda. I don't mean you to tell your parents anything at all about you-know-what. It just seemed to me that if we were here, it would be a pity not to see them. Linda's going to be there, if she can. I said we'd be there about seven."

And they showered, and put on their crumpled clothes, and ordered a cab. A black cab, for fear of offending the hall porter. While they were waiting, Lloyd began to look very pale and seedy, so she felt his forehead. Then she rang reception for aspirin, her parents to say that they wouldn't be coming after all, and the hall porter to tell him to cancel his flashing beacon. Half an hour after that, she put Lloyd to bed and rang reception and asked if the hotel ran to medical help. By the time the doctor came, Lloyd had every blanket in the room on him, he was shivering and delirious, and she was panicking.

"It's a forty-eight-hour thing," the doctor said. "It's got a name, but I won't bother you with it. A flu-type virus, we call it in the trade. Don't worry. I've given him something that will bring his temperature down, and then he'll sleep. Probably feel right as rain when he wakes up, if the symptoms began yesterday. People usually do, I've found."

253

Judy looked at Lloyd, his teeth chattering, listened to him mumbling, watched him toss and turn and tried very, very hard to be unselfish, but it didn't work. "Am I going to get it?" she asked.

"Probably not. It isn't particularly virulent, but there have been a few cases up and down the country. Enough for me to recognize the symptoms. Thirsty, headachy, then a fever, then they're better, providing they're under seventy-five. If the sufferer is going to pass it on, it's during the first twenty-four hours, and you would probably be coming down with it yourself by now. It has a very short incubation period."

Did she feel headachy? No. Thirsty? No. She hadn't had anything to drink since she'd got here, and Lloyd had gone through two bottles and three cans of fruit juice, with her pointing out that it was costing him as much as a six-pack would cost every time. But there was another problem. She looked at the doctor, and uttered the actual words for the very first time. "I might be pregnant," she said.

"Oh, don't worry about that. There's no danger there." He smiled. "Congratulations."

"Thank you," said Judy, weakly. Lloyd was tossing and turning and muttering, and she wished she could make him feel better, more comfortable. It was hard to believe that he would be as right as rain tomorrow. "Are you sure he's all right like that?"

"I'm sure you have no need to worry about him," the doctor said. "But he should take it easy for a day or two when he recovers, however well he feels. Post-viral fatigue will get to him if he tries to do too much, but he'll be fine. If he's still like this in two hours, then call me again, but he won't be."

Judy tucked him in every time his uncomfortable writhings threw off the bedclothes. Eventually, he stopped shivering and muttering. And then he slept. She watched television with half an eye, creeping into the bedroom to check on him every ten minutes until she felt that she could get in beside him without waking him. She would have slept on the sofa, but she wanted to be with him, in case anything happened.

She lay stiff and awake, frightened to move in case she disturbed him, and then after what seemed like a month, she finally got some sleep herself.

# CHAPTER TEN

THE LIGHT SHINING THROUGH THE CRACK BE-tween the heavy curtains landed on Judy's face, and she opened her eyes. What time was it? Where was she? She glanced over, glad to see that it was Lloyd she was with, because she didn't recognize that window, and she did hope she hadn't taken to letting strangers pick her up.

Then her brain began to function, and she remembered where she was. She checked Lloyd, who was still sleeping peacefully and normally. Good. Now. What time was it? Why did they never have clocks in hotel bedrooms? She reached gingerly over Lloyd to pick up his watch, and smiled as he stirred, then settled down again.

She would never have arranged all this when she was coming down with a flu-type virus. She *was* selfish, she knew that. She just didn't know how to go about not being, really. But then, she would never have arranged it in any circumstances; it simply wouldn't have occurred to her, because she was also irredeemably unromantic. Romance always seemed slightly comic to her; and what had happened last night proved that it was just as difficult to plan as murder. Romance happened when you least expected it.

Half past four. She had loads of morning, and she didn't feel sick. Good. If she didn't feel sick when she woke up, then she was all right. She inched out of the bed, and went out into the little corridor, into the bathroom. She was going to enjoy this. An hour and lots of toppings-up and an entire facial with the goodies at her disposal later, she emerged, wrapped in a wonderfully heavy bathrobe, wearing the towelling slippers she was invited to keep with the hotel's compliments, and padded into the sitting room. She had hung her clothes up last night, and she didn't want to go back into the bedroom in case she wakened Lloyd. Besides, it was still only twenty to six, and she wasn't going to get dressed yet.

She pushed up the window, and smiled at another bright, sunny, warm day. Early morning London rumbled gently past, and she stood there for a moment, watching as delivery trucks arrived and turned into various courtyards and sidestreets, as the newsagent and the breakfast house across the road opened for business, as the road gang arrived, with a bright yellow tiny little excavator, and an equally bright yellow, remotely operated roaddrill, and two compressors. They began setting up barriers and stop and go signs, and she closed the window. The noise of a road being dug up was another one that mattered not a jot to her, but it might disturb Lloyd.

She jumped when the door opened, and turned to see Lloyd, fully dressed, and entirely well.

"What are you doing up?" she said.

"Good morning to you, too." He came over, put his arms round her. "You smell gorgeous," he said.

"Well, I don't know how much that stuff costs, but I made the most of it," she said. "What are you doing up?" she repeated.

"I'm not only up," he said. "I have had the executive breakfast."

"You never have breakfast. What's the executive breakfast?"

"Cornflakes, orange juice, and really good black coffee."

Judy's face fell. "Do I have to have the executive breakfast?"

He grinned. "No. Full English breakfast, German breakfast, American breakfast, Japanese breakfast—you name it. We execs have ours in a little room along the corridor." He kissed her, then kissed her again. "You know the sexual harassment part? Is it still on?"

"That's something else you don't do in the morning."

257

"I've not usually gone to bed at half past seven in the evening," he said. "I woke up at quarter to five, couldn't get into the bathroom because some woman was in there who locks the door, so I just got dressed and went in search of a loo. What I found was the executive shower room. Complete with shaving facilities. I don't think it's for policemen who find women locked in the bathroom—I think it's for executives falling off overnight planes and going to meetings first thing when their rooms aren't available, but they let me use it anyway. Then I had some sustenance, because I was hungry."

"Cornflakes?" she said. "You call that sustenance?"

"They're very good for you. And I asked about the car park. They said I can talk to the security manager at half past seven when he comes on. So, I thought, what can I do to while away the time? Sexual harassment, that's what. So—is it still on? Then I promise you can have the full English breakfast, and the full German breakfast, and the full—"

"You're supposed to be taking it easy—the doctor said."

"It is easy. Come on." He took her by the hand and led her towards the bedroom. "I'll show you."

She couldn't remember ever having had a nicer start to the day, and she told Lloyd that as they lay, still entwined, on the bed. It was too hot like that really, but she didn't want to let him go. There had been a dreadful thirty minutes last night when she had thought he might be dying, before the wonderfully reassuring doctor of the sort she had thought was extinct had come along. It was Lloyd, eventually, who moved, who went off and returned with the champagne and glasses, and the only can of orange juice that he hadn't got round to last night.

"They're setting up a sort of information network as a result of Curtis Law's programme," he said, pouring the orange juice, then expertly addressing the champagne cork.

Judy frowned. Work? Lloyd never did this. She did. It usually annoyed him. "Are they?" she said.

"And there's to be a working party, and all that—you know the sort of thing. It'll have twelve months to do something that

258

should probably be given twelve years, if it's to be done properly." The cork left the bottle with a satisfying pop. "It's supposed to come up with a computer system that will plug all the gaps," he said, topping up the glasses with champagne.

"Yes?" she said. Sometimes conversations that started like this ended up being jokes, but she couldn't see this one's potential.

"They intend seconding you to head it," he said. "Sit up," he said, handing her her glass. "Or you'll spill it."

It had better be a joke. She sat up. "Me?" she squeaked.

He nodded.

"I hope you said no!"

He shook his head, sitting down beside her.

"Well, I *will*! I'd hate it. I hate committees. I hate computers. I hate paperwork."

He drew in his breath. "I really don't think you should turn it down," he said, and touched her glass with his. "Your health, Detective Chief Inspector Hill."

She stared at him as he drank. He wouldn't joke about that. Would he? No. He wouldn't. "Honestly?" she said.

"Honestly."

"Wow." She sipped her Buck's Fizz, then set it down. "That's the fastest promotion sexual harassment's *ever* got me."

He kissed her, held her close. "Am I allowed to mention you-know-what?" he asked.

"Yes, of course you are."

"Well, for a start, I want to tell you that you mustn't think for one moment that I meant any of that nonsense the other night."

"You must have meant some of it."

"Judy!" He smacked her gently. "You know me far too well to think I had to mean any of it at all. When I saw the pregnancy-test thing, all right, I felt . . . well, left out. Which is something you do to me that I don't like, and that made me angry. The only bit I meant was that you should have told me. All the rest was rubbish."

"What about the bit about having your baby?"

259

"That's the bit I meant least of all! You don't have to have my baby to prove anything to me."

"But I *am* having your baby." She disengaged herself from him, and sat back so she could see his face. "I want to know how you feel about that," she said, looking into the blue eyes which she had never been able to read, so this was probably a waste of time. He'd say whatever he wanted *her* to believe, whether he believed it or not. "About abortion," she added sternly. "Let's stop refusing to use the word."

"You know how I feel about abortion. I think it's up to the individual."

"Oh, Lloyd! You *are* an individual. So what are your individual feelings about this individual baby?"

"Exactly the same. I want you to do whatever you feel is best for you."

Maybe. She wished she really knew how he felt, but she never would, and it was just typical. He made all that fuss about her not telling him, and now he was just loading it all back on to her anyway. It was her decision.

"What I'd really like to know is how it happened," he said.

Judy smiled. "Well," she said, "I've been thinking about that, and I think it's got something to do with what we were just doing."

"Very funny. I thought you were supposed to be on the pill."

She sighed. "I forgot to take it, didn't I? It was your fault. I've got a routine when I go to bed, so I *don't* forget. But you turned up to watch me make my television debut, and . . ." She shrugged. "I forgot," she said.

"You've forgotten before. You always just took two the next day."

"I wasn't forty before. He wanted me to come off the pill altogether, but I said no, so he put me on some other kind. It's more critical. So will he be, if I go saying I want . . ." She tailed off, and didn't use the word.

She was just finishing her full English breakfast when Lloyd joined her with the intelligence that the security key for the Executive Wing allowed access to the car park at any time, since they were simply inserted at the barrier.

"So she could have taken the car, driven home, bumped off hubby, and driven back with no one any the wiser," he said. "The latest sighting we've got of them is when dinner was delivered to their suite at eight. But Law could have been here on his own from then on. She could have driven home, given her husband a fatal injection of morphine before half past ten, which is why the tapes weren't changed, and been driving away from the farm at ten to eleven when Nicola saw her. Nicola really did think the house was empty. She didn't know her father was unconscious somewhere. And Law could have gone home on the train, and done what he did in order to confuse us."

Judy shook her head. "I'm no doctor," she said, "as I proved yesterday, when any fool could have seen that you were coming down with something, but if Bailey had been drinking heavily, and then was given barbiturates and enough morphine to kill a horse at half past ten, I don't think he would still have been conscious four hours later. So how did Law get in?"

"Nicola says the alarms were off. Rachel could have put them off, and Law could have got in the back way, then put them on again before he stabbed Bailey. He'll know where all the cameras are, as Tom pointed out, so he could avoid them with no trouble."

"Mm." She put down her cup. "Why would they kill him twice? Do *I* get to mention you-know-what?" she asked.

"I'm not being paranoid! It's possible."

Judy conceded that it was possible, though hardly likely. For one thing, Rachel's hysterics had been too convincing. Her doctor had said that she had been given a real fright.

"Law didn't tell her what he was going to do," said Lloyd.

"Then she didn't put the alarms off for him," said Judy.

Lloyd smiled. "How can you think that quickly?" he said.

She didn't always think quickly. Judy's thoughts went back to last night. Why hadn't she called a doctor sooner? What sort of mother would she be if her child had to be delirious before she worked out that he needed medical attention? But Lloyd wasn't a child, she argued back. He must have known there was something wrong. He should have been going to the doctor himself, not organizing romantic nights in five-star hotels. She frowned as she thought about that. Bailey must have known there was something wrong, too. Something a great deal worse than a flu-type virus.

"Why do you suppose Bailey didn't call a doctor?" she asked.

Lloyd shrugged. "Maybe he was too ill to get to the phone," he said.

"But according to Freddie, it would have been fairly gradual. He might not have been able to carry on much of a conversation, but there must have been a time when he knew he was desperately ill. He could at least have dialled nine-nine-nine, surely? If he could let Curtis Law in when he was barely conscious, he could have called for help at some point before that."

"See? Maybe he didn't let Law in, as I have just suggested."

Maybe he didn't, thought Judy, as they left the hotel. Maybe Lloyd's weird scenario was right. Maybe Rachel Bailey was a brilliant actress into the bargain. They were pulling out of the courtyard, very nearly on their way back to Stansfield, with her at the wheel, having told Lloyd that he was supposed to be taking it easy, when he told her to stop.

"Look," he said, pointing at a security camera.

"Yes," she said, her voice flat. "What about it?"

"Do you think they've got them in the car park?"

"Possibly," she said, with a sigh. "More videos. I don't think I can take it." But she reversed smartly back in, and invited the young man who whisked the cars away and brought them back to show her the way to the car park.

And there were more videos. Judy would pay a lot of money never to have to look at a jerky security video again in her life. And this one, run through at top speed, showed that Rachel

Bailey's BMW had sat in its space in the car park, untouched by human hand, from two-twenty-one on Friday afternoon until seven o'clock on Monday morning, when it was driven out by a member of staff.

"Does this mean we can forget Rachel Bailey and Curtis Law?" Judy asked, as they went back into the breakfast room for a cup of tea in order to recover from a surfeit of security videos.

But even as she asked the question, Judy knew she didn't want to forget about Curtis Law. He had been on the ten o'clock news last night, being magnanimous, saying that he didn't think for one moment that the *Law on the Law* special had in any way affected Chief Inspector Lloyd's judgement; he had simply moved too fast, and jumped to a wrong conclusion. The item was by way of being a sort of trailer for the network showing of *Mr. Big? What Mr. Big?* which would now get a much bigger audience than it would have done. Then he had oh-so-casually mentioned the death threats about which nothing seemed to be being done. *She* was beginning to feel paranoid about Law, never mind Lloyd.

"You can't clone people," said Lloyd. "But you can clone cars."

"Oh, Lloyd!" said Judy, as a middle-aged man approached them.

"Excuse me," he said, "are you the police officers from Bartonshire?"

"We are," said Lloyd.

"It's just that I was told you were asking if anyone had seen Mrs. Bailey on Sunday night, and I did. I wasn't actually on duty, which is why no one told you to talk to me. I'd been to the pub, which is just round the corner from the Executive Wing, so I nipped in the private entrance as she was coming out. You're not supposed to do that, but it takes a good five minutes longer to walk round to the front, so I always do, if I get the chance."

"You're certain it was Mrs. Bailey?"

He smiled. "Yes," he said. "She was looking for a cab. She said her husband had ordered one for eleven o'clock to go to St. Pancras, but there weren't any there. But his train wasn't until half past, apparently, so I told her not to worry, because it was only a ten-minute run at that time of night, and one would be there any moment."

"Thank you," said Lloyd, and the man left. Lloyd looked at Judy and shrugged. "Nicola Hutchins," he said. "We have to have another word with her."

"My problem is that I still can't see Nicola doing all that."

Lloyd smiled. "You've changed your tune again."

"I know. Because while I don't see how it could have been anyone else, I still can't make sense of it. Not after putting up with it all her life. Why now? Like that? Concocting this story about a sheep. Going up there in cold blood to kill her father. I just can't see it."

"It might not have been in cold blood," said Lloyd. "Perhaps there was a sheep, like she said. Perhaps her father did go out— we don't know that he didn't. He could have rung from anywhere. But we know the sheep was supposed to have been seen right beside his land. What if it was just . . . winded, or something? Just got up and went back through whatever gap it had come out of in the first place? She really wouldn't have been able to find it, and all the sheep would have been present and correct next day. And what would she be doing when she failed to find it? She'd be going to the farm to find out where it was supposed to be, armed with the very things she would have taken to deal with an animal in pain. A fast-acting barbiturate. Morphine."

Maybe, maybe. Judy wasn't sure what you took to deal with a badly injured sheep, and neither was Lloyd. But she always let him ramble on with his scenarios, because there was usually something useful in there.

"So, supposing *she's* the one he started knocking about?" he said. "You said her husband shot out of the house as soon as Rachel mentioned bruises. What if that was because Nicola

264

had come home with bruises after she'd gone to deal with this sheep? She had failed to find it, hadn't she? I expect that was worth a hammering. And what if she decided that she had had enough? Bailey was very drunk. He would be far from alert, and she had the means of his disposal with her. A few minutes' premeditation. Not planned. Not intended, when she went in there. Last straws exist. Worms do turn."

"Mm," said Judy, then laughed. "But I doubt if I've ever heard anything less likely than the winded-sheep theory."

Lloyd smiled. "All right," he said. "The sheep didn't exist. But that means she presumably did go there to kill her father, because I can't think why else she would make it up. And we know she didn't see Rachel's car, so . . ." He shrugged again.

At half past nine, they finally drove away from the hotel. Judy was still at the wheel, despite Lloyd's protests that he felt perfectly all right, because she didn't suppose he would be taking it very easy when they arrived, which they did, one hour, fifty minutes and the odd complaint about her driving later, stopping only to confirm to their colleagues that they were back, before continuing north to Harmston, and Nicola Hutchins.

Gus Hutchins was on reception; Nicola was with a patient, he said, and told her they were there. He showed them into the sitting room, waiting with them, making sporadic and unsuccessful attempts at conversation before Nicola joined them.

"I don't have much time," she said, apologetically. "I've got another appointment in ten minutes."

"This won't take much time, Mrs. Hutchins," said Lloyd, standing as she came into the room, remaining on his feet, as did she. "We have this morning spoken to a witness who saw Rachel Bailey at the hotel at eleven o'clock on Sunday night. We have further watched surveillance videos from the car park of the hotel in which Rachel Bailey's car sat from Friday afternoon until Monday morning, without moving from the spot."

She frowned slightly.

"Perhaps you can explain how you could have seen it leaving your father's farm at ten to eleven on Sunday night?"

She blinked a little. "I couldn't have," she said interestedly, disconcertingly. "Could I?"

"Are you saying you lied to us, Mrs. Hutchins?"

"No," she said quickly. "At least—not . . . not deliberately. I'm sorry. I must have been mistaken."

"Mistaken?" said Lloyd. "And were you mistaken about anything else? About the house being empty, perhaps? About the alarms being off? About this sheep that no one has seen hide nor hair of before or after it was supposed to have been injured on the road? About this phone call that no one can trace?"

"No." She stepped back a little. "No. I don't think so. I got the call. I . . . I thought the house was empty."

"*Thought* it was empty?" said Judy, looking up from her notebook. "Do you mean you were wrong about that, too?"

"No. No, it was empty. There was no one there. I waited for him, and when he didn't come back—"

"You left," Judy finished for her.

"Yes." She looked back at Lloyd. "You *do* think I murdered him, don't you?" she said.

Lloyd sighed. "Until some part of your story checks out, I have little alternative but to work on that assumption. I think you've been lying to us, Mrs. Hutchins. I think you still are."

Gus Hutchins got up and left the room. Nicola looked after him, then turned back to Lloyd.

"I didn't mean to mislead you about Rachel's car," she said, then smiled, a little tearfully. "I really believed I'd seen it. It must be because she's a gypsy."

Judy glanced at Lloyd, who was looking at her, his face as baffled as she felt.

"I'm sorry?" he said.

Nicola's hands clasped and unclasped as she spoke. "When I was five," she said, "there were gypsies on the farm. We had free-range hens, then, and I was allowed to collect up the eggs. And one day, I saw one of the gypsies stealing eggs. He

266

dropped some when he ran away, and when my father saw them, he said I had broken them. I told him about the gypsy, and he stopped hitting me."

Judy glanced again at Lloyd. Once again, he was looking at her. Once again, his face mirrored her feelings.

"For a while after that if I was being punished for something I didn't understand, something I didn't think I'd done, I'd tell him I'd seen the gypsies do it. And it wasn't a lie. I believed it. I made myself believe it, because I thought it would make him stop. But I'd just get punished twice. Once for what I'd done, and once for blaming the gypsies. But I really believed I had seen them, so that's what I told him. I grew out of it," she said. "Or learned not to say it, even if I did believe it, because it meant getting two beatings, one after the other."

Her hands fell still.

"But I think I must have done it again," she said. "Because Rachel's a gypsy, and you were telling me I'd done something I hadn't done, something I didn't understand, and my mind must have played tricks on me. I'm sorry if I've caused you unnecessary work." A bell rang. "That's my appointment," she said. "I really must go. Unless you're arresting me."

Lloyd shook his head, looking bemused at her sudden change of manner. "No," he said. "We're not arresting you. We still have further inquiries to make. But I imagine we will want to speak to you again."

"I'm not going anywhere," said Nicola, and went back through to the surgery, leaving them to find their own way out.

Neither of them spoke until they were in the car.

"Well, now we know what Rachel meant about lasting damage," said Judy, fastening her seat belt. "What do you think?"

Lloyd shrugged. "God knows. But I'm making damn sure of my facts before I arrest anyone else for this murder. You said you thought Jack Melville was lying to you about his visit to the farm, didn't you?"

"Well, yes, but I imagine he's been taking too healthy an interest in Rachel Bailey," said Judy. "Like every other man who meets her," she added.

Lloyd smiled. "And Tom's convinced that McQueen's not been straight with him," he said. "So we have further inquiries to make. We still don't know why Bailey got drunk, do we? Maybe one of them had something to do with it."

Yes, thought Judy. That was a little puzzle that they had rather overlooked.

Nicola's appointment took less than five minutes; she went into the empty waiting room to find a message on her answering machine, asking her if she could oversee that afternoon the repossession of livestock at Bailey's Farm, as an urgent favour for Willsden and Pearce, one of whom had gone down with some sort of bug. She frowned, then smiled. There had to have been a mistake.

But when she rang, Rachel told her that there was no mistake. That her father had gone bust, that the bailiffs had just been waiting for the fortifications to come down so that they could descend, and they would be descending that afternoon.

"Didn't even wait till we buried him," she said.

Nicola discovered that even the land was worth nothing, because McQueen had lent her father the money on it in the first place, held the title deeds already, and was taking possession of it as soon as the creditors had taken everything away.

"Isn't there something about leaving you the tools of your trade?" she asked.

Rachel laughed. "I don't have no trade, Nicola."

"But Rachel—what are you going to do?"

"Mr. McQueen's lettin' me keep the house," said Rachel. "And a bit of land. I'll be rentin' it from him."

"Oh. Well—I suppose that's quite good of him, really."

"Yeah," said Rachel. "Providin' I can pay the rent," she added, with commendable cheerfulness.

Oh, God. Rachel had no money. She had nothing at all.

Nicola hadn't known that this was going to happen. "But how *can* you pay the rent?" she asked.

"I'll manage."

Nicola felt terrible. This was all her fault. And she ought to set Rachel's mind at rest about her car, now that she knew she couldn't really have seen it.

"Rachel, I'm sorry I told the police I saw your car," she said. "I couldn't have, because it was in the hotel car park all weekend. They've just told me. And someone saw you there, too. But I didn't lie," she said anxiously. "I don't think I did. Not on purpose. They think I said it to get you into trouble, but I didn't. I think it's just because you're a gypsy. I tried to explain. I really thought I saw it. They think I murdered him. I don't think I did, but I'm not sure now. Do you think I did? Gus does."

"The bastard," Rachel said, her voice just a whisper.

Nicola frowned. "Who?" she asked. "Gus?"

"No. No one. Nothin'. Don't worry 'bout it. Don't worry 'bout nothin', Nicola. You just come over here this afternoon, and we'll talk. I got to go out for a little while, but I'll be here later. If I'm not here, you wait for me. All right?"

"All right." Nicola put the phone down, and walked slowly out of the waiting room, into the house. She was going to come out of all this with nothing, not even Gus, she discovered, when she found the note on the kitchen table. He had gone home to his parents, and didn't, as far as she could see, intend coming back. She barely registered that, throwing the folded paper down again, and went through to the dining room, pulling the shoe box out of the sideboard. Four thousand, six hundred pounds. She had counted it as she had taken it from her surgical bag and put it in the shoe box. But then she hadn't known what to do with it; she couldn't put it in the bank without Gus finding out, and Gus was almost painfully honest. She supposed that was why he hadn't been a terrific success as an accountant. She could use it now he'd gone.

But it wasn't her money. It was Rachel's. And Rachel needed

269

it desperately. Much more desperately than she did. No one was taking her furniture away, or her car. No one was going to repossess her house, or the surgery, not yet, anyway. And they wouldn't, because she had a job. A trade. Something that brought money in, that kept the wolf from the door, that stopped the debts getting out of hand. Rachel hadn't. And they weren't even her debts.

She would take the money back.

"Could I see Detective Inspector Hill?" asked Jack.

"Oh, I'm sorry," said the girl on the desk. "I'm afraid she's at lunch at the moment."

That was a good start. "I believe you've been making inquiries about money that went missing from the safe at Bailey's Farm," he said. "Perhaps I could speak to whoever's dealing with that?" That was probably who he should be talking to anyway.

The girl had a consultation with someone else, then invited him to take a seat. In a few moments, a man with riotous blond curls appeared.

"Sergeant Finch," he said. "I believe you wanted to talk to me?"

Not really, thought Jack. I don't really want to do this at all. He had told Terri last night, but he hadn't had to sleep in the spare room. Because she had walked out, saying she couldn't live with a man she couldn't trust. She had spent the night with one of her SOWS buddies. He wasn't sure if it was what he had actually done, or the lies he had told about Rachel that had been the clincher. He suspected it was the latter, and that this was the first recorded instance of a woman leaving her husband because he hadn't had an affair with the woman next door.

He followed Sergeant Finch into the interview room, and they sat down amid a small electrical storm.

"It's on the blink," explained Finch. "It'll settle down in a minute."

Jack waited until it had, being unable to talk to someone

who looked as though he was in a stage representation of a silent movie. "I believe you're looking into the disappearance of some money from Bernard Bailey's safe," he said, when the light came on and stayed on.

"That's right," said Finch. "Do you know something about it, then?"

Jack almost laughed. "Yes," he said. "I know something about it. I took four thousand, six hundred pounds in cash to Bernard Bailey on Sunday evening."

"Well, at least we know how much is missing now," said Finch. "And the thing is, Mr. Melville, normally it wouldn't be any of my business what you did with your money, but Bernard Bailey has been murdered. Did anyone else know about this money changing hands?"

Jack smiled at the expression, redolent with skulduggery and dirty work at the crossroads. Which it was, he supposed, but it wasn't illegal, which was clearly what Finch was assuming. "No," he said. "No one knew. No one but me, and Bernard Bailey."

"Thank you," said Finch, in a winding-up tone. "We might want a statement from you—it depends really, on what happened to the money, and why."

"That isn't all," said Jack. "Your Inspector Hill told me that I should allow you to decide what is and isn't relevant to your murder inquiry. And I have some information which I suspect I should have given to her before now."

"Fire away," said Finch.

"I am the director and major shareholder of a company called Harmston Estates," he said. "My wife is the other director, but she didn't actually know that until last night. I asked her to sign something a long time ago, and she did, without even looking at it, because she trusts me. At that time, I had no intention of compromising her," he added. "It was just routine. And I've done nothing illegal, you understand."

Finch nodded.

"But Harmston Estates wholly owns another company

271

called Excelsior Holdings. And Excelsior Holdings owns the woodland through which the road to the so-called Rookery would have to pass if Bernard Bailey had refused to sell his land."

Finch started making notes.

"Bernard Bailey and I both took a considerable knock-back about two years ago," Jack went on. "A risky speculation that failed. He lost just about everything, and I lost very much more than I was prepared to admit. McQueen was offering enough money for the woodland for me to recoup my losses, and make a profit, but his real intention was to take the road through Bailey's Farm. The route through my land was just back-up if Bailey refused to sell."

Finch looked a little lost, as he tried to keep up.

"Bailey was in desperate financial difficulties, and he was going to lose the farm if he defaulted on the loan he had taken out on it, so he approached me with a deal. He asked me to pay his loan instalments, and his farmhands' wages. He showed me proof that he would come into a very large inheritance if and when his wife produced a son, and he would have been able to repay me with interest, provided he could hang on to his farm, and his wife did her bit. I could afford to take the gamble, providing the road did go through the wood as a result, so it was in my interests to help him, and I gave him the money in cash every month."

Finch looked up from the notebook over which his hand had been a positive blur. "So Mrs. Bailey might have known about the arrangement?"

"Only if Bailey told her, and I think that most unlikely."

"Thing is," Finch said. "We've reason to believe that Mrs. Bailey quite often overheard business transactions."

"She didn't overhear this one," said Jack. "She wasn't there."

"But there had obviously been previous transactions."

"Yes, every last Sunday in the month. But Bailey had always come to me before. The day was chosen because my wife chairs her committee meetings on Sundays, so I'm alone in the house. The repayments had to be made by the last Monday in the month. But Bailey wouldn't leave the house for anything or anyone last Sunday, so I went to him."

"Why did you lie to Inspector Hill about what you were doing at Bailey's Farm?" said Finch.

He was direct, thought Jack. It made it easier, somehow, if you called a spade a spade. "I lied about it because the committee my wife chairs is the Save Our Woodland Sites committee, and if my plan had worked out, she would have been, in effect, selling the very woodland she was pledged to save. I really didn't want her to know that. That was what I meant by compromising her."

"Yes," said Finch. "I can see that it would."

"I also financed Mrs. Bailey's trip to London," Jack went on. "Bailey was anxious that his wife shouldn't be there if there was to be a demonstration of any sort, because she was at last expecting a baby, and he rang me to see if I could let him have some cash. I saw him on Thursday, with the money for the trip, and he was, for him, almost cheerful. But on Sunday night, he had had a lot to drink, and he was threatening her. I did tell Inspector Hill that," he said. "What I didn't tell her was that he seemed to think she had gone away, not to avoid the demonstration, but to have an abortion."

"Did he say why he thought that?"

"No. He just kept saying that he'd found out that she'd had an abortion. Got rid of his son. And that he was going to kill her. I only knew about this baby because it was . . . collateral, I suppose, and that's why I didn't mention it before, because I was trying to keep my involvement in repaying his loan quiet."

"I think we will take a formal statement, Mr. Melville, if you wouldn't mind waiting there."

Rachel had got rid of Curtis because McQueen had told her to, and now, armed with her information, she was going to get rid of McQueen, too, after going to such lengths to get him. But

273

her mother had brought up seven kids on the road; she came from hardy stock, and she could survive without anyone's help, if she had to.

Inspector Hill sat opposite her in the interview room; Lloyd stood looking out of the window as she explained the circumstances under which she had overheard McQueen's conversation with Bernard, and her decision to abort the baby she had been carrying. She tried to sound unconcerned about that, but she didn't. It had hurt her deeply, and it always would. "Shouldn't've done that," she added. "But I did. Too late now."

Inspector Hill had been jotting down notes. Rachel saw her pen stop for a moment, then she carried on.

Lloyd was listening, despite his apparent absorption in what was going on outside. "I don't think that really affects the investigation," he said.

"Wasn't no way I could go to my doctor, because she wouldn't have let me do it without us speakin' to Bernard first, so I had to get it done private. And I'd got no money. So I went to McQueen. Told him if I was having a boy there wasn't no way he'd ever get Bernard's land, because Bernard'd get millions from his grandfather's will so long as he still owned it. Turned out he knew that already."

Lloyd turned then, came to the table, and sat down.

"I knew from how he'd talked to Bernard that he was desperate for him to sell him that land," Rachel said. "That's why I went to him. And he never even thought twice. Sent me off to a clinic where they didn't ask no questions, paid for the lot. Turned out it was a boy," she added. "And I didn't ask them 'bout that. I didn't want to know. But he did." She looked away. "He was glad."

Lloyd had tipped his chair right back, and was rocking gently. Inspector Hill was looking thoughtful. "Why have you come here with this now, Rachel?" she asked.

" 'Cos now I know somethin' else 'bout McQueen," she said. "Somethin' I reckon *you'll* want to know."

\* \* \*

Curtis hadn't gone in to work. He had rung in, said that he had caught this virus that was going round.

It was all happening on the work front, but right now he didn't care about any of it. They wanted to get *Mr. Big* out on the network next week, on the August edition of *Monthly Fact-file*, in order to cash in on the publicity surrounding him. He should have been at a meeting about it right now, but he hadn't been able to make himself go in.

He had been awake all night, thinking about what Rachel had done without a second thought, while he was locked up because of her, charged with murder because of her. He had thought that Rachel, beautiful though she was, fixated on the money though she was, sexy as she was, had been, in a way, unworldly. She would listen to him, and he had enjoyed explaining things to her. He had thought that she needed a champion, a knight in shining armour, a protector.

She had needed no explanations, no protection. He had offered himself up to her, told her that he was going to be in possession of a whole pharmacopoeia of drugs. She had seen her way out; she had come up with her ridiculous notion of slipping Bailey a lethal Mickey Finn, because she knew he would come up with something better, and that he would take all the risks for her.

And what had she been doing while he was taking those risks? He couldn't bear to think of it, but he couldn't get the image out of his mind. He hated McQueen. And he hated her.

Mike had just finished lunch when Lloyd and Inspector Hill had arrived. They knew, somehow, about the photograph, and Rachel was the only person who had ever been in the bedroom besides himself and Shirley. Shirley had never liked the idea of a cleaning lady; the one they had had to employ for this big house did what Shirley called the public rooms, as though they lived in the White House. Mike found it hard to believe that Bailey had kept a photograph of her, but perhaps he had, because Rachel must have recognized it somehow.

275

"Her name was Margaret," he said, picking up a cigar, coming out onto the terrace, handing them the photograph. "She was fifteen years old when that was taken, and she was fifteen years old when Bernard Bailey got her pregnant for the first time. She was my step-daughter."

He sat down, took out matches, and lit the cigar. "She came to me and told me she was going to have a baby. I think she chose me in preference to her mother because I was always as soft as butter with her. And she was right; I wasn't angry. Bailey was handsome, when he was young, and I think I understood. But she wanted to marry him, and her mother and I both said no. We didn't want to separate them or anything—we just wanted her to wait. But that row was the last conversation we ever had with her. It was the last time we ever saw her."

Chief Inspector Lloyd stood; Inspector Hill sat opposite him as Rachel had done last night. He didn't suppose the same service was on offer, but he certainly wouldn't turn it down if it was. She was a nice-looking woman; well dressed. Good clothes. Shirley had taught him to appreciate dress sense, and he had taught her about what made a match and what didn't. He could have advised the inspector that those shoes didn't quite go with the dress. The colours quarrelled a little. Not much, but Mike had noticed. Some people had an eye for shades and colours, some didn't. He always had had. Shirley hadn't. Rachel Bailey had.

"Didn't she keep in touch at all?" asked Inspector Hill.

Mike shook his head. "She vanished," he said. "They vanished. We had no idea where she was, or what was happening to her. And we tried, believe me, we tried to trace her. But there was a slight problem."

"And what was that?" Lloyd asked.

"Bailey wasn't called Bailey when we knew him," said Mike. "His name was Hawthorne. We spent years checking what must have been nearly every Hawthorne in the United Kingdom. Cost a fortune, and got us nowhere. In the end, we gave up." He drew on his cigar, and watched the smoke drift up into another golden day. "We only ever had Margaret," he said. "Shirley lost one baby after we were married, and she couldn't have any more. Well, she passed that particular problem on, didn't she? So everything revolved round Margaret, and . . . and Hawthorne *stole* her. She was still a child." He inhaled some smoke. "She might just as well have been kidnapped. Shirley . . . Shirley *died* a little with every month that passed, and we didn't hear from her."

"Even kidnappers contact their victims," said Inspector Hill.

Mike nodded. "And you know that the hostage wants to be returned," he said. "Margaret didn't want to come back to us, or even see us, or she would have got in touch. That was the hardest thing to take. And our marriage survived it, but it was never the same. We'd lost . . ." He tried to think of a way to explain. "We'd lost the future, I suppose," he said. "Seeing her grow up, having grandchildren . . ." He shrugged. "But that wasn't to be, anyway."

He saw the inspector frown very slightly, but she didn't speak.

"Life's very odd," he said. "I came here because there was a greenfield site to be developed. I looked at the plans, and I saw a stumbling block. The only possible routes to the development went through, in the one case, some very old and pretty woodland, and in the other, a farm called Bailey's Farm. So I did some asking around, and established that the woodland would meet with considerable opposition. But it was possible that the farmer might be prepared to part with his land, at a price, so I went to see him. That is, I, as the representative of MM Developments, went to see him. I doubt if the name seemed like anything other than coincidence to him. And I found myself looking at my son-in-law."

Inspector Hill looked up from her notebook. "Did you see your step-daughter?" she asked.

"No. I asked to see her, but he said she didn't want to see me. Physically barred my way. Got the shotgun when I tried getting physical back. I said that at least he could tell me how she was.

And he said, 'She's never carried a live one full term yet.' "
Mike shook his head. He had thought he might manage this bit
without feeling the impotent rage he had felt then, but back it
came, just as strongly, just as overwhelmingly. He took a moment to get himself together. "He might just as well have been
talking about a sheepdog, and I—I just went for him. The
shotgun went off, and people came running, dragged me off
him, and kicked me out." He relit his cigar, inhaling some more
of the strong smoke. "Margaret was just upstairs," he said.
"But she didn't come down to see me, not even to ask about
her mother. There was plenty of time when she could have
come down, before it got heated, but she didn't. And that hurt.
It hurt me, and you can imagine what it did to Shirley."

Again, a little frown. But the inspector didn't speak.

"She was sure that Margaret would come round, given time,
that Hawthorne or Bailey or whatever he called himself had
poisoned her mind against us because she was just a child
when he took her away. She insisted that we move here to be
close to her, but by the time we had arranged it, and sold our
house, bought one here, Margaret had died. He hadn't told me
she was pregnant again. I'd had no idea that she was still
trying. She was nearly forty."

The inspector and Lloyd exchanged glances.

"Do you blame the money?" he said. "It wasn't the money's
fault. It was Bailey's greed for it that caused Margaret's death."

Lloyd looked round at the opulence of his surroundings, and
nodded. "Yes," he said. "I'm not much of a man for the bible,
but I think that the love of money is probably the root of all
evil, as it says."

"I use it, Chief Inspector. I don't worship it. Anyway, I
didn't realize any of that at the time. And Bailey seemed to go
into some sort of mourning after Margaret died—he even
made a suicide attempt. He didn't plant the fields, he sold off
a lot of his stock and machinery, he went into a sort of semi-
retirement. I made a formal, written approach to him for his
land, but I had no heart for the development project by then—

278

I almost dropped out. Shirley and I went back north, and we were going to put this place on the market."

Lloyd sat down beside the inspector, his elbows on the table, his chin on his clasped hands, and watched him as he spoke.

Mike tried not to feel self-conscious. "Meanwhile, I had had a private investigator on to him, to find out why he'd changed his name, and it turned out that it was required under his grandfather's will. Bailey was his maternal grandfather. Bailey's mother had married some Yorkshire farmer that she'd met at a Young Farmers conference, and gone off to his place. The grandfather had wanted to found a dynasty, and had left everything to his grandson, providing he changed his name, farmed the land here, had a son of his own, made the same provision for him, and so on. That was when I realized why Margaret had died."

Lloyd sighed. "I think I actually hate money," he said. "Maybe that's why I spend it whenever I've got it."

"And she hadn't been dead six months when we heard that Bailey had a new wife, and he was back on course to becoming a multi-millionaire. I wasn't going to let that happen if I could help it."

Lloyd looked faintly baffled. Mike smiled briefly. "Back to the bible," he said. "An eye for an eye. He took Margaret from Shirley, and I was going to get that land off him if I could. So I made sure of the woodland, and met stern opposition from one Mrs. Melville. I told her I'd made an offer to Bailey, sat back, and let the sparks fly."

Inspector Hill smiled. "I hope you retired to a safe distance."

"You've met the lady? Well, then I learned that Bailey's suicide attempt had not been because Margaret had died. His semi-retirement wasn't because he had lost the will to carry on. It was because he had speculated and had lost every penny he had, and it had all come crashing down round his head on the day of her funeral. And I learned that he'd borrowed on a loan that made the land forfeit if he missed one payment."

"I'm glad I'm just a simple copper," said Lloyd.

279

Mike doubted that he was simple. He'd watched that programme about him, but it hadn't convinced him of Lloyd's stupidity, just of Curtis Law's callow approach to life, which was infinitely more complex than Law gave it credit for.

"I found out who had financed him, and one of my companies bought the loan. But he kept paying up," he went on, "in cash, paid into the company's account, every month without fail. So I went to see him again, and I took some pleasure in telling him that it was me he was in hock to, that I was the one who would be repossessing his precious land the day he failed to make a payment."

Again a look passed between his visitors. A faintly puzzled look this time. Mike thought that Lloyd was going to ask a question, but he didn't, so he ploughed on.

"But since he had shown no sign of failing to make the payments, I made him an offer that I really did believe he couldn't refuse. Enough to clear his debts to me and everyone else, and still have money in the bank. Nothing like he would get from his grandfather's will, of course, but a whole lot better than repossession. I thought he would *have* to sell to me. So did his new wife."

He dropped his cigar on to the terrace, and stepped on it, smearing tobacco shreds and leaves over the pale pink stone.

"I presume it's Rachel who told you about Margaret, and I imagine she's told you that I paid for her to abort the baby she was carrying."

Lloyd nodded.

"But he did refuse it. And he still managed to come up with the repayments. So then I tried to scare him out, give him cash-flow problems. Anything that might work. I even had his machinery vandalized."

This time the look that passed between them was the baffled look he'd seen before, when he had been hunting through Hawthornes for Margaret. Perhaps he was as much of an obsessive as Bailey himself. Other people certainly seemed to

280

think so. Even Shirley. But he had been doing it for her. It had all been for her.

"So he put up his alarmed fences. And that's when Rachel suggested the death threats."

Lloyd's eyebrows rose.

"I thought she might not have told you that," said Mike.

"What did she hope to accomplish by them?" asked Lloyd.

"She said it would frighten him to think that someone could get past his security, and that my offer might begin to seem more attractive to him if he thought his life was at risk. But . . ." Mike shrugged. "You tell me," he said. "I think she was laying the groundwork for murder. Because she thought she would get even more money if Bailey was dead than if she gave him his son. But she was wrong, as she discovered."

Lloyd looked even more puzzled. He got up from the table, and walked to the edge of the terrace, looking out at the immaculate garden. "Would it surprise you to know, Mr. McQueen, that Rachel Bailey heard every word of that conversation you had with her husband?" he asked.

Mike frowned. "But she was still trying to sell me that land yesterday morning," he said. "Why would she do that if she knew that it was already mine?"

"I don't know," said Lloyd, turning. "Perhaps she hoped to salvage something."

And she had salvaged something, thought Mike. She had *still* been manipulating him, God damn it. He had been congratulating himself on putting one over on her, when all the time . . .

"Why did you go to see Bernard Bailey on Sunday night, Mr. McQueen?" Lloyd asked.

"It was over," said Mike. "Somehow, the payments kept coming, and unless I could make him sell to me right then, I was going to have to go through the wood. I wanted to have one last go. I was just going to up the offer, that's all."

"Why did he let you in?"

"He'd won. As soon as he saw it was me, he opened the gate.

He wanted to tell me to my face that he had won. That he had hung on to the land. He said he would eventually get his grandfather's money, too, because this one *could* give him a son, unlike that useless bitch he'd had off me. Those were his words, Chief Inspector. And I felt just as I had the day he wouldn't let me see her. But I didn't hit him this time. I told him that Rachel had no intention of giving him a son. That she had been colluding with me to send the death threats. That she had aborted the son she had been carrying. That he had been that close to his millions, and she had snatched them away."

Inspector Hill stood up, walked a little way away.

"I felt very guilty afterwards," said Mike, when she turned to look at him. "He was threatening to kill her, and I believed him. But as it turned out, I needn't have worried. Rachel can take care of herself."

"Can she?" she asked.

Mike shrugged. "She's alive. He isn't. Who else do you suppose killed him?"

"How does this sound?" asked Lloyd. "You go to Bailey, not to up the offer, but to kill him before he can make this month's payment."

Mike shook his head. "If Rachel Bailey overheard that conversation I had with her husband, then she can tell you that once Bailey was dead, I had no more interest in his land."

Lloyd looked a little baffled again.

"I didn't want Bailey dead," said Mike. "An eye for an eye, Chief Inspector. I wanted to concrete that place over in front of his greedy eyes. Bury it. Without remorse. Just like he buried Margaret. Rachel Bailey may not have known why I wanted to do that, but she knew that that was all I wanted to do. And I can never do it now, because he's dead. I was the last person who wanted that, Chief Inspector. The very last. And Rachel Bailey knows it."

Lloyd nodded briefly, and turned to go, but Inspector Hill turned back.

"Mr. McQueen," she said. "Do you know Nicola Hutchins?"

Mike thought. The name was familiar, but he couldn't quite . . . yes. He remembered now. "The vet," he said. "No. I've never met her."

She came back, sat down again. "I don't know of a tactful way to say this," she said. "Nicola Hutchins is Bernard Bailey's daughter. Margaret's daughter. The baby she was expecting when she married Bernard."

Mike stared at her, shaking his head. "She's my . . . my wife's granddaughter?" he said.

She nodded.

"But—but why? Why would he tell me Margaret hadn't carried a baby full term if she had?"

"I think he'd be talking about boys," said the inspector, and stood up again. "I don't think he counted Nicola."

They left then, and Mike sat at Shirley's rustic table, his chin resting on his hands, his mind racing. He had a granddaughter. Well—a step-granddaughter. She must be . . . must be twenty-five. He didn't even know what she looked like. Like Margaret? Like Shirley? Like Bailey?

He smiled. It would be a grand*daughter* that he suddenly found he had. Another woman whose bidding he would do. He'd have to go and see her, work out how to introduce himself. He'd have to tell Shirley.

But first, he had another call to make, and an arrangement to cancel, and then he could prepare his introduction of himself to Nicola Hutchins. He drove up to the farmhouse to see Rachel sitting on the porch, unsurprised to see him, and got out of the car, walking up the steps toward her. "You set the police on me," he said.

She looked up, the sun sparkling in her eyes before she shaded them, and nodded. "Just thought some things were better out in the open," she said.

"You do realize that our arrangement won't now be going ahead? I can't trust you to keep private things private."

"Reckoned it might not. But I got a tenancy agreement. Legal and bindin'."

"For which you will now have to find the rent."

She nodded again. "You let me worry 'bout that," she said. "You've done more than enough for me already, Mr. McQueen." She smiled. "No hard feelin's?"

Mike looked round at the land he possessed and didn't want, then back at the woman he still wanted and had been foolish to imagine he could ever possess, and shook his head. Then he saw Shirley's sister's girl coming out of the house. No, no, Shirley's niece was years older than this girl. My God, it was her. It had to be.

"You two know each other?" Rachel asked.

"No," Nicola Hutchins said. "I don't think we've met."

"This is Mike McQueen," Rachel said, and rose. "This is Nicola Hutchins, Mr. McQueen. Reckon I'll leave you to get acquainted."

Mike was thrown; he had had no time to prepare, no carefully constructed overture. Haltingly, inadequately, he explained who he was. The resemblance to her second cousin made him realize that Nicola Hutchins had a whole host of blood relations she knew nothing about, and it was hard for him to grasp, so how much harder must it be for her? How could Margaret have done that to her?

"I tried to find you," she said. "Well—not you, exactly. I was trying to find someone called Bailey who had farmed in Yorkshire. I couldn't really try to trace my mother's family, because all I knew was her maiden name, and that she was from Newcastle originally, and her parents moved round a lot. I didn't know what her fath—what you did for a living."

"It wouldn't have got you very far anyway," said Mike. "With her name being different from mine."

"No. But Bailey didn't get me very far either. I must have telephoned every Bailey in Yorkshire."

Mike smiled. "And I was looking for Hawthornes," he said. "But at least we've found one another now."

She looked at him. "You might wish you hadn't."

"I doubt that."

"You ought to know that my husband left me today," she said. "And both he and the police think I murdered my father. And I stole four thousand, six hundred pounds from my father's safe, but I've given it back now, so I'm broke."

Oh. Well, he hadn't supposed this would be straightforward. Mike took her hands in his. "You mustn't worry about any of it," he said. "You're not broke anymore, for a start. You've got a grandfather with more money than he knows what to do with. Except now he does know what to do with it, and you don't ever have to worry about money again."

Nicola almost smiled. "I don't think money's going to help, though," she said. "Not if I murdered my father."

"Money always helps." Mike looked at her worriedly. "*Did* you murder your father?"

"I don't know. Maybe I did."

Mike frowned. "What do you mean?" he asked hesitantly.

"I just wanted him to die. I just wanted not to be frightened of him anymore."

"Why were you frightened of him?"

And he listened, appalled, as she told him why. He had beaten her all her life. He had beaten Margaret. He had once beaten Rachel so badly that she hadn't been able to walk unaided.

"He never did anything like that to me or my mother," Nicola said, by way of making him feel better. "Just . . . you know."

No. No, he didn't know. He couldn't imagine it. Margaret, who had been cosseted and cared for all her life, had suddenly found herself at the mercy of some bully's fists. And Nicola. A child. A baby. His mind shied away from that altogether. "Why didn't she leave him?" he said. "Why didn't she come home?"

Nicola gave a short sigh, and looked down at the table. "I told someone the other day it was because she was frightened to," she said. "But it wasn't just that. She blamed herself. She thought if she gave him a son everything would be fine. She loved him when she married him. Maybe there was still something there."

But she must have known that he had been here, in Harmston, the day her husband let off the shotgun at him. He had thought she had chosen to remain upstairs, but Nicola had been right the first time. She had been too frightened of her vicious husband to defy him. Rachel wouldn't have been, he thought. Rachel wouldn't have let anyone or anything keep her from her father. But Rachel didn't even know who her father was. Life really was very odd indeed. He wasn't looking forward to telling Shirley any of this, and it might be worse even than that, if Nicola had killed the man. "*Did* you kill him?" he asked again.

"I suppose I did."

Oh, God. Mike was way out of his depth.

"I was there," she said. "I took the money. I remember wanting him to die. But I didn't think I'd *murdered* him. I said Rachel had been there, but she couldn't have been. She was in London. The police know she was."

Oh, he wouldn't put anything past Rachel Bailey. Not even being in two places at once.

"I think I made that up. Imagined it. Said I'd seen her car, because she's a gypsy, and I used to blame . . ." Her fingers were being tied in knots as she spoke. "It was stupid. I just got punished twice. But I really believed I'd seen them. I thought I saw Rachel's car, but I couldn't have. I suppose I did murder him. Rachel wants me to go to the police, tell them what I did."

"Does she, indeed?"

"But I think I should stay here. Rachel's livestock's being moved, and I should be here. The RSPCA like a vet in attendance. It's terrible—everything's being repossessed. Everything. But she says you're letting her rent the house from you. That's kind of you."

"Aye, well . . ." Mike felt a little ashamed of the interpretation she was putting on his arrangement with Rachel.

"Do you think I should go to the police?"

"We'll see. Look—just you take it easy. Don't worry about anything. Everything's going to get sorted out. All right?"

"All right," she said, as trusting and defenceless as a puppy.

He wasn't sure what to do with her. "I'll just have a word with Rachel," he said grimly. "You wait here, pet."

"I don't really think I *did* murder him."

No. Neither did Mike. He strode into the house, found Rachel sitting behind Bernard Bailey's desk.

"She's having some sort of breakdown," he said, jerking his thumb in the direction of the porch.

Rachel shook her head. "That's what Gutless Gus said in his note. But she's not havin' no breakdown. Just the opposite. Bernard Bailey broke her down years ago. Now she's tryin' to start herself up." She smiled. "Like our old camper when we got it," she said, and nodded towards him. "You'll need a lot of patience, if it's anythin' to go by. But it went in the end."

He nodded back, and looked at her, trying to make her out. "Did she murder her father?" he asked.

Rachel shook her head.

"Did you?"

"You don't 'spect me to answer that," she said, with a slow smile.

"She says you want her to tell the police that she killed him."

"No, I don't. Nicola didn't kill no one. But she won't tell me nothin' 'bout what went on in here that night. That's why I want her to go to the police. There's a lady inspector there'll *make* her tell the truth. Not all this stuff 'bout gypsies and chickens."

Mike hadn't heard the bit about the chickens. He frowned. "Won't that be a bit risky?" he asked.

"She's got to tell someone. Don't do herself no good keepin' it all bottled up, you can see that for yourself. Inspector Hill won't frighten her or nothin'. She'll just make her sort out the truth from the other stuff, once she knows she's got somethin' *to* tell. She's got a knack of gettin' under Nicola's skin."

Mike smiled. "I meant risky for you."

287

"Maybe. Maybe not." She shrugged. "I got to stay here," she said. "Don't know if you've heard, but all my worldly goods are bein' repossessed today. If she'll go with you, will you take her to the police? Ask for Inspector Hill, and don't accept no substitutes. Nicola's got pretty good at stonewallin' everybody else. Got so good at it with Gutless that he ran home to Mummy and Daddy. Thinks he's married to a murderer."

Mike looked at her for a long time, trying to gauge whether or not he was being manipulated once again, and decided that he really didn't care. She had probably murdered her husband, and he certainly didn't care about that, not anymore. And she was right; Nicola had to tell someone what had happened to her on Sunday night, whatever it was. He had a strong suspicion that there was something more to Rachel's advice that Nicola go to the police than that, but whatever it was, he was still a sucker for those eyes, and that voice, and he would do her bidding. "Aye, all right, pet," he said. "You've talked me into it."

Nicola agreed, with some gentle persuasion from both of them, to go to the police, complete with her pathetic shoe box. Mike drove off with her in the Cherokee, aware that he was taking on a very big project indeed for his retirement. But he and Rachel could take care of things in the short term, and Shirley would come home now. Then they could think of the long term.

That might be very long indeed if they were to undo twenty-five years of abuse, but they would cope with it, and Nicola would get better. He would see to it that she did.

They were in Judy's office, and the sequence of events had become clear, at last.

McQueen had visited Bailey, and had told him that he had been within an ace of his multi-million-pound prize, and that Rachel had snatched it from him, and Bailey had thought that he was talking about the baby Rachel had told him she was expecting. As he had done the last time he had lost a great deal of money, he had sought solace in the whisky bottle.

Then Melville had come to give him this month's loan instalment and wages, and had been treated to what Bailey intended doing to Rachel as a result of what he had learned, something Lloyd was profoundly glad he had not been able to carry out. There was no pregnancy, no baby to abort, not this time, but it came to the same thing in the end. Bernard Bailey *would* have broken every bone in Rachel's body, if Nicola hadn't seen fit to do away with him first.

"It has to have been Nicola," Lloyd said, but it was as much to convince himself as Judy. "We've completed our other inquiries, and all the evidence points to her. The drugs, the time of death, her story about the sheep, her nonsense about the alarms, saying she saw Rachel's car—everything. She must have killed her father."

"Why?"

"Just because she wanted to, and who can blame her? It'll be a plea of diminished responsibility. But it has to have been her, or someone who was there before her. And neither of the ones we know about murdered him, even if they could have procured the means, because they had both wanted Bailey alive. So unless someone else altogether visited Bailey between Melville's leaving and Nicola's arrival, then it has to have been Nicola. And the only other person with half a motive is Mrs. Melville, who was at a committee meeting with a dozen witnesses."

"Killing him because she just wanted to is all very well," said Judy. "A spur-of-the-moment thing. But she didn't have a motive for planning it, for producing an elaborate story about a sheep! She just didn't. And I doubt very much if she has the cunning to do that, anyway."

"There are no other candidates," Lloyd said. "Even if Rachel Bailey could have been in two places at once, her only hope of getting her hands on some money was if Bailey stayed alive, and she knew it. That's why she had hysterics when she found him dead. Law was frightened for her safety, tried to kill Bailey, but he was too late, because Nicola Hutchins had already done the deed."

"But *why* had she done it?" asked Judy, for the umpteenth time. "What had happened that would have made her kill him now? This was premeditated murder. She had to have a motive."

"There is a motive," said Lloyd. "She knew about Rachel and Curtis Law. And then she saw Law's programme, all about drugs. Drugs that *he* could pick up any time he liked, and which *she* had access to every day. *She* wasn't in her father's will, but she knew that Rachel was. And she believed that that land would be worth a fortune to McQueen. If she could kill her father and make it look as though Rachel had done it with Law's help, Rachel wouldn't inherit, and she'd get the land as his next of kin, whether she was in the will or not."

Judy was shaking her head. "She isn't capable of that, Lloyd."

"Not now," said Lloyd. "Not now she's done it. Now she's backtracking, saying she made it all up about Rachel's car, because it's got too much for her to handle. But she indicated right from the start that Rachel had been there, and then she reluctantly told us about Rachel's affair with Curtis Law. And we arrested Law, but we let him go. So she had to remind us that he had access to drugs."

Judy got out her notebook.

"The first thing she said when I told her Law had been released was 'What about Rachel?' " Lloyd reminded her. He didn't need a notebook to remember what people had said. "And then she said she had seen Rachel's car. Because Rachel *herself* had to be guilty of murder, if Nicola was going to get anything. That's why she bungled the injections and used more drugs than she needed, so it would look like an amateur's work. And it could perhaps have come off," he said. "If that car park hadn't had surveillance cameras."

"Mm," said Judy.

"She may even have convinced herself that she didn't do it," he said. "Like she did when she was little. But there was her obvious confusion when she discovered that her father had been stabbed," he said. "You mentioned that yourself. And no surprise at all when we told her that he'd died from an overdose."

"I know," said Judy. "But I think she really believed he had committed suicide. She wasn't surprised about the overdose itself, but she was surprised that we thought *she* had given him it. I think she *still* thought he'd committed suicide, until you mentioned that the hypodermic was found on the road outside. And that's when she began not to understand, and blamed the gypsies."

"But *why* would she think he'd committed suicide?"

"Because he'd tried to do it before, and he was drunk, and she thought that must be because he'd found out about Rachel and Curtis Law."

"Oh, come on!" said Lloyd, getting up, restless, as he always was when the solution seemed just beyond his grasp. "She was the only one who knew about Rachel and Curtis Law! How *could* he have found out, except from her?" He looked out of the window at the summer sunshine glinting on the cars, and sighed. "Perhaps Bailey went to see her, forced her to tell him, and she went to the farm and killed him before he got to Rachel, like Law tried to do. That would explain why she would make up the sheep business. But when we faced her with it, she knew she had done something very wrong, and blamed Rachel. I'm not saying she's responsible for her actions, Judy. I'm just saying that she must have done it."

"I still don't like it," said Judy, continuing to leaf through her notebook. "You're the one who says if you clear up the little puzzles, you'll get to the big one, and if it was Nicola, that just gives us more puzzles."

Lloyd continued to look out of the window as she went through the puzzles.

"Why would Nicola say she saw Rachel's *car*, rather than Rachel herself, if she wanted to shift the blame? Why mention suicide, if she knew she'd ditched the hypo outside the farm?

291

Why didn't Bailey ring a doctor, if he was conscious from when she left until Law arrived? And we don't even know who took the money," she concluded.

Lloyd continued to look out of the window as he spoke. "Rachel Bailey's car is considerably more of a puzzle if Nicola Hutchins really did see it," he said, watching as a big, expensive off-roader tried to find a space in the car park. "Since it didn't move from the hotel car park. She said her mind plays tricks on her. I don't suppose she can pick and choose what she imagines she saw." The off-roader squeezed into a space, inching past someone's wing mirror. "Bailey didn't call a doctor because he was too ill. She mentioned suicide, because she really hadn't meant to get Rachel into trouble, but she had." He mentally checked off her objections, and thought he'd pretty well covered them, except one. "Nicola killed him, and then *she* took the money," he said. "Alan says she's operating on a shoe string. She needed money, and there it was, in the safe. So she took it."

"A nice, neat theory," Judy said. "Clears everything up. There's just one problem with it. If Nicola Hutchins took the money, then how did Curtis Law see it? It was only there from ten o'clock until midnight, and he was on a train—" She broke off, and there was a little silence broken only by the pages turning in her notebook. "You can clone cars," she said, almost to herself. Then: "Why *didn't* he ask Rachel just to get rid of the newspaper when she got home?"

Lloyd turned, saw her face, and heaved a huge sigh of relief, not just because his gun dog was pointing at last, but because she was pointing right at Curtis Law.

"You always home in on the right things," Judy said.

Yes, sometimes he did, but that was because he blasted away at anything and everything, so he had to wing something now and again. It took his gun dog to find them.

"That money was never reported stolen," said Judy, after she had gone through her notebook, and found all the puzzles had been answered, even ones they thought they had already answered.

"No," said Lloyd.

"So if we can get our evidence some other way, we can deal with that on an unofficial basis."

"True. I'd rather we did, anyway," said Lloyd. "Nicola wouldn't make the most reliable of witnesses."

They went into the CID room, and Judy told Tom Finch exactly what had to be done by his small workforce in order to get the hard, rock-solid evidence that they had to have if they were to prove it, and he wrote out a list as she spoke.

The post-flu-type viral fatigue that Lloyd had been warned to expect was beginning to catch up with him; it looked and sounded like a horrendous amount of work to him. But Tom saw no reason why in this age of faxes and computers and information highways they couldn't wrap it up today. They had three hours before people began shutting up shop, he said, and if he couldn't galvanize into action the various organizations and companies involved, no one could. At least, that was Lloyd's translation. What Tom actually said was, "No sweat, guv. Three hours till knocking-off time for most of that lot. We can get most of this stuff down the line. Consider it sorted." Then he had sucked in his breath. "Could take a while to find this outfit, though," he said, tapping one of his tasks. "Is that a problem?"

Judy checked her notebook, then wrote three names on his pad, at the bottom of his list. "Try them first," she said.

Tom raised his eyebrows.

"Just a hunch."

Tom's phone rang, and he picked it up. "Yes," he said. "Yes, she's here—hang on." He looked up at Judy. "McQueen's just come in with Nicola Hutchins, guv," he said. "She wants to talk to you."

Downstairs, Nicola Hutchins was waiting in an informal interview room.

"What did you want to see me about, Mrs. Hutchins?" Judy asked, as they went in.

"I took this from my father's safe." She pushed a shoe box across the table. "He owed me at least that," she said, as Judy opened the box and took out the bundles of notes. "He set me up in the practice as a wedding present, so he'd look big to his friends in the Masons, and then he expected me to tend his animals for nothing for the rest of his life. I don't think I took anything that wasn't owing to me."

"This money was never reported missing," Lloyd said. "So, if you want to return it to Mrs. Bailey, then you can do that."

"I tried to. Because I found out that Rachel has no money at all. They're taking all her stuff away this afternoon—her furniture, and everything. They've already repossessed her car. So I took it back to her. But she said I had to tell you about it."

Well, well, well. Lloyd could see only one reason why Rachel Bailey would want Nicola to do that.

"It wasn't really a lie about her car."

"It wasn't a lie at all," said Judy. "Was it?"

Nicola shook her head slightly, her lips tightly shut, her hands clenched into fists.

"You did see her car, didn't you?"

Nicola's hand went up to her hair, and was brought down again.

"Mrs. Hutchins," Judy said, her voice holding the nanny-like firm-but-fair warning note that she could do to perfection.

Nicola looked at her, her eyes wide with misery. "I don't want to get Rachel into trouble," she said.

"But Rachel told you to come here. So she can't think you'll get her into trouble."

Her hand hovered once more, and was put firmly back in her lap. "But—but I don't know what she wants me to tell you!"

"Then tell us the truth, Mrs. Hutchins. You know what you saw. You're trying to make yourself believe you didn't see it, but you did."

"But you said her car was in a car park all weekend! And she said, yes, it probably was. But I had to tell you what had happened. But if I do that—" She broke off.

"Just tell me everything you remember about going to the farm on Sunday night," said Judy. "All of it. Whether you think you must be making it up or not. Everything you remember, Nicola."

And at last, Mrs. Hutchins put her hair firmly behind her ears, and said nothing at all. And neither did Judy. The next person to speak in this room would be Nicola Hutchins, if they were there until midnight.

# CHAPTER ELEVEN

NICOLA TRIED NOT SAYING ANYTHING, BUT SHE couldn't do that, not yet. Maybe not ever, but then she would have thought that she could never have done a lot of the things she had done recently. She didn't have to do anything she didn't want to do, she reminded herself. And she had handled Finch. But that wasn't going to work, not this time. She couldn't make it work with Inspector Hill.

There had been a little while today when she had thought that her childish fantasy about the gypsies had returned to haunt her. Because she had lied over and over again about what had happened that night, and when they had said that Rachel's car had been in the hotel car park all weekend, she had thought she must have lied about that, too. She couldn't believe that she would have done it to get Rachel into trouble, so it had to have been a throwback to her childhood, and the non-existent gypsies who might, just might, stop him hitting her, like they had once before. But they never had again.

Bleak memories crowded in on her as they had done on Sunday night when she had stood over her father, helpless for the first time in his brutal, bullying, melodramatic life. She had lied about that until she had almost believed that he really hadn't been there. But it had to stop now. She had to tell the truth now, while she still knew which was which.

But she hadn't lied about the car. Did Rachel really mean her to tell them about that? It didn't matter what she had meant, because Nicola knew she was going to tell them the truth, like the inspector had asked. And now that she knew she wasn't going to try to lie anymore, she was all right. She could hold herself together. She wasn't a confused, frightened five-year-old, inventing gypsies. She knew what she had done. She just didn't know if it was murder, that was all.

"When I got to the farm, I saw Rachel's car leaving," she said. "I know I did. It was her car. I saw it. I know its number. I know you say it was somewhere else, but I saw it. The sitting-room door was open, and the light on, but he wasn't in there. I saw the light from under the office door, and I went in, but the office was empty. Everywhere else was in darkness, so I thought he must have gone after Rachel, that he'd been hitting her or something. And that's when I saw the money."

"Is that when you took it?" asked Inspector Hill.

Nicola shook her head. "I went back out into the hallway, and I saw that the alarms were off, which I couldn't imagine him having done. Then I realized that I would have seen the Land Rover if he'd gone after Rachel, so I thought he'd gone to meet me, crossed the fields. I had to wait for him, because I hadn't found the sheep, and he'd blame me for that anyway. It would only be worse if I wasn't there when he got back."

Failing to find the sheep would have constituted an offence; failing to wait for his return would have constituted a greater offence. The greater the offence, the more severe the punishment; Nicola had been frightened not to wait.

"So I went into the sitting room, and waited for him. Then I saw the whisky bottles, and I wasn't sure what had happened. If he'd been drinking as much as it looked like he had, it had to have been something bad. I thought it must have had something to do with Rachel, or why else would she be driving away so late? Then I heard a noise in the hallway, and I went out, and he was there. He was drunk, swaying about. I could smell it. He pushed past me, and went into the sitting room."

"Did you speak to him?"

"I asked where he'd been and he said he'd been in the kitchen, but it had been in darkness, so I don't know if he really was in there. He was very drunk. Or—rather, I thought he was just drunk. I asked about the sheep, and he said to forget about the sheep, there was no sheep. He said something about Curtis Law, and told me to get the doctor."

Inspector Hill nodded, noted something down.

"I went to the phone, but it wasn't working, and I was on my way out to go to the pay phone in the village when I heard him being sick, so I went back in. He was on his knees on the floor, and I helped him up, and got him to the sofa. He was saying he was cold, so I put on the radiators, and then he fell asleep. I thought he would just sleep it off, but I waited, in case he was sick again. And when he opened his eyes again, I could see the pupils were contracted, and I thought he'd taken something. I thought he'd done it again."

"Done what again, Mrs. Hutchins?" asked Lloyd.

It was Inspector Hill who answered. "A sort of a suicide attempt," she said. "Is that what you thought it was?"

"Yes," said Nicola. "With him having said something about Curtis Law. I thought Rachel must have told him about her and Curtis. I thought she must have told him she was leaving him, and that he'd taken something to try and stop her going, because he *couldn't* beat Rachel into submission, not like he could my mother. And when she just ignored him, he'd rung me with this story about a sheep, just to get me there so I would get a doctor for him before whatever he'd taken actually worked. I thought that Rachel had left because she knew I'd be there, and I'd deal with it."

She saw Chief Inspector Lloyd smile a little when she said that.

"Then next day, when you told me he'd been stabbed," she said, looking at Inspector Hill, "I thought maybe she'd gone back to him, found him on the sofa, and just . . . you know. And I didn't want to get her into trouble, because I thought that was what had killed him."

"Was your father lucid when he woke up?" asked Lloyd.

"Oh, yes," said Nicola. "He said he'd told me to get a doctor, and I hadn't, and when he was strong enough, he'd give me a

298

hammering I wouldn't forget, and to fetch one now if I knew what was good for me, and I . . ." She closed her eyes, made herself tell them. "I said no." She opened her eyes then, and looked at their faces, but it was serious, professional, unshockable expressions that they held. "And I told him I was never taking another order from him, or another hammering from him, because he was going to die, and it was his own fault. I told him that all I was taking from him was what he owed me. I told him I was taking the money from the safe." She paused, aware that Inspector Hill was taking notes, feeling that she should give her time to catch up. "By the time I'd finished talking he had started rambling about Curtis Law again, but I couldn't make anything out. Whatever he'd taken was working fast, because of the alcohol. Well—whatever he'd been given, I suppose, but I didn't know that. Not then."

"Did you know how ill he was?" asked Lloyd.

"Yes. I knew he would go into a coma if he didn't get help. I knew he would die. I wanted him to die. But I thought he'd taken something himself. I thought it was his own fault. When he finally lost consciousness, I took the money from the safe, and closed the office door again. Then I went home. Gus was back from the pub, complaining that I hadn't rung him, and . . . and it was as though it had never happened."

Lloyd nodded slowly, and got up, came round to her side of the table. The inspector was still writing.

"Is that murder?" she asked him. "Did I murder him?"

"No," he said quietly. "You didn't murder him."

"But it is against the law, isn't it? To leave someone like that? Without getting help?"

"Well, don't worry about that just now."

Nicola saw his hand come towards her, and her arm automatically went up to ward it off. But he just patted her shoulder. She felt herself blush hard. That was silly of her. He hadn't been going to hit her. She had known he wasn't going to hit her. Why had she done that? She'd stopped doing that a long time ago.

Inspector Hill took her hand. "I think perhaps you need some help, Nicola. Would you like me to phone your doctor?"

Nicola shook her head. "I'm all right," she said. "I know what I did just now, but I'm all right." She saw the inspector look worriedly up at Lloyd, and she, too, looked up at him. "I'm sorry," she said. "I used to do it to Gus if he reached out to me like that. He always just pretended I hadn't. I'd stopped myself doing it. I don't know why I did it just now."

"Is your husband at home?" asked Inspector Hill.

"He's left me," Nicola said, then almost laughed. "I've lost a husband and found a grandfather. Mr. McQueen says he's my grandfather. Well—his wife's my grandmother. He's worried about me. He wants me to stay at his house tonight. He says his wife will be there, and we should meet. But I don't know them. I don't really want to go there."

"Do you have someone else you can go to? Or someone who can stay with you? So that you're not on your own?"

"Rachel," she said, and then she remembered, and her hand flew to her mouth. "I'm supposed to be there," she said. "I'm supposed to be at the farm. Mr. McQueen's waiting to take me back. They're coming to take the—" She saw Inspector Hill's concerned face. "Am I free to go?" she asked.

"Yes," she said, doubtfully. "If you think you're all right."

"Most of the time." Nicola smiled briefly, a little tearfully. "I see dogs like me in the surgery," she said. "Ones people have rescued. But they get better, once they realize it's stopped. So will I."

"I'm sure you will," said Lloyd. "But perhaps you shouldn't try doing it all on your own. Or it'll keep coming back. Like the gypsies."

"I will get help. Counselling. Whatever. If I'm not in prison. Well, I suppose even if I am, they might let me have . . ."

"I don't think it'll come to prison," said Inspector Hill. "And as far as counselling goes, Rachel's probably as good as you could get anyway. Have you told her all this?"

"No."

300

"Perhaps you should."

Mr. McQueen drove her back to Rachel's, then went wandering off while she and Rachel sat in her father's office.

"They don't want the stuff in here," Rachel said. "Too old and battered for them to be interested in it. Reckoned I might as well sit somewhere that wasn't goin' to disappear from under me."

Nicola told Rachel what she had told the police, and Rachel looked as unshocked as they had. But it was a shocking thing to have done, wasn't it? She thought it was. Rachel just said that she should never have been there, but Nicola didn't understand what she meant.

She watched as all Rachel's lovely stuff was being carried out of the house, and looked back at her. "I caused all this, didn't I?" she said.

"No."

"But if I hadn't taken the money, you could have paid this month's instalment on the loan, and maybe you could have found a way to keep this from happening."

"The money wouldn't've made no difference."

"It would have made a difference to you. You've got to find the rent for this place."

But Rachel just smiled. "Don't worry 'bout it," she said. "Don't worry 'bout nothin', Nicola. It's not your problem." The smile went, and her face grew serious. "It never was," she said.

Curtis was back in Stansfield police station. He had been arrested again, cautioned, and the tape was being set up. By Lloyd's feet there was a small pile of stuff: papers, videos. A TV and video recorder were sitting on a table in the corner. It looked a little ominous. Attack, he decided, was the best method of defence. "This is harassment," he said.

"Is that right?" said Chief Inspector Lloyd. "And what would you call what you've been doing to me, Mr. Law?"

Curtis shrugged.

Lloyd sat down opposite him. "A word," he said. "Off the

record. You're a good journalist, Mr. Law. You know your subject. You knew how I would react to that programme, even if it never got shown, because *I* would have seen it, and it would have done nothing for my self-esteem."

"You don't seem lacking in that," said Curtis.

"No. It can afford to take a knock or two. Unlike some people's. You knew it wouldn't stop me coming after you when you began to emerge as the prime suspect. But you thought that it would stop me coming after you a second time, didn't you? And you were wrong about that, because here you are."

"You might regret it yet."

"I doubt it. And let's get one thing straight from the outset. For the first time in my career—and I mean for the first time—I couldn't care less about the fact that you killed in cold blood, because your victim was Bernard Bailey, and I actually think it's a great pity someone didn't do it sooner. What I object to, Mr. Law, are your methods."

"I don't know what you're talking about. I tried to kill Bailey, but I failed. I don't know why I'm back here."

"You're back here because you sadly underestimated Detective Inspector Hill. I make mistakes, Mr. Law, as you were only too pleased to point out in your programme. But I have *never* made that mistake."

Inspector Hill started the tape, and sat down. "Interview with Curtis Law, Thursday, thirty-first July. Present are DI Hill, DCI Lloyd, and Curtis Law. Mr. Law, you are not obliged . . ."

Curtis listened again to the rigmarole, then smiled. "How can I help you this time, Chief Inspector?" he asked.

"Let's see." Lloyd went through a lot of mannerisms. Head scratching, finger steepling, hand clasping. "It's difficult to know where to start, really," he said, sounding as though he had just arrived at the pit head after a night at the coal face. "Videos," he said, and sighed. "I have seen more videos this week than the most ardent of blue-movie fans."

Curtis raised an uninterested eyebrow.

"You wanted to murder Bailey," Lloyd said. "But Bailey

was having closed-circuit television installed, and that obviously presented a problem. So you thought you would turn this disadvantage to your advantage. You decided that the whole *thing* would be recorded for posterity. Everywhere you went, you were going to be on video. Video was going to prove you had been on a train when Bailey was really murdered. Video was going to prove that Mrs. Bailey's car hadn't moved from the moment she arrived at the hotel until the moment she left. And video was going to make me suspect you of murder, and look for all those clues you had so obligingly left me."

"I don't know what you're talking about." Curtis removed a cigarette from the packet, and lit it.

"But we'll come to the videos presently," said Lloyd. "Let's start with the red BMW two-seater that was seen driving away from Bernard Bailey's farm at approximately ten minutes to eleven on Sunday the twenty-seventh of July. Were you driving that car, Mr. Law?"

"No," said Curtis. "At ten to eleven on Sunday I was in a hotel suite with Rachel Bailey."

"Well, let's go back a bit. Where were you at, say, twenty past ten?"

"The same place, with the same person."

Lloyd shook his head.

"For the tape, Chief Inspector," said Curtis, archly.

"For the tape, I am shaking my head," said Lloyd. "At twenty past ten, you were at Bailey's Farm. You were driving a red BMW with false number plates, and you parked in the road at the front of Bailey's property."

Curtis didn't like the accuracy of his timing, or his geography. Surely Bailey hadn't had a camera installed that he knew nothing about? "Do you have some evidence of this?" he asked.

"Evidence? Certainly." He went into the pile of stuff, and pulled out a sheet of paper in a plastic folder. "I am showing Mr. Law a faxed invoice from Wicked Wheels Ltd., a car-hire firm, addressed to a Mr. Roger Wheeler, at the address of the flat owned by Aquarius Television in Barton. It is for the twenty-four-hour hire of a BMW sports car of exactly similar specification to that owned by Bernard Bailey, driven by Rachel Bailey, and repossessed by the finance company this afternoon."

Curtis breathed a silent sigh of relief. No evidence that he had been at Bailey's Farm, thank God. He had had no idea that Rachel's car was in imminent danger of repossession until he'd seen the repo man on the video Gary took. That would have ruined everything.

Lloyd stood up, flexed his back, and stepped over the pile. "It could have taken us a lot of man-hours to find the hire company," he said. "Naturally, you wouldn't have used the same one that supplied Roger Wheeler with his Jaguar. But we knew it would be a London firm, we knew it hired upmarket cars—we would have found it in the end. Fortunately, thanks to DI Hill here, we didn't have to."

Curtis blew smoke in DI Hill's direction.

"She makes notes—I expect you've noticed. Well, she's making them now, isn't she, even though we've got a tape running. And she made a note of everything she found in your flat. Including a mail shot from Wicked Wheels lying in the waste bin along with a couple of other car-hire firms hoping to get Mr. Wheeler's business. Try these ones first, she said. So we did. And bingo. I imagine the false number plates have been destroyed, but we'll keep looking in likely places, just in case. And of course inquiries are proceeding in an effort to find where you had them made up."

"What false number plates? I hired a car. That's all you know."

"You hired this car from seven o'clock on Sunday evening to seven o'clock on Monday evening. And shortly after you had received dinner in your suite together with Mrs. Bailey, you left the hotel by the Executive Wing door, picked up that car and drove it to Harmston." He turned away, and seemed to be reading a notice about AIDS.

"Prove it," Curtis said to his back, then turned to Inspector Hill. "Prove that car ever left London. I hired a car, using an alias. Perhaps I was hoping to defraud Aquarius TV. That's all you've got."

"You left the car," said Lloyd, still with his back to him, "and you went to Bailey's gate. You told Bernard Bailey that you had just seen a badly injured sheep on the road. Not one of his, of course, or the alarms would have been set off, but that wouldn't matter to Bailey. He liked animals. Not so keen on women, but he liked animals."

Curtis shook his head. "No," he said. "No—you're mixing your suspects up. That's his daughter's story."

Lloyd turned, his face like thunder. "No, Mr. Law," he said, his voice low and threatening. "That is your story. The one you told Bernard Bailey to get yourself through his gate and into his house in order to murder him, the one that you hoped would make Nicola Hutchins look a liar."

Curtis smiled.

"Now, I don't know exactly how you did it, but the pegs are very conveniently situated. I think I would hang up my jacket, perhaps drop something, bend to pick it up, and remove the phone connection from its socket."

Spot on. Prove it. Curtis said nothing.

"Bailey would, of course, attempt to phone his daughter. But the phone would be dead, since you'd just pulled it out of the socket. And you would kindly offer your mobile phone."

Curtis lit a cigarette. "I left Rachel the mobile," he said.

"For the tape," said Lloyd, "I am shaking my head again. You didn't leave Rachel the mobile."

"Then how did I ring her about the newspaper? Doubtless you've checked. She didn't receive any phone calls through the hotel switchboard."

"You didn't ring her about the newspaper," said Lloyd. He sat down again. "If you really had had occasion to ring her about the newspaper, you would have told her that you had inadvertently dropped your newspaper at the scene of the crime,

305

and asked her to get rid of it. Much simpler all round. But you didn't want her to get rid of it, because it was very important that we find that newspaper, wasn't it, Mr. Law?"

Oh, Jesus Christ, thought Curtis as he looked at the blue eyes that looked coldly into his. Lloyd knew exactly what he'd done. He'd slipped up somewhere. He must have. But they had to prove it, he told himself. They had to prove it. Guesses weren't worth anything.

"Oh, Mr. Law," Lloyd said, shaking his head. "You thought you had been so terribly clever, didn't you? But you have been found out. And the beauty of it is that it was Nicola Hutchins whose actions found you out. Poetic licence may be foreign to your journalistic nature, Mr. Law, but I'm sure you recognize poetic justice when it jumps up and bites you."

Curtis decided that from this point on, he should say nothing. He hadn't asked for a solicitor. Perhaps he should ask for one, but he wouldn't, not yet.

Lloyd reached back into the pile of stuff. "I am showing Mr. Law a fax of the printout of calls made on the mobile phone issued to Roger Wheeler. At ten-twenty-nine on Sunday evening, a call was made from that phone to the surgery of Mrs. Nicola Hutchins."

Shit.

"We weren't supposed to check the calls made on this phone, were we, Mr. Law? You knew that as soon as we suspected you of stabbing Bailey, we'd search that flat, knew we'd find the phone charged up. But you *confessed* to leaving it with Rachel. We had had to wring that confession out of you. So why on earth would we check that it was the truth?"

That had been the general thinking. Curtis stubbed out his cigarette.

"Shall I tell you why? Because Bernard Bailey hadn't rung a doctor. He had to have known that he was very ill for some time before he became too disoriented to deal with it. But he hadn't rung a doctor. Why? It had to be because his phone wasn't working, we thought. He'd rung his daughter from some other phone, which further suggested that his phone wasn't working, but since he hadn't left the premises all day, how had he done that? Answer. Someone brought a phone to him. And that's why we checked Roger Wheeler's charged-up mobile phone to see exactly what calls had been made from it, and when. And the silly thing is, that isn't why he hadn't rung the doctor at all. I doubt if he even tried."

Curtis lit another cigarette, drawing calming smoke into his lungs. "You can't prove where the phone was when that call was made," he said. "Or who made it. You can't prove that Rachel didn't have it. She might have called Nicola for a chat. She might be knocking off Gus for all you know, and called him."

"Quite true, Mr. Law." Lloyd sat back. "Which is something you may live to regret. But let us return to our sheep," he said, and smiled broadly. "Bailey tries to ring his daughter about it, finds the phone isn't working, and you offer your mobile. But you wanted the house to appear empty, and Mrs. Hutchins would be bound to look in the office, and the sitting room, so you chose the kitchen. She would see that it was in darkness through the hatch so she wouldn't try there. He'd be unconscious, or as good as, so with luck she would never know he was in the house."

Very, very good. And all totally unprovable. Did Lloyd seriously think he would break down and confess, or what?

"So . . . how to get him there? I think you would take him to the back door, where you would try to show him where exactly you had seen this poor, distressed animal that urgently needed veterinary attention. You showed him, he rang Nicola, and as soon as he had relayed the sheep's position . . ." Lloyd smiled. "You jammed a hypodermic into his neck, and knocked him out. Now," he said. "Which of us should tell the rest of this story, Mr. Law? You or I?"

"I'm fascinated," said Curtis. "Why don't you carry on telling it?" He still wasn't convinced that Lloyd had real evidence. It was psychological trickery.

"Then you injected the morphine, taking care this time not to find a vein, because he might have died there and then, and that wouldn't do. That wouldn't do at all. He had to stay alive for several hours if your plan was to work in its entirety."

Curtis tried to look calm and unruffled. It was as though he really had carried out this murder on camera.

"You left the back door unlocked, took his key to the alarm system, and switched off the alarms by opening the box on the wall, so you could leave the back way, over the fence, dodging the cameras that you helped set up in the first place."

He had told Bailey that blind spots were inevitable, as he had positioned the cameras to leave himself a clear run, not to the fence, but to and from a gap in the hedging. He hadn't wanted to be spotted climbing over a ten-foot fence by some courting couple.

"You then ran the tape back, and recorded over your arrival. We all missed that, I have to confess, because of course by the time we saw it, the tape had been recorded on again, and there was no jump in time to give us a clue. But the tape didn't run itself back until ten thirty-nine, and a twelve-hour tape running from ten-thirty in the morning would normally run itself back three or four minutes past the half hour at the most. That one ran nine minutes past the half hour, and a test has revealed that six minutes of that tape must have been run back and recorded over. We should have spotted that at the time, rather than in retrospect. But as you pointed out in your programme, we do make mistakes."

So, someone had tampered with it. It wasn't proof that he had. Inspector Hill might have worked it all out, but that was no good without proof, and that she hadn't got.

"You amused yourself in the meantime by working out what clue you were going to leave for me on your voiceover for your report of the murder, and you saw the open safe, and the money that was lying in it. So you closed the office door. But we'll come back to that."

Curtis lit another cigarette.

"And then you left by the rear, ran round to the front, waited until you saw Nicola Hutchins's car in your rear-view mirror. You knew she would be arriving sooner or later, as she would not, of course, have found the sheep. Once you saw her, you drove off, making certain that she saw *your* car."

And it had worked beautifully. Nicola had driven towards the farm, obediently going to confess to Daddy that she hadn't found his sheep, and get herself beaten up for it. The woman needed her head tested.

"You knew that naturally, she would assume that it was Mrs. Bailey that she had seen," Lloyd said. "You knew that naturally, whether she wanted to or not, she would tell us that, and that the alarms had been off, and the house empty. Naturally, we would suspect her, especially when we checked up on the whereabouts of Mrs. Bailey's car. There she was, telling us about a sheep that didn't exist, and a phone call that had never been made, and alarms that had unaccountably been switched off in an empty, unlocked house, when we had been told that Bailey had been in mortal fear all day, and would never have put the alarms off or left the farm late at night. And we would conclude that since she was there at the material time, complete with drugs, that she had had to lie about the alarms to explain how this mythical sheep had got out in the first place, lied about the car to incriminate Rachel, and lied about the house being empty because she had murdered her father."

So how come he was here and she wasn't?

"She had the motive," Lloyd went on. "She had been abused all her life, had been deliberately omitted from her father's will. We would think that she was hoping to lay the blame at Rachel's door, knowing, as she did, Rachel's relationship with you, and knowing, as everyone did, your relationship with drug suppliers. We were supposed to think she was trying to frame you, when all the time you were framing her." He leant forward. "And there was the possibility that sooner than incur anyone's displeasure, she would actually confess to murdering her father, wasn't there? You knew that. She might give the impression of being in control, but you know just how unstable she is, because Rachel had told you, hadn't she?"

Curtis smiled again. This was all guesswork. It was right, but it was guesswork.

"And—most importantly—you knew that she would be too frightened of her father to put the alarms back on again without his permission, which he would be unable to give, since he wouldn't, as far as she was concerned, even be there."

Curtis stubbed out his cigarette, and sat back, arms folded. "I don't see you producing evidence of any of *that*," he said.

"No," said Lloyd. "And I can't produce evidence that you then drove the car to Barton, almost certainly to the Aquarius flat, changed out of your jeans and into a suit, then drove away again and parked close to the station. Or that you joined the passengers leaving the eleven-thirty from St. Pancras, and drove back to where you had parked the BMW, stopping only to pick up your accomplice on the way."

No proof. No evidence. As long as he kept his mouth shut, they could prove absolutely nothing. All Lloyd was doing was digging a great big hole for himself.

Lloyd got up again, walking round the little room as he spoke. "Your accomplice gave you the newspaper and the cancelled return ticket, and drove the BMW back to London, to be collected by Wicked Wheels later that day, and you drove back to Bailey's Farm. You parked on the road, this time at the rear of the property, for an hour and a half, and you did the *Times* crossword. You smoked and drank Coke, and for someone with a conscience about forest fires, you have very little regard for the litter laws, because you threw out your Coke cans, you emptied your ashtray . . . in other words, you left clues. Big, bold clues that even an incompetent copper like me couldn't miss."

Curtis looked away. Lloyd was enjoying this. He was centre stage, and loving every minute. But he wouldn't enjoy it for very long, because providing he said nothing, it was all just guesswork, however clever his detective inspector had been.

"Then, when you felt you had crossed off enough clues in your crossword, and left enough clues on the roadway, you let yourself in to Bailey's property the same way you had left it. If the alarms had all gone off, you would have driven away before anyone got there, but they didn't. True to form, Nicola had interfered with nothing. Or so you thought."

Now, they were coming to whatever it was he had done wrong. He was supposed to ask what she'd done, he supposed. Lloyd really was skating on very thin ice. He wondered how much the tabloids would pay for his story after this.

"You went in by the back door, locked it, went to the drawer and chose a knife entirely unsuited both to cutting apples and to murdering anyone. An old, blunt, short-bladed vegetable knife. The last thing you wanted it to do was finish him off, or even be capable of doing him much damage. But it couldn't look as though you'd *chosen* it. It had to look as though you had just picked it up, so you hacked an apple in two with it, and put it on the coffee table."

Now, Curtis lit another cigarette. Pretty good, except that he had chosen the knife weeks before, when he was helping Bailey with the cameras. He had taken it away, deliberately blunted it, kept it. Rachel, if she had missed it, would just think she had mislaid it. That wasn't it, wasn't what had got Judy Hill on to him. It was something to do with Nicola Hutchins, but he couldn't imagine what. It didn't really matter. Proof was what Lloyd needed.

"Then you switched the alarms back on, pushed the phone connection back into the socket, gave the now comatose Mr. Bailey his key back, and stuck the knife into him four times. When you had done that, you took your newspaper, and you smeared it with blood, and left it lying on the floor." Lloyd perched on the corner of the table. "This was the window-dressing. And it was done for three reasons. One was to make me suspect you of a murder that never happened, the second was to leave a clue that would give you an alibi for the real murder, and the third was to give Rachel Bailey a real, honest-to-God fright."

And it had worked, Curtis thought. On all counts.

"This time you ran the tape back thirteen minutes," said Lloyd. "Not to remove the recording of your arrival as before, and as you would subsequently say, but rather to mask the fact that you had not arrived by the gate, which was, of course, going to be your story. Because the longer Bailey had appeared to remain conscious, the later he would be assumed to have been given the drugs, which would have the effect of isolating Nicola Hutchins as his murderer." He got off the table. "Then you *left* by the front gate, concealing your identity to some extent, but knowing that you would be faintly recognizable, and that together with all the other clues, you were certain to be suspected of the murder of Bernard Bailey."

Curtis lit a fresh cigarette.

"And it was, you thought, foolproof. The worst that could happen would be that Nicola would find Bailey, and get help in time to save him. Then when Bailey recovered and accused you, you would simply deny ever having been there, and you would have an alibi to prove it. However, none of that happened. As far as you were concerned, everything had gone as hoped for. But it hadn't, Mr. Law. It hadn't."

Presumably Rachel had been right. Nicola had found her father. So what? She hadn't done anything about it. Curtis had been a bit worried about how long Nicola had been in the house, but not too worried, because nothing had come of it. He had assumed that Nicola had thought her father was drunk, and that Rachel had been involved in his subsequent stabbing; that she had said nothing in order not to get Rachel into trouble. But he had known that she would crack, that she would tell them in the end about seeing the car, and that the hotel car-park videos would apparently prove she was lying.

"You thought Bailey would still be unconscious by the time his daughter left, but she, afraid of offending him, waited

312

longer than you thought, and Bailey was conscious and lucid long enough to get himself from the kitchen to the sitting room, long enough to try to tell Nicola what you'd done to him, and long enough to issue a final threat. And that was the straw that broke the camel's back, Mr. Law. The worm turned. But you weren't to know that."

Curtis didn't know what he was going on about with his camels and worms. He was still waiting to see some evidence.

"So you thought it had worked. But in order for me to suspect you, you had to catch my attention, didn't you, Mr. Law? So you did a voiceover for the news report, mentioning money in a safe that you couldn't have seen through a closed door. You knew Gary would get the camera rolling as soon as he got to the farm, and we would confiscate the tape, and, of course, watch it—video of a murder scene is very helpful. And the first thing the camera would see would be the closed door to Bernard Bailey's office."

Curtis didn't react at all.

"What you didn't know," Lloyd went on, "was that the money wasn't *there* any more. And what you still don't know is that it was Nicola Hutchins who removed it."

"So?"

"We have two statements, Mr. Law. One is from a Jack Melville, who called on Mr. Bailey at ten o'clock on Sunday evening, in which he says that he gave Mr. Bailey four thousand, six hundred pounds, and one is from Nicola Hutchins, who says that she removed four thousand, six hundred pounds from Mr. Bailey's safe at about midnight that same evening. And if you saw that money, Mr. Law, then you couldn't possibly have been on the eleven-thirty from St. Pancras."

Was that it? Were they going to have to rely on Nicola Hutchins giving evidence? Someone who stole from her own father? Someone who would agree that the moon was made of green cheese if it meant avoiding an argument? Someone who every now and then lost it altogether? Curtis smiled. "How do you know she removed it at midnight?" he said. "*She* could

313

have put the alarms off. She could have come back later, once she was certain he would be in a coma, gone in the back way, and taken the money *after* I stabbed him. A good brief would get her admitting that in five minutes flat."

"For the tape," said Lloyd, "I am shaking my head. A good brief would know that she couldn't possibly have done that. How did she leave? If she had left the back way, the alarms would have had to remain off. If she left the front way, she would have been on the video."

Shit, shit. Curtis thought furiously. "How do you know Rachel didn't turn the alarms back on when she got home?" he said, beginning to hear a note of desperation in his voice. "Just because she says they were on doesn't mean they were. You can't trust her an inch. She and Nicola could be in this together."

"But the alarms were on when *we* got there," said Lloyd. "And when Bernard Bailey was examined by the pathologist, the key to them was in his shirt pocket. That key was in there when he was stabbed, Mr. Law. And no one had removed it, because it was covered in undisturbed blood. Therefore the alarms were reset *before* you stabbed Bailey. No one turned them on after that. Mrs. Hutchins took the money when she says she did, and you were not on that train."

Curtis closed his eyes. Sod's Law. Sod's Law had got him. Law on Sod's Law, he thought. Maybe he could do a series when he got out of prison.

"But." Lloyd reached down and picked up a video. "Thanks to Inspector Hill, we can prove that by more solid means."

Barton station concourse, timed at eleven twenty-five, when the station was busy with people catching last trains. Curtis watched as he walked into camera range in a crowd of other people. There simply wasn't a way on to Barton station by which you could avoid the cameras, but he had taken precautions. He had worn a different hooded jacket from the one he had been wearing when he had left Bailey's Farm, and had ditched it on platform three.

With the hood up, he couldn't be picked out from the crowd

just by running through the security videos, because his face was in shadow. He had given Rachel the Roger Wheeler disguise, because there was no way in the world that he was recognizable on the video as it stood. So how the hell had they picked him out? But they had. They could, and would enhance it.

"It's good to know, isn't it," said Lloyd, "that there are some honest people left in the world? An anorak was found on platform three, Mr. Law, and handed to a member of staff, who handed it in to Lost Property, as we saw when we were anxious to prove that you *were* on that train. And it occurred to me that it was a very warm night on which to have worn such a garment. Inspector Hill even found herself reflecting that she had only seen one other person wearing a hooded jacket recently, and that had been to conceal his identity. She remembered that, Mr. Law, when we began to piece things together."

Curtis crushed out his cigarette.

"It was, as I've just said, a very warm night. Once they knew what to look for, it took the station security staff no time at all to find you, because absolutely no one else was wearing a jacket with the hood up. And, of course, as I'm sure you know, security video pictures can be enhanced. We're assured that this one will blow up quite effectively, and that quite enough of your face is showing for you to be identified."

He knew that.

"Unfortunately, that was the one thing that Sergeant Finch couldn't arrange in time for this interview, but we know that's you, Mr. Law, and we are going to prove it, make no mistake about that."

Curtis was under no illusions about the weight of Lloyd's evidence, but there was even more.

"A bonus," said Lloyd. "The jacket has gone to forensic. The hood yielded two head-hairs. So if you want to fight this, Mr. Law, your brief will have to challenge not just the unstable Mrs. Hutchins, but documentary evidence, video evidence, and forensic evidence, all proving beyond a doubt that your alibi was faked. And I believe there can only be one reason for

315

faking an alibi for murder. But that will be up to the jury to decide."

It *was* happening. It really was. This wasn't a nightmare. This was for real.

"So that's why you're sitting here. Because Inspector Hill doesn't miss a trick, and because Nicola Hutchins, whose total lack of confidence in herself you hoped to exploit, whom you hoped to frame for murder, defied her father for the first time in her life."

Curtis nodded. He wasn't going to try to deny anything. They had enough evidence to sink him. But he wasn't going down alone. "I trust you've arrested her, too," he said.

"Who?" asked Lloyd.

"You know damn well who!" shouted Curtis. "You can't play favourites! I did it for her. And she had better be charged too, or you'll be in deep shit."

Lloyd looked faintly puzzled. "I'm sorry," he said. "Who are we talking about?"

"My accomplice, Mr. Lloyd," said Curtis. "As you've just demonstrated, I couldn't be in two places at once."

"Ah, yes, your accomplice," said Lloyd, and picked up another tape, ejecting the one already in, pushing the new one in.

The station concourse once again. People coming through the doors from the platform. Lloyd froze the picture. "Well," he said, "it has to be one of these people. Which of them would you like me to arrest?"

"Rachel Bailey is the one carrying the hand luggage," said Curtis, through his teeth.

"Oh, the girl who walked past the taxis?" said Lloyd. "Is she?" He got up and bent over, peering at the screen. "Are you sure?" he said. "You can't see her face with that sunhat, and of course, she's walking away from the camera, unlike you, so there's no point in enhancing the video still, because we'd just get a better picture of her hat. But anyway, she's got long dark hair, and she must be at least a size larger than Rachel Bailey. What do you think, Inspector?"

DI Hill looked over at the screen, and spoke for the very first time. "At least," she said. "Maybe two sizes larger."

"She's wearing the padded waistcoat and wig that I used as Roger Wheeler," said Curtis. "As if you needed telling."

"Well!" said Lloyd, shaking his head. "I'd never have recognized her. Indeed, I *didn't* recognize her, when I saw this video before." He took off his glasses and looked at Curtis. "And you know something? I don't think anyone else would recognize her. I've a feeling that she will deny absolutely that it *is* her. And there won't be much we can do about that if she does."

Curtis stared at him. "Are you saying you're going to let her get away with this?"

"No," said Lloyd. "Not if she's involved, and we can prove it. What I'm saying is that *that* isn't evidence of her involvement that would stand up in court. So unless she admits that she is this woman . . ." He shrugged. "Do you think she will?"

Curtis turned to Inspector Hill. "Then I'll ask you what you asked me," he said. "How did I know she would ring the café? If I didn't leave her the mobile, if I didn't ring her at the hotel, then she already knew to do that, didn't she?"

Inspector Hill nodded. "*If* you didn't ring her at the hotel," she said. "But as you pointed out yourself, we have absolutely no proof that you didn't leave her the mobile. What you did or did not do with the mobile won't form part of the case against you, because we can't prove where it was when that call was made, or who made it. I believe you pointed that out, too. Besides, that was in order to set up your deliberately transparent alibi for the stabbing, on which no charges are being brought."

Jesus. He stared at them. "Rachel Bailey got me to murder her husband, and you're going to do nothing about it?"

Lloyd sat back. "Did she? In your last statement, you said that she had *not* asked you to murder her husband."

"She said I could kill him and get away with it! She said I could run rings round the police!"

"A rare lapse of judgement on her part," said Lloyd. "But

did she actually *ask* you to murder him? You told us repeatedly that she knew nothing whatever of your plan to murder her husband."

Curtis stared at him. "But she *did* know!" he shouted. "I even told her I was going to poison him! She bought the paper, brought it to me! And after I'd done it, I made her believe that I had stabbed him *instead* of doing what I'd said I'd do, that I hadn't done it right, and I hadn't killed him after all, so that even *she* wouldn't know what had really—" He broke off.

Lloyd nodded. "You thought of absolutely everything, Mr. Law," he said. "You covered every angle you could possibly have foreseen. You set up clues and alibis and red herrings like nobody's business. I think you may actually have made it impossible for us to implicate Rachel Bailey in her husband's murder. You've run rings round yourself, Mr. Law."

Christ. Lloyd was right. She really believed that she *hadn't* murdered Bailey, and innocence was the best defence of all. He couldn't be certain that she *wasn't* innocent of Bailey's actual murder. But innocence was not a word he would associate with Rachel Bailey.

"Do you know what she was doing, the last time I was in here?" he shouted. "Screwing McQueen, that's what she was doing! Because he'd said he'd buy her land if she did. And do you know what that makes her? A whore. She's nothing but a whore who murdered her husband for money, and you're going to let her walk away from it!"

Lloyd gave a short sigh. "I can only assure you, and hope that you accept my assurances, that we have not yet finished our inquiries, and that we will be questioning Mrs. Bailey further, in view of what you have told us. That if we do uncover any evidence of her involvement, the appropriate charges will be brought. But for the moment, you're on your own, Mr. Law. Interview terminated at 17.15 hours."

Curtis was taken away, and charged for the second time with the murder of Bernard Bailey. Last time, when he had been asked if he had anything to say in answer to the charge, he had said nothing. This time, he said that he had done it for her.

But he was on his own, and that was the way he was going to stay, if he knew Rachel Bailey at all.

Mike watched as two bailiffs supervised the removal of everything they thought was worth anything. Rachel had told him what Nicola had done, what it was that she had been bottling up, what it was that had pushed her to the very edge of her reason. Served the bastard right, that was what he had said. Rachel had agreed. But it should never have happened, she had said. Mike chose to let that pass.

Nicola was behaving exactly as you would expect a vet to behave when supervising the removal of a herd of cattle, as though nothing at all was wrong; Rachel stood, leaning against the porch railing, watching her peach armchairs being loaded up into a removal van.

"This has nothing to do with me, you know," Mike said, joining her on the porch. "I'm strictly land and buildings."

She smiled. "I know that," she said.

"I could maybe buy some of it back for you."

She looked up at him. "You hagglin' now?"

"Yes."

She shrugged. "Reckon it's a buyer's market this time," she said. "I got no money for the rent. Seems that money forms part of Bernard's estate. It'll go to creditors."

"Same arrangement as before about the rent. And make a list of the stuff you want back, if you like. I'll go to the auction."

"Depends," said Rachel. "What do I have to do for it?"

"Shirley and I are going to need your help with her," he said, nodding across at Nicola. "You know her. We don't." He sighed. "You'd swear there was nothing wrong with her, most of the time. But there is."

"She's always fooled folk," said Rachel. " 'Cos she did so good at school and college and all that. But that's because she didn't want no comeback from Bernard 'bout wastin' his money. She don't know who to be frightened of now, and she can't keep up the act like she could." She looked up at him again. "D'you think they'll do anythin' 'bout her not gettin' help for Bernard?"

Mike shrugged. "I'll take her to my solicitor this evening, see what he has to say. Whatever happens, she'll need professional help. But I think we can probably do more good than they can, in the long run." He watched the last of the cows being loaded up. "Will you let me buy you a cow back?" he asked.

"What do I have to do to get a cow?"

"Give us a drink of real, unpasteurized milk straight from her udder now and then. There's nothing like it. Margaret used to bring me it from Hawthorne's. I haven't tasted it in twenty-five years."

Rachel smiled. "Done," she said, and spat on her hand.

Mike smiled, spat on his, and they shook on it.

Lloyd smiled tiredly as Judy came into his office. They hadn't had any chance to talk since their interview with Nicola; they had had to assemble the interview room, and Tom had surpassed himself with his evidence-gathering; they had been under way with Curtis Law before they'd had time to get their breath back. "Thank you," he said.

"What for?"

"Giving me the floor with Law."

"You're welcome."

"When I think what he tried to do to Nicola Hutchins . . ." Lloyd was lost for words, as he thought of her cowering away from his hand after having so bravely got herself together, calm and assured, even when she was confessing to what she had done. It took so little to knock her off balance, and Law had known that, used that. But he hadn't realized how deep it went. He shook his head. "I don't think even Rachel knew the extent of the damage," he said.

"No," said Judy. "When you come to think of it, perhaps Bailey did commit suicide, in a way."

Yes. More poetic justice. "But she was the only one who knew Nicola *was* damaged," Lloyd said. "And she was right about Gutless Gus. Off like a shot as soon as he sussed she wasn't quite the ticket."

"I think Rachel's right about most things," said Judy. "And if she gets it wrong she puts it right. She sent Nicola to us to nail Curtis Law, because she realized what he'd been trying to do to her."

"And it cost her four thousand, six hundred pounds to do it." Lloyd smiled. "That must have hurt."

"I think this business cost Rachel a lot more than that," said Judy, standing up. "Can she wait till tomorrow? We're not going to get a thing on her anyway, and I'd like to be excused, if I may."

"Where are you going?"

"I've just rung the ACC. He says he can see me if I leave now. His door, he assured me, is always open."

"It *is*," said Lloyd, pulling a face. "Literally. He closes it when you go in. Well, he does when it's me. Maybe it's politically incorrect to close doors with a woman in the room." He looked at her. "Does this mean you've made your mind up?"

"No," she said. "I just want to know where I stand."

"Good. I'm sure he will applaud your making an informed decision. He's very fond of them."

Judy smiled. "And you should go home," she said, getting up. "See you later."

But Lloyd had no intention of going home, leaving things half done, and he took his mobile phone with him when he went to talk to Rachel Bailey. He had rung Wicked Wheels in the vain hope that the car might still yield evidence, but the managing director had told him that cars were usually washed and valeted on the day after collection. However, he had said, sometimes there was a backlog, and it was just possible that it hadn't been done yet. He would ring him back.

321

He didn't really *want* evidence of Rachel Bailey's involvement, but it was his job, and it was against the law to murder your husband. He shook his head as he drove through the gate. He knew Rachel Bailey to be guilty of the cold-blooded murder of her husband, and he was hoping that she would get away with it. Because he fancied her? Because he loathed what he had learned about Bailey? A little bit of both, he thought. And right or wrong, he did hope she would get away with it.

The house was unrecognizable. Virtually nothing remained of its elegant, comfortable furnishings. The hallway, of course, was bare of the paintings, he noticed as he followed Rachel into the office, the only room that seemed to have any furniture in it at all. Other things were piled up in it; some clothes, a suitcase, Rachel's personal belongings. This time, she sat behind the desk, and he sat down opposite her.

"We re-arrested Curtis Law this afternoon," he said. "He has been charged with your husband's murder. I think this time it will stick."

She gave a brief nod of acknowledgement, but said nothing.

"He's given us a statement which strongly implicates you, Mrs. Bailey," he said.

She shrugged slightly. "Helped him out over the business with the newspaper," she said. "You know that."

"The newspaper was a deliberately planted red herring, and Mr. Law insists that you knew that. That you knew of his plan in its entirety."

She frowned. "What plan's that?" she asked.

Lloyd smiled. "We have reason to believe," he said slowly, "that Curtis Law did not ring you about the newspaper. That you purchased that newspaper, and brought it to Mr. Law on the eleven-thirty train from St. Pancras, in order that he could establish an alibi for the time the actual murder was committed. Mr. Law says that he furnished you with a disguise in order to carry out this task. He says you helped plan and execute the murder of your husband, Mrs. Bailey."

She sat back in the chair, and looked at him. "You got proof of any of that, Mr. Lloyd?" she asked, her eyes amused.

"Not yet."

"You expectin' to get some?"

Lloyd patted his mobile, which he had placed on the desk. "I'm expecting a phone call," he said. "From a car-hire firm. We can have that car forensically examined. If you left any trace of your presence . . ."

"What car's that?"

Lloyd sighed. "I think you know what car, or we wouldn't have had a visit from Nicola Hutchins." He looked at her, his head slightly to one side. "I'm curious," he said. "Curtis Law had hired a car exactly like yours in order for you to get back to the hotel. Did you ask him why? What excuse did he give you? You were a bit slow off the mark, whatever it was."

He still couldn't fathom Rachel Bailey. Everything about her was slow, except her mind, and it was hard to believe that she had swallowed whatever Law had told her about that car. But she would never have allowed Nicola Hutchins to get to the very brink of mental collapse before rescuing her, not if she could have avoided it.

"Don't know nothin' 'bout any car," she said lazily. "I was in London all the time, Mr. Lloyd, and I don't reckon you can prove no different, or you wouldn't be here. I'd be at your police station, under arrest, just like Curtis."

Lloyd knew that was all he was going to get. All anyone was ever going to get. There were so many things he wanted to know, wanted to understand, but Rachel Bailey wasn't going to explain herself to him or anyone else.

"I thought Nicola would be here," he said. "Is she all right?"

"She's fine. Mr. McQueen's taken her to see his lawyer, find out how much trouble she's in. Nell and me'll be stayin' with her tonight."

"Good. I think that would be best for all three of you." He looked round the dingy little office. "Is this it?" he said. "Is this what you're left with?"

"I'll be gettin' some of my stuff back. Me and Mr. Mc-Queen've got an arrangement," she added candidly. "Curtis didn't like it when he found out about McQueen." Her eyes widened in would-be innocence. "D'you think that's why he's tellin' lies about me?"

Lloyd didn't dignify that with an answer.

"But Mr. McQueen's been good to me. He's even buyin' me a cow so I can start a smallholdin'."

Lloyd heard the sarcasm, shook his head. "That's what stands between you and poverty?" he asked. "A cow and McQueen's good will?"

"Reckon so."

He might have tried to tell her that she was worth more than that, but she must know that herself, and anyway, his phone rang. "Excuse me," he said, picking it up. "Hello, Lloyd here."

"Mr. Lloyd. It's David Bingley, Wicked Wheels. I've checked up on that car, but it's no go, I'm afraid. It was put through the car wash and valeted on Tuesday morning."

What a shame. His last hope of evidence against Rachel Bailey had gone. "Ah, well," Lloyd said. "You win some, and you lose some."

"Sorry," said Bingley. "But I'm glad you rang. It seems that we've been trying to get in touch with Mr. Wheeler. In fact, the secretary at the depot says she caught the late post on Monday with a letter to him, but there's been no reply. It's just that we've retrieved some lost property from the vehicle, and it looks as though it might be quite valuable, so . . ."

Lloyd didn't want to hear this. He really, really didn't want to hear this.


Jack looked up as Terri came in. She walked in slowly, almost hesitantly, an adverb that he had never found himself applying to his wife's way of behaving before. She sat down, and looked at him for a long time without speaking.

"Have you come to discuss divorce?" he asked, after a few moments of that.

"No," she said. "I've come to make a confession."

"You were having an affair with Bernard Bailey," said Jack, with a grin. Humour usually helped, though he wasn't sure if anything would now.

She pulled a face at the very idea. "But it has to do with him," she said, and took a deep breath. "I told Mike McQueen his financial position. Told him who he'd borrowed from, what sort of loan it was. You told me that in confidence, and I told Mike McQueen, because it would give him leverage. I think that bit of untrustworthiness probably cancels out Excelsior Holdings."

Jack had reflected on how devious they both were a couple of months back, he remembered. Neither of their devious tactics had paid off. Because someone had murdered the man, and not before time, even if he had lost a great deal of money over it.

"And while your capacity for lying startled even me when I discovered that that story about Rachel Bailey was invented from beginning to end," she said, "I was even more startled that you had actually kept your promise."

Jack cast wildly round his memory for any promise he had made, never mind kept, and was unable to locate it.

"You really haven't had an affair since the last time we spoke about it," she said.

Oh, that. True.

"You really did manage to live in the same village as Rachel Bailey without adding her to your list of conquests."

Ah. Well. Sort of true. In that Rachel Bailey had steadfastly refused to be added. Still. Terri didn't know that. She thought that the story about the pass was a lie, too. Did that make the truth a lie? Or a lie the truth? He really had lost the place now.

"I'm quite proud of you for that," she said.

"Does this mean you're not leaving me?" he asked.

She smiled. "How can I leave? I've got a painting to finish before we have to sell this place and move to a semi in Stansfield." She got up. "And the shadows should be right just about now."

Rachel shaded her eyes from the setting sun that slanted through the office window as Lloyd concluded his conversation with the car-hire firm.

"Right," Lloyd said. "Well, if you could just hang on to it for now, Mr. Bingley, someone will be collecting it from you. Yes. Yes. Thank you. Yes, I think it will be of assistance. Thank you again, and goodbye."

He put the phone down and looked at her. "The car *had* been valeted," he said.

"Reckoned it most likely would've been," she said.

"But they did find some lost property."

Rachel nodded. She'd gathered that.

"And you rang the hotel with a description of *your* lost property," Lloyd said. "I don't know if you realize it, but . . ." He waved a hand at the fireplace. "It works both ways," he said. "I overheard you."

Rachel glanced at the fireplace, then back at Lloyd. "Never thought 'bout that," she said.

It was true; she had never thought about it. As far as she could recall, no conversation had ever taken place in the bedroom, unless you counted Bernard's quietly spoken threats, and her desperate phone call to Nicola the next day. It had never occurred to her that her call to the hotel might have been overheard. But it had.

"Then perhaps you should think about it now," he said.

Rachel nodded, thought about it, then made a small bet with herself. If she was wrong, it wouldn't be for the first time, and she had always been, would always be, a gambler. "Seems to me," she said slowly, getting up from the desk, "that you and me and the man you were talkin' to are the only folk who know 'bout this."

Lloyd's eyebrows rose very slightly.

"And only you and me know what it means," she said. "So?"

"So if you collected it from him yourself, you could get rid of it, and no one'd ever know *nothin'* 'bout it 'cept you and me." She closed the blinds, doing the old, neglected office a favour, as the rose-tinted light was softened and diffused. She turned to look at him, and smiled. "Would they?" she said.

Lloyd's face held a would-be puzzled frown. "And why would I do that, Mrs. Bailey?"

Rachel walked over to him, sitting on the edge of the desk as she had sat on Mike McQueen's garden table. But this evening she was fully clothed, and her shoes stayed on. The highly unsubtle methods she had used on McQueen wouldn't go down too well with Lloyd. "Maybe 'cos I'd be real grateful," she said.

"A bribe, is it?" said Lloyd, sounding very Welsh.

"Don't reckon you'd take no money, even if I had any," she said. "But maybe I got somethin' you want."

"Are you offering to go to *bed* with me, Mrs. Bailey?" he said, as though the thought had just that moment occurred to him.

"Don't think they left no beds," Rachel said. "Reckon we could manage without, don't you?"

Lloyd shook his head. "Thank you," he said. "But no, thank you."

"Don't have to be here," she said. "Don't have to be now. Don't have to be just the once, neither. I'm not goin' nowhere, 'less it's to jail. You want me to end up there, Mr. Lloyd?"

"No," he said. "I don't. But much as I don't like the idea of your going to prison, and much as it grieves me to have to decline your offer, the answer's still no."

Rachel shrugged, pushed herself away from the desk, and sat on the safe, deemed too heavy for the truck by the bailiffs, reaching behind her to pull the blinds open again, angling them so that the sun's dying rays fell away from Lloyd. "That all right?" she asked.

"Fine," said Lloyd. "Mrs. Bailey, did you ask Curtis Law to murder your husband for you?"

"No," she said. "But he offered." Her eyes held his, and she gave the tiniest of shrugs. "Offer I couldn't refuse," she said.

"What about the death threats?"

"They were just to get Curtis here." Because seeing Curtis reminded her that real life was going on beyond Bailey's Farm. Because she had to have some respite from Bernard Bailey. Because Curtis had taken away her prescriptions, and had brought her six months' supply of pills at a time, in a spirit of self-interest. "Wasn't thinkin' of killin' no one, not then."

"So when was it all planned?"

"In the spring. Curtis reckons it took him a week's solid thinkin' to work it all out. Then he booked the suite, and came here, tellin' Bernard 'bout this demonstration that was planned, how some of them had said they were goin' to get him, get me, even. Got him all worked up, so when I said I'd go away for the weekend, he jumped at it."

Lloyd nodded. "And that was when you were given your instructions? At the weekend?"

"Yes. Told me we had to talk to folk at the hotel, make sure everyone saw us, remembered us. That we'd order dinner on Sunday night, and he'd order a cab for eleven, then leave right after they brought in the food and go back to Harmston. Said he was goin' to poison Bernard. He'd get here just before he went to bed, put somethin' in his whisky." She got up, and switched on the desk lamp, sitting on the corner of the desk. "But he reckoned we'd be the first people you'd suspect, 'cos Nicola'd never be able to keep quiet 'bout us. And she'd tell you 'bout how Bernard treated me. And everyone knew how Curtis could get hold of drugs, and how much the land was goin' to be worth to McQueen."

Lloyd looked as though he was going to say something, but he didn't, so she carried on.

"And he said you'd be able to find out when he'd been given the stuff, so we had to have alibis. I had to take the cab to St. Pancras, walk over to King's Cross, buy Monday's *Times*,

328

and bring it to him on the train. I had to get clothes a couple of sizes bigger'n I take, so I could wear them over his waistcoat thing, and change on the train. I had to use his return ticket, and that way it'd look like he was on the train when it happened. Then I had to drive back to London, and phone room service at half three. That way it'd look like I'd never left the hotel."

She hadn't liked it. She had said so, but he'd just kept saying that it would work. And it very nearly had. Very, very nearly.

"It was OK to start with," she went on. "But on Sunday, I didn't want him to go. I didn't want him to do it. I didn't know nothin' 'cept what he'd told me, and it didn't sound like an alibi to me. But he said to trust him." She gave Lloyd a brief smile. "Didn't have no option, so I did. I got the paper, and I caught the train, and I met him. Gave him his paper, his ticket, his waistcoat and his wig, and that was when he said 'bout ringin' Steve."

"Did you ask why?"

"Said he was goin' back to the farm, goin' to make it look like it happened in the middle of the night. Said it wouldn't be no good if he just gave you the paper, that you'd get suspicious if he produced somethin' that gave him an alibi. But you'd find it, and he'd tell you a lie 'bout droppin' it there that mornin', so you'd prove he couldn't have. And when you found out when Bernard really died, you'd already have proved he couldn't've done it."

"Why couldn't you have just brought the newspaper with you in the morning, left it there yourself?"

"I asked that. He said someone might find Bernard 'fore I got home, and the paper had to be there if they did."

Lloyd gave a reluctant smile. "I have to hand it to Mr. Law," he said. "He really did think of everything. I think you really were as much in the dark as we were."

Rachel nodded almost vigorous agreement. "When I did get here, it wasn't like he'd said it would be at all. I thought it'd all gone wrong, and I just lost it. Never had hysterics before—

wondered who was makin' all the noise. Never cried so much in my whole life as I cried this week. Never felt so scared, neither." She shrugged. "Never murdered no one before, though."

"I should hope not," said Lloyd.

"Don't do your nerves no good. Anyway, Curtis told me that he'd never meant to poison him. He'd just said that, so I'd react right. I didn't know nothin' 'bout no overdose of morphine till Nicola told me."

"But the post mortem was delayed," said Lloyd. "So we knew nothing about the overdose either. And Mr. Law found himself being arrested, which was the last thing he'd meant to happen."

"I was sick as a dog after you left that flat," she said. "Scared out of my wits all week."

Lloyd got up, started walking round the room again. "But I understand you still found time to take care of business," he said, looking at the small collection of things she had managed to hang on to. "Your arrangement with Mr. McQueen, for instance."

"Didn't have no option 'bout that, neither."

"But you knew that land was already McQueen's," he said. "What was the point of trying to sell it to him?"

"He didn't know I knew. Thought he was gettin' somethin' for nothin'." She shrugged. "It was another gamble," she said. "Reckoned once he'd had me, he'd want more, and he did. So I kept a roof over my head."

Lloyd shook his head slightly. "So," he said, "you had manipulated Curtis Law, you had manipulated McQueen, and then you manipulated me." He shook his head tiredly. "Don't tell me," he said, leaning on the filing cabinet. "You didn't have no option."

"I didn't," she said.

"You knew McQueen didn't want Bailey dead."

She nodded. "Had to get you off Nicola's back, while I thought what to do. You thought she'd done it. She thought

330

she'd done it. Thought she'd been imaginin' things . . . I had to do somethin'."

Lloyd looked weary as he walked slowly back to the chair, and sat down again. "Rachel," he said, "why did any of this have to happen? Why did Bailey have to die? Why didn't you just leave him? Stay away? Go and set up home with Curtis Law, steal McQueen away from his wife—anything? Why did he have to die?"

Rachel walked back round the desk. "Thought you were a detective," she said, opening the drawer, pulling out the folder of photographs, taking out the top one, pushing it over to Lloyd. "You think I carried on takin' the pill after he'd done *that* to me?" she said, tapping it. "First thing I did soon's I could move was burn every packet I had, case he found them. First thing *he* did soon's I could move was carry on tryin' to get me pregnant. And he did."

"You don't look pregnant."

"Well, I am. Thirteen weeks. You can check with my doctor if you want. My mother was the same. A month 'fore she was due, wasn't no one could tell she was pregnant, 'cept me. So I could've hung on, if I hadn't had to tell him 'bout it. But I did." She smiled. "Didn't have no option." She picked up the photograph, putting it back in its folder. "He got me to the doctor, got it confirmed. Soon's they could tell the difference, he made me have a scan." She glanced back at Lloyd. "I'm carryin' Bernard Bailey's son," she said. "And he knew it." She shook her head. "Told you, Mr. Lloyd. Wasn't no amount of money'd make me give Bernard Bailey any baby of mine to damage."

That was what Judy had meant about it costing Rachel a lot more than four thousand, six hundred pounds. She had already worked out Rachel's motive. He hadn't exactly been on the ball over this one. But then, he hadn't been well.

"If I'd stayed away, he'd've found me. No way he'd let me leave him when I was having his son. Or give up what was his once he was born. Wouldn't let his first wife take Nicola away from him, so there was no way he'd let me take a boy away.

And Nicola would've sworn blind that he never laid a hand on her if it come to a custody fight."

Lloyd nodded.

"Would've been my word 'gainst his. And what am I? A tinker. A traveller. With six half brothers and sisters, and not one of us got a father we'd know if we saw him in the street. Someone he paid to have his baby for him. No way I'd win. Couldn't leave my baby with him, couldn't stay and watch him hammer all the guts out of him like Nicola's mother watched him do to Nicola." She put the folder back in the drawer, closed it, and sat down. "That's why he had to die, Mr. Lloyd. Couldn't see no other way of dealin' with it." She shrugged. "Didn't have no option."

"And Curtis Law? Did he know all this?"

"No. Wouldn't've done it for me if he'd known I really was pregnant. He thought I was goin' to get kicked half to death again, that's why he offered to kill him for me. But I never said I wasn't pregnant. Never lied 'bout it. Not to him, not to you. Not to anyone."

"No," said Lloyd. "You just manipulated everyone."

She sat back. "You goin' to arrest me?"

Lloyd sighed, rubbed his eyes, and shook his head. "I could," he said. "I could arrest you, get you to repeat everything you've told me on tape. But your confession would be inadmissible, because I'm afraid I tricked it out of you. They didn't find your pendant in the car."

Rachel smiled. "I know," she said.

Lloyd looked really puzzled this time. "Then why the inducement?"

"Had a bet with myself that you wouldn't take me up on it. Even though you'd like to. Even though you didn't really have to get rid of evidence, didn't have to break no rules, run no risks. You could've got it for nothin', just like McQueen. But I reckoned you had too much respect for your lady inspector. For yourself. Maybe even for me."

Lloyd's tired face broke into a smile. "I should have known

332

I was being manipulated again," he said. "Is there anyone you haven't manipulated, Mrs. Bailey?"

"Your lady inspector," she said. But she had plans for her, if she got the chance.

"What were the terms of the bet you had with yourself?"

"You won either way," said Rachel. "If I lost, you got me. If I won, you got told what you wanted to know. But I'll deny every word if you try takin' it further. And I didn't have no motive at all, did I? I'm carryin' his son, and the only way I was goin' to get anythin' out of him was if he stayed alive and farmin' this land. No reason I'd want him dead."

"No," said Lloyd. "I doubt that I can take it any further. I can't prove a thing, thanks to Mr. Law."

"What did they find in the car?"

"A gold cigarette lighter. Mr. Law's, I presume, since I notice he's reduced to matches these days. I take it the hotel found your pendant?"

"No," said Rachel. "Reckon someone found it, though. Someone got lucky, maybe, walkin' along the Embankment or somewhere. Hope it was someone homeless. But I couldn't afford to be homeless, not with a baby on the way. That's why I had to work on McQueen. I thought I'd have the pendant to fall back on, but I don't."

Lloyd frowned. "But if you really have lost your pendant, how could you be so sure that they didn't find it in the car?" he asked.

" 'Cos I never drove that car, Mr. Lloyd. Wasn't slow off the mark, just never knew nothin' 'bout it. It was Curtis's car I drove back to London."

"Ah," said Lloyd. "The one that was in for service, according to him."

"He went to collect it when he'd finished here on Monday. I thought he was gettin' the train. But he must've driven this BMW back then."

"So how did you find out?"

333

"To start with, I really thought Nicola had murdered Bernard. Didn't know why she would suddenly take it into her head to do that, but it was obvious there wasn't no sheep, no way Bernard would've had the alarms off. So I thought she'd done it, and got so frightened she lied 'bout seein' my car. And I could understand that—I was frightened, and I'm not Nicola. It's a frightenin' thing to do, murderin' someone."

"I imagine it would be."

"Then McQueen told me to get rid of Curtis if I wanted our arrangement to go ahead. Reckoned the quickest way to do that was tell him 'bout McQueen. Kindest way was like I'd told him by accident, so he'd think he was ditchin' me. So I told him 'bout the photograph, said I thought McQueen had done it. It was just so I could tell him where I'd seen it. But he said McQueen didn't come here with a bag full of drugs." She shrugged again. "You hadn't told him how Bernard'd died, and I'd only just found out from Nicola. That's when I realized that he *had* poisoned Bernard, just like he said he would, that Nicola hadn't done it at all. So there was no way she would say she'd seen my car 'less she had. I didn't know how he'd got here from London on Sunday night, but then I reckoned he must've taken my car, didn't get away from here fast enough, and Nicola saw him."

Lloyd nodded, the frown between his dark eyebrows almost permanent now.

"Then Nicola told me that she couldn't've seen my car after all, that you'd checked up on it, and it hadn't left the car park. The poor kid thought she'd been seein' things, or lyin' without even knowin' she was doin' it. But she *had* seen it, and if my car hadn't gone from the hotel, that meant he'd got one just the same, and he'd made *sure* Nicola saw it, so she'd look like she was lyin'."

Lloyd got up again, stiffly, holding his back.

"And he'd got you suspectin' her, and Gus suspectin' her, and me suspectin' her—he'd even got her so she wasn't sure herself what she'd done, because she *had* done somethin'. And

334

she should never've been here to do that. He'd no business draggin' Nicola into this. Wasn't her problem, it was mine. She was right on the edge as it was, and he knew that. He'd no right messin' about with her, Mr. Lloyd. No right at all."

Lloyd drew the sheet away from the paintings, but it didn't matter, because the sun had gone down now.

"If you'd arrested her, I would've told you all this on tape, and that's the truth. Wouldn't let Nicola take the blame for somethin' I did. But she came and told me 'bout takin' the money, and I reckoned you'd put two and two together quick enough if I sent her to you. I didn't know what she was keepin' back, or maybe I would've done it different. Kept her out of it."

"But you'll see Curtis Law go to prison without a qualm?"

Rachel nodded. "He wouldn't *be* goin' to prison if he hadn't tricked Nicola into comin' here on Sunday night," she said. "Reckon it's his own doin', not mine."

"Poetic justice," Lloyd said, carefully separating the canvasses, looking through the paintings.

"But it would've worked," said Rachel, pleased at least to know that she hadn't lost her touch after all. "If I'd just hung on to that money, he *would've* run rings round you. I read him right."

"Yes," said Lloyd. "He would have run rings round me." He smiled. "But no one runs rings round my lady inspector, Mrs. Bailey. She was on to him before Nicola arrived, and she didn't need the money to prove it. You could have had four thousand, six hundred pounds stashed away for a rainy day, if you'd read *her* right."

Rachel smiled. "It don't matter," she said. "And I reckon Nicola's better off with it out in the open, anyway. Couldn't get her to tell me nothin'."

Lloyd straightened up from the paintings, and rubbed his eyes. "I think perhaps I'd better leave my car here, if I may," he said. "And get my lady inspector to come and pick me up. I think I'd be a bit of a liability on the road."

"Sure. I won't be here tonight, but it won't come to no harm.

335

I can lock it up in the barn. Can't put no alarms on though. They took all the security stuff."

"Why didn't they take the paintings? Are they coming back for them, or what?"

"They didn't belong to Bernard," Rachel said. "They're mine."

"Well," Lloyd said, stepping back, looking at the top one. "I can see you might not want to pawn one, but it'll get you as much as your pendant would, I'm sure. And you always got it back, didn't you? So perhaps you'd get the painting back, too."

Rachel smiled. "They're not worth nothin'," she said.

Lloyd frowned. "How much did you pay for them?" he asked.

"Nothin'. They're mine, like I said."

Lloyd pointed at her. "*You're* Trelawny?"

She nodded. "Goin' to call myself that again, now," she said. "Don't want his phoney name. Don't want my baby havin' it, neither."

"But they're wonderful," he said. "You must know how good they are. Have you studied art?"

Rachel shrugged. "In a manner of speakin'," she said. "A lot of artists in Cornwall. Got to know one pretty well. Taught me a lot."

"Another arrangement?" Lloyd shook his head. "But he must have told you that you were good, surely?"

She smiled. "Told me I was a lot of things when we split up," she said. "Don't recall good bein' one of them. But they're not worth nothin', are they?"

"I'm not an expert," said Lloyd. "But I'd expect to pay at least as much for one of them as I'd pay for a gold pendant, however thick and solid. And, if I hadn't just treated myself and my lady inspector to a night in that hotel, I might be offering to buy one."

"You can have one," said Rachel.

He shook his head.

"I'm not offerin' no inducement this time," Rachel said. "I'd

336

like you to have one. You're a nice man. Don't know many of them. Maybe just you."

"You haven't got that kind of money to throw away yet," Lloyd said. "Take them round to some art dealers. See how much they think you can get for them. Please don't rely on Mike McQueen and a cow to keep you and your baby fed."

Rachel looked at the paintings. She thought they were good. Good enough to hang. Good enough to make sure they didn't get taken away. She'd just never thought she could sell them. But it would be nice to be able to pay McQueen's rent in cash and tell him to stuff his arrangement.

"I'll try that," she said.

"Good," said Lloyd, going out to the telephone.

Judy drove up to the farmhouse, frowning as she saw the building in virtual darkness. Lloyd's car was outside, as was the old sheepdog, sound asleep on the porch.

The front door stood open, and she could see a faint light from the office. She knocked, called.

"In here," said Rachel Bailey.

Judy saw the long room to her right virtually empty, and walked towards the office, tapping on the half-shut door, pushing it open. It was lit by one desk lamp. "Taxi for Lloyd," she said, a little surprised by the subdued lighting, and the general atmosphere, as Rachel and Lloyd sat sipping lemonade, easy in one another's company. It wasn't a lot like a police interview, she thought. Rachel Bailey ate men for breakfast, he was ripe for compromising himself, and he had come here at night to interview her alone. But it looked innocent enough now, and if it hadn't been, she didn't want to know.

Lloyd got up, holding on to the desk as he pushed himself wearily off the chair. "Perhaps we could give you a lift?" he said.

"No, thanks, all the same," said Rachel. "Don't take much time to walk to Nicola's, and Nell could do with the exercise."

She came with them to the door; Lloyd said good-night, and went down the steps to the car.

"Is Mr. Lloyd all right?" asked Rachel.

"Yes," said Judy. "He's just tired out. He had this virus that's going round. He shouldn't really have been at work today."

"He's a good man," said Rachel. "You want to hang on to him."

There was very little point in standing on ceremony with Rachel, Judy thought. "Yes," she said. "I do."

Rachel smiled. "You got no call to worry," she said. "He don't want no one but you."

So she had put him to the test. Judy had known she would, as soon as they had met. She was used to Lloyd's frank appreciation of other women, and had known he would fancy Rachel as soon as she had clapped eyes on her. It was when she had discovered that Rachel fancied him that she had begun to worry. Purely on a professional level, of course. Because that sort of thing didn't mean anything, wasn't important. But she was pleased she had no call to worry, all the same.

"Tell me something," she said. She might as well, since they seemed to be on very intimate ground already.

It was when she had bought the pregnancy-testing kit that she had first wondered. Because she had been sneaking into the chemist, hoping no one saw her. And lying to Bernard Bailey about being pregnant would, she had thought, have been suicidal; she didn't think Rachel was into suicide. Then Jack Melville had said that Bailey had told him he was going to have a son. He wouldn't have said that just because Rachel had told him she was pregnant. He must have known she was, known the sex of the baby. But she had lied to him about being in the chemist, and Judy knew why.

"You really are pregnant, aren't you?" she said. "You'd bought a pregnancy-testing kit in the chemist that day. You didn't want Bailey to know that you might be."

Rachel nodded. "Was goin' to leave him if I was," she said. "But I still didn't want to give up on the money, not if I didn't have to. Not on what might've been just another false alarm. But 'fore I knew it, he was kickin' me again. Had to tell him." She smiled. "You told your chief inspector yet?"

Judy stared at her.

She shrugged. "I'm a gypsy," she said.

"You're the eldest of seven children," Judy said. "If anyone knows the signs, you do."

The long dimple appeared. "That, too," she said. Then her face grew serious. "Just don't do nothin' you'll regret," she said, and closed the door.

Judy walked slowly down the steps, and made her mind up. She got into her car to find Lloyd asleep in the passenger seat; he woke up as she got in, and rubbed his eyes, sitting up, putting on his seat belt. "What did he say?" he asked.

"He said he doesn't think it would make any difference. That working parties don't convene in smoke-filled rooms any more, except right at the start. Once it's up and running, as he says, it's all conducted through computer conference facilities and cyberspace, so they could fix me up with a computer and a modem at home, if I didn't want to take the full maternity leave." She started the car, and set off down the farm road. "And I am going to have the baby," she added.

Because a gypsy told her she should have it? Maybe. She tried to push all the doubts to the back of her mind, because of the one certainty that Rachel Bailey had put there. She would feel guilty for the rest of her life if she didn't have it, whatever her enlightened views about other people's freedom of choice. Enlightened views were all very well, until they came up against reality. Like real babies. And real Rachel Baileys.

"Aren't you going to say anything?" she asked, glancing at him, thinking he'd gone to sleep again, but he hadn't.

"This computer," he said. "*Are* you going to have it installed at home?"

That seemed an odd thing to be exercising his mind. "I should think so," she said.

"And . . . where will home be, Judy?"

She didn't answer. That was another problem, for another day. One that hadn't started at half past four in the morning. Her selfish soul wanted to have its cake and eat it, wanted Lloyd to be around when she wanted him, and not when she didn't, and she was going to have to wrestle with that some other time.

But she had made a start on trying to reform. She had spent what had possibly been the longest working day of her life walking round in shoes that clashed with her dress. And if that wasn't an act of pure selflessness, then she didn't know what was.

**SCENE I—BARTONSHIRE**
**Saturday, September 27th, 11:00 A.M.**
**The garage and various rooms of a semi**
**detached house in Stansfield**

Detective Chief Inspector Lloyd looked at the two bodies in the elderly Ford Fiesta and sighed.

The man, he had never met. He was about Lloyd's own age—late forties, early fifties; difficult to say at the best of times, and this was not the best of times. He had more hair than Lloyd, but most people did. He had the same dark colouring, but he was much bigger, taller. The car had been specially adapted for a disabled driver; he was in the driving seat.

The woman he *had* met, and had worked with, but that was a long time ago now. She had been twenty-four when he'd seen her last; she had left the job to marry the man whose hand she had been holding while their car had filled up with lethal fumes, pumped through a vacuum-cleaner hose from the exhaust pipe.

"Their daughter found them this morning, sir," said the constable. "She walked along the passage between the house and the garage, to the back door of the house, and heard the engine. She pulled the hose from the exhaust, but she couldn't get into the car to turn off the engine."

The garage, its overhead door closed and firmly locked, still held the heavy odour of exhaust gases; the small door at the rear stood wide open to admit as much fresh air as possible, but even diluted and dispersed, the pollution in the atmosphere was unhealthy. Undiluted, confined in the small car, it would have been lethal in about ten minutes.

"It wouldn't have made any difference if she had. They'd been dead for hours by the time she got here," said the Forensic Medical Examiner, straightening up from the car. "Life pronounced extinct at . . ." She looked at her watch. "Eleven-seventeen A.M.," she said, and smiled at Lloyd. "I'm a bit puzzled about why you're here, Chief Inspector. How come you got called out? Am I missing something?"

"No," Lloyd said. "You're not missing anything. I'm not here on duty—the officers dealing thought I'd want to know, that's all."

He could hear his own Welshness when he spoke; usually his accent was very carefully controlled, ranging from barely discernible to impenetrable, depending on the impression he was choosing to give. It was when he got what Detective Sergeant Finch called a gut feeling that it popped out all by itself. From his soul, he liked to think, rather than his gut.

"I knew Kathy—twenty years ago, admittedly, but I knew her." He smiled at the slightly wary look on the FME's face. "I wouldn't rush 'round to see all my friends' dead bodies," he said. "But I want to be sure that this really is a suicide pact, because I don't think Kathy was a quitter."

"Oh, I'm sorry," she said. "I didn't realize you knew her. But there's nothing to suggest that she didn't go through with it of her own accord."

"No," sighed Lloyd. "But it doesn't add up," he said, almost to himself, then smiled apologetically at the doctor. "Kathy always had a tendency to wade in first and think second," he said. "She never thought ahead. She survived by finding a way out of whatever problem she found herself with. She was famous for it."

"Well," said the doctor doubtfully, "this *is* a way out."

"True," Lloyd conceded. "And I don't know what her problems were yet—this may have seemed the *only* way out." He took the notes that she had made. "Thank you, Doctor," he said, lifting a hand as she left. "Where's the daughter now?" he asked the constable.

"She's with Sergeant Alexander in the house, sir."

Mary Alexander had joined Bartonshire Constabulary on the same day as Kathy White, as she then was, and Lloyd, and there was a bond between raw recruits all learning the ropes together that never quite went away; she had known that Lloyd would want to be sure of this one.

Lloyd walked past the young man and stood in the open door at the rear of the garage. "Odd, about this door being unlocked," he said. "Don't you think?" He didn't wait for a reply. It was just a little puzzle. "Don't stay in there," he said. "You can keep an eye on things in the fresh air." He went along the pathway to the back door, knocked, and let himself in.

"The electric's off, sir," said Mary, coming into the kitchen and closing the door behind her. "They came to cut it off just before we got here—about an hour ago, I suppose. Lucy— that's Kathy's daughter—said they might as well go ahead and do it."

"Money," said Lloyd, like an oath. "Was that the problem? I can't believe that."

"Big money. The house was about to be repossessed. But— it seems that Kathy was running some sort of detective agency, and the front room's been turned into an office. It's absolutely full of brand-new office equipment. I can't work that out. Why would she buy all that stuff when they were broke? The agency wasn't getting a lot of business, according to her daughter, so she couldn't have had much hope of paying for it."

Another little puzzle, like the unlocked door. Judy was who he needed on this, but he was going to have to get used to doing without her soon. Still, he'd try them out on her when he got home; it would help take her mind off all the things that were worrying her. Her late, unplanned pregnancy had been confirmed at virtually the same time as she had been offered a

344

year's secondment to HQ and the promotion that went with it; Judy found change of any kind unsettling, never mind whole-sale change. That was why she and Lloyd still lived in separate flats, a situation he hoped the baby would remedy. But she was at his flat now, as she usually was at the weekend, and he would see what she made of all this.

"How's Kathy's daughter?" he asked. "Is she all right?"

"Yes, sir. Well, as all right as you can be in these circum-stances. She's in the living room with the Coroner's officer—he's explained about the need for a postmortem and an inquest. She's not taken it too badly, considering. But—" She wrinkled her nose, shook her head. "No," she said. "Forget it."

Lloyd smiled. "You know no one can, once someone's said that," he said.

"Well, it's probably nothing. But I was going to make her a cup of tea, before Lucy remembered about the electricity being off, and she told me the tea bags were in that tin. It was empty, and she said there would be a new packet in this cupboard." Mary opened the cupboard, which had various tins and packets in it. "But it wasn't. It was up here." She pointed to the shelf on the unit. "So she started checking, and lots of things weren't where she expected them to be."

Lloyd lived on his own, hopefully not for too much longer now that he and Judy were to be blessed with issue, but he lived on his own, and had for several years. He had decided the day he moved into the flat where he kept everything in the kitchen, and that was where it had stayed. But perhaps having a change-round helped cheer Kathy up, or something. That hardly counted as a puzzle.

"And some things are in two different places," Mary went on. "Beans, for instance. There was one tin in this cupboard and two in this one down here. That just seemed a bit strange."

"I agree. You keep tins of beans wherever you keep tins of beans," said Lloyd. That *was* another puzzle.

"Lucy says her mum and dad always went shopping on a Friday night," Mary said. "And there's some cold ham in the fridge still in its supermarket deli bag. That's another thing she was surprised about, because her mum always put stuff like that in clingfilm before she put it in the fridge. And the eggs are in the fridge—she says her mum usually kept them in the larder. Of course, it's been very hot—"

"Right," Lloyd said, making his mind up. "I want the duty inspector informed, and I want the SOCOs down here, and the pathologist."

"Scene of crime people? To a suicide?"

Lloyd sighed. "There are too many little puzzles for my liking," he said.

## PLOTS AND ERRORS
### by Jill McGown

**Published in hardcover by Ballantine Books.**
**Available in bookstores August 1999.**

# Murder on the Internet

## Ballantine mysteries are on the Web!

Read about your favorite Ballantine authors and upcoming books in our electronic newsletter MURDER ON THE INTERNET, at www.randomhouse.com/BB/MOTI

Including:
- ☠ What's new in the stores
- ☠ Previews of upcoming books
- ☠ In-depth interviews with mystery authors and publishing insiders
- ☠ Calendars of signings and readings for Ballantine mystery authors
- ☠ Announcements of online activities
- ☠ Profiles of mystery authors
- ☠ Excerpts from new mysteries

To subscribe to MURDER ON THE INTERNET, please send an e-mail to **join-moti-dist@list.randomhouse.com** with "join" as the body of the message. (Don't use the quotes.) You will receive the next issue as soon as it's available.

Find ou        r sample chapters f        Ballantine

www        stery